PRAISE FOR *TYPECAST*

"A smart, endearing heroine; an enjoyable, entertaining story; and a hopeful, satisfying ending. Callie revisits the past with her ex to make sense of her present love life, making *Typecast* a fun mix of rom-com and women's fiction. Full of heartfelt charm, humor, and truth, Stein's debut is exactly the book I'd been craving. Perfect for fans of Marian Keyes and Josie Silver. A very delightful read!"

—Angela Terry, award-winning author of *Charming Falls Apart* and *The Trials of Adeline Turner*

"With patience and realism, Andrea J. Stein explores the complexities of first love, family dynamics, and adulting. A relatable journey fraught with growing pains, *Typecast* reminds us that in order to truly evolve—and find new, lasting love—we must first accept the past and ourselves."

—Nora Zelevansky, author of *Competitive Grieving*

"Insightful and bighearted and oh-so-deliciously page-turning, *Typecast* is like a road trip with friends, complete with detours and surprises and wildly satisfying moments. A perfect next read for fans of Camille Pagán and Kristy Woodson Harvey, Stein's *Typecast* is a don't-miss debut!"

—Amy Impellizzeri, award-winning author of *I Know How This Ends* and *In Her Defense*

"In lively, sparkling prose, Andrea J. Stein's *Typecast* offers keenly observed insights about family, friendship, and figuring out who you want to be when you grow up. Alternating between the heroine's past and her present, *Typecast* is a portrait of a woman rewriting her own future."

—Jenn Stroud Rossmann, author of *The Place You're Supposed to Laugh*

"*Typecast* is an excellent first novel! I could totally see this in movie form . . . It would surely be a standout rom-com that everyone would love."

—Kyle Wendy Skultety, gimmethatbook.com

"I adored this book! . . . Callie was a fantastically written character whom I grew to love as each chapter went on. I highly recommend!"

—@doingitbythebook

TYPE-CAST

a novel

Andrea J. Stein

GIRL FRIDAY BOOKS

 **GIRL FRIDAY BOOKS**

Published by Girl Friday Books™, Seattle

Produced by Girl Friday Productions

Cover design: Bailey McGinn
Production editorial: Laura Dailey
Project management: Kristin Duran

ISBN (paperback): 978-1-954854-65-9
ISBN (e-book): 978-1-954854-66-6

Library of Congress Control Number: 2022901292

First edition

For Bablu, Ravi, and Kieran

CHAPTER ONE

Before

When I woke up, my arm was asleep. It was neither surprising nor unusual, considering Ethan and I were snug against each other in the twin-size dorm room bed. It would be the last morning we'd wake up together on this thin mattress sagging in the center, tilting us toward each other more than strictly necessary in the narrow space.

I opened my eyes and took inventory of the institutional square I'd worked hard to turn into a home. The framed *Spellbound* poster I splurged on for Ethan's twenty-first birthday hung across from the bed. Other movie posters—*Marathon Man* and *Jaws*—decorated the other walls, and the huge bulletin board for which I had painstakingly chosen fabric was a collage of photos—mostly of Ethan and me—flyers for rallies, on-campus plays, and concerts I meant to attend but never did; takeout menus; birthday cards; and hastily scribbled notes so heartfelt they became keepsakes. A gauzy piece of batik-printed fabric draped the window, hiding the plain white window shade. Two blond wood dressers stood side by side near the closet with its accordion door, the trio of them housing our clothes—Ethan's jeans, plaid shirts, and white T-shirts, and my random assortment of hoodies, loose sweaters, flippy skirts, tights, and a handful of body-hugging scoop-neck tops that I wore occasionally because Ethan liked them. I preferred my "girls"—bigger than oranges but not quite grapefruits—to be a little less conspicuous.

Ethan and I moved in together at the beginning of junior year. Well, kind of. The truth was we each had a single room across the hall from one another. This one we used as our bedroom. The other, as our study. That's where our two desks lived, along with a mini fridge and the other twin bed—which we'd tried to move into this room to create a king, but gave up on when we discovered we'd never be able to open the closet. Besides, we didn't mind having to sleep so close together. A few of my sketches and paintings hung on the walls of the study. A few were from a drawing class I took, and a couple I did on my own, when I realized how much I enjoyed trying to capture images on the page—Ethan's profile when he was studying, his brow furrowed; my favorite tree near the library entrance with its gnarled roots and twisted branches.

This room with this boy had been my home for two straight years, and we'd been together for nearly all four years of college. But yesterday we graduated, and today we were moving out. I was going back to Brook Hill, New Jersey, and Ethan was returning to the suburbs of Chicago. Soon he'd drive out to San Francisco and get us an apartment. The plan was for me to meet him there in September, after spending the summer temping, reconnecting with my parents, and visiting my older sister, Nina, in Manhattan—if she could tear herself away from her office in one of the city's ubiquitous glass towers.

I felt Ethan stir behind me; his hand, which had been resting on my hip, slipped down onto my belly and then slid up toward my breasts. I didn't think our bodies could get any closer, but instinctively, my lower half pushed back toward his as he caressed me exactly the way he knew I liked. I turned toward him, and he pulled my T-shirt over my head.

Afterward, we lay naked and spent. Ethan pushed my hair off my forehead. I'd conducted an unfortunate experiment with bangs a few months prior—they were finally growing out and were at that awkward stage.

"Wow," he whispered. "How am I going to live without that for the next three months?"

I smiled and reached for his hand. "There's always this," I said, giving it a squeeze.

"Ha, ha. As if it's the same." He grinned, his eyes crinkling, but then his face turned serious. "Come on, Callie, spend the summer with me. You can still go home and see your folks first. And then fly out to Chicago so we can drive to California and start our life together." He ran a finger down the side of my face, along my neck, and past my collarbone. "Just think of all the fun we can have on the road."

I giggled. "I'm sure we could," I said, brushing my own hand across the junction between his thighs. But then I looked into his blue eyes, their sandy lashes visible without the barrier of his glasses, and something clenched deep inside me. I swallowed. "But you know I need to spend some time at home. I *want* to spend some time at home. I've barely been there since I left for Welford. Besides, you know what my mom would be like if I changed my plans. She can't stop talking about having her baby back, even if it's just for the summer. If I'm moving all the way across the country from her and my dad, the least I can do is be with them for a while before I go."

Ethan sighed. "Fine—but don't forget, you're *my* baby, too. And come September, you're *all* mine."

CHAPTER TWO

After

"Do you know what I have in my pants?"

Jacob looked up at Callie with a cherubic smile, his formerly round cheeks having recently thinned as he proceeded through the predictable transformation from squeezable toddler to more angular preschooler. She smiled at him.

"No, Jacob. What do you have in your pants?"

He grinned. "A green snake! Do you want to see it, Miss Callie?" His hand started to slide into his waistband.

It was not unheard-of for her three- and four-year-old students to display a completely age-appropriate lack of embarrassment about their private parts, and Callie immediately started to shake her head. "No, Jacob, why don't you keep it—"

But he beat her to it, quickly pulling a piece of yarn out of his jeans. "Look! My green snake!"

Callie laughed and made a mental note to share this story with Tess later.

Jacob rewarded her with another big smile before turning

toward the boys playing on the carpet with cars. Teachers aren't supposed to have favorites, but they're human, so of course they do—and Jacob was one of Callie's. How could this good-natured child, whose cowlick caused his brown hair to perpetually stand up in the middle of his crown, not be any teacher's pet? There was no question that Callie would have preferred to focus on him and his classmates, but instead, to her annoyance, she was preoccupied with the voicemail message her sister, Nina, had left her earlier that morning.

"Hey, Callie. It's me. Look, I stopped by yesterday to drop off a few things, and it doesn't look like you've done anything about moving out of Mom and Dad's room. I thought we'd agreed on that, but if you've changed your mind, you need to tell me. The movers are coming next week, you know. I mean, I know you know that. Anyway, give me a call."

Callie sighed deeply, wondering if it was fair to be irritated that Nina had let herself into the house while she'd been at work. True, it really wasn't Callie's house—it was their parents'. And come next week, Callie would be sharing the space with a pregnant Nina; her husband, Michael; and their four-year-old daughter, Zoe, while their own home was undergoing a major renovation.

As she watched Jacob and the other boys racing Matchbox cars, Callie once again sought to forget what she had begun to think of as "the Invasion." It became easier as one of her charges appeared before her, looking indignant. The blonde-haired and blue-eyed girl was wearing a frayed yellow dress-up gown over her clothes.

"Miss Callie! Emma took the hat that I had first!"

Callie squatted down. "Did you ask her to give it back?"

The little girl nodded vigorously.

"And what happened?"

"She pignored me."

Callie bit her lip and tried not to smile. If there was one

thing she'd learned in her decade as a preschool teacher, it was that children don't like to think that you're not taking them seriously.

"Ignored you," she corrected gently. "Okay. Let's see what we can do." And with that, she banished Nina and her impending invasion from her mind.

Later that day, Callie sat in the weekly Bouncy Castles staff meeting. For the third time in the three weeks since school had started, the focus was Liam Switzer, a student in Robin Vitale's class. Liam had regular tantrums when he didn't get his way, periodically pinched other children who "bothered" him, and had even more trouble sitting still than the average four-year-old. But the biggest problem was Liam's parents—they hadn't been receptive to calls or emails from Robin or even from the school's director, Judith Preston, who typically had a way of making parents feel like disobedient children themselves.

"I think we need to put our foot down," said Robin. "It's getting worse. He was so disruptive today I could barely get through story time. It's like he knows his parents aren't on board."

"Of course he knows." This voice was that of the school's veteran teacher, Denise. "They pick up on everything," she added darkly. Callie couldn't tell if this was intended to be laudatory or pejorative.

"I agree," said Judith. "They're going to have to come in for a meeting with both of us."

"Do we think he needs to be evaluated?" Tess Morrison, another teacher, asked. Tess was Callie's closest friend both in and outside of work.

"I do," said Robin, looking pointedly at Denise, who pursed her lips. The teachers at Bouncy Castles had mixed feelings about the current rage to diagnose children with all sorts of behavioral issues.

"Perhaps you're right." Judith sighed. "I'll put a call in to

Liam's mom as soon as we're through here. Does anyone have anything else?"

Callie glanced around, hoping that no one did. While she loved being in the classroom with the kids, she didn't enjoy sitting around with other teachers talking about them. In fact, she and Tess had initially bonded over their shared dislike of these meetings. She frequently had to look away from her friend, who had a tendency to cross her big brown eyes while the other teachers were talking.

Fortunately, the meeting adjourned, and Callie headed back to her classroom to change one of the bulletin boards. She carefully took down the kids' blue collages and began to pin up their pumpkin stencils.

Callie heard a sound behind her and turned. Tess had perched herself on one of the kids' tables, her feet on a small chair and her full skirt swirling around her. Callie loved Tess's habit of wearing billowy Indian cotton skirts—she never told her friend that they reminded her of Anna in *The King and I* sitting on the floor in an enormous hoopskirt, singing "Getting to Know You" with all the king's children—but her own primary clothing goal was comfort. Sometimes that meant a sweater with shorts and tights; sometimes it was a skirt with boots; sometimes it was pants with a long-sleeve tunic. She tended to grab whatever was handy, and as long as it was comfortable and looked okay when she glanced in the mirror, she was good to go.

"I don't think Robin knows how to handle that kid." Tess examined her fingernails through the magnifying glass Callie kept on the science table.

"She's doing her best." Callie turned back to the board and shifted a couple of pumpkins around before pinning them up. "She just wants them all to like her. And the parents, too." She stuck the last pushpin into the last pumpkin stencil.

"No kidding. And it's the parents that you *really* need to

be strict with!" Tess chuckled, replacing the magnifying glass. Callie joined her friend's laughter, although, having experienced New York City parents in her previous job, she couldn't complain too much about the crop they had to deal with at Bouncy Castles.

An hour later, Callie pulled her champagne Toyota Corolla into her driveway, gathered her things from the passenger seat, and got out of the car. As she ascended the old Victorian's porch steps, she absently noted, yet again, the peeling paint on the railings, and wondered if she should talk to her parents about having the house painted in the spring.

After opening the door with its leaded-glass panes, she dropped her bag and keys on the table beside it. As she walked into the kitchen to get a drink of water, the phone rang. Glancing at the caller ID, she was puzzled to see *Hartford Courant*—the newspaper where her friend Jenna worked as a reporter—pop up.

"Hey, Callie." Jenna's voice was almost as familiar to her as her own.

"Is everything okay? It's not like you to call me from work."

"Oh, everything's fine with me," Jenna answered quickly.

"And Rob's good?" Callie asked, her mind jumping to Jenna's husband of three years. He was a journalist, too, but wrote for an online sports news site.

"Oh yeah, he's fine. Super busy with baseball season, but that's typical." She paused. "How about you? How are you doing?" There was something in Jenna's voice that Callie couldn't identify.

"Good—just got home from work. It's beautiful out."

"Yeah, here, too." There was a silence that ran a beat too long. "So," Jenna began again. "Did you see the new *Quarterly*?" she asked, referring to their college alumni magazine.

"Not really. It came the other day, but I just glanced at it. Why?"

"Well." Jenna paused. "There's an article about Ethan."

Callie hated that her pulse immediately quickened. "What about Ethan?"

"Well . . . he's written a screenplay, and the movie is about to come out."

Callie's heartbeat resumed its normal pace. "That's great," she said, meaning it.

"You might want to read the article."

"Sure, I'll check it out."

"The thing is," said Jenna cautiously, "I think the movie may be about you."

"About me?" Callie tried to say it lightly but felt a sudden sinking feeling in her gut. "It's been ten years. What could it have to do with me?"

"Well, according to the article, it's about a guy who just graduated from college and is planning to move to California with his girlfriend. And then she dumps him." Jenna stopped, as if expecting Callie to interrupt, but then continued. "He goes on this cross-country road trip with his friends. Looks like they're billing it as a unique combo of a guy movie and a chick flick—adolescent humor plus flashbacks of his college relationship."

Callie sank heavily into a kitchen chair. "Oh God."

"Are you okay?"

Callie swallowed. "Oh, yeah, fine." *What right do I have to be upset about this? After all these years? After how things ended?* There was a weighty silence on Jenna's end of the phone line. "It's just weird." Callie knew Jenna expected her to go on, but she didn't know what to say—or even what to feel. Instead, she cleared her throat and changed the subject. "So, what's up with you?"

As Jenna complained about how little she and Rob got to see each other now that, in addition to baseball season heating up, she was swamped covering a growing story about a city official's silent partnership with a local developer, Callie struggled to listen and respond appropriately. Jenna might as well have been telling her that she was about to expose the biggest scandal to hit the tristate area since Anthony Weiner's sexts for all that her words were cutting through the buzzy hum in her brain. Callie had to suppress her sigh of relief when her friend had to hang up abruptly to take a call from a source at city hall.

After the phone nearly slipped out of her sweaty palm, she replaced it in its cradle and wandered around the house, slowly at first, then with increasing frenzy. She searched through stacks of mail and the recycling bin, on the coffee table, the kitchen table, the nightstand, the back-patio table, any place she could think of where she might have left her latest copy of the *Welford Quarterly*. When she finally caught sight of the magazine on the desk in her old bedroom, she pounced.

Flipping through the pages as she returned to the kitchen, she quickly found the article: "English Major Turns Screenwriter: Ethan Rendel Pens Forthcoming Feature Film." It occupied a full column and included a head-and-shoulders photograph of Ethan with what she assumed was the Pacific Ocean in the background.

Callie's mouth went dry, and her pulse rattled a rapid staccato. She dropped the magazine onto the table as if it were aflame, and then turned her back on it for good measure. She wasn't ready to step on that land mine just yet. What better way to avoid it than by focusing on what needed to be done before the Invasion next week? She couldn't help but smile at the irony that something so onerous had now actually become appealing.

When she'd moved into her parents' house seven years

earlier, Callie had settled in the master bedroom. Because it was just too weird to sleep in the bed with the carved oak headboard in which she was presumably conceived, she'd bought herself a white Pottery Barn look-alike and moved the old bed frame up to the attic. It was that bed, along with the quilt in tones of deep blue, buttery yellow, and cream, that made the house feel a little bit like her home rather than her parents'. But now, with Nina and Michael moving in, Nina had made a hard pitch—which she attributed to Michael's "need for space"—to have them take over the master bedroom. "It's only temporary, Callie," Nina had cajoled. "And you've certainly had the run of the house for plenty of time," she'd added, a not-so-subtle reference to the financial inequity of the arrangement their parents had devised. Lorraine—perhaps out of her own guilt at her unequal treatment of her daughters, not to mention her recognition of her sole son-in-law's intractability—had backed Nina up: "It's probably easier if you just go along on this one, Callie. They'll be gone before you know it."

Once the determination had been made, Callie knew she had to empty the closets in the master bedroom and move the contents into her childhood room down the hall. Although it was the smaller of the two additional bedrooms in the house (Lorraine always referred to it as "cozy"), she chose not to question the assumption that Zoe would set up temporary lodgings in the room that had been her own mother's. Besides, it meant Callie didn't have to move her makeshift art studio. Her old desk was stocked with art supplies, sketch pads leaned against the wall, and a standing lamp with an adjustable neck provided sufficient light for her to draw indoors when the weather outside wasn't cooperative.

She carried a jumble of skirts and scarves and blouses down the hall and dumped them on her childhood twin bed. She had visions of hanging them up in their new, temporary home in an organized way, grouped by color. Why should picture-perfect magazine closets have anything on hers? But when she opened the closet door and was confronted by the reality of the undersized storage space, it was all she could do to tamp down the resentment that rose in her.

Sighing, Callie returned to the kitchen and filled the kettle with water to make herself a cup of tea. Once the vanilla maple tea bag was steeping in the steaming water, she brought the stoneware mug over to the table and sat down, the alumni magazine taunting her. She picked it up and braced herself.

She studied the photograph of Ethan—same sandy-brown hair, a bit windblown. Same blue eyes, but no glasses. Did he finally get contacts? His face had filled out a bit; it wasn't as angular as she remembered. It was weird seeing his face again. It was so familiar—she could almost feel the texture of his skin under her fingers—and yet almost alien. A face she hadn't looked at, except in her mind's eye, for years.

It was strange that someone who had been such a huge part of her life had been so entirely excised that she hadn't seen his face—or even heard his voice—for ten years. She wasn't on Facebook, Twitter, or Instagram, and the last time she had spoken to him was when she'd ended the relationship by phone, halfway into the summer after they graduated—also known as the summer she planned to spend with her parents before moving three thousand miles away to be with him. Of course, Ethan had tried to call her after that, but she knew talking wouldn't help either of them. Nothing could have changed her mind, and anything else she could have said would only hurt him more.

Looking at his photo now, she lingered on his half smile. Someone who didn't know him might think it was the real thing—but she knew it was only the beginning of the huge grin that spread across his entire face when he was truly happy. Cute as he was, it was hard to imagine he was single, but she didn't think he was married. There had been no report of it in the *Quarterly*, and she assumed that news would have reached her somehow, although, as far as she knew, none of her girlfriends had ever communicated with Ethan beyond the phone call Jenna had received immediately afterward. But Jenna couldn't answer his big question—*why?*—because she didn't know. During the many times she and her friend had spoken in the aftermath, Jenna checking in with her to make sure she was okay, Callie couldn't bring herself to tell her the truth. It was just too painful. And she didn't want to know what Jenna would say if she knew. She didn't think she could stand losing anyone else.

Taking a sip of tea, Callie couldn't restrain herself any longer. She had to see what the article said. She read about how Ethan had exhibited his love for movies while at Welford by attending the weekly film series—a fact she knew quite well—and how, after a few years of using his English degree to write for online magazines, he pursued his MFA in film at the University of Southern California. *Huh*, Callie thought, surprised that he had ended up in that part of the state—a place he had frequently mocked as offering nothing but beautiful people and highways. As Jenna had explained, the movie he penned—called *Rerouting* and scheduled to be released right after New Year's—was about a guy ditched by his girlfriend before they were supposed to move across the country together. His friends convince him to make the move anyway, to start his life over, and decide his big send-off will be an unforgettable road trip. Callie's stomach clenched anew as she read, "Rendel explained that the film departs from the traditional road movie as it shifts back and forth between the guys' escapades on the road and flashbacks of the relationship the lead character is mourning."

She closed the magazine and sat back in her chair. What she'd said to Jenna was true—she truly was happy for Ethan.

But there was another emotion pinging around her insides. There was something oddly unsettling about how he'd achieved such success without her having the slightest inkling it was going on. She knew it made no sense—but yet, the feeling was there. And if she were honest, there was another feeling—like the one you get when you have an instant connection with someone you've just met. Not that Callie could remember the last time that had happened, but she knew the sensation. The fluttering in her stomach. This had been her guy. The guy who was madly in love with her. And he'd written a movie about her. There was something a bit, well, something a bit *wow* about it.

Her intestines began to relax, and Callie felt herself starting to smile—and then the bucket of icy water hit. This wasn't the story about how they fell in love. It was the story of what happened after the bitch broke up with him. That new thought certainly didn't sit well—at all.

CHAPTER THREE

After

Callie spent the night obsessing about Ethan and his movie. When she wasn't dreaming about it, she was staring at the ceiling, trying to picture what they'd been through on the big screen. She couldn't stop wondering how exactly he had portrayed their breakup. Had he made her out to be the bad guy? Or was she the one who got away? At work, even the distraction of a classroom full of four-year-olds proved no match for what had become a nearly word-for-word recitation of the alumni magazine article spinning through her head.

She was dying to talk about it, but it wasn't until snack time, potty time, and story time had come and gone, and the children were on their mats for nap time, that she was able to fill Tess in on this strange new development.

"Wait, what?" Tess whispered, rising from her position on the floor where she was straightening the picture books.

"I said, my ex-boyfriend has written a movie based on our relationship. Or at least on our breakup. And it's going to be released nationwide in January," Callie repeated, her voice low.

"That's insane! Did he tell you he was doing it?"

Callie shook her head. "We haven't talked in years. Not since I was twenty-one."

"Jesus! He should have had the decency to call you! What the hell?" The fury Tess managed to inject in her whisper was commendable.

Callie responded with a shrug. She didn't want to say she wasn't sure she deserved any "decency."

Tess raised her eyebrows at what she surely saw as Callie's feeble reaction and then pushed her dark curly hair behind her ear. Callie once again marveled that her friend's large hoop earrings had never once been caught in the tenacious grip of one of the small children in her care. "How did you find out?"

Callie explained about the article in the alumni magazine, not mentioning the very flattering photo of Ethan that had appeared alongside it.

"Did it say who's playing you?"

Callie looked quizzically at her friend.

"In the movie, silly! Who'd they get?"

An interesting question. "It didn't say." She surmised this meant that the actress wasn't a big-name star. The lead role—the Ethan character, whose name in the movie was Will—was played by Nick Sykes, who had originally made it big as a brooding teen on a television drama about rich kids with too much time on their hands. Clearly, they were casting Ethan as a heartthrob. Now Callie wondered who her alter ego was—and what she would look like. And did Ethan have any role in casting this person? Would he have chosen someone with a gorgeous face and a rocking body to make him look like a stud to have had her as a girlfriend, or would he have gone for an unattractive girl, as a "screw you" shout-out to Callie?

"Well? Will you go see it?" Tess asked, her voice louder now. Callie realized she must have been tuning her out.

Before she had a chance to respond, there was a tap on the window of the door. It was Judith, who raised her eyebrows and pointed to the children curled up on their mats. Tess turned toward Callie and crossed her eyes. Callie bit down hard on her lip and nodded at Judith before moving away from Tess to sit in the chair closer to the mats.

As they walked out to their cars later that afternoon, Tess picked up right where she had left off. She was nothing if not tenacious in her pursuit of information, especially about her friend's life. Tess had started at Bouncy Castles the year before Callie and was three years older. Callie had attended her low-key beach wedding a year earlier. Tess and Brett had been together for nearly a decade—having met at an outdoor concert—and lived together for most of that time. Tess thought marriage was completely unnecessary and joked that she'd never told Brett that he'd "better put a ring on it," but Brett finally talked her into it. Callie was sometimes surprised that she and Tess were so close, despite one of them being coupled up and the other not. But Tess was a fierce friend. For her, the idea that being in a relationship would interfere with a friendship was nonsensical. The couple frequently invited Callie over for brunch on Sundays, or to go out for drinks on Thursday or Friday nights. Remarkably, she (almost) never felt like a third wheel when she was with them.

"So, why do you think your ex made a movie about you?" Tess asked as they crossed the small parking lot.

Callie considered Tess's question and shrugged. "Beats me," she said. "I mean, we were together for four years. Don't they say writers should write what they know? He certainly knew me." She laughed self-consciously, thinking of all the time they'd spent in bed. "Anyway, he was an English major, and he loved movies, but he never talked about actually wanting to write them. He was more interested in journalism—and had been planning to get into broadcasting."

"And you haven't talked to him since you broke up?"

Callie shook her head. It sounded preposterous to her, too. Ethan had been her world. They ate together, studied together, and slept together. After their first date freshman year, they spent virtually no time apart, even summers. One year, they spent six weeks driving around in his Volkswagen Beetle, visiting friends throughout New England, and camping out in Maine and the Adirondacks. The next year, they spent their break in San Francisco doing separate programs at Berkeley, hers on education, his studying German. And the summer before their senior year, they stayed on campus while she worked at the farm stand of a nearby orchard and he did an internship at the local radio station. Not for the first time, Callie considered how extremely odd it was to have that person gone from her life—the person who listened to her blather endlessly about the children in the campus day care at work, who could always amaze her with his ability to come up with the right movie reference for any situation, who joined her for long rambles in the woods—even if she was the one who had jettisoned him from her daily existence.

"Do you know where he lives?"

"California."

Tess nodded and leaned against the side of her car. Abruptly changing the subject, she spoke again. "Oh, hey, I never asked you—how was your apple-picking date?"

Callie wrinkled her nose and slowly shook her head.

"No good?"

Callie paused, wondering how to explain Adam. Should she begin with the fact that he was obsessed with the mud on his perfectly polished loafers? Or how every little thing out of his mouth verged on a complaint? "You'd think they'd provide better bags," he'd muttered as he struggled to open the plastic bag. "Why don't they tell you which aisles are already picked over?" he'd said as they walked along a row of denuded trees.

Callie didn't point out that he had zoomed away from the wagon that had carried them out to the trees without pausing to ask the driver for suggestions. And then there was lunch at a sandwich shop in the little town near the orchard, where he'd inspected every utensil, sending back the fork for a "clean" one after he'd noticed what Callie was sure were water spots.

Callie knew that describing any of these incidents would lead Tess to say she was being too critical. That everyone had their quirks. That she looked for reasons to dismiss every man she met. And Tess might take it personally since she was the one who finally convinced Callie to register on the Connections dating app, where she'd met Adam. It would be hard to explain that it wasn't any one of these comments that sounded the death knell for a wedding invitation announcing the impending nuptials of Callie and Adam. It was that all of his little remarks, taken collectively, made her skin crawl.

Instead, Callie told Tess about Adam's one cardinal sin— the fact that on date number one he chose to talk about his past experiences with online dating.

"So, have you been with Connections long?" he'd asked as he carefully inspected the straw that he'd just removed from its paper wrapper before plopping it into his diet soda.

Callie had shaken her head. "No. A friend has been trying to talk me into it for ages, but I only recently signed up."

"Ah, a newbie," Adam said, smiling in a way that rankled at Callie. "I started off with Synchronicity.com, and then I tried HandInHand. I was going to do eDuets, but when I found out they don't do same-sex relationships, I didn't want to support that."

Callie gave him points for that, but then he continued.

"You should be careful, you know. Lots of people aren't what they seem."

Callie stopped herself from rolling her eyes. "Really?" she asked politely.

He nodded, then took another sip of his drink and glanced around. "How long does it take to make a sandwich?" he muttered. "Anyway. Yeah. I've probably met a hundred women by now. I'd say at least half of them posted photos of themselves when they were younger. Or thinner. And they must get their friends to write their profiles so they seem funnier or smarter. And then you meet them and they're, well, they're duds."

He looked at her, and she became conscious of how silent she had become. She knew she would never see him again, but she didn't want to end up in the dud column. Not in his book, anyway.

"Yes, I can see that happening a lot." But before she could go any further, perhaps even to suggest that he was not exactly the happy-go-lucky guy his profile made him out to be, the sandwiches arrived.

"Finally!" Adam exhaled, after the server walked away and as he lifted the top piece of bread to inspect the slightly wilted lettuce beneath.

"Maybe it's not dishonesty," Callie continued. "It could be that's how they genuinely see themselves. Sometimes people think they're low maintenance when they're really high maintenance."

Adam shrugged. "Maybe a few. But all I know is, I've been pretty disappointed by most of the women I've met."

Looking back, Callie wished she had asked him how those women felt about him. But now, telling Tess about it, she said only, "I think he's one of those serial daters. No one is ever good enough. They just keep trolling for someone better."

Tess cocked her head. "And how is that different from what you do?"

Callie made a face at her friend—the kind of face she would have reprimanded the children in her class for making. "I may be picky, but I don't spend my time purposely meeting men just to find fault with them."

"No, you purposely don't meet men," Tess said dryly.

"That's not true!" Callie protested.

Tess raised her eyebrows, clearly disagreeing. "Well, either way, I have to say that talking about your other dating exploits on a first date is pretty tacky."

"Thank you."

"Well, onwards and upwards," Tess declared, spreading her arms wide to encompass the parking lot. "Plenty more fish in the sea. Or online."

Callie shook her head. "I don't know, Tess," she sighed. "All the emailing, and then setting up the drinks date, and then holding your breath before they actually come through the door . . . It's exhausting. I would rather just . . . meet someone, I don't know . . . the old-fashioned way. This feels too forced. There's no spontaneity."

Tess sighed. "You're a preschool teacher. You live in the 'burbs. The only time you ever go out is with me and Brett. How and when is spontaneity supposed to happen?"

"That's not true. I go out sometimes. I go into the city to meet up with Jenna . . ."

Tess's eye roll was impressive. "Yeah, another married friend. I'm sure you and she are going all kinds of places where you could hook up with someone."

"You never know! And I go out to draw—I go to parks. To the botanical garden. I go to my art classes . . ." Callie trailed off.

"Hotbeds of men, all those places. Look, Callie, as far as the online thing goes—you went on one date. And you've emailed, what, half a dozen guys? I have friends who have gone through fifty people before finding the right one."

"I don't have the energy for that. At least not now. Nina and her family are moving in next week, I have to get the house ready, my whole routine is going to be turned upside down . . ."

"Excuses, excuses. If you want to meet someone, you have to put yourself out there and put in the time. It's like looking for a job. It's not going to fall into your lap."

Callie dug into her oversized shoulder bag to retrieve her car keys. "Geez, Tess, you make it sound so romantic. I'm tempted to run home and hop online right now."

"Ha, ha. Very funny, Ms. Dressler," Tess replied, placing her hand gently but firmly on Callie's shoulder. "I just want you to be happy . . . *really* happy. Like Brett and me. And I want to go on double dates with you and be the go-between when your sister and your mother both try to take over your wedding."

"Let's not get ahead of ourselves, Mrs. Morrison." Callie smiled as she wagged her finger at her friend. "But I promise you, we will go on double dates, and I will not become a cat lady, if that's what you're worried about. In fact, I don't even like cats. I'm a dog person."

Callie joked, yet she was having trouble remembering the last time she'd had sex. Had it been that long, or was it just not very good? Back when she lived in the city, there were a couple of short relationships. She spent a few months with Dan, who was a friend of a friend. Though he was enthusiastic about sex, he was one of the laziest people she'd ever met. And there was Philip, who was a waiter/actor at the diner she and her roommates frequented. He was cute, but things never quite clicked—particularly when it came to his figuring out what worked for her in bed. After things with Philip petered out, she was sadder about the prospect of giving up the diner than she was about the loss of his company.

Since she'd been back in Brook Hill, there had been a string of first and second dates. There was the divorced dad whose daughter had been in her class a few years ago; when the school year ended, he'd asked her out, but she couldn't get past the fact that he'd been one of "her" parents. There was the former high school classmate who she'd bumped into at the supermarket, but after only one dinner, Callie remembered why she'd never been interested in anyone she'd gone to high school with. And there was the carpenter friend of Brett's who he sent over when the porch railing had come loose. As soon as Joel showed up, with his chiseled cheekbones and impressive biceps, Callie knew why Brett had sent him. And while he was as sexy as they come, they had absolutely nothing to talk about. Truth was, she'd considered finally investing in a vibrator.

"Ugh. Can we stop talking about this now?" She clicked her key fob and her car chirped.

"Suit yourself. But I'm going to log on to your profile and start emailing people for you."

This time Callie smacked her friend on the shoulder. "Don't you dare!"

Tess winked at her and got into her car.

That evening, after a distinctly college-era dinner of tuna fish on a bagel with cheddar cheese melted on top, Callie logged on to her Connections account. She had two new "nudges" and a new message. The message was essentially a catalog of basic facts, written with so little humor that the voice she imagined going along with it was the monotone of the teacher in *Ferris Bueller's Day Off*: "Bueller? Bueller?" She clicked through to the profiles of the two "nudgers," even as she continued to wonder about the philosophy behind "nudging" someone. As far as she was concerned, a nudge essentially meant "There's something mildly interesting about you, but not enough that I'm actually going to take the time to write one sentence, maybe two, introducing myself."

Scrolling through the first profile, she couldn't imagine why this guy thought they had anything in common. From taste in music (heavy metal) to movies (action), and the fact that under books he'd written "None," there wasn't a thing they meshed on. She heard Tess's voice in her head: *Maybe*

he believes in opposites attracting? Wondering what in the
world might have prompted Mr. Heavy Metal Action Movie to
nudge her, she clicked on her own profile. There was her photo
and the basics: thirty-one, Jewish, never married. She jumped
past the *Favorites* section where she had written "See below,"
referring to her detailed response to *What you should know
about me*: "When I'm not teaching a classroom full of preschoolers, you'd likely find me outside sketching or walking. I
hesitate to call it hiking because it's not all that strenuous, but
I do like a nice trek in the woods. I'm a huge reader—but I'm
often the last one to pick up a bestseller. I've found my favorite books—from *Isabel's Bed* to Dennis Lehane's Kenzie and
Gennaro mystery series—by wandering the library shelves.
When it comes to movies, I have a soft spot for the '80s movies
my older sister introduced me to . . ." Nope, she couldn't find
anything in common with Mr. Heavy Metal Action Movie.
Perhaps he just liked how she looked?

Callie didn't think about her appearance much. She'd cut
her long hair a few years earlier and donated it to Locks of Love.
She never let it grow as long again—too much trouble—so now
it reached just past her shoulders in brown waves. She thought
her eyes were her best feature—big and brown with flecks of
gold. Her lips were a little too full, but her nose was small and
straight. In her photo, she was laughing—a genuine laugh at
goofy faces her niece, Zoe, had been making one afternoon at
the botanical garden. Nina had been snapping pictures of her
daughter with her iPhone, and then she turned it on Callie.

Callie had been wearing a forest-green top with bell
sleeves, and there had been a gray-and-burgundy scarf (which
Nina insisted didn't "go") looped around her neck, but she had
taken it off so Zoe could make it into a cape as she ran through
the explosion of daffodils. The top had a lower neck than Callie
would typically wear—hence the scarf—so she couldn't help

but wonder if that's what caught this guy's eye. And she didn't mean her fine collarbones.

She turned her attention to the profile of the second nudger. This one was more intriguing. Jason claimed to be in advertising and enjoyed travel, hiking, and murder mysteries. The travel comment appealed to her—she had a long list of places she wanted to visit, from Denmark to New Zealand to Belize—but, thus far, the lack of budget and of a travel partner had held her back. Jason's profile photo was taken at a distance, so his appearance was hard to judge. Though Tess would have advised her to message him, she clicked "Nudge back."

Then, before she could talk herself out of it, she opened a new window and typed "Ethan Rendel" into the Google search box. Right at the top of the results was one for IMDb. "Ethan L. Rendel. Born: Wilmette, Illinois. He is a writer known for *Rerouting*." The rest of the profile was empty—no trivia or personal quotes.

As she clicked back to the Google page, her cell phone pinged. It was Tess: I have some free time if you want me to log on to Connections for you ;). Callie smiled and rolled her eyes. Tess was incorrigible. Then as she glanced at the computer, she heard her friend's voice in her head: *Are you seriously spending time Googling your* ex?

Tess was right. Callie firmly closed the laptop. Continuing to transfer her belongings from master bedroom to childhood bedroom was suddenly a much better use of her time. And would probably cause her less heartburn.

CHAPTER FOUR

Before

Week three of freshman year. I was sitting alone in the cafeteria with my turkey on rye waiting for Jenna, who was still making her way down the salad bar, when a flood of ice-cold liquid cascaded down the back of my T-shirt.

"What the . . . ?" I yelped as I heard a crash behind me.

"Oh geez, I'm so sorry," said a male voice. I turned and saw the perpetrator scramble to clean the mess of his tipped tray off the floor. He looked at me with bright blue, bespectacled eyes. "Let me get you some napkins . . ."

I peeled my soda-soaked shirt away from my skin. "Don't worry about it. I'll just go back to my room and change."

"Are you sure? I can get you some paper towels," he offered, looking somewhat helplessly at the detritus of his lunch.

"No, really—I can't go around all afternoon like this anyway." I felt sorry for him as he bent to retrieve a hamburger bun from where it had skittered under a nearby table.

"Yuck. What happened here?" I knew Jenna's voice before

I turned to see her head tilted to one side, her blonde ponytail hanging over one shoulder, her nose wrinkled. We'd become fast friends when we sat down next to each other on the first day of First-Year Seminar.

"Just an accident—I'm going to get a clean shirt. I'll be back," I explained as I pushed my chair out and got up from the table. "Watch my stuff?"

"Sure," Jenna said, eyebrows raised while she watched the flustered boy—whose hair cutely flopped into his eyes—assemble the carnage back onto his tray.

I made my way out of the cafeteria, weaving around the line of students scanning their cards to enter. As I headed across the stone patio outside the exterior doors, a voice called out, "Hey, wait!"

It was the soda-spilling guy, combing a lock of sandy-brown hair off his forehead with his fingers. If I weren't sticky and wet, I might have just stood there and focused on the unruliness of his mass of hair. His T-shirt was half tucked into his jeans.

"I am *so* sorry," he began.

"It's okay. Accidents happen. At least it wasn't syrup." I offered him a smile.

He smiled in return. "Well, I guess if I had to spill something on somebody, I'm glad it's someone who can be laid-back about it."

"It's one of the qualities about myself I'm most proud of. 'Doesn't take spills seriously.'" I pushed my own hair behind my ear and resisted the urge to pull my wet shirt away from my skin again. "But I have to go get changed if I want to have time to eat before class."

I turned in the direction of my dorm, and the boy fell into step beside me. I didn't entirely mind.

"What class?" he asked.

"Child Psychology."

"Cool. Is it good?"

I shrugged. "So far. The professor's nice—and we're going to start working in the on-campus childcare center soon, which could be fun. Or awful, I guess." I laughed, and he laughed, too.

"I guess it all depends on if you like kids." He followed me as I headed past the student center. It was a fairly new building, and its modern architecture didn't match the school's older, ivy-covered aesthetic. I'd been trying to convince myself that the mix of styles was interesting, but mostly I thought it was strange.

"Well, I do like kids, in general—but that doesn't mean they're easy."

"I could say that's how I feel about girls." The boy winced as soon as the words were out of his mouth.

I raised my eyebrows, my eyes widening. *Really?*

He shook his head. "Sorry, that was stupid. Open mouth, insert foot." He squeezed his temples as if he wanted to punish his brain.

I turned away, biting my lip to hold back a smile. "You could say that." I glanced back at him, and he looked like he wanted to crawl into a hole. "Look, don't worry about it," I said.

We continued along the path that crisscrossed the grass. The row of mostly freshman dorms lay ahead of us. They weren't as classically pretty as the older dorms, but they were cute—sand-colored stone punctuated by brick accents. The roofline made it look like the top floor was under the eaves, but those rooms—including mine—were as boxlike as all the others. And while it might have been nice to live in a space with more character, I wasn't sure how my roommate and I could have managed with even *less* elbow room. Beyond the dorms was a forest; if you followed the road that ran between the dorms and the woods, you'd reach the art building where I would have been taking a studio drawing class if I hadn't gotten closed out as a first-semester freshman. Beyond that was a popular upperclassman dorm that had once been a Hudson River Valley mansion, alongside the Hudson River itself.

We walked in silence, and I wondered why he was following me. I kept expecting him to turn back toward the dining hall, but he was still beside me when we got to Carter, my home away from home.

"Well, this is me," I said, one hand on one of the short stone pillars that bracketed the steps leading to the front door.

He glanced up at the windows and then back at me. "Oh, right. Okay." He cleared his throat. "Well. I'm Ethan, by the way."

"I'm Callie. Nice to meet you." As soon as the words were out of my mouth, I wanted to bite them back. They sounded so . . . uncool. Darn my mother for all those good-manners reminders.

But he grinned. "I don't know about 'nice'—there's got to be a better way to meet someone than having them pour Coke down your back."

"True. Maybe you can work on that." I laughed. "Anyway, I've gotta get changed. I'll see you around." I turned to go up the steps and couldn't help but smile when I heard him behind me:

"I hope so."

CHAPTER FIVE

After

When Nina had approached Callie about moving in with her during the construction, it didn't seem like something she could say no to. Callie had been living in the house they grew up in for seven years—ever since she left her teaching job at Pemberley, one of New York City's leading private schools, and moved back to Brook Hill.

Callie had initially thought the job at Pemberley was a dream come true. It wasn't one of the *most* coveted programs in the city, so she assumed that the families there wouldn't be like the wildly wealthy, wildly competitive ones that had made it into the top two schools on everyone's list. And since children could stay on for eleven years—from age three through eighth grade—she figured the pressure would be off and they would be allowed to be three-year-olds.

As it turned out, many parents were already thinking ahead to high school applications—not to mention Harvard, Yale, or whichever Ivy League school they wanted for their unsuspecting children. Callie lost count of the conferences she had with parents who were concerned about their little ones' "academic" work. Even the ones that started out as reasonable—"Of course I realize that little Claudia shouldn't be reading now"—ended up on the dark side: "But I've heard about programs where children even younger than her *are* actually reading. I'm planning to hire a tutor."

As far as Callie was concerned, her students lived in an alternate universe from the one in which she and her fellow struggling twentysomethings resided. The children all had the latest hundred-dollar boots, which they were destined to outgrow in three months, and multiple winter coats of different colors and weights. And while Callie and her friends were thrilled to get an invitation for a weekend at an overcrowded beach house in the Hamptons—where a spot in a sleeping bag on the floor of a bedroom was more coveted than the living room sofa since at least it afforded some privacy—the Pemberley kids were constantly flying off to Turks and Caicos, Vail, and Paris.

Callie frequently shook her head in disbelief and amusement as she shared these stories with her three roommates— her college friend Amy, a friend of Amy's from high school, and a fellow Pemberley teacher named Emily. They lived in a tiny apartment on the Upper East Side, a long trek from the subway. The only shared living space was a shoebox-sized kitchen, and what had once been two bedrooms had been divided into four with thin, sound-conducting partitions so that each of them had her own private space. Nonetheless, Callie felt lucky to have a place she could afford (sort of), with roommates who weren't weirder than average.

For three years Callie lived a budget version of *Sex and the City*—largely without the sex. Amy had a boyfriend who occupied her spare time, but the others sought out the bars that offered the best combinations of cheap drinks and potentially appealing men. They had a standing date for Sunday brunch at a diner down the block from their apartment, and gathered on the small sofa in the kitchen to watch *Veronica Mars* and *American Idol* every week. Emily shared Callie's interest in art, and the two liked to check out the exhibits at the Met—paying significantly less than the "suggested" donation—and wander around the galleries in SoHo and TriBeCa. Callie took some drawing and painting classes at the Ninety-Second Street Y, and when the weather allowed, she brought her sketchbook outside on weekends—to Central Park if she was in the mood for nature, or to one of the pocket parks in the canyons of Midtown if she wanted to sketch their angles and shapes. Jenna sometimes took the train down from Connecticut to spend the weekend. On those occasions, Callie splurged on a fancier restaurant or an off-off-Broadway play.

Among the things she *didn't* spend much time doing was hanging out with Nina. They occasionally met for dinner, when her sister could tear herself away from work. Nina had devoted several years to getting her MBA at night, and when she graduated, she simply put the hours she had dedicated to school into her marketing job at a pharmaceutical company. And then, while at a company retreat in Phoenix, she met Michael Kagan, who was there on a guys' golfing weekend. Suddenly, she was able to make time for a social life—but it didn't involve Callie.

When Amy and her boyfriend decided to move in together and the remaining roommates had to figure out what to do about it, Callie realized that adjusting to sharing their tiny bathroom with someone new or increasing her share of the rent by a third were equally unappealing options. She was tired of spending half of her salary on a tiny room with an even tinier window. She was tired of having to walk a mile to see greenery. She was tired of having the sense that she kept meeting the same men over and over again, even if they had different names. And she was tired of feeling increasingly lonely, even as she was surrounded by people.

Briefly, she entertained the idea of becoming a live-in nanny—from what she'd heard, the pay was as good as or better than she was getting at Pemberley, the accommodations would certainly be a step up, and first-class travel would be included. Of course, those jobs weren't easy to come by, especially as parents looked for candidates who had not only college degrees and backgrounds in education but preferably a variety of other skills as well: fluency in a second, if not a third, language; the ability to play—and teach—a musical instrument (ideally one that was less common and therefore more useful for school admissions, like oboe or French horn); and, of course, the aptitude to tutor the children in advanced calculus and physics. Callie knew that she was great with kids and that she could offer up her college-level French and drawing lessons. But before she could give it serious thought, her parents announced that they were moving to their Boca Raton condo—which they had bought as a winter escape—year-round.

"Most of our friends in New Jersey have downsized away from us, and I'm tired of living in two different places," Lorraine had announced on the phone. "Now that your dad has retired, what's keeping us here?"

Callie was momentarily speechless. "You're selling the house?" she asked, unable to wrap her head around the loss of her childhood home.

But apparently Lorraine couldn't wrap her head around it either. "Oh, I couldn't do that!" she exclaimed. "The place where I raised my babies? How could I give that up? And besides, we can stay there when we come to visit you girls."

A few days later, as Callie walked to her apartment in a drenching May rain, rivulets of water finding their way into her boots, she decided she was done. If this was the glamorous city life, glamour wasn't for her anymore. There was about to be an empty house across the river in New Jersey—with a bathroom she wouldn't have to share, a yard where she could spend time outdoors without a moment's thought, and an actual living room with an actual full-size sofa. It would give her the opportunity to regroup and figure out her next move.

Lorraine was thrilled, and wouldn't hear of Callie paying rent. "The house would just be empty otherwise! It will make me feel better knowing it's being looked after," she said out loud. But Callie could hear her thoughts, as clearly as if she had spoken them: *What a relief that my baby who can barely support herself will be safe and sound.*

Callie gave her notice at Pemberley, where neither the director nor her colleagues could believe that she'd leave without a job lined up elsewhere. But the luxury of rent-free living gave her freedom, and she took advantage of it. As soon as the school year ended, she rented a U-Haul, packed up her meager belongings, and headed through the Lincoln Tunnel. Remarkably, only days later, she discovered that Bouncy Castles was in search of a new teacher.

So she moved into her parents' house, intending it to be a temporary way station. But, now, here she was, approaching her midthirties—and the only move she was making was back into her childhood bedroom.

Callie pushed that thought from her head as she spent much of the weekend working on two art projects. She finished the "Zoe's Room" sign she'd made as a surprise for her niece—the words in the kind of bubble letters the little girl liked, with ballerinas perched on the *Z* and the *R*. And on Saturday afternoon she brought the photos she'd taken of all the kids in her class to a picnic table at a nearby park so she could work on drawings of them while sitting beneath the warm end-of-summer/start-of-autumn sun. The leaves hadn't yet begun to turn, but there was a bite in the air signaling that it wouldn't be long before the trees would shimmer in yellows and reds and oranges.

She'd been doing this for the past four years—sketching photos of each of her students and then coloring them lightly with watercolors. Once she was finished, the drawings would hang next to the kids' cubbies, above the rectangles printed neatly with their names. The children thought they were great, but the parents especially loved them. Her last art project of the year was always having the kids decorate inexpensive frames she brought in from the craft store—and then Callie's drawings would go home in their custom frames. Part of her wished she could keep them herself—on some kind of "wall of fame" in her classroom—but she also loved the looks on the parents' faces when their kids presented the gifts to them on the last day of school.

On Sunday, Tess and Brett invited her over for brunch—Brett made a mean chocolate chip pancake, and Tess poured a mean mimosa—and in the late afternoon, she luxuriated in her empty house while she still had the chance. She lost herself in a book, carrying it with her from the living room sofa to the kitchen table, where she ate her dinner—Trader Joe's had just brought back one of her favorite soups—and then up to bed, where she finally closed the book long after she should have turned out her light.

When the alarm awakened her on Monday morning, she was loath to get out of her cozy, queen-size bed for the last time in what would be months. But she dragged herself up, knowing she'd promised herself that she'd put fresh sheets on the mattress for Nina and Michael. She had debated bringing her beloved comforter to the room down the hall and doubling it up on the twin bed, but then decided she was being petty.

She quickly stripped off the sheets, put on new ones, smoothed the duvet, and fluffed up the pillows. Satisfied, she went downstairs to put coffee on before going back up to shower and dress.

The first text came as she headed out the front door. She glanced at her phone.

> Up all night packing. Movers on their way. Everything ready on your end?

Callie shook her head. Nina had been preparing for the move for the past six weeks. It was hard to imagine there was any packing left to do. But her sister always made it sound like every minute of her day was so chock-full of activity that sleep was rarely an option. She stuck her phone back into her purse and got into the car, where she listened to it continue to ping over the course of the short drive to school. When she pulled it out again after putting the car in park in the Bouncy Castles lot, there was a series of no fewer than eight more messages.

> Is the bedroom ready for us?

> Michael ended up having to go to work for a while. Can't believe I have to do this alone.

> We're doing the drop-off at the storage unit first.

> Should be at the house by noon.

> When will you be home?

> We're wiped out. I hope there's nothing for me to do when we get there but unpack.

> Movers just got here. Wish Michael were here. I don't think they're taking me seriously at all.

> Where ARE you?

Callie typed back, Just got to school. Was driving. Everything is all set for you. See you when I get home. Then she turned the sound off on her phone and put it back into her purse.

The moving van was gone by the time Callie returned home after school around three o'clock, a headache nagging behind her eyes. She took a deep, bracing breath before walking up the porch steps.

Suddenly the front door burst open. "Aunt Callie!"

Callie smiled in spite of herself. Clearly, Nina hadn't overseen Zoe's clothing that morning. The little girl was wearing pink-and-green-striped leggings with a yellow sundress. A blue cardigan was half on and half off. Callie crouched down and her niece ran into her arms. She breathed in the barely-there scent of the all-natural baby shampoo Nina special-ordered.

"Hi, Binks," she said, giving her a squeeze.

Zoe pulled away from her embrace and then grabbed one of Callie's hands and pulled. "Come see my new room," she urged.

"Just a minute, kiddo. Let me see how your mom is doing."

Zoe put her hands on her hips. "She's *working*," she declared, her tone on the second word remarkably like Nina's.

Callie suppressed a smile. "Still, let me check in with her," she said, calling then in a louder voice, "Neen?"

"Upstairs!"

Callie dropped her jacket and purse on the armchair in the foyer and headed up, barely registering the sunlight that filtered through the door onto the hallway rug and continued to fade the fibers in exactly that spot.

Lorraine and Martin had moved to this house from an apartment in New Brunswick when Nina was a baby, forty years earlier. Lorraine had left her position as a librarian in one of Rutgers's many campus libraries when Nina was born, and Martin's commute to his job as an engineer at Lockheed

Martin was only a little longer from their new home. (For years—encouraged by Nina—Callie was convinced that their dad was co-owner of the firm he worked for. Why else would it have Martin in the name?)

The couple had met when Martin was pursuing his PhD in physics at Rutgers, and they didn't marry until he completed his degree—which meant they were a little older than most newlyweds at the time. Nina was born a couple of years later, and while Martin would have been happy staying in the apartment, Lorraine wanted to raise her family in a house. To her—as Callie had heard the story told many times over the years—a home was only a home if you went upstairs to go to bed.

Callie couldn't count how many times she'd heard what a state the house had been in when they moved in. Built in the 1890s, like a stretch of other Victorians on the block, it had known only a few owners in its lifetime, but they hadn't done much to it other than basic maintenance. Lorraine would have preferred one of the homes of 1960s or '70s vintage in Brook Hill's newer neighborhoods, but Martin—the family's number cruncher—couldn't resist the good deal they could get on the Victorian, despite its sagging front porch. And engineer that he was, he insisted on teaching himself to do many of the upgrades. Much to Lorraine's unending chagrin, Martin left the walls open—revealing the plumbing and electrical systems—until he could find enough spare time to complete the job. But by the time Callie came along when Nina was eight—"Better late than never!" Lorraine liked to sing—the walls were closed up, and her mother had spent a couple of years throwing herself into decorating their finally presentable home.

Now, seven years since Callie had moved back home, the same paintings that Lorraine had chosen hung on the walls, the same framed photos stood on the half-moon-shaped hall table near the stairs, and the same figurines were displayed in the breakfront in the dining room. The living room sofa was the same one that Callie had sprawled on when she was doing her homework, that Nina made out with her boyfriends on when their parents were out and she was babysitting Callie, and that their dad used to fall asleep on while he was "watching the game." As an adult, Callie could frequently be found curled up on that sofa with a good book.

Arriving on the upstairs landing, Callie turned left at the top of the staircase toward what, that very morning, had been her bedroom. In the doorway, she stopped. On the bed was a paisley Ralph Lauren bedspread in tones of burgundy and navy. Her impeccably put-together sister was crouched on the floor near the closet, stacking taupe canvas shoeboxes neatly on top of each other. Through the clear windows in the ends of the boxes, a variety of pumps, Top-Siders, and Tory Burch flats were visible.

"Hey, Nina," Callie said.

Nina turned, the five-month baby bump visible under her scoop-necked eggplant maternity tee. She blew wisps of hair out of her eyes. Her brown hair—the same natural color as Callie's—normally glinted with golden highlights, but as she had when she was pregnant with Zoe, Nina was eliminating them from her routine for the sake of the baby. "Hey," she said.

"You look tired. Why don't you take a break?" Callie asked, stepping into the room.

Nina shook her head. "I won't be able to rest until things are in some sort of order."

Involuntarily, Callie glanced at the bed, wondering where her own comforter was. Nina followed her gaze.

"And on top of everything else, I had to strip the bed. I thought you said everything was ready," she said testily.

"I *made* the bed for you," Callie retorted. "You made extra work for yourself."

"Why would we want to use your bedding?" Nina asked, as if the linens in question were riddled with bedbugs. "We have our own." She looked Callie up and down. "Is that what you wore to work today?"

Callie looked down at herself. She was wearing a flippy short skirt with a black-and-white harlequin print—one of her favorites—a lightweight maroon sweater with three-quarter-length sleeves, and high-tops. Looped around her neck was a bright yellow scarf with pinpoint black polka dots.

Callie felt her blood pressure rising. She had wondered if the upside of this new living arrangement might be that she and her older sister could rediscover some of the closeness they had once had. Or rather, the closeness Callie had once felt for Nina.

With eight years between them, the sisters had lived largely parallel lives when they last resided in this house together. But elementary school Callie was awestruck by her high school sister. As long as she could remember, Nina always had a cute boyfriend in tow and was always winning something—a trophy for cross-country, a prize for math. In the moments when Nina paused to braid Callie's hair, or ask her about her second-grade teacher—whom Nina had had nearly a decade earlier—Callie was over the moon. And when things went south with the cute boyfriends and Nina would briefly wallow in sadness, she'd let Callie snuggle next to her while they watched videos of Nina's best-loved movies—*Pretty in Pink*, *When Harry Met Sally . . .*, and *The Breakfast Club*. One of Callie's favorite memories with her sister was when Nina took her to see *Sleepless in Seattle* right after Nina graduated from high school. Callie was ten, and thought Jonah Baldwin was super cute and his best friend, Jessica, was the epitome of cool.

When Nina went away to college in Maryland, it seemed to Callie as if she'd gone to some amazing alternate universe full of fun, friends, and no rules. On Family Weekends, Callie felt like queen for a day—or, more accurately, princess for a day—while Nina's friends exclaimed over her cute little sister and

asked her questions about her favorite TV shows and books
and if she wanted to go to Loyola, too, when she grew up.

Callie had always assumed that when she got older and
"caught up," she and Nina would have a relationship more
like her friends did with their sisters—with whom they could
share clothes and secrets. But Nina moved to Manhattan right
after college graduation and threw herself into her first job,
in the marketing department of an insurance company. She
started her MBA program while Callie was at Welford, and
was still juggling both that and her new job with "Big Pharma"
when Callie herself graduated. When Callie and Ethan broke
up, Nina invited her little sister to spend a weekend with her
in the city. She took her to Serendipity for one of their ginor-
mous sundaes, they binge-watched some of the same movies
they used to watch after Nina's high school breakups, and—
uncharacteristically gingerly for her—Nina poked around the
edges of Callie's thin story about why she'd ended things. But
the last thing Callie wanted was for Nina to know the truth.
She felt sure that polished, put-together Nina would never
have done what she had.

Once Callie moved into the city herself, the sisters occasionally met for Saturday dinner at the apartment Nina had
proudly bought for herself in TriBeCa—Nina was starting
to get adventurous with cooking, and would try ever-more-
challenging recipes out on Callie—and they took the train
home to Brook Hill together periodically to spend a weekend
with their folks. And Nina sometimes suggested that Callie
come running with her. If it had been a leisurely loop around
the park, Callie might have given it a try—she had run a bit
in college with Jenna when she'd first arrived—but Nina was
always in training for a 5K, and then for a half-marathon, and
finally, a marathon. Once Nina met Michael, what little free
time she allowed herself away from work and running was
suddenly swallowed up. And gradually, the gulf between them

just seemed to widen, especially when Callie moved back to
Brook Hill.

Despite the fact that Callie's career choice was something
Nina couldn't quite take seriously ("My friend's retired mother
works at her daughter's preschool to fill her time"), her older
sister also couldn't understand why she would have given up
her position at Pemberley ("Do you *realize* how hard it is to
get a teaching position in a place like that?"). And it didn't help
that Callie was literally living "on the house" in their family
home—though it certainly fit the narrative of Nina working
hard at her storybook life while Callie bumped along without
a care in the world.

Now, as Callie looked down at her outfit, the hope that this
might be a time for things to change between them fizzled.
She didn't see anything wrong with what she was wearing.
In fact, two of the girls in her class had actually told her they
loved her scarf.

But before she could snap back at Nina, Zoe appeared,
hopping on one foot. "Aunt Callie! I'm *waiting.*"

Callie tossed one last glance at her sister before turning
to her niece. She reached out her hand. "Okay, Binks, let's go."

Callie and Zoe walked down the hall to the room where
Nina had spent her formative years, the little girl tugging on
her aunt's hand. "Come *on* . . . ," she urged.

At the doorway, Callie had to silently give her sister credit.
She'd clearly tackled her daughter's room before her own.
On the bed was Zoe's familiar pink comforter, a patchwork
of gingham, flowers, and bright suns. Lined up on top of the
bookcase was a collection of her favorite stuffed animals, and
the bookshelves were stocked with her books—many of which
Callie recognized as gifts she herself had bestowed.

Zoe ran over to the bed and leaped onto it. "Look, Aunt
Callie—it's just like my room, but in Gamma and Grampa's
house!"

Callie smiled grimly. Of course Nina continued to refer to it as their parents' house, although they came up now only for the holidays and a week here or there. Not, she had to admit, that she had done much to make this house her home—but still, it irked.

She watched her niece cuddle a floppy-eared bunny, and her smile softened. "Wow, sweetie, it's great," she said as she stepped across the threshold. "By the way, I have a surprise for you. Wait here."

After a quick trip down the hall to her own room, she returned with the sign behind her back. Zoe had hopped back off the bed and was bouncing up and down on her toes. "What is it? What is it?"

Callie held out the sign to her.

Zoe's smile was wide. "My name!" she exclaimed, pointing at it.

"Yup. It says 'Zoe's Room.'"

"Thank you, Aunt Callie!" she yelled, flinging her arms around Callie's thighs before her aunt could bend down to her level.

"You're very welcome, Binks. Let's figure out where to put it."

Once they'd concluded that propping it up on the dresser was best, Callie suggested that they read some books. The two settled in on the bed, Callie happy that one of the very books she'd given her—*A Bad Case of Stripes*—was on the top of the pile.

A little while later, the doorbell rang. Callie pushed herself off the bed to head downstairs. Through the wavy glass in the diamond-shaped panes in the front door, she recognized the bulky figure of her brother-in-law. Apparently, he didn't yet have his own key.

As she opened the door, she started to say hello, but Michael raised a finger to hold her off.

"Right, right," he was saying, and she realized he was speaking via the Bluetooth transmitter perched in his ear. "Okay, then. I gotta go. I have another meeting to get to."

Momentarily puzzled, Callie realized that his family was Michael's next "meeting." Heaven forbid his colleagues or clients realize he had a life outside his office.

"Hey, Cal," he said, leaning in to give her a peck on the cheek. In her entire life, no one had ever called her Cal until Michael came along. She hadn't been sure how to correct him at the time and had been stuck with it ever since.

"Hi, Michael. Seems like you're busy." She inclined her head toward the earpiece he was now removing from his ear.

"Always. How're things here?"

Callie shrugged. "You know Nina. She's practically finished unpacking already."

Michael deposited his briefcase on the floor next to the door. Callie knew Nina would find it there and silently pick it up later. "That's Nina. So, what's for dinner?"

Callie raised her eyebrows. *Is dinner my responsibility?* "Umm, I don't know. We could order pizza . . . ?"

"Sounds good," he grunted. "Nina's upstairs?"

Callie nodded. "And Zoe," she added. She often thought that her niece was an afterthought as far as her brother-in-law was concerned.

"Thanks." He dismissed her by heading up the stairway.

She went into the kitchen to look for the menu from her favorite local pizzeria, shaking her head—not for the first time—at her brother-in-law.

Although she wanted to like him, she couldn't quite get there. Michael was just a little too loud and too self-important for Callie's taste. He had opinions about nearly everything, whether or not he was hampered by any actual facts. She never understood what he did for a living—she knew he worked in finance—but clearly it was *extremely* important and demanded that Michael work long hours and check his BlackBerry every three or four minutes. As far as Callie could gather, prior to meeting Nina, Michael's life was his job and a weekly, well-lubricated poker game with friends who still went by nicknames like Worm and Gator. She assumed there had been women, too, but didn't get the sense that any of them had lasted very long.

Now that Zoe had come along, Michael's parenting style had done nothing to change her view of him. As far as Callie was concerned, he was interested in Zoe on his terms—when it suited him. And the bulk of the heavy lifting was on Nina's shoulders. Callie wasn't sure she had ever seen him change a diaper or prepare a meal, causing her to often wonder how her sister had ended up in some sort of 1950s marriage. But as Lorraine frequently reminded her when she made noises about Michael's shortcomings, Nina seemed happy.

Once again, as she located the pizza menu, Callie steeled herself for the coming months of cohabitation with the mantra "This is all for Nina and Zoe."

Hours later, after pizza was eaten, Zoe was tucked into bed surrounded by a menagerie of stuffed animals, and Michael was camped out in front of the television, *Monday Night Football* on and stacks of paper surrounding him.

During dinner, they had all listened to his lamentations about the deal he was in the midst of. Apparently, it was on the verge of "blowing up," thanks to the many "stupid" people involved on all sides. Callie realized she was the only one at the table who was glancing at Zoe each time her father described another one of the "idiots" he had to deal with. Zoe appeared to be paying no attention as she picked the cheese off her pizza, eating that and leaving the crust behind. But Callie knew she was absorbing every word. Finally, Michael's eyes followed Callie's gaze, and he suddenly seemed aware of his daughter's presence. Something changed in his face—maybe he had finally realized that his tirade was not appropriate for four-year-old ears. Then he spoke.

"Zoe!" he said sharply. "Don't do that with your pizza."

Zoe looked up, startled. "The bread part is yucky."

"What you're doing is disgusting." Michael's tone suggested there was no distinction between Zoe's actions and nose picking. "Stop playing with your food."

"I'm not playing," she said plaintively. "I only like the cheese."

Callie bit the inside of her cheek to keep herself quiet.

Nina sighed. "Let me scrape the cheese off for you and cut it up," she said, reaching for Zoe's plate.

Michael shook his head, clearly not approving of this solution, but he remained quiet. *Thank goodness for small favors.*

"Anyway, I've got to get some work done," he said, rising from the table and heading out of the room. Callie was torn between thanking him for gracing them with his presence and suggesting that he not let the door hit him on the way out—but said nothing.

Now, Callie and Nina sat in the kitchen with cups of tea. Like the rest of the house, the kitchen remained unchanged. The same wallpaper with sprigs of flowers covered the walls, the same dishes still lived in the same oak cabinets, and the same toaster still sat on the same speckled countertop that bore a burn mark from one of Callie's first attempts to use the iron. Callie suspected that Nina would not be using this kitchen as a model for the one in her soon-to-be-renovated home.

Callie put her cup down on the table that was scarred from years of art projects and homework. "You look exhausted, Nina. Why don't you go to bed?"

Nina sighed. "There's no point. My indigestion is so bad I can't lie down properly, and it takes me forever to fall asleep. This pregnancy thing isn't a whole heck of a lot of fun."

"Can you take something?"

Nina shook her head. "Pregnant, remember?"

"Ah," Callie replied.

Nina leaned back in her chair, gently rubbing her sternum, and closed her eyes. Callie knew that, no matter how uncomfortable she was, Nina was thrilled to be pregnant again.

When Nina and Michael got married, Nina was thirty-four, and she made it clear that the next step for them was a baby. Callie sensed that her sister felt behind schedule—and when pregnancy didn't come easily, it was the first time she had seen anxiety bleed through Nina's mask. Lorraine confided that Nina was obsessed with finding a solution: changing her diet, cutting back on running, trying acupuncture. But the biggest shock came when Nina announced that what she really needed was to cut stress out of her life.

Nina downsized her job, took a pay cut, and talked Michael into buying a house in Wolcott, New Jersey—a diverse suburb with a bit of an urban vibe, a short(ish) train ride away from Manhattan. Callie still wondered how in the world she had convinced her husband to bookend his day with a commute.

But Nina's plan did the trick. A few months later, she called Callie to tell her she was pregnant, her voice filled with a mixture of joy and relief. Before they knew it, she'd quit her job altogether, throwing her considerable energy and organizing skills into her new home, her new community, and then her new baby. Zoe was two when Nina talked to Callie about wanting her daughter to have a sibling—but this pregnancy didn't come any quicker than the first one had. So as Nina sat across from her, her hand resting on her baby bump, Callie knew she was overjoyed.

After a few moments' silence, Nina opened her eyes and spoke again. "Oh! So, I saw that article about Ethan."

Callie's heart quickened. *Why does it* do *that?* she asked

herself, annoyed. *And why does Nina have to know* everything?
"What article?" she asked her sister. *Better to play dumb.*

"In your alumni magazine." Nina sighed impatiently.

"How did you see that?" she asked, mystified.

Nina waved her hand vaguely in the direction of the recycling. "I was putting the pizza box in the recycling. The magazine was on top. Open to that page."

Shit. Callie had to start thinking like someone who had
roommates rather than someone who lived alone. Then she
realized that Nina was looking at her, clearly waiting for a response. "Yeah, seems like he's doing well."

Nina cocked her head, her eyes still on Callie. After a long
moment of silence, she spoke again. "Seems like that movie of
his is about you."

Callie swallowed. "Yep, could be," she said noncommittally.

Now Nina raised her eyebrows. "That's all you have to say?"

Callie shrugged. "What's there to say?"

"Your ex-boyfriend writes a movie about you, and you
don't care? You don't wonder what it means?"

"What it means?" Callie was beginning to feel like an echo.

"Yes, what it *means*," her sister replied, crossing her arms
over her belly.

Callie bit her lip. Of course she'd wondered what it meant.
Of all the things he could have written a screenplay about, he
wrote about a relationship that had ended ten years earlier?
Did he still think about her? Had he not gotten over her?

But she simply shrugged. "I'm sure it doesn't mean
anything."

Nina frowned. "Hello! This is your sister speaking. The
guy you were practically joined at the hip with for four years
has been out of your life for what, ten years, and now here he
is, writing a love letter to you, and you don't think it means
anything?"

"A love letter? The movie's not out yet. It could be a big 'fuck you.'"

"I doubt it. I don't think people hold grudges that long. At least not when it's over a failed college relationship."

"But you stay in love that long after a breakup?" Callie made a face.

"Maybe. Look at you."

"Look at me, what?" Callie crossed her own arms, mirroring Nina's.

"Ten years later and have you gotten serious about anyone else? That's got to mean something."

"It means I haven't met anyone. You know what that's like. It took you a while to find Michael," Callie said, looking down at the table and tracing one of the bigger scratches on the surface. Talking about her love life—or lack thereof—with her happily married sister was not exactly how she wanted to spend her evening. Particularly since, even now that they were both adults, Nina clearly remained the older sister—the responsible one, the sensible one, the successful one, at least in her own eyes. *Oh, Callie,* she always seemed to be saying—whether aloud or telepathically—in a slightly bemused, slightly disdainful tone. And Callie knew that it didn't help that she was living rent-free in their childhood home. Evidence, as far as Nina was concerned, that she had yet to grow up.

"Riiight," Nina said, drawing the word out so it would sound as incredulous as possible.

Callie felt a spark of anger and looked up. "Hey, I broke up with him, remember?"

Nina sat forward in her seat. "Yes, I remember. I also remember that no one could understand why." Nina looked intently at Callie as if waiting for her to say something, but Callie couldn't imagine what. Then she lifted her shoulders so slightly it was almost imperceptible. "Anyway, you were a mess afterward. For a long time. And," she added, "it looks like you might still be. You've lived here for seven years. *Seven years*, Callie, and you've done nothing in this house. Probably the only rooms you use are your bedroom and the bathroom. All you've done is turn Mom and Dad's house into a dorm. There wasn't even any food when I got here. What do you eat?"

The spark of anger Callie had felt a moment before burst into flame. "I eat. And as far as the house goes—that is *totally* unfair!" she exclaimed, even as she was thinking that, perhaps, *totally* was the wrong choice of word. She really hadn't made much of an imprint on the house in seven years. *Why is that?* "So I don't really cook. It's just not my thing. Trader Joe's has great stuff you can just heat up. Nothing wrong with that. And I do takeout. And what am I going to do to the house? It's only temporary anyway. And you know how Mom is—she wants everything as it is."

"Temporary? Since when is seven years temporary? And you know perfectly well Mom would be okay with some changes. She's just happy you're here and she doesn't have to worry about you scrambling to make rent. You could buy new towels, for God's sake," Nina said, gesturing toward the dish towels hanging on the handle of the dishwasher, the same faded plaid that had hung there longer than Callie could remember.

Callie pushed her chair away from the table and carried her cup to the sink. "So I don't care about dish towels. What does that matter? I'm busy—I have work, and my art classes . . ."

"Geez, Callie, I saw all the artwork you have stacked up in your room. You could hang *that* up around the house. Some of it isn't half bad. But you just exist here. It's not living. Which is what I was saying about Ethan—that ended, and you were a mess for so long . . ."

Callie looked over her shoulder and cut her off. "I was not. It's always hard moving on from a relationship. Especially one that lasted so long." She turned back to the sink, where she finished rinsing the cup and put it in the dishwasher. Then she turned around. "Anyway, that's all ancient history."

Nina opened her mouth, and closed it again. Then, clearly having decided to end the argument, she stood up, put her hands on the small of her back, and arched slightly to stretch her muscles. "No, it's current pop culture," she said, smiling.

Callie grimaced, not in the mood to find the quip amusing. Nor was she about to concede any point Nina might make on the topic. "Movie aside, it's in the past."

"There's no such thing as 'movie aside.' It's out there." Nina pushed her chair neatly back under the table. "Don't tell me you're not going to see it."

Callie shrugged. "I dunno," she said noncommittally, knowing immediately how implausible her response sounded.

Nina pointed at her chest. "Again, sister here. Has known you your entire life. If you don't see this movie, then I'm type B."

Callie managed a laugh. Her sister smiled.

"All right," Nina added. "I'm off to bed to try to sleep in an upright position." She headed out of the kitchen, but turned back at the doorway. "And when you do see that movie, maybe you can finally move on."

Callie opened her mouth to speak, but Nina had turned away again. Besides, she didn't know what else to say. Except that if this was the kind of after-dinner conversation she'd have to endure with the new living arrangement, this was going to be a long four months.

CHAPTER SIX

After

Callie had trouble falling asleep that night. And it wasn't just because of the narrow twin bed to which she had been relegated.

Ever since the call from Jenna, she had been pushing aside the question that kept popping into her head. But now, thanks to Nina's prodding, she had to face it. *Why?* Why, after ten years, would Ethan have written a movie that kicked off with their breakup? Could it be, as Nina said, that he was still thinking about her after all this time? It didn't take much reflection for Callie to answer that with a resounding no. It could have been years since he'd written the screenplay, after all. Everybody knows films take forever to make. What if she was wrong, and he was married? What if he had kids? Callie was well aware of how Ethan had felt about her—and how much pain she caused him back then—but that didn't mean he had any feelings at all for her now. And if he did, why hadn't he ever contacted her? What kind of person would make a movie for the purpose of it being some sort of love letter, as Nina put it, when all he had to do was write an *actual* love letter? Or an email? Or pick up a phone? Aside from a few agonized voice-mail messages and a single hurt, angry letter right after the breakup, she hadn't heard a word from him.

She tossed and turned, trying to push these thoughts from her head. She didn't care what Nina had to say—this was not a *Say Anything* moment, and Ethan was no Lloyd Dobler standing outside her window with his boom box. If only she had taken out the stupid recycling.

When she dragged herself out of bed the next morning, it felt like she'd nodded off only moments before her alarm went off. Hearing movement downstairs, she decided to alter her normal routine and head straight for the shower. She was definitely not ready for human interaction.

She turned on the water to let it heat up and peeled off her nighttime costume of T-shirt and plaid boxer shorts. Then she put her hand under the spray, expecting it to be hot. It was not. She closed her eyes, realizing that two showers may well have been taken before hers, draining the old water heater lurking in the corner of the basement. Gritting her teeth, she stepped into the tepid shower and proceeded to wash herself as speedily as she had when, as a teenager, she went on a school trip to a rustic sleepaway camp and the only option was a communal washroom. Just as she was rinsing the shampoo out of her hair, the door to the bathroom flew open.

Callie shrieked. Then she saw a small figure through the translucent shower curtain.

"Hi, Aunt Callie," Zoe said, proceeding to pull down her pants and perch herself on the toilet.

"Zoe! You need to knock before you come in!"

"I had to pee." She hopped off the commode and finished her business.

Callie's heart slowed to its normal speed, and she kicked

herself for not locking the door. *That's a mistake I won't repeat,* she thought as she turned off the water and grabbed her towel. She dried herself off as briskly as possible as the chilly air raised goose bumps on her wet skin.

A few minutes later, she was downstairs, wearing a pale yellow T-shirt and a pair of black leggings. Over the T-shirt was her super-soft baby-blue cashmere cardigan—the only cashmere she owned, which she had treated with kid gloves to prolong its life span for the six years she'd had it. After a night of no sleep, a comfy, cozy outfit was definitely in order to get her through the day. On her feet she wore her favorite cowboy boots because they made her happy. What hadn't made her happy that morning was her hair. She was typically okay with how it fell around her face, but today it was completely uncooperative. She'd given up and twisted it into a messy bun on the back of her head.

In the kitchen, Nina was decked out in a pair of dark-rinse skinny jeans (skinny except for the swell under what was certainly a maternity panel concealed under her top) and a camel-colored ribbed turtleneck. Her bobbed hair was smooth and tucked behind her ears, in which she was wearing small diamond knots. She was zipping up a pink canvas lunch box bearing the initials *ZJK*—Zoe Jillian Kagan—stitched in green. She turned at the sound of Callie entering the room and raised her eyebrows. "Nice outfit. Are you going line dancing, or back to bed?"

Callie resisted the urge to say the first thing that came into her mind. "Rodeo, actually," she replied instead. "And good morning to you, too." She went to the coffeemaker, where she imagined there would be coffee brewing. There wasn't. "No coffee?"

"Well, I'm not drinking it." Nina patted her belly. "And Michael is very particular." She pointed. A Keurig was now sitting on the counter beside the toaster. "He'll only drink this specific dark roast."

"Ah. You think I could grab one of his? It would be faster than putting up a pot."

A shadow crossed Nina's face. "Fine, but not all the time, okay? We get them at this shop up near our house, and I don't want to have to be going there all the time."

"Never mind. I'll stop at Dunkin' on my way to work." Callie thought Nina would respond, *Oh, no, just take one*. But she didn't.

"Oh, okay. That's great, thanks" is what she did say. Then she suddenly turned toward the hallway and screamed, "Zoe! Are you ready?" Silence. "Zoe!"

Then there was a *clump, clump* down the stairs and Zoe appeared at the doorway.

"Come on, we've got to go," Nina said in the direction of her daughter. Then she turned to Callie. "We've got to run. I have to drop Zoe at school and then I have an appointment with the decorator. We're starting to look at tile."

Callie nodded. "Sounds like fun."

"Hardly. I'd like to be able to have one day without running around."

Then have one, Callie said to herself, suspecting that if the tile wasn't discussed today, the world wouldn't collapse. But she knew better than to suggest such blasphemy to her sister. Instead, she smiled. "Well, have a nice day anyway."

Nina snorted as if that were hardly possible.

"Bye, Aunt Callie!" Zoe said.

"What kind of goodbye is that?" Callie opened her arms.

Zoe ran into them, and Callie gave her niece a big squeeze. "Have fun at school."

Zoe looked at her very seriously. "Okay. But snack is a problem."

"What kind of problem?"

But Callie wasn't destined to find out that morning.

"Let's *go*, Zoe. We're going to be late."

Zoe turned and skipped after her mother.

Later that day, while the kids were having lunch and she was on her break, Callie found herself alone in the school office. She bit into her apple and idly opened the browser on the desktop computer. All morning, her conversation with Nina had been lurking at the corners of her mind, so before she could type "Ethan Rendel" into the Google search box, she opened the Connections website. She had received an email notification that morning that Jason the advertising guy had messaged her.

> Hi, Callie. Thanks for the nudge back! I still find writing these emails so weird, and I never know where to start. So I'll tell you that I nudged you because I think you're very cute, and, like you, I enjoy reading (especially a good mystery) and good conversation. Have you read anything good lately? I also think it's cool that you're a preschool teacher; kids are so funny. I have two nephews that I love to take to the park. How old are the kids that you teach? As you know from my profile, I'm in advertising—which has its good and bad days. But I work with some great people. I've been in the New York area for a couple of years. I used to live in Chicago. It's also a great city (have you been there?), but I'm liking my new home a lot, as well. Are you from this area? I hope to hear back from you and get to know you better. I'm more interesting than this in person, I promise.
>
> Cheers,
> Jason

Callie smiled at the last line. Until then, she'd been thinking, *Well, he's awfully . . . earnest.* Before she could decide not
to, she clicked Reply.

> Hi Jason. Thanks for the message. Glad you're
> liking this area—I'd have to wonder about
> anyone who doesn't enjoy New York, at least
> during the "honeymoon" phase. I stayed up
> way too late this past weekend with Fredrik
> Backman's new book. In the mystery cate-
> gory, I like everything from Agatha Christie to
> Tana French. My classroom is full of 3½ and
> 4 year olds. On any given day, they are hilari-
> ous, exasperating, adorable, and noisy! I love
> my job—but I am definitely happy to give them
> back to their parents at the end of the day.
> (Just like they're probably happy to give them
> to me in the morning!) How old are your neph-
> ews? I have a 4-year-old niece who I love to
> death. What brought you here from Chicago?
> Is that where you're from? I'm writing this on
> my break, so I'm going to sign off here. I'll end
> with a "dating show" sort of question. If you
> could plan your ideal weekend, what would it
> be? Enjoy your day.
> Best,
> Callie

She reread her message. She'd sidestepped the question of
whether she'd been to Chicago, preferring not to think about
trips with Ethan that had brought her there. Reasonably satisfied, she clicked Send, and glanced at the time. No time for
Google now—she had to be back in her classroom.

• • •

When her school day ended, Callie stopped again at the school office. Judith had asked her to come by before she went home.

"You wanted to see me?" Callie asked, hovering in the doorway. At least now the pit in her stomach had nothing to do with Ethan.

Judith looked up and ran a hand through her short, spiky hair. "Yes, please, sit down." She waved a hand in the direction of the single chair in the corner of the small office, as if there were anyplace else to sit—other than in her own lap.

Callie sat, first placing her hands under her thighs, and then, deciding that was unprofessional, she put them in her lap, clasped loosely.

Judith took off her glasses and tapped a pencil against her teeth. Then she sighed. "I'll just get right to the point. As you know, we've been having a challenging situation with Liam Switzer. After school yesterday, his mother met with me, and then with Robin. We've decided that the best thing at this point is a fresh start."

Callie cocked her head. "A fresh start?"

"Yes. As of Monday, Liam will be in your class."

Callie's heart sank. Nearly a month into the school year, she and her kids had fallen into a good rhythm. Overall, they were a nice group that meshed well together. She wouldn't have relished adding anyone to the mix at this point, but especially not a boy who was, well, challenging.

"Are you sure that's best?" she asked diplomatically.

Judith took a long breath. "In this case, yes. I know it's unusual for us to juggle classrooms, but honestly, I think it's the right thing to do. Liam's mom isn't comfortable with Robin, and she promised she'd be more on board with working together if we could start over."

"Since when does a mom get to decide?"

Judith arched her eyebrows. "*I* decided. But you're right, we wouldn't normally make a switch like this so early in the school year, without trying to build on relationships that are just starting to gel and giving things more of a chance to work themselves out. But there are some extenuating circumstances."

"Which are . . . ?" Callie probed.

"Robin is having some . . . health . . . issues, so I think it may be best to take some of the burden off her."

Callie's eyebrows knitted together. "Is she okay?"

Judith nodded. "Yes. I think so. It's not my place to discuss it, but since you're directly impacted by this decision, it's only right that you know that that's a part of it."

Callie felt a pang of guilt at having been annoyed by the change. "Thanks, I appreciate that."

"Of course. And you know that you have our support."

They talked a bit more about the change, and the dynamics of Callie's class and how it might be best to try to integrate Liam. But she still felt frustrated—and a bit overwhelmed—when she drove out of the parking lot in the direction of home.

Letting herself into the house, she was surprised by the quiet. For a moment. Then there was a shriek.

"Aunt Callie!" Zoe yelled. "Come see!"

She followed the voice into the dining room, where the table was covered with paper and markers.

"I'm writing a book!" her niece announced proudly.

Callie noticed that some of the sheets of paper had drawings on them. Others were marked with random letters.

"Wow!" she said. "You're working hard! What's your book about?"

Zoe looked up at her, her eyes shining. "It's all about how me and Mommy and Daddy moved in here." She pointed at a page with a stick figure and a crooked box colored pink. "This is me in my new room."

"I can tell. What a great picture!"

Callie waited patiently for Zoe to explain another dozen pages before she managed to extricate herself and go into the kitchen. There, she found Nina chopping vegetables.

"Hey," she said, sneaking a carrot stick off the cutting board.

"Hey," Nina replied, putting the knife down and walking to the cupboard to retrieve a bottle of olive oil.

"How was your day?"

"Exhausting. The traffic was terrible driving Zoe to school, so we were late. Then I was with the decorator for probably two hours. I brought some tile samples home." She pointed vaguely toward the hallway. "Then I had an hour to kill where it made no sense for me to drive back here before I had to get Zoe. Then the two of us had *another* hour to kill before her dance class. All I want to do is sit down, but now I have to make dinner."

"I'm tired just listening to you, and I'm not even pregnant." Callie started to sit down herself, but then straightened up, not wanting to throw it in Nina's face. "Can I help?" she asked instead.

"No, it's fine. I have a system."

Of course you do, Callie thought. Then she did sit down. She was going through her mail when Nina suddenly said, "Oh!"

She turned to see her sister holding the countertop with both hands. Callie rushed over to her. "Are you okay?"

Nina's knuckles were white. "I was just dizzy for a second. I'm okay."

Callie put her hand on Nina's back. "Why don't you come and sit down?"

Nina took a shuddery breath. "I'm okay."

"Still. Humor me." Callie put her arm under Nina's elbow to nudge her to release the countertop. Then she led her to the table and eased her into the chair she had just vacated.

Nina passed a hand over her face while Callie got her a glass of water. She took a sip and put the glass back on the table. "Thanks."

"Better?" Callie pulled out another chair and sat down herself.

Nina nodded. "I just got a little light-headed."

"Has this happened before?"

Nina shrugged and picked at the pale polish on one of her fingernails.

"It has."

"It's no big deal." Nina raised her eyes to her sister's. "Sometimes I forget to eat."

Callie closed her eyes and shook her head. "For someone who won't take so much as a Tylenol because of the baby—you *can't* not eat!"

"I know," Nina said, looking down.

Callie stood and went to the refrigerator. She found a package of organic string cheese. After ripping open the red package—and accidentally decapitating the happy cow—she pulled one out and brought it to Nina.

"Those are Zoe's."

"Eat it," Callie replied firmly.

Nina glanced at her, then silently peeled off the plastic wrap and took a bite.

"I'm going to finish making dinner," Callie announced.

Nina quickly swallowed the piece of cheese in her mouth. "No, I'll do it." She started to push herself away from the table.

Callie put her hand on the back of Nina's chair. "You will not. I've got it. Just tell me what to do."

Nina sighed, clearly deciding not to fight her sister. Callie silently thanked her years of preschool teaching for enabling her to develop a tone of voice that compelled even stubborn big sisters to obey.

"When is Michael coming home?" Callie asked as she poured the wild rice into boiling water, per Nina's instructions.

"Not till after we eat. I'll warm up a plate for him later."

"Is that every day?" Callie put the lid on the pot and turned the fire down.

"Pretty much. He was early yesterday because of the move."

"Wow. Long hours."

Nina nodded. "I'm used to it. He's used to it."

Callie wasn't disappointed to hear she wouldn't be having dinner with her brother-in-law on a regular basis, but she couldn't help but wonder when Zoe saw her dad. "We might as well eat in here, if it's just the three of us. There's plenty of room, and then Zoe can keep her book project set up in the dining room. How are you feeling?"

"Better. Thanks. Oh, by the way—I saw the sign you made for Zoe's room. It's adorable. I love it!"

Callie flushed with pleasure. "Thanks."

Zoe slid into the kitchen on her pink-socked feet. "I'm *hungry.*"

"Dinner's almost ready, Binks."

Zoe climbed into her mother's lap while Callie finished the preparations, and then the three of them had a quiet meal.

Later on, when Zoe was in bed, Callie was reading in the living room when she heard Michael come in. She listened to him grumble about the mess of papers and crayons on the dining room table before he sat down to eat the dinner Nina heated up for him.

"I was looking at tile for our bathroom today. I brought home a couple of choices for you to take a look at." Nina's voice carried into the living room.

"Seriously? You want me to look at them now?" Michael's voice was both incredulous and annoyed.

"I didn't say you have to look at them now. I'm just letting you know that they're here."

Callie closed her book to go upstairs.

CHAPTER SEVEN

Before

"Guess who I just saw?" Jenna asked, plopping down next to me on the bench and twirling her ponytail in what I'd come to recognize as one of her signature mannerisms.

"Who?" I put down the copy of *Emma* I was reading for my Victorian lit class. Though I liked the book, I was having trouble not picturing Alicia Silverstone in *Clueless*—one of my sister's favorite movies.

"Soda Boy."

"His name is Ethan," I replied automatically. I hadn't seen him since the day of the "cola calamity"—another Jenna-ism. I'd become used to them over the many hours we'd spent together.

She waved her hand as if swatting a fly. "Yeah, whatever. Anyway, he was in the library."

"So?"

"So nothing. Just saw him. Luckily, he wasn't carrying any liquids."

I laughed. "I'm sure it was just an accident. He may not be congenitally klutzy."

"Or maybe he is." Jenna's eyes widened in mock horror.

"I guess we'll just have to wait and see."

"We can observe him, like a science experiment. Maybe we need to buy lab journals."

"Don't we need a control group or something to make it valid?"

Jenna shrugged. "Don't ask me. I don't even know where the science building is."

"It's right there." I pointed at the ivy-covered building behind us.

"Good to know. Now I can avoid it."

I shook my head. "It was your idea to create an experiment!"

"Yeah, well, no one ever said I'm consistent," she said flippantly.

I didn't see Ethan myself until about a week later, when a group of us—Jenna, Amy, Shauna (Jenna's roommate), Jade, and I—decided to check out a dorm party. My own roommate, as usual, wasn't around. She was a music major and spent hours on end with her viola in the music department's practice rooms, and she went home most weekends to play in a community orchestra. I barely needed to know her name, for all the time we spent together. I might have felt a little lonely had I not found Jenna, but I was feeling more at home at Welford than I ever had back in Brook Hill. There, it always seemed like a competition about who could be the preppiest, and it was all about getting good grades to get into college—never about figuring out who you really were or what you wanted to do.

The party that night was much like the others we'd been to. The floor was already sticky with spilled beer, and the music was loud and not what I would have picked. Even though I felt like a good fit for Welford's quirky world, I had to admit I was a fan of pop music—Matchbox Twenty, Creed, 98 Degrees. The alternative stuff they played at parties was definitely not my thing, and I was starting to wonder if we should have just gone to the coffee shop instead.

I was standing in the corner, no longer even trying to hear what the other girls were saying. Instead, I was watching a couple of people who had gotten drunk enough to attempt dancing. One guy, completely independent of the beat of the music, flung his head back and forth, shoulder-length hair swinging into his face and then down his back, over and over again.

Next thing I knew, someone was saying something to me. I turned, and it was Ethan. Even in the semidarkness, I could see his hair flopping into his face in that endearing, tousled way.

"What?" I asked, leaning toward him.

He bent his head toward the guy with the hair. "Clearly a dance major," he replied louder.

I smiled. "Talented. Probably here on a scholarship." I pushed my own hair behind my ear.

He nodded seriously. "Definitely." He took a sip of his beer from the shiny red cup in his hand and then looked at me again. "Don't worry, I don't plan to spill this on you."

I giggled. "I don't know, maybe we need to maintain a safe, arm's-length distance as long as you're holding that cup."

"Yeah, but then we wouldn't be able to hear each other. Do you know sign language? Or semaphore?" He swung his free arm around, as if signaling a passing ship.

I shook my head. "I guess I'll take my chances." Then I looked around. "Maybe there's a raincoat somewhere I can borrow?"

He grinned. I liked his smile. Just when you thought he'd finished smiling, it got even wider.

"So, child psychology," he started. *He remembers what I said.* "Are you planning to major in psych, or . . . ?"

"Education, I think. I've always wanted to be a teacher."

"Ohhhh . . . Are you one of those kids who played school

all the time? Made their friends do 'homework' when they came over to play?"

"I don't think I was that bad . . . ," I protested.

"That's what they all say." He put his cup down on the windowsill behind him and stuffed his hands into his jeans pockets.

"What about you? Do you know what you're going to major in?"

He shrugged. "Not sure. English maybe. Or philosophy."

I nodded. "Both very marketable degrees."

"Absolutely. I can quote either Shakespeare or Hegel while I serve up Whoppers." He retrieved his beer, drained it, and then nodded toward mine. "Want another?"

I glanced into my own half-full cup. I was definitely a lightweight when it came to this drinking thing. "I'm good."

"I'll be right back."

"I'll try to find an umbrella while you're gone," I teased.

Ethan laughed and headed in the direction of the keg.

As soon as he was gone, Jenna sidled over to me. "So, Soda Boy?" Even with the loud music, I heard the mischief in her voice.

"We're just talking." I took a swallow of my beer. With no real dating history to speak of, I often had no clue when it came to guys. Did they like me? Or were they just being friendly?

"Is he nice?"

"Seems to be. Kind of funny."

"Funny's good."

"Yeah, funny is good."

At that point, Ethan came back, and I introduced him to Jenna. They did the whole "where are you from" and "what are you studying" thing, and Jenna told a story about her professor in American Lit. While she was talking, I took a closer look at Ethan.

He was a few inches taller than me, which put him at

around five foot nine. Oddly, I liked his chin. It was square, but not obnoxious. He was a little thin, but the hand holding his beer looked strong. Bottom line: he didn't have heartthrob looks like Josh Hartnett or Jason Behr (who in real life did?) but he was cute, in a slightly dorky sort of way.

We talked awhile, and our little group of three got bigger—first Ethan's friends Peter and Tim joined us, and then Amy, Shauna, and Jade. When none of us could take any more noise or stuffiness, we headed outside.

Shauna and Tim peeled off, talking intently with their heads close to each other. Shauna's hand was on Tim's arm, and next thing I knew, they were wandering away on their own. Shortly afterward, the rest of us made our way toward the freshman dorms.

By the time we got to Carter—where Jenna lived on the second floor, immediately beneath me—Amy and Jade had already gone into their dorm, next to ours.

"You ready to go in?" Jenna asked, looking at me. I had my arms wrapped around me; the night air had gotten chilly.

I nodded. "I'm cold." I glanced at Ethan and Peter. Were they going to invite themselves in? I wasn't sure if I wanted them to.

Ethan pushed his hair off his forehead. "This was fun," he said. Then he paused and bit his lip. Was he nervous? Then he spoke again. "Hey—are you going to the movie on Wednesday?"

Every week, they showed an old movie in the campus center. "I don't know," I began. I hadn't yet been to the weekly movie—my tastes ran more to the '80s and '90s films I grew up with. "I haven't thought about it. What's playing?"

"*Spellbound*. Hitchcock. Gregory Peck."

The only Hitchcock I'd seen was *Psycho*, which had totally creeped me out. But it might be nice to spend more time with Ethan. And besides, wasn't college supposed to open your horizons? "Sounds good. Why not?"

Ethan smiled. "You want to meet up?"

I smiled back. "Sure."

He lifted a hand in a wave goodbye.

I waved back, and as I turned to walk up the steps to the dorm, Jenna was looking at me bemusedly.

"What?" I asked as a smile played around her lips.

"Just be sure Soda Boy doesn't bring a drink into the theater," she said, heading inside before I could respond.

CHAPTER EIGHT

After

Over the remainder of the week, with some bumps along the way, Callie, Nina, Michael, and Zoe settled into a regular routine. Every morning, Michael departed first for work, and then Nina and Zoe left the house ahead of Callie to make the half hour drive back to Wolcott, where Zoe's nursery school and their family house was located. They'd decided it wasn't worth the upset to switch Zoe's school for the few months they'd be in Brook Hill. After school drop-off, Nina spent time checking out the construction at the house, taking care of errands, or meeting friends, before retrieving Zoe and then bringing her to whatever activity she had scheduled for the day, to a playdate, or back down to the Victorian in Brook Hill.

Nina cooked dinner every night. The evening after Callie prepared the meal under Nina's direction, Callie came into the house with a rotisserie chicken. Nina was dredging chicken breasts in panko bread crumbs as Callie pulled it out of her reusable grocery bag.

"What's that for?" Nina asked.

"Dinner."

"What are you talking about?" Nina's voice was irritated. "I'm making chicken parmigiana."

Callie folded the bag and put it in the drawer beneath the oven where it lived. "I don't expect you to cook for me every night. I'm not your child."

Nina expelled a long breath. "Callie, don't be ridiculous. I'm cooking. It's as easy to cook for four as it is for three."

Callie didn't know what to say. Of course that made perfect sense, but it also made her feel like she had lost all autonomy in her own home. "Well, how about I make dinner sometimes?"

Nina raised her eyebrows and was silent.

"I could follow a recipe if I wanted to. Or I could get takeout."

Nina just continued to stare at her, and Callie threw up her hands, exasperated. "Okay, how about you at least give me a grocery list, and I do the shopping?"

She could see Nina hesitate. She was sure her sister was wondering if Callie would pick out the right produce. If she'd buy the correct brand of couscous.

Finally, Nina spoke. "Okay, deal," she said, with the same tone of frustration that had marked Callie's words. The similarity in the pitch of their voices almost made her smile. Almost.

But the cooking issue wasn't the hardest for Callie. It was the fact that she rarely had any time to herself. She was used to eating her evening meal with a book. That wasn't happening anymore. And she liked the quiet in the house in the morning, before work, when she could have a peaceful cup of coffee. That *certainly* wasn't happening anymore.

At any time of day, if she wanted to be alone in what felt increasingly like the incredible shrinking house, she had to be in her bedroom. And although she'd spent a lot of time there when it had just been her art studio, it wasn't the same with the door closed, and the knowledge that if she stepped out, she was likely to bump into someone. On the upside, she did enjoy spending more time with Zoe, getting to experience the everydayness of her. At least, she enjoyed it *most* of the time.

As she sat holed up in her room, Callie devoted a lot of thought to how to integrate Liam into her classroom, and expended a lot of effort *not* thinking about Ethan. And she continued her email correspondence with Jason the advertising guy. She hoped his ad copy was more exciting than his emails, but at least they were polite and written with correct grammar and spelling.

"So, are you going to meet him?" Tess asked her on Friday afternoon when they went for coffee after school. They had driven into downtown Brook Hill—so small that *downtown* was hardly a suitable term—to go to Sip, a cute café with cozy round tables and chairs with rattan seats.

Callie swirled her pumpkin spice latte before removing the stirrer from the cup and laying it on the table. "We made a date to go for drinks next week."

"Drinks? Not dinner?" Tess broke off a piece of her biscotti and dunked it into her coffee before taking a bite.

"It's like *Sleepless in Seattle*: 'If it's just a drink, if you like them you can always ask them for dinner, but if not, you can just say, "Well, that was great," and then you go home.'"

Tess raised her eyebrows. "And *how* many times have you seen that movie?"

Callie laughed. "Enough, I guess. I still remember the first time I saw it—Nina took me when it had just come out. It's sort of funny—for a long time, I was way more into Jonah than Tom Hanks, and I was obsessed with their house, just right there on the water."

"Hmm. I always thought that movie was kind of creepy."

"Creepy? Really?"

"Well, isn't Meg Ryan sort of stalker-ish? She gets obsessed with this guy she hears on the radio and then actually tracks him down through a private eye? And *flies* across the country to spy on him?"

Callie laughed again. "I never thought about it that way. For me it's more about the 'magic.' You know, when he puts his hand in hers."

Tess swallowed the piece of biscotti she had just popped into her mouth. "And *that*, my friend, is why you are single."

Callie picked up the discarded stirrer and folded it in half. "And how do you figure that?"

"The whole thing about destiny. Fate. That there's one man out there who's right for you. When you have such high expectations, how is anyone ever going to measure up?"

"Come on, that's not fair. Just because I like a movie doesn't mean it says something about my relationships."

"Maybe, maybe not," Tess replied, one eyebrow raised.

Callie took another sip of her latte. If she had said what she really thought, she would have added that, when it came to relationships, what she actually worried about was: How do you *know* when someone is *the one*? And what if you think someone isn't—and then it turns out he was, all along? Maybe that's what the universe was trying to tell her with this whole *Rerouting* thing. Maybe she had been right in her argument with Nina, and Ethan's movie shouldn't be interpreted as a love letter to her. But maybe it was a sign that she needed to reach out to him. That she needed to answer that "what if" question. What if they were meant to be together after all?

"Anyway," Tess continued, interrupting her musing. "Whose idea was it to meet for a drink?"

"His," she replied, then paused. "Well, maybe mine."

Tess looked puzzled.

"He suggested that I come into Hoboken to meet him. I said we could have a drink. He didn't propose dinner."

"Okay, so you're both taking the cautious route. He lives in Hoboken?"

Callie nodded. "Made more sense for me to go there than for him to come out here to suburbia."

"Agreed." Tess popped the last of her biscotti into her mouth. "Well, hopefully it will go better than the apple-picking date."

"*Anything* would go better than the apple-picking date."

"Aren't you the optimist." Tess grimaced at Callie.

"That's me. Mug always half full." She lifted up the ceramic cup and then peered inside. "Or not." She grinned.

"Ha ha. Oh, hey! I meant to ask you—any word from that filmmaker ex of yours?"

Callie shook her head.

Tess's eyes narrowed. "What's that look?"

"What look?" Callie attempted to wipe her face clear of any emotion but confusion.

"Oh, come on, girl, I know you too well. Your face suddenly caved in."

"Please." Callie didn't intend to sound so annoyed, but the tone in her voice was unmistakable.

"Ooh—looks like I hit a nerve. What's going on?"

It had only been a few days since she'd gone through this with Nina, and the last thing she wanted was to hash it out again. She knew Tess would see right through her if she tried to pretend it was nothing. She went for lighthearted instead. "Oh—that's a subject to be talked about over a cocktail," she quipped.

Tess raised her eyebrows. "Well, you know I never say no to a cosmopolitan, but I think someone's avoiding the subject."

Callie shrugged and took a hard right turn, hoping Tess would go with her. "Well—anyway, I'll probably need a drink after a few days with Liam in my class."

Tess gave her a long hard stare, the wheels in her brain

visibly turning. Callie could see the moment when her friend decided to let her off the hook. Tess mirrored her shrug. "No kidding. Actually, you should probably keep a thermos of wine on you."

"Somehow, I don't think that would go over very well if Judith caught wind of it."

"Maybe she'd be okay with it if you offered to share with her." Tess grinned.

"Sure. I'll give that a try. And then will you be my reference when I'm looking for a new job?"

"Of course. As long as you share the wine with me, too."

"Yeah, I don't think I'll be able to afford wine when I'm unemployed." Callie unfolded the coffee stirrer, which she had creased into quarters. "Seriously, though," she said then, no longer smiling, "I'm not looking forward to figuring out how to deal with Liam."

Tess reached up and pulled her thick hair behind her, twisting it into a knot that actually stayed in place for a moment before falling down. "Come on, you'll be fine. You've handled tough kids before. And you're not Robin."

"I know. It's probably scarier in the abstract than it will be in reality."

Tess nodded. "Absolutely."

Callie started to speak again and then paused, hesitant to reveal anything told to her in confidence.

"What?" Tess looked at her curiously.

Callie lamented her friend's powers of observation. "Nothing . . . I just wondered if you'd noticed anything different about Robin lately."

"Different? Like how?"

"I don't know. Does it seem like she's let this kid get under her skin more than you would have expected?"

Tess looked thoughtful. "Maybe so," she said slowly. "It's like she doesn't have the energy to try to figure it out."

Callie nodded. As for her, when it came to kids, she *did* have the energy to deal with what was thrown at her. But when it came to everything else going on in her life, she wasn't so sure.

That weekend, Zoe was invited to a birthday party at Got Paint?, a paint-your-own pottery studio near her school. As Callie poured herself a glass of orange juice, Nina spoke to Michael, who was on his BlackBerry. "Could you take her to the party?" she asked. "I've been driving up to Wolcott every day. I could use a break."

Michael looked up. "Come on, Nina—I've been in the city every day. And I don't know these women. I'll be standing around like a sore thumb."

You'll be standing around looking at your BlackBerry, Callie thought. *Just like you would be at home.*

Nina sighed. "Fine," she said. "I'll go."

Callie looked at her sister, who was once again rubbing the small of her back with the heels of her hands. Without thinking before she opened her mouth, Callie spoke. "Hey, why don't I take her?"

Both Nina and Michael looked at her, surprised.

"No big deal. I don't have anything going on today."

"Are you sure?" Nina asked. "It'll be pretty boring."

"Hey, if she wants to go, let her go," Michael said.

Callie resisted shaking her head in annoyance. Of course Michael would be delighted. It got him off the hook. She directed her answer only to Nina. "Sure, no problem. What time's the party?"

"Eleven o'clock. The present's all ready to go. I really appreciate this, Callie."

"Happy to help."

As Callie got dressed, she once again wondered what Nina saw in her husband. So many years had passed since the wedding, and his attractive qualities continued to elude her. Objectively speaking, Michael *was* reasonably nice looking, though not at all her type. Tall and muscular, he still resembled the college baseball player he had once been. He had a square jaw and perpetual five-o'clock shadow. Not so bad, actually. *But looks only go so far.*

She pulled on a slouchy gray V-neck sweater and her black skinny jeans. The outfit felt a little drab, but she thought Nina would approve. To spice it up, she put on a chunky silver bracelet and a pewter pendant with a geometric design that hung on a long leather cord. Then she brushed her wavy brown hair, peering at herself in the mirror hanging over her dresser. Maybe it was time to do something different with her hair. She hadn't grown it long since college, and she certainly wasn't going to go through another disastrous experiment with bangs. Maybe if she flipped her part to the other side? She tried it, shuddered, and flipped it back.

She sighed. Though she couldn't pinpoint what it was exactly, she just didn't look as young as she used to. She sucked in her cheeks thoughtfully and glanced down at herself. There was no full-length mirror in the bedroom (how had she gotten through her teenage years without one?), but she'd never had issues with her body. She could still fit into most of the clothes she wore in college—and even some from high school. She always felt a little self-conscious about her C cups, so she usually wore loosely fitted tops. But overall, she could pull off most any outfit she was in the mood to wear. Which was a good thing, she thought wryly, since it had been a very long time since anyone had seen her *out* of one.

She wished she were at least looking forward to her date with Jason, but it just felt like work. Getting to know someone new. Learning their tastes, food preferences, sense of humor. There was a time when all of that was exciting, but the thrill just wasn't there anymore—or at least it wasn't right now. She would humor Tess, but deep down she was convinced there were far better ways she could be spending her time.

As had become inevitable lately, her thoughts turned to Ethan. The comfort of being with someone who was one hundred percent a known quantity. The ease. The simplicity. Had Ethan found that with someone else? She certainly hadn't. And did she really want it anyway? Maybe that was part of the problem. After all this time, she still didn't know.

Zoe was tickled to go with her aunt to her friend's birthday party. As for Callie, she didn't mind being in a room full of preschoolers and not being responsible for managing them. Although she introduced herself to some of the moms, she wasn't surprised that they stayed among themselves, so she occupied herself watching the children create designs on their ceramic plates, after which the Got Paint? staff painted the kids' hands so they could add handprints to their creations. There was pizza for lunch, and then cupcakes. The children happily licked the frosting off the baked goods and then left the naked cupcakes on the paper plates decorated with *Frozen* princesses Elsa and Anna.

After the favor bags—full of plastic toys destined for the recycling bin as soon as their recipients were looking the other way—Callie helped Zoe zip up her jacket, and they stepped outside. Heading toward the car, they walked past trendy boutiques, a wine bar, a cigar store, an antique dealer, and a consignment shop. Wolcott was definitely more bustling than Brook Hill. It wasn't surprising that it had become such a mecca for young families moving from Manhattan and Brooklyn.

"Did you have fun, Binks?" Callie asked as they strolled down the sidewalk, hand in hand.

"Mm-hmm. I want to have my birthday party there."

"You'll have to tell Mommy that."

"Mommy doesn't like messy parties," Zoe said solemnly.

"So, do you think it would be too messy for her?"

Zoe considered the question, her face screwed up in thought. "Maybe not. Because she wouldn't have to clean it up."

They arrived at the car, and Callie strapped her niece into her car seat. She had just pulled away from the curb when Zoe announced, "I have to go pee."

Callie kicked herself for not thinking to ask her if she had to go before leaving the pottery studio.

"Right now? Can you wait till we get home?" Even as she asked the question, she knew what the answer would be. It was a half hour ride back to Brook Hill.

"I have to go right now."

Callie glanced in the rearview mirror and saw Zoe dancing a bit in her seat, her knees pressed together. Up ahead was a sign reading "Cuppa Joe." She put her signal on and turned into the parking lot. "Okay, Binks, let's go."

They ran to the front door and then straight toward the back of the café, fortunately finding the single restroom unoccupied. When they emerged, Callie led Zoe to the short line at the counter.

"What are we doing?" asked Zoe.

"It's not right to use the bathroom if we're not customers. And besides, I'd love some coffee." Although she knew Nina wouldn't be pleased in light of the fact that Zoe already had a belly full of frosting, she added, "You can pick something out of the case if you want," pointing at the variety of pastries behind the glass.

Zoe scooted over to examine the cake pops and decorated cookies. "Ooh, look, Aunt Callie!" she said loudly, turning and walking smack into a pair of male legs.

"Whoa there! Are you okay?" the man asked.

Zoe looked stricken.

"I'm so sorry!" Callie interjected.

"No worries—as long as she's okay."

The "she" in question was now at Callie's side, half behind her leg.

Callie looked down at her. "What do you say to the man, Binks?"

Zoe peeped out. "Sorry," she said, barely audible.

"Zoe?" the man said then.

Callie quickly looked up at him, wondering how he knew Zoe's name. He was tall and lean, probably midthirties, with thick dark hair shorn close on the sides. Nice looking. He was wearing a half-zip fleece pullover and jeans. Perhaps a dad from Zoe's preschool?

"Hi," he said, putting out his hand. "I'm Ben Perlow. If this is Zoe, I'm with the architecture firm that's handling her family's addition."

Ohhh. Callie took his hand, which was warm. "I'm Zoe's aunt. Nina Kagan's sister."

"Ahhh—the sister who took them in in their time of need." Ben smiled. He had a nice smile. And kind eyes. Callie had the sudden, unexpected thought that if she could look at the world through his eyes, everything would somehow appear brighter and shinier.

"That's me." She smiled back, noticing a single dimple in his left cheek. "So, how's the project going? Is it really going to be only four months? Or should I figure they'll be with me till this one goes to college?" Callie ran her hands through Zoe's curls. She knew Zoe would fight to tame them one day, but hoped she'd come to appreciate them sooner rather than later.

"Oh, I'm sure they'll be out by then. Maybe when she's graduating from middle school." Ben winked. "But, seriously, so far so good." He held up his hand, fingers crossed.

"I guess that's all I can hope for."

"I hope for it, too. Otherwise, we'll have cranky clients." Ben grinned.

Callie thought of her brother-in-law. She wondered if Ben had seen a glimpse of Michael's true colors beneath the charm he trotted out when necessary.

Zoe tugged on Callie's sleeve. "Aunt Callie," she whispered. "I know what I want. One of those leaf cookies."

Callie glanced at the case and spotted the leaf-shaped cookies decorated with orange, red, and yellow icing.

"How do you ask?" she said automatically.

"Please . . . ?"

Callie nodded. "Okay, Binks." She turned back to Ben. "Well, duty calls."

"I can see that." He glanced at Zoe, who was jumping up and down.

"Anyway, it was nice meeting you."

"Nice meeting you, too—is it Callie?"

"Yes, Callie Dressler."

About half an hour later, Callie unlocked the front door, and Zoe zipped past her. "Hellooo!" the little girl yelled.

"Zoe! Quiet!" It was Michael's voice, in a loud whisper, coming from the living room.

Callie sighed as she put her handbag down on the hall table and began to take off her jacket. She peered around the doorjamb to see what required such silence, and immediately felt remorseful. There on the sofa, Nina was curled up in a fetal position, asleep, with her head on a pillow and her feet in Michael's lap. He had the laptop propped next to him, and he was turned at an awkward angle to do whatever he was doing on the screen. *I guess everyone has their moments,* she thought guiltily.

"Is Mommy sleeping?" Zoe asked softly.

Michael nodded. "How was the party?" he whispered back, moving the laptop so Zoe could sit next to him.

Callie left them to their unusually sweet family tableau and turned to hang up her jacket. The phone rang as she went into the kitchen.

"Hi, sweetie," her mom's voice said brightly as she picked up the receiver. "How's the extended family reunion going?"

Callie cradled the phone on her shoulder as she automatically started to clean up the crayons Zoe had left on the kitchen table that morning. "Fine."

"Fine?" Lorraine said skeptically. Callie could picture her sitting at the breakfast bar in her cheerful white kitchen, the Florida sun streaming through the French doors that led to the small, maintenance-free patio. The absence of lawn work and raking leaves was one of the things that had helped convince her dad to abandon the Northeast permanently.

"Well, it's not all perfect. Like the fact that there isn't enough hot water for three showers in a row. But we're getting into a routine. It's nice to spend this much time with Zoe, anyway."

"I miss that cutie patootie," Lorraine said wistfully.

"It'll be Thanksgiving before you know it. Or you could come up sooner . . ."

"Right—just what you all need, another person in that house!" Lorraine snorted.

Callie laughed. "True! You'd have to sleep in the garage."

"I don't even get the basement?" Lorraine asked, with faux petulance.

"Okay, the basement. But you can only come upstairs at your scheduled time."

They chatted awhile about Lorraine's new interest in mahjong and her frustration that Martin spent so much time reading. It felt like the conversation was wrapping up when Lorraine suddenly announced, "Oh, I forgot—I saw that article about Ethan."

Callie's heart rate quickened . . . again. *Why do my parents keep donating to Welford? If they didn't, they wouldn't get the stupid alumni magazine.*

"Oh yeah?" Callie struggled for nonchalance.

"Sounds like he's doing well," Lorraine said evenly.

"Yes, it does."

"Do you ever hear from him?"

"Nope. Not since . . ." Callie cleared her throat to dislodge the lump that had risen unexpectedly. "Not since we broke up," she continued, telepathically willing her mother to drop the subject.

Lorraine sighed. "Do you know anything more about this movie, beyond what they say in the *Quarterly*?"

"I don't. I've been trying my best to avoid the subject, to be honest."

There was a brief silence, during which Callie knew Lorraine was hoping she would say more. When she didn't oblige, her mother spoke again. "So, anyone on the horizon now?"

Also not a great topic, but less tricky. "Not really, Mom, but I'm dating."

"Well, that's good, at least." She paused again, perhaps deciding how much to torture her younger child. "Is Nina around?"

Callie exhaled. "She's napping."

"That's great. She does so much, I worry about her. It's like she doesn't know she's pregnant."

Seriously? "Oh, Ma. She knows she's pregnant." Callie didn't want to go down this road.

Lorraine heaved an exaggerated sigh. "Obviously she knows she's pregnant. What I mean is she's not slowing down."

Callie swallowed the words that came to her first, which were that her sister didn't have it so bad. Considering that she spent hours a day with a roomful of children Zoe's age, Callie knew that being on call for miniature people with endless demands wasn't easy. But plenty of the moms at Bouncy Castles negotiated pregnancies along with multiple children at home, or juggled full-time paying jobs with their full-time mommy jobs.

"She's fine, Mom," she said instead. "Don't worry."

"It's my job to worry about my girls," Lorraine replied. "You'll understand when you have kids."

"Right, Mom," she said flatly. "I can't possibly get it." She couldn't believe Lorraine would go there.

Lorraine expelled an exasperated sigh. "Oh, don't be so sensitive, Callie. You know I didn't mean—"

Callie cut her off. "Fine, Mom."

Lorraine sighed again. "I only want the best for you and your sister. You know that."

"Yes, Mom."

"One of these days we'll have a phone call where I don't become the bad guy."

Oh my God, I love you but you're impossible. "Don't worry about it, Mom. I'll tell Nina you called."

"Okay, sweetie. I love you."

"You, too." Callie replaced the cordless phone in its cradle, and took a deep breath before heading up to her room.

CHAPTER NINE

After

Callie awakened early Monday morning, before her alarm went off. She had spent Sunday in Manhattan. Her former roommate and Pemberley colleague Emily had told her about an exhibit by an artist who was being called the Twenty-First-Century Magritte. It intrigued them both, so they met for brunch and then explored the gallery. Callie walked back to Penn Station from TriBeCa—enjoying the crispness in the air and the buzz of the city. Although she didn't necessarily want to move back, she did find herself wondering why she had stayed so long in her parents' house. In the town she hadn't liked much when she was growing up there. Was it only convenience? Or something else?

When she got home, she begged off having family dinner with Nina & Co., instead carrying half of a leftover sub sandwich to her room under her sister's disapproving gaze. She went to sleep early with her mind on Liam joining her classroom the following morning, thinking about strategies that had worked in the past with challenging kids and hoping that perhaps simply the change of room would be what Liam needed.

Going straight into the shower, Callie enjoyed the hot water for a change. She felt a twinge of guilt that Nina would probably be the one relegated to the lukewarm water—and hoped it would be Michael instead.

She put on a blue-and-green-striped button-down over a ribbed tank top and a pair of slim-fitting black pants before heading downstairs, where she found Michael in the kitchen. So it would be Nina in the tepid shower.

"You're up early," he said, taking a sip of his coffee.

"I guess so. Do you have a busy day?" Callie asked, knowing what the answer would be.

"Oh yeah. Conference call after conference call."

Callie nodded in a way she hoped conveyed genuine interest and silently thanked the universe that her work life didn't require sitting at a desk participating in conference calls.

Michael left for the train shortly thereafter, and Callie decided she might as well go to school a little early. When she arrived, a few children who had early drop-off to accommodate their working parents were already there, but Callie's classroom was, as she had expected, empty.

Although she enjoyed "her" kids, one of the things Callie loved best about being a preschool teacher was her classroom. While she could never be sure of finding what she was looking for at home, at school there was no doubt where she'd find the Duplos or the pipe cleaners—in the Lucite drawers bearing their names.

Her favorite spot was the reading corner, where a few years earlier she'd painted a mural of a big tree, with rolling hills in the distance. Hanging from one of the tree branches was a painted swing, and on the real-life floor beneath it were a couple of cushions—big and squishy—for the children to sit on.

Next to the cushions was a bookcase designed for books to face out, rather than displaying only their spines. Callie had painted that, too—her own renditions of some of the kids' perennial favorite fictional characters: the cap seller from *Caps for Sale*, Sylvester and his magic pebble, Corduroy and his missing button, and Peter in his snowsuit, all ready to enjoy the snowy day.

Callie took out the vinyl orange circles that the children would sit on for gathering time and arranged them in a half circle on the floor. On each circle, she placed a piece of poster board on which a child's name—first and last—was written. She put the one marked "Liam Switzer" nearest to the chair where she would sit to lead them in their daily conversation about the day of the week, the weather, how many children were present, how many were absent, and what activities would be available to them at playtime.

A few minutes before it was time for the children to arrive, there was a knock on the door. Through the glass pane, she could see a woman with shoulder-length reddish hair. Her skin was pale and her features sharp. Ellen Switzer, Liam's mother.

Callie walked to the door and opened it.

Liam was standing behind his mother, wearing a gray shirt with a big orange basketball on the chest and a pair of black track pants with yellow stripes up the sides.

"Hi, Mrs. Switzer," Callie began.

"Oh, I wasn't sure if you'd know who I was. But, please, call me Ellen." The other woman produced a small smile. "I'm sorry to bother you, but I thought it might be a good idea to chat for a few minutes before school starts. I should have thought of this before and made arrangements, but, well . . . things have been hectic."

Callie nodded. "No problem. Come in." She opened the door wider, but Ellen hesitated and glanced down at Liam. "How about if Liam comes in to explore the classroom and you and I can chat in the hallway?"

Ellen looked relieved. "Great idea."

Callie squatted down so she was at Liam's level. "Hi, Liam. I'm Miss Callie. Do you want to come into your new room?"

Liam looked at her but didn't respond.

"Let's go, Liam—I bet there are fun things inside," his mom added, putting her hand on his shoulder.

"I don't want to."

His mom took a deep breath, as if this wasn't the first time she'd dealt with this today. "Come on, Liam, it's time to go in."

He bit his lower lip and looked away.

Callie went back into her room to the drawer marked "Cars." She took out a handful of Matchbox cars and Hot Wheels—many of them scarred from years of use—and lined them up on the table. She knew without looking that Liam was watching her. Then she grabbed a length of wood that was leaning against the wall and propped it up on the table, making a ramp. She perched a bright yellow car at the top and let it go.

Liam put one foot into the classroom, and Callie knew she had him. She let another car go down the ramp, and then Liam was at the table, trying it himself.

Callie stepped back into the hall.

"Wow," said Ellen. "I was getting ready to just drag him in."

Callie shrugged. "Sometimes it works and sometimes it doesn't."

"I bet you have a bunch of tricks up your sleeve."

"I try," Callie said offhandedly.

Ellen nodded. "Anyway, I wanted to tell you that I know Liam hasn't been . . . easy. And I know I haven't been around much." She hesitated. "My life has been . . . complicated."

Callie waited. She was no longer surprised by what parents chose to share with her. Perhaps because they were entrusting their children to her for a few hours each day, they felt a closeness they might not achieve so quickly with others.

But Ellen veered away from whatever was on her mind. "I'm hoping that a new classroom is what Liam needs. And I think Robin and I got off on the wrong foot. I really do want to help, if I can."

"Thanks, Mrs. . . . I mean, Ellen. I appreciate that. Will you be picking him up?"

"No—I'll be at work. My babysitter will get him. But, please, call if you need me." She gave Callie her business card, on which she'd written her cell phone number.

Callie slipped the card into her pocket. "Why don't we plan to touch base in a few days, unless there's a more immediate reason to talk?"

Ellen nodded. "Sounds good. Thank you. Can I say goodbye to Liam?"

"Of course." Callie stepped aside and gestured Ellen into the classroom. She stood in the doorway while Ellen went inside and bent over to her son.

"You be good, okay? Mommy loves you."

Liam's lip quivered a little.

"See you later, sweetie." She hugged him and stepped back out of the classroom.

Callie left the ramp up, and as her other students began to arrive, they joined Liam there, some dropping cars down the ramp, others zooming them around on the tabletop or the rug. When everyone had arrived, Callie clapped her hands, and the children—with the exception of Liam—turned to look at her.

"Okay, everyone, let's put the toys away. Gathering time!" The swarm of little people began to carry the cars to their assigned drawer. Liam watched them, holding a small blue convertible in his fist.

"Okay, Liam," Callie said cheerfully, "time to put that away." Liam looked at her, and Callie wondered if he'd be defiant. But after a long moment, the blue car quietly joined its brothers and sisters.

The children took their assigned seats, and Callie pointed out Liam's circle to him.

"We have a new friend in class today," Callie announced once everyone was settled, crisscross applesauce. "Can we all say hello to Liam?"

"Hello, Liam!" they said, mostly in unison.

"Since Liam is new to our room, we're all going to help him learn how we do things here, right?"

Grave faces nodded all around her.

Callie had planned this the night before and hoped that it would have an impact. "So, when two people want to play with the same toy, what do we do?"

Little hands went up in the air. When she called on them, Jacob announced, "Share," and Emma declared, "Take turns!" Callie smiled inwardly. It was nice to hear that even though Emma wasn't so good at it herself, at least she knew what she was supposed to be doing.

After leading them through some other golden rules, like listening when our friends speak and keeping our hands to ourselves, Callie set them loose to play. Liam sat on his circle.

"What would you like to do, Liam?" Callie asked him.

He shrugged, but then looked at the boys who had taken the cars back out.

"Do you want to play cars with Jacob and Noah?"

Liam shrugged again, and Callie led him over to the other two children and got him settled.

When Judith stopped by her room at the end of the school day, Callie was unclipping now-dry artwork from the cord that stretched across her classroom so she could deposit it in the children's mailboxes in the hall. Judith stood in the doorway, her arms crossed. "So, how did it go?"

Callie took the clothespin out of her mouth. "Not bad."

Judith raised her eyebrows.

"We had our moments. A tussle over which chair to sit in for crafts, and some trouble joining in to clean up, but overall okay."

Judith nodded.

"Honestly, I'm not sure why Robin was having such trouble."

Judith sighed. "I'm not sure how focused she is right now. And I do think Liam isn't the easiest kid."

"Well, we'll see. It was just the first day."

"I'll check in with you again tomorrow."

"Thanks, Judith."

"No, thank *you*."

Though Callie had entered into this with her doubts, it felt good to be appreciated.

The following days passed similarly, and while Callie wasn't as relaxed as she'd been the week before, things were going reasonably well, which was what she told Tess when they walked out to their cars together on Thursday afternoon.

But Tess wasn't interested in talking about Liam. "So you're headed into Hoboken tonight?"

"Yep. Shoot me now."

"Oh, stop it! You could be meeting your future husband."

"Or I could be spending an excruciating evening listening to some guy talk about his collection of taxidermy specimens."

Tess wrinkled her nose. "Ew. Does he really do that?"

Callie laughed. "No. Or at least, not that I know of."

Tess shook her head. "You need a better attitude about this, you know. This is the exciting part—not like Brett and me, sitting around on the couch in our sweats eating potato chips and watching season four hundred and twelve of *Survivor*. You've got the first date, the first kiss, the first . . ." Tess made a gesture.

"Seriously? I don't think I've seen anyone do that"—Callie pointed at Tess's hands—"since elementary school."

"That's where my brain stopped developing." Tess smirked.

Callie rolled her eyes, even as she felt her stomach clench. Tess was right—beginnings could be exhilarating. But that was where the trouble lay. It didn't always lead to the smartest decisions, as she knew all too well. She mentally shook herself. "Anyway, I better get going if I'm going to have time to change and catch the train."

"Text me from the bathroom if you need to be rescued. I'll call you and say I need you to take me to the hospital. 'The baby's coming!'" Tess winked as she turned toward her car.

CHAPTER TEN

Before

When Wednesday night rolled around, I headed over to the student center to meet Ethan for the movie. I didn't know what to expect—and had floated the idea to Jenna that maybe Ethan was just looking to hang and even invited her along. She rolled her eyes at me, but I truly wanted her take on the situation. The truth was, high school had been pretty much a desert for me when it came to dating. I was fairly quiet, and the boys I thought were cute were also jerks. A couple of guys had nosed around me a bit, but I was never attracted to them.

It was always so much easier for Nina—boys flocked to her, and she jumped from one steady relationship to another. Of course, the downtimes in between were miserable. She'd get cranky and slam doors and fight with our mother. But there was a part of me that liked those times when I was the only one she could stand, and she'd spend hours with me watching movies.

A couple of my girlfriends dated, but I didn't envy them. They spent more time speculating about their "relationships" than they did with their boyfriends. One snuck around with a boy for weeks because her parents didn't want her to date, only to have him dump her for someone else. It took her longer to stop crying about it than the length of time they'd actually been together. It was nothing like the romances in the teen movies Nina and I watched, and none of the boys were Andrew McCarthy or Eric Stoltz. Filling my evenings with babysitting definitely seemed the way to go.

When I looked at myself in the mirror before leaving my dorm room, I wondered if I looked like someone going out on her first date. To mark the occasion, I swiped on some eyeliner. I'd never been big on makeup, but it brought out my eyes. I'd always liked my eyes; they were brown like my mom's. Nina got my dad's blue ones. I stared, then pushed my hair off my face and tried to imagine myself with bangs before letting the waves drop.

I pushed open the student center door, trying to ignore the nervousness in the pit of my stomach. Some people were sitting in the lounge area downstairs—a few were alone, reading, but another group was clustered at a table playing some kind of strategy game. I went upstairs to the screening room and saw Ethan waiting by the door. He was wearing a rugby shirt and jeans, and his face—which had seemed anxious as he peered down the hallway—relaxed. I felt a little rush realizing he was so happy to see me. I smiled and waved, and Ethan grinned back.

"Hey . . . I thought you might have forgotten."

I had to give him credit for honesty. "Nope. I'm here."

We went inside. The theater was small, maybe fifteen rows of ten seats each, and we took seats somewhere in the middle.

"What's been up with you?" Ethan asked, once we were settled.

"I started at the preschool this week, so that was new."

"How was it?"

"So far, so good. We go in groups of two or three and basically help out the teachers. The idea is that we start observing and getting to know the kids a little. Later on we have to do some sort of project."

"Cool." He bent his head toward the screen at the front of the room. "Have you seen this before?"

"Nope. I can't say I've seen many of the classics."

"Oh wow, you don't know what you're missing!"

But before he could tell me what, exactly, the lights dimmed and the opening credits began. It was funny to see a movie that didn't start with a dancing popcorn bag singing that we should go out to the lobby to get ourselves a snack.

As I watched Ingrid Bergman help amnesiac Gregory Peck regain his memory, I couldn't help being distracted by Ethan sitting next to me. His jeans-clad leg was near mine, and he kept glancing my way. As the credits rolled, he turned again. "So, what did you think?"

"I liked it—though the whole dream-symbolism thing was pretty heavy-handed."

"Ya think?" he said, cocking his head.

I laughed. "Just a bit."

"So." He paused. "Do you want to get a coffee or something?"

"Sure."

We went downstairs and, crossing the lounge, passed the same group huddled around their board game as we headed toward the café. During the day, they sold some premade sandwiches and salads as an alternative to the dining hall, but at that time of night, the case was empty save for one sad-looking sandwich in plastic wrap. I hoped it would get tossed before they closed up for the night. Near the cash register was

a row of dessert choices—cling-wrapped brownies and cookies, along with a few muffins likely left over from the morning.

The guy behind the counter appeared to be close to thirty,
but his red hair was in dreadlocks. He was wearing a tie-dye
shirt that looked like an enormous yellow-and-orange sun and
had a name tag that read "Garth."

"Hey, dudes," he said upon our approach, lifting his hand
to high-five Ethan. Ethan glanced at me as he touched palms
with Garth before handing him the chocolate chip cookie and
brownie we'd selected.

"Two coffees?" Ethan asked.

"Sure, dude. No problemo."

I was trying not to laugh as Garth turned to the coffeepot
to pour out two cups. Ethan pulled out his wallet to pay, and
Garth nodded his head rhythmically while watching him. He
seemed to be bopping along to a song only he could hear. He
dropped the bills into the cash register drawer and retrieved
some change.

"Here you go," Garth said as he deposited it in Ethan's outstretched palm. Then he took a quick look at me, turned back
to Ethan, and in a lower voice said, "Nice one, dude."

"Uh, thanks," Ethan replied as I bit my lip, again trying not
to laugh.

We found a table in a corner of the lounge. "I hear that
guy's been at Welford for, like, ten years. Can't quite get his
credits together," Ethan said as we sat down.

"Gee, what a surprise. He's not exactly a great advertise-
ment for a Welford education."

Ethan laughed. "No, I guess not. Maybe that's why he only
works nights—so he's not here when the tours go through.
Anyway, how do you like it here so far? The school, I mean, not
this lounge," he clarified, gesturing around the room.

I ripped open a packet of sugar and poured it into my coffee.

"Yeah, I knew what you meant. It's good, I guess. Classes have been fine. I like the people, for the most part."

"And . . . ?" Ethan peeled the wrap off his brownie and smoothed it out on the table.

"And?" I looked at him quizzically.

"That's the answer you'd give your parents. Or your great-aunt Millie. What do you *really* think?"

I laughed. He was right. "Well, honestly, I think it's kind of weird."

"Weird?" He popped a corner of the brownie into his mouth and licked crumbs off his fingers.

I hesitated. "So . . . it's like we're in the Twilight Zone or something. This strange place that's only open to people between eighteen and twenty-two. Where we go from having other people constantly watching over us to being on our own—but in this limbo where the decisions we make don't really matter. We don't have to worry about taking care of ourselves because there's food three times a day and a place to live, but otherwise it's just us. Kids pretending to be grown-ups." I looked down, surprised at myself for sharing this thought with someone I barely knew. On what was presumably a date. Clearly, Garth thought it was.

Ethan suddenly laughed and I looked back up, trying to read his expression. "Are you making fun of me?"

Ethan stopped laughing but was still grinning as he shook his head. "Not at all. It's just that's exactly what I've been thinking. Although I don't think I ever put it together until you said it so well."

I relaxed.

"But I think it's a good thing, right? That we get this practice run at life before we go out into the real world." Ethan ran his hand through the hair that flopped in his face. A piece of it was sticking up when he took his hand away.

"I don't know. It seems like it'll be so different when we're actually 'out there.' Like at the day care center. The parents come in with their kids, and they're not necessarily all that much older than we are. But it's like they live on a different planet."

"Well, yeah—they're *parents*. Totally different." Ethan took another bite of his brownie. "Do you want kids?"

I nodded. "I love kids. But not anytime soon."

"My cousins are older than me—two of them are already married with children. We only see the kids at the holidays and stuff. They seem . . . exhausting."

A loud laugh escaped me. "They are. I've been babysitting since I was twelve. And there are lots of times I can't wait for the parents to come home." I paused. "But I guess what I like about them—the kids, I mean—is that they're so funny. The things they say, the way they see the world. They're so honest."

"Last summer, we went to visit my one cousin and his family. They took us to their community pool. My cousin is, well, he's losing his hair. His son looked at him in his swim trunks and asked him, 'Did the hair on your chest used to be on your head?'"

I giggled. "Exactly. See what I mean?"

Ethan smiled at me, and it sparked a warm glow. Before I could stop myself, I reached out to smooth down the piece of hair standing at attention on the top of his head. "It was sticking up," I said by way of explanation. Then I quickly looked down at my cookie, my face warm. I wanted to take another bite just to have something to do, but I was afraid I might choke.

Ethan cleared his throat. "So, do you have sisters or brothers?"

Relieved that he didn't comment on the unexpected intimacy of my gesture, I told him about Nina, who was living and working in Manhattan. Ethan talked about his two younger brothers. One was a gamer who rarely left the basement. The other sounded like the boys I went to high school with—a three-season athlete who took each sport he played more seriously than the one that came before.

Eventually, we left the student center and took a meandering route back to the dorms. I told him about my virtually nonexistent roommate, and he told me about his, who never left the room and apparently slept all day. We talked about our favorite cafeteria foods (we both thought the "frost your own cupcakes" totally rocked). And we talked about, of all things, *Star Trek*. Because he liked it, too, I didn't mind admitting it was one of my guilty pleasures. Even though it was just chit-chat, it felt like something was simmering, just beneath the surface. How intently he looked at me when I talked about how Lwaxana Troi sometimes scarily resembled my own mom, and how much I laughed when he admitted to having frequent conversations with himself in the voices of a Ferengi, a Klingon, or Data.

Then, despite how unhurriedly we were walking, we got back to my dorm.

"So . . . ," said Ethan.

"So . . . ," I replied, feeling my pulse quicken.

"This was really nice."

"It was."

He was looking at me so steadily that I had to drop my eyes. When I raised them again, he was still looking at me.

As dorky as it sounds, I'd only been kissed twice before. Despite all the media hype about how sexual today's teens are, my group of friends back in Brook Hill were *mostly* "good girls." Still, it was sad that my two kisses were nothing to write home about. Once, we were hiking with family friends, and when everyone else had gone ahead while I was trying to get a photo of a butterfly, I ended up alone with their teenage son.

Out of nowhere, he lunged at me, and I got a peck that landed on the corner of my mouth. It was just weird and embarrassing. The other time was at a graduation party. One of the boys in my class suddenly revealed that he'd had a crush on me for years, and he leaned in to kiss me. He smelled and tasted of beer, which was probably what gave him the courage to make his confession. I felt bad about it, but I spent the next two weeks dodging his phone calls.

It sounds like a cliché, but as Ethan bent toward me, it was like the world slowed to a steady crawl. At the last minute, I remembered to close my eyes, and I felt his lips, warm and dry, on mine. He pulled back and looked at me quizzically. I realized I was holding my breath and wasn't entirely sure I'd kissed him back, but I smiled, and thankfully he leaned in again. This time, I met his kiss, pressing back against him. His hand cupped the side of my face oh so gently as he pulled me closer, his kisses growing more intense. Involuntarily my lips parted. Ethan sighed deeply as our tongues met, and I felt the buzzing all through my body as his hand tangled in my hair. *So* this *is what a kiss should be.*

CHAPTER ELEVEN

After

Callie was on the nearly empty train to Hoboken, riding the commuter route in the reverse direction. She'd nearly missed it while waffling over what to wear, despite ending up in an unimaginative black three-quarter-sleeve top with skinny jeans and tall boots with chunky heels. Her biggest quandary had been the appropriate amount of cleavage. The V-neck she wore offered some, but not enough that she felt self-conscious. Hearing Tess's voice in her head about trying to be at least a little enthusiastic, she added a teardrop pendant on a short chain and dangly geometric earrings. She suspected Nina wouldn't have put the two together, but she thought they worked. She brushed smoky-gray shadow on her eyes and light plum blush on her cheeks. As she'd headed out the door, Zoe told her that she looked pretty—and even Nina glanced up at her and, after an appraising look, gave her a thumbs-up.

Callie wasn't a big fan of Hoboken, at least not anymore. Located right across the river from lower Manhattan, it had been transformed in her lifetime from a run-down industrial city whose biggest claims to fame were Frank Sinatra and the filming of *On the Waterfront,* to a bastion of postcollege twentysomethings, with enough bars and restaurants that you could probably avoid any regretted one-night stands long enough for memories to fade. At the same time, it still had the overtones of the old Italian city it had long been—with amazing bakeries and delis.

Callie had spent time there the summer after college, while she was living at home and temping. She had landed a weeks-long assignment at an insurance agency where she became friendly with the other young women working there, and they had included her on their excursions to the Hoboken bars. At first it was exhilarating—feeling like a part of this crowd of people just out of college who were taking the "Work hard, party hard" motto to heart. But the way things turned out, Callie was never sure if it was a good thing that she had been part of that scene. Now being there just made her feel old and jaded.

As the train pulled to a stop at the station, she rose and walked to the exit. Outside, it had begun to grow dark, and she bypassed the taxi line to pick her way across the cobblestone street.

Weaving through the crowded sidewalks, she arrived at the bar Jason had suggested. Glancing at her watch, she saw she was about five minutes late. *Perfect.* It was crowded, the bar already two deep. Briefly, she felt like she was going to throw up, and wished she could step back outside for a breath of fresh air, but she thought that would look weird, especially if Jason was watching for her. He'd said he would be waiting off to the right near the "Dead End" sign hanging on the wall. *Hopefully that isn't a portent.*

Callie looked over that way. There were several men, but three of them were clearly together. The fourth was alternating between glancing at his phone and watching the door. She wondered if he was actually doing something on the mobile device or just trying to look busy. Her initial impression—in the moment she had to observe him before he caught sight of her—was that she could understand why he'd used a distant photo of himself on his Connections profile. There was nothing particularly unattractive about him, but the word that came to mind was *ordinary*—that is, ordinary for a man approaching forty. Even in his suit, she could tell that he'd thickened in the middle, and he didn't look like he spent time engaging in any physical activity other than rolling around on his desk chair. His hair was cut short and looked a bit like a Brillo pad. If Tess asked her to describe his face, she would have been at a loss. It was just . . . *there*.

He looked up from his phone and his eyes sought out the door. He smiled at her tentatively, and she gave him a small smile back as she walked toward him. He stepped forward as if he might shake her hand or give her a hug, and then stepped back again, clearly unsure what the protocol was.

"You must be Callie?" he said, the inflection in his voice making it a question.

She nodded. "Yes. So you must be Jason."

"Well, at least we found each other. Maybe this will be the most difficult part of the evening."

She raised her eyebrows. "Maybe."

"We can always hope, right?" He smiled wryly and pointed with his chin toward the bar. "Should we try to get a drink?"

"Sure." Callie let him lead the way.

It took a while to get the bartender's attention, but they were lucky that when they finally did, a tall table had just been vacated near the end of the bar. They sat there with their drinks—a Beck's for him and a Corona for her.

"So . . . ," he began, his right leg bouncing up and down. "Thanks for meeting me."

"Thanks for inviting me." Callie took a sip of her beer. She thought about her conversation earlier with Tess and wondered what "getting to know you" question he would lead off with—or which she should choose if he didn't take the initiative.

"How was your train ride in?"

"Fine, no problem." She ran her finger around the lip of her glass, remembering how, as a child, she used to do that to make whistling noises. "Do you like living in Hoboken?"

He nodded, his knee still jiggling. "It's super convenient for getting into the city. And I love the fact that literally every single restaurant delivers. I don't cook, so it's great for me."

"What kind of food do you like?"

As they talked about restaurants—Dabbawalla, Jason's favorite Indian place in Hoboken; Cadillac Cantina, Callie's favorite Mexican in the city—Callie found herself thinking about Ethan. About their attempts to cook in the dorm kitchen, including a disastrous effort to make tandoori chicken that was so spicy they ended up ordering pizza, about their rare excursions to restaurants, and about how easy it was to talk to him, right from the beginning. She honestly couldn't recall a time when they ever had to fill the silence.

"Refill?" Jason asked.

"No, thanks," she replied, maybe too quickly as she wondered whether his leg had stopped bouncing for even an instant since they'd sat down.

"Would you like to get some dinner?"

Extending the evening into a meal was the last thing Callie wanted to do. But she felt guilty. Jason seemed like a nice enough guy, and she had spent the last half hour distracted by ridiculous memories of an ex-boyfriend she hadn't seen in ten years.

"Sure. Where would you like to go?"

They decided on one of Hoboken's many Italian restaurants, and after a short walk, they were seated at a small table with a votive candle in a jelly jar and a sprig of fake flowers as a centerpiece. Callie couldn't help but notice the continued jiggling of his knee—especially as it set the small bud vase rattling as well. After they'd placed their orders—baked lasagna for him and mushroom ravioli for her—Jason asked where Callie had gone to college.

Inwardly, she groaned. So much for pushing Ethan out of her thoughts. "Welford. In upstate New York."

"I've heard of it. Isn't it sort of a hippie place?"

"I think of it as 'crunchy granola.' Not as much as it once was, though."

"You don't look like you would have gone there," Jason commented, his leg momentarily stilled.

She raised her eyebrows. "Well, I was going to wear my Birkenstocks and tie-dye, but decided against it at the last minute."

He looked at her as if he were trying to imagine her at a Phish concert, and his knee started up again. Callie wondered if his left one ever got in on the act.

"Um, I was kidding," she felt obligated to say.

"Oh, of course, right, I knew that." *Clearly, he didn't.*

In the silence that followed, Callie noticed the strains of a Katy Perry song she liked playing over the restaurant's speakers. "Oh, I love this song." She pointed toward the ceiling.

Jason's eyebrows drew closer together as he listened. "Oh, yeah, it's okay. But I'm more into stuff like Green Day, Bad Religion . . ."

Wow. It had been a while since she'd listened to that music. Whether she'd wanted to or not. It described Ethan's entire music library.

Callie decided to change the subject as the waiter brought them a basket of bread.

"So, advertising . . . Are you on the creative side or the business side?"

"Account management. I basically do client service."

Callie wanted to ask if his leg bounced like that in client meetings. "In certain industries, or all kinds of things?" she inquired instead.

"Lately it's been a lot of cleaning supplies and personal care products."

Callie poured some olive oil on her bread plate and took a piece of bread. "Anything I'd know?" she asked as she broke off a corner of the bread and dipped it in the oil.

"Let's see—Sparkle 'n' Shine . . . ?"

Callie finished chewing. "Wait, is that the commercial where those women are standing around in the kitchen talking about how shiny the floor is?"

"That's the one."

"Cool." Callie waited to see if he had anything further to say on the subject. Then she cleared her throat and resisted taking another piece of bread just to have something to do. "So, do you enjoy it?"

They managed to keep the conversation going through dinner, but Callie begged off dessert, saying that she couldn't possibly eat another bite.

"Coffee, then?"

"I'd love to, but if I miss the next train, there isn't another one for almost an hour, and I have work in the morning."

"Oh, sure, I understand," he replied, pulling his wallet out of his pocket with one hand while reaching for the check with the other.

Callie thanked him for dinner, and a few minutes later they stepped back outside. Jason walked her to the train station, and they talked about how chilly it had gotten and what the weather was predicted to be on the weekend. *It's never a good sign when you start talking about the weather.*

"I can take it from here," she said when they reached the door to Hoboken Terminal. "Thanks again."

"Thank *you* for meeting me. I hope we can do this again?"

"Sure. That would be nice."

"I'll call you," he said.

Her heart sank. *Maybe he's just being polite?*

CHAPTER TWELVE

After

When Callie got home after eleven o'clock, she was surprised to see a bluish glow in the living room. When she investigated, she found Nina on the sofa, covered by a blanket, watching a reality cooking show. Callie wasn't sure if it was the one where contestants were asked to invent meals based on famous literature, and open and operate restaurants with only twenty-four hours to prepare, or if it was the one where candidates had to create dishes using unappetizing combinations of ingredients—like salami, sriracha, Cheetos, and maple syrup.

"You're still up?" she asked, realizing as she said it that it was a ridiculous question. *No,* she imagined her sister saying, *I'm upstairs asleep.*

Nina twisted around to look at her. "I can't sleep. How was your date?"

Callie plunked down in the armchair facing the sofa. "Ugh."

Nina reduced the volume on the TV, so the tattooed chef

on the screen trailed off saying, "Somehow, the clams didn't make it into my bag. I'm totally f— . . ."

"It couldn't have been that bad."

Callie raised her eyebrows. "It couldn't? You've been out of the dating world a long time, big sister."

Callie pulled her knees up to her chest and pushed her hands through her hair. It suddenly struck her how the tables had turned. In another lifetime, Callie had asked Nina about her dates. And Nina was evasive and mysterious. Back then, Nina was also a source of wisdom. A dazzling beacon of knowledge for her clueless little sister.

When Callie was sixteen, she had spent a weekend in New York with Nina—who, at the time, was twenty-four and living in a fourth-floor walk-up in SoHo. It was the first time Callie had been in the city without her parents, and this glimpse into the glamorous life her sister led was like nothing she had ever experienced. Nina had taken her to a party that was a crush of bodies and loud music. At the time, she was dating an assistant district attorney Callie thought was gorgeous. Some of his friends came along with them, and in retrospect, she realized they were probably under strict instructions to keep Nina's little sister safe. Although, truthfully, Callie wouldn't have minded if one of them had been a little dangerous. When they got back to the SoHo apartment, Nina and her boyfriend had a lingering kiss at the door before she sent him on his way. And then she and Callie stayed awake talking for hours. Callie thought it was the first time Nina had *almost* spoken to her as if she were her contemporary, not as her little sister.

Now, sitting in the darkened living room, with just the flickering light of the TV, Nina was not about to let her younger sister off the hook. She made a face at her. "Come on. What happened?"

Callie expelled a long sigh. "I suppose you're right. It wasn't that bad. It was just . . . boring. He's a nice enough guy, but we didn't connect."

Nina cocked her head. "And did you give him a chance to connect with you?"

"What's that supposed to mean?"

"You know exactly what I mean." Nina matched Callie's annoyed tone note for note. "I wasn't kidding the other day when I said you're still hung up on Ethan."

"I am not," Callie said immediately, feeling as she said it that it was like Zoe denying she was tired, even as she yawned so large she could swallow a grapefruit whole. Nina's expression indicated that she found Callie's denial as convincing as she would Zoe's. But having started down the path, Callie felt compelled to continue. "It's been ten years."

Nina pushed her hair behind her ear and sat up straighter. "Ten years in which you haven't gotten serious about anyone else. At all. Have you even dated anyone for more than six months since then?"

"It's not easy meeting someone once you're out of school, unless you're working someplace with lots of people," Callie said defensively. "I'm a preschool teacher, Neen. You know, practically a nun."

Nina rolled her eyes. "Plenty of people meet people. I did."

"Yes, you did. While you were working with dozens of other adults and wearing high heels like a grown-up."

"You could wear high heels like a grown-up, Callie. What's stopping you?"

Callie said nothing.

"Look, I know you don't like Michael." She raised her hand to stop Callie, who had opened her mouth. "Come on, let's be real. You don't like him. That's fine. The point is *I* like him. I love him. He's right for me. And I managed to meet him and marry him. And here you are, holing yourself up in Mom and Dad's house, making no effort to find anyone."

Callie felt something rising in her throat. So much for living under the same roof helping them to find closeness. "What does the fact that I live here have to do with anything? I know you're pissed that they don't charge me rent, but—"

"Whoa, whoa, whoa!" Nina interrupted. "Don't try to change the subject. All I'm saying is that you live here in suburbia where you're never going to meet anyone."

Callie took a deep breath. "Look, I live here because New York is New York. It was fun for a while, but I got tired—literally and figuratively. I needed a break."

"I would say you've taken it," Nina said dryly.

"Don't start with me. This is my life. I love my job, and preschoolers need to be taught whether they live on the Upper East Side or not," Callie retorted. "And I'm doing the stupid online dating thing now."

"Exactly!" Nina said triumphantly. "The 'stupid' online dating thing. If that's what you think about it, do you think that means you're seriously trying to meet someone?"

"And if I'm not?" Callie heard her voice rising. "So what? Maybe I'm happy by myself."

Nina took a deep breath and sighed. "That would be fine. If you were. But I don't think you are."

"And who are you to say I'm not?" Callie's voice rose a few more decibels.

"Shh!" Nina pointed at the ceiling, indicating the people above. "Look, I'm not trying to start a fight with you. Honestly." She looked at her sister's narrowed eyes. "All I'm trying to say is that I think there's unfinished business with you and Ethan that's keeping you from moving on. And his movie coming out isn't helping."

Callie didn't know what to say. She would be lying if she said she'd completely put Ethan behind her. Jason was hardly the first date who suffered by comparison. Of course he wasn't. Ethan had been her first boyfriend and her first love. He was the first person she shared a real kiss with, the first person she made love to. And she'd never found anyone else she felt as close to since.

She had been trying to keep *Rerouting* out of her mind. But it had remained there, bubbling beneath the surface, regardless. It suddenly occurred to her that maybe she was going about this all wrong. Maybe she needed to find out more about the movie, instead of avoiding it. Maybe if she could find out more about Ethan, and how he'd been able to get on with his life, she would move on as well. She knew she was in a bit of a rut. She wasn't as oblivious as Nina made her out to be.

"See? Even you can't deny it," Nina said pointedly.

It was true. She couldn't. But now at least she had an idea of what to do about it.

When Callie came downstairs the next morning, she was surprised to find Michael in the kitchen. Zoe was eating her cereal, her legs pumping back and forth beneath the table. "Guess what?" she exclaimed, half-eaten Cheerios visible in her mouth. "Daddy's taking me to school!"

Callie looked at Michael. "Is everything okay?" she asked, immediately sorry for having argued with Nina the night before.

He put down his coffee cup. "Oh, fine. Nina couldn't sleep last night and she's exhausted. I'm going to take Zoe so she can rest."

Callie was skeptical. Michael going in late just because Nina was tired didn't ring completely true. "But she's okay?"

"Yeah—she's fine. Don't worry." Michael turned his attention to Zoe. "Hurry up, kiddo. We need to get going." Then he turned back to Callie. "Hey, could you make lunch for her? I don't know what to send."

And I do? Callie fought the desire to respond to her brother-in-law and instead turned to her niece. "Zoe, what does Mommy send for lunch for you?" she asked with exaggerated patience, knowing full well what answers she'd give.

"Hmm . . . sometimes cheese sandwiches. Sometimes mac and cheese. But *no* peanut butter. It's not allowed. 'Cause of kids who are 'lergic."

See, how hard was that?

"Thanks, Binks. I'll make you a cheese sandwich. Do you want fruit with it? Strawberries?"

"'Kay. But no apples. They get brown." Zoe wrinkled her nose, as if biting into a brown apple was on par with biting into an apple and finding a worm. Or half a worm.

Callie had just finished packing up Zoe's pink-and-green lunch box when Michael came back into the kitchen with his coat on and briefcase in hand.

"Let's go, Zoe!" He clapped his hands twice. Zoe didn't move. "Zoe!"

"I have to drink my milk." The two adults watched her slowly drink the glass of milk that had sat untouched all through breakfast. Michael's eyes rotated heavenward as he shook his head slowly. Zoe finally finished, set the glass down, and pushed herself off the chair. While she went into the hall to get her shoes, Callie pressed the lunch box firmly into her brother-in-law's hands.

"There you go," she said with a saccharine smile.

"Thanks, Cal," he replied, with a similar expression.

Once she had quickly looked in on Nina—who was sound asleep—Callie drove to school consumed by thoughts of her discoveries from the night before. After leaving her sister on the sofa downstairs, she had powered up her laptop and started poking around. There was still disappointingly little about Ethan on IMDb. Googling, she found a link that brought her to an item on the USC News page for alumni, announcing that his film, *Rerouting*, had been optioned, and another one announcing that the film was set for release. Both links were accompanied by photos—the first was the same one that had appeared in the *Quarterly*; the second looked like a professional headshot. In this one, his smile was one of mild amusement, and he had a brooding look about him. Still no glasses. It barely resembled the Ethan she knew.

Having uncovered so little about Ethan, Callie typed "*Rerouting* movie" into the search box. This yielded pages and pages of results, including many items about its heartthrob star, Nick Sykes. She looked at photos of him as Luke, the misunderstood wild boy in the teen drama *The Summit*. She knew it was silly, but she kept studying him, trying to imagine Nick as Ethan. She also found some publicity shots of Nick as Will, the Ethan character in *Rerouting*. His hair was shorter in those photos—and shorter than Ethan's had ever been, at least when she knew him. It was spiky on top, in a style that clearly cost more than the ten-dollar haircuts Ethan used to get. She watched a video of Nick talking about the casting process and the experience of filming, hoping he'd mention the screenwriter, but he only explained how he saw this as a natural continuation of his prior work—playing someone a few years older than Luke—and how he enjoyed the challenge of being the "straight man" in a group of rambunctious friends, rather than the rowdy one. He also talked about what a pleasure it was to work with the actress who played his vanished love interest—Sarina Apple. *Could that be her real name?* According to further internet digging, it was.

Callie then found herself reading about Sarina Apple—who had played only bit parts in a few television dramas prior to this. Like many young actresses, she had been one of the special victims on *Law & Order: SVU*. Callie had sort of expected Sarina to resemble her, but beyond the slim body type, she didn't see anything of herself. The actress had unruly red hair, fair skin, and hazel eyes. Unquestionably gorgeous, though—which made Callie feel oddly gratified. Stumbling on the Twitter handle @imsarinaapple, she discovered that the actress was also an avid social media user—tweeting about how much she loved the cast and crew and, more intriguing for Callie, sharing some photos from the filming.

She pored through the images and found Ethan in two of them. One in a group shot with the cast—Nick, Sarina, and the actors playing Will's friends—and one where he was just in the background, appearing to be in conversation with a blonde almost precisely his height. Was she involved in the production? Or was she someone in Ethan's life? Finally, Callie forced herself to shut the laptop and get into bed—before she was entirely sucked into the black hole of internet entertainment news.

These thoughts still swirled in her head as she readied the classroom for the kids and as they began to trickle in and take their seats on their orange circles. But once the school day got underway, she was shaken out of such ruminations.

"OWWWWW!" Emma shrieked before she burst into tears. Callie ran over to her. Liam was standing nearby, a scowl on his face as he kicked at a pile of blocks with his toe.

"What happened?" Callie rubbed Emma's back, which heaved with sobs.

"He . . . he . . . pinched me!" Emma's face was red and wet with tears.

Not wanting to make any assumptions, Callie asked who "he" was.

"Liam!" Emma yelled, pointing at him.

Liam's scowl deepened as Callie turned to him. "Did not," he said stubbornly.

Callie raised her eyebrows.

"She had all the blocks I wanted," he added defiantly.

"All the blocks? We have enough to share. And we never put our hands on each other."

"He pinched me!" Emma shrieked again, holding out her pudgy arm to display a red mark.

Callie took a deep breath. Apparently, the Liam honeymoon was over.

"Liam. Pinching is definitely *not* okay." She crouched down and looked into the little boy's eyes.

He refused to meet her gaze. "She wouldn't give me the blocks."

"That doesn't matter, Liam. If you're having trouble sharing and can't work it out with words, you come and ask me for help."

"You were busy!"

"Liam. You can always come to me. Even if I'm doing something. And if I can't help right away, it's still not okay to put your hands on someone. You need to go sit in the peace chair for five minutes, and then you're going to say 'sorry' to Emma."

"It's not fair!" he yelled, balling up his fists.

Callie pointed to the peace chair in the corner. "Go," she said sternly, breathing a sigh of relief when he did.

After the five minutes had passed, Liam gave Emma a grudging apology, but even before snack time, there was another incident in which he grabbed a dinosaur out of Jacob's hands and pushed him. Callie felt a headache coming on and was grateful to take her break at lunchtime. Some of the kids went home then, but the "lunch bunch" that stayed joined Tess's class for their meal and Callie got a short respite.

She used the computer in the office to email Liam's mom, filling her in on the morning's events and asking to meet with her. As she typed, her cell phone pinged. She looked down at the screen. It was Nina.

Hi Callie. Can I ask you a big favor? I'm really not feeling well. My friend Holly is picking Zoe up from school

> and taking her home with her. Could you go up and get
> her when you finish work? Please please?

Callie didn't love the idea of making the hour-long round trip, but she agreed to do it anyway. Nina never asked for favors. *Except for the one about staying at my house for four months.*

Okay, she typed back. Text me Holly's address.

Right away, an address appeared on her screen. Almost immediately, another message followed.

> Since you'll be up there, could you also stop at our ar-
> chitect's office to pick up our kitchen drawings? We're
> meeting with a cabinetmaker this weekend.

Seriously? Considering that Nina so rarely asked anyone for help—no one was as capable as she—it was as if her sister had been taken over by a pod person.

> Fine.

Thank you, thank you! came back, along with the address for HMK Design Group. And a follow-up text—Please make sure they've made all the changes—with a list of items that could only be characterized as minutiae as far as Callie was concerned.

She massaged her temples, made a mental note to find some Tylenol in her handbag, and finished her email to Liam's mother.

Driving up to Wolcott after school, Callie decided to go to the architect's office first. She figured it would be easier to run in there alone than with a four-year-old dragged away from a playdate.

HMK Design Group was tucked into one of Wolcott's side streets, above a perpetually going-out-of-business rug store. Callie climbed the stairs to the frosted glass door and went inside. The girl at the reception desk looked up at her. She had unnaturally red hair, cut in a severe asymmetrical bob.

"Hi," Callie said. "I'm here to pick up the kitchen drawings for Nina Kagan?"

"Oh, right." The girl pushed herself away from the desk on her wheeled chair and stood. As she walked away, Callie noted her remarkably high heels, which were paired with patterned leggings. She'd have no desire to totter around on heels like that, but was intrigued by the tights.

The girl stuck her head into one of the offices. "Ben, do you know where Margo left the Kagans' kitchen drawings?" A low voice responded, and then the girl turned to Callie. "Ben has everything in here."

Uncertain about what she was supposed to do with this information, Callie hesitated, but then decided she was meant to follow. As she approached the door, Ben came out with a rolled-up sheaf of papers. It was the architect Zoe had literally run into in the café following her friend's birthday party.

"Oh! Hello!" Ben said, his eyes widening. "I didn't know it was you."

"It's me," Callie said, smiling, surprised he remembered her.

"Margo had to run out; she left everything with me." Ben clearly assumed Callie knew who Margo was.

"Thanks. Um, Nina asked that I check on a few things . . ." Her voice trailed off.

Ben chuckled. "Of course. Why don't we go to the conference room?"

Callie followed him into a room with windows on three walls—some looking outside, and others looking into the interior of the office space. A beautiful wooden table sat in the center. Ben rolled the drawings out onto the table and secured the corners with stone paperweights.

"Okay, I have no idea what I'm looking at," Callie said, peering at the documents.

Ben bent over the table next to her and pointed. "So, these are the floor plans of the kitchen. And these are the various elevations—showing what the room looks like as if you're standing in it."

Callie tried to get her bearings, figuring out which wall was which. As if reading her mind, Ben guided her through. "Here's the rear-facing wall, with the box window over the sink. The dishwasher was moved to the other side of the sink. And here in the island, the drawer sizes have been changed." Ben pointed to another drawing. "And the double oven has been flipped from here to here. Which means that the pantry only has one door now instead of two."

Callie looked at all the pictures, checking off everything on the list her sister had given her and doubting that any of these changes would really make a difference in the function-ality of the kitchen. "Just curious—why all the changes?"

Ben looked at her. "Because your sister asked for them."

Ah. Callie smiled and glanced down again at the draw-ings, wondering how many variations they had gone through already. "So, how have Nina and Michael been to work with?"

Ben gave her a funny look.

"Oh, come on, I know what they're like." Callie laughed.

Ben laughed then, too. "They're okay. I've had worse."

"Really?"

"It's not like they asked that we flip the house around so ev-erything on one side is on the other. And the back is in the front."

Callie immediately recognized the reference to *Sleepless in Seattle.* "Or that the front of the house opens on a great big hinge so she can get in with a garage door opener?"

Ben laughed again, bigger this time. He had a nice laugh.

"I didn't know guys liked that movie," Callie remarked.

"Oh—guys only like *The Dirty Dozen*?"

She shrugged.

"Well, I don't know what other guys like—but, as an architect, I can certainly appreciate Tom Hanks's pain in that movie."

"Got it. It's like—'My job would be great if it weren't for the clients'?"

"Hey, your sister is one of my clients. I plead the Fifth." Ben winked. "But aren't most jobs like that?"

"A lot of them, I guess. Happy to say mine isn't."

"Wow—what do you do where you don't have to answer to other people? And are there any openings?"

Callie laughed. "Well, I definitely have to answer to people. I'm a preschool teacher."

"Oh my God. The worst clients of all."

"What, the kids? They're not so bad."

"No—their parents."

Callie burst into laughter. "They're okay where I teach now, but you're definitely right about that."

Ben nodded knowingly.

"You have kids?"

He shook his head. "No, I'm not married. But I see it with my brother and his wife. And from the stories they tell. But they're in the city, so it's probably worse there."

"Where do their kids go?"

Ben sucked air in through his teeth. "Now you're asking the hard questions. Some private school. Starts with a *P* . . ."

"Pemberley?"

"That's it!"

"Small world. I used to teach there."

Ben assumed a serious expression. "I'm so sorry," he said gravely.

Callie giggled. "You're not kidding."

"I can only imagine what it would be like to deal with a whole set of parents like my brother and sister-in-law. And their little rug rats who wouldn't know the word *no* if it bit them on the face."

"I was lucky to get out alive."

Ben took a half step back and assessed her. "And looking pretty unscathed."

"Well, I've had a few years to recover." Callie tossed her hair over her shoulder.

"It looks like you have. Quite nicely."

Callie's face got warm, and she looked down at the drawings on the table. "So." She cleared her throat. "Is this everything they need?"

Ben took a moment to regroup. "Oh, um, yes." He removed the paperweights and rolled the documents up again. "Here you go." He held them out to her, and she took them.

"Thanks." She glanced up at him. He was a good five inches taller than she. "And thanks for the compliment." She smiled. "Nice to know those viper parents didn't mutilate me permanently."

Ben smiled back. "Not at all," he said. He tapped on the end of the roll of paper. "And if Nina has any questions, Margo or I are around."

Callie nodded and thanked him. She left the office with the sneaking suspicion that he was watching her go.

CHAPTER THIRTEEN

Before

It had been hard to pull away from that delicious first kiss, but I did, and I went upstairs to my room alone the night of our first date. After that, Ethan and I were rarely apart. We ate most of our meals together in the dining hall—sometimes just us, sometimes with friends. We went to the campus movie every Wednesday. Ethan said they were all classics. Most were new to me, but he had already seen a lot of them. He was always eager to introduce me to the ones he knew, though sometimes I just didn't get them. Like *Marathon Man*. Or *Marnie*. Of course I loved *Casablanca*—one of the few I had already seen. And I wished they would sometimes show something more my speed, like John Hughes. But occasionally I was pleasantly surprised—like by *The Godfather*. Mostly it was just so cute how excited Ethan got, telling me about what he thought made each movie special.

Most nights, we studied together—usually in my room because my roommate was so conveniently absent. Of course, this meant that we were doing less and less studying, and more and more making out on my bed. At first, I was shy about it, but the more we kissed, and the more he figured out just how to touch me, the more okay I was with him sliding his hand under my shirt up my back, then around to the front, then taking my top off entirely. The first time he unhooked my bra and I let it slip down my arms, and he murmured how beautiful I was, I flushed with pleasure.

It was getting harder and harder to keep my eye on the clock and my ear on the lock in the door as we shed more clothing and Ethan's hand was between my legs. Soon, he was regularly whispering in my ear how much he wanted to have sex with me. But I kept telling him no—even as my humming body was threatening to undermine my resolve.

I may not have been the last American virgin, but I knew there weren't that many of us left. Nonetheless, I wasn't ready to cross that line. You could have only one first time. And even though I was almost sure I wanted it to be with Ethan, I was scared. A little part of me liked how it was all up to me. That he was asking for something that was totally in my control.

I wouldn't be Ethan's first, which also made me nervous. He'd slept with a girl he dated that past summer. Honestly, I worried I wouldn't do it right. That he'd compare us, and I'd come up short. I wished I could talk to someone about it—but Jenna had so much more experience than I did that I didn't think she'd get it, and Nina felt more and more like a stranger. And even though my high school friends and I were talking a bit when we first got to college, those phone calls had dwindled to practically nothing.

We didn't often get to leave campus on anything resembling a real date. The nearest town, Glover, was three miles away, so without a car—which not many freshmen had—we were stuck. However, when my birthday came in December, Ethan borrowed a friend's Mazda so he could take me out.

I put on the one dress I had hanging in my closet. It was some sort of shimmery fabric in a deep eggplant shade with a billowy scoop neckline. It hugged my waist and hips, and came to just above my knees. I fell in love with it when I'd seen it on a sale rack and bought it not knowing when I might wear it.

Looking at myself in the mirror, I thought it was probably a bit overboard for a birthday dinner, but I decided to go with it. I slipped on my trusty Doc Martens to dress it down and brushed my hair. It had gotten very long—reaching past the middle of my back—and I pulled it over one shoulder before putting on my coat and going downstairs to meet Ethan.

"I like your hair like that." He kissed the exposed part of my neck, making me shiver. "Happy birthday," he whispered into my ear, before taking my hand so we could walk to the parking lot.

We drove the ten minutes into Glover, and Ethan found a parking spot, only then removing his hand from my knee— which felt lonely without it. It was Saturday evening, and some of the shops along the quaint main street were still open. Twinkly white lights were strung between lampposts, and big red bows punctuated them every fifty feet or so. We had time before our dinner reservation, so despite the cold, we walked past the brightly lit windows—many of them decorated with small Christmas trees or spray-painted snow—and enjoyed the change from being on campus.

We entered a gallery that showed work by some Welford alums. One wall was entirely covered by paintings of gourds in different shapes and colors.

"How many gourds can you paint before going insane?" Ethan whispered.

"Shh!" I said, before adding, "Clearly, at least"—I counted softly—"seventeen."

We left the gallery and wandered into a shop that sold things made by area artisans. A display of simple jewelry caught my eye.

"Look," I said, reading the information displayed in a small frame. "She makes these from stuff she finds—pebbles and sea glass." I picked up an earring made of wire twisted around an unusual stone and held it up. "Isn't this cool? You can even provide your own rock."

"Interesting," Ethan replied. I thought he was just humoring me, but when we went back outside, he pulled me to him and kissed me.

"What?" I asked when he slowly drew back.

"I just had to do that. I'm so lucky to be with a girl who actually means it when she says she wants a rock. Not a diamond." He kissed me again. "I love you, Callie."

"I love you, too," I whispered back. He'd said it before, but it still flooded me with warmth. I especially liked hearing it at times like these—and not when we were naked in bed.

He took my hand and we continued on to the restaurant where he'd made reservations, an Italian trattoria in what had once been a church. The interior walls were roughly hewn stone, and the floor was dark-stained wood. They had a Christmas tree in the corner, decorated with white lights and red and silver balls. I smiled when I noticed there was also a menorah on the mantel over the fireplace.

I took off my coat when we got to our table.

"Wow," Ethan said, looking at me. I'd forgotten about the dress.

"I didn't know what to wear."

"You look amazing."

My cheeks grew warm. The maître d' was hovering, holding our menus, so I sat down, and Ethan followed.

"Kind of a step up from the cafeteria, right?" Ethan observed a few moments later, looking up from his menu.

"Just a little." I grinned. "We don't have to get our own food."

"And hopefully it won't be served on orange plastic trays."

After a distinctly non-cafeteria-like dinner—shrimp scampi for me, chicken saltimbocca for Ethan—the waiter brought a slice of chocolate mousse cake with a candle.

I closed my eyes, but at that moment, I didn't feel like there was much left to wish for. So I opened them and blew out the flame. Ethan reached into the pocket of his coat, which was hanging from the back of his chair, and pulled out a small wrapped box, which he placed on the table. "Happy birthday, Callie."

Grinning like my face might break, I carefully unwrapped the package, slitting the Scotch Tape with my fingernail and peeling away the wrapping.

"You can rip the paper, you know," Ethan said, amused.

"I've got it." Inside was a box.

"It's not a rock," he said as I lifted the lid to reveal a bracelet made of linked silver hearts.

"It's beautiful! Thank you!" I leaned across the table to kiss him, and then fastened the bracelet on to my wrist.

"You like it?"

"I love it," I said, admiring its shine in the light of the fire. "Now, I can't possibly eat this whole piece of cake by myself."

Ethan picked up his fork. "I was hoping you'd say that," he replied as he speared a bite and popped it into his mouth.

When we got back to campus, he found a parking space and we walked up to my dorm.

"Is your roommate here?" he asked as we approached the front steps.

I squeezed his hand. "She's gone for the weekend."

"Excellent."

A few minutes later, I was unlocking the door to my room and stepping inside to remove my coat and boots. And then Ethan's arms were around me, his lips finding mine. We fell onto the bed, kissing.

"My dress!" I whispered as the fabric crushed beneath me.

Ethan drew back and raised one eyebrow. I loved that he could do that. "Then we'll have to take it off."

"Turn off the light."

While Ethan took the two steps to the light switch, I pulled the dress over my head and tossed it onto the desk chair. Ethan removed his plaid shirt and returned to me in a T-shirt and jeans. He ran his hand over my hair, and bent to kiss me again, his tongue tangling with mine. Then his hand ran down my neck and slipped my bra strap off my shoulder, sliding around to cup my breast.

"Wait!" I pulled away from him, breathless. I wanted to make this decision when I was still reasonably clearheaded.

He looked at me quizzically.

"Do you . . ." I bit my lip. It felt like the point of no return, but I was as ready as I'd ever be. "Do you . . . have something?"

His brows knit together. "Something . . . ? Oh!" A smile spread over his face. "You mean a condom?"

I nodded and ducked my head, suddenly embarrassed.

He put his hand under my chin and tilted it back up toward him. "Always prepared. Like the Boy Scouts," he said solemnly, removing his hand from my chin to pat the pocket of his jeans. "Are you sure?"

"I think so."

He hesitated a moment and then kissed me again, even more deeply. He unhooked my bra and slipped it off, his hands and lips finding my breasts and my brain fogging up, as I knew it would. Then he pulled off his T-shirt, and my hands explored the skin of his back.

In what felt like moments but also like days, we were both naked, and I was finding it hard to catch my breath. "Are you ready?" he murmured.

I nodded, not trusting my voice.

He fumbled with the foil package he'd pulled out of his pocket before removing his jeans, and then was poised over me. I looked up at his face, which was tensed with—what? Desire? The fear of hurting me? I closed my eyes. And then, there it was, not nearly as painful as I'd expected.

"Are you okay?" he whispered.

I looked at him and nodded. He smiled and started to move, slowly. "Just relax," he breathed, shifting a bit and adjusting his motion until I was moving, too. His breathing grew more rapid, and then, more quickly than I imagined it would be—and just as I was starting that delicious climb—it was over. Ethan collapsed on top of me with a groan, his chest heaving.

"That was great," he whispered when he could speak again. He kissed me on the forehead, then raised himself up to get out of bed and crossed the room to the wastebasket. When he'd discarded the condom, he got back under the covers and curled himself around me. "Was that all right?"

"Mm-hmm."

"But you didn't, um . . ."

"It's okay."

"No, it's not. That's not how your first time is going to end." He kissed my forehead, and then my eyelids, and then his mouth captured mine again. And his hand was moving down my body, down to the junction between my thighs. Almost immediately, he brought me back to where I'd been when he was inside me, and then . . . the intense explosion followed by sweet release.

When I opened my eyes, he was smiling at me. "Now *that's* the way I want to make you feel," he said. "My gorgeous birthday girl."

Sighing, I stretched out my toes lazily and then tangled them with his.

"Come here," he said, and I slid into him, his arm swallowing me up. "Thank you for letting me be your first."

I laughed softly. "Anytime," I said with a smile. And then, with my head on his chest, we both fell asleep.

CHAPTER FOURTEEN

After

That Saturday was a quintessential autumn day. The sky glowed blue, and the intense hues of the foliage burned against it. The delicious aroma of waffles met Callie as she went downstairs. At the kitchen table, Zoe happily munched on one. Michael sat opposite, neatly cutting his up, while Nina lifted a fresh waffle from the iron and dropped it onto a plate. Callie couldn't remember the last time that old waffle iron had been used. *But why not? I could do that.*

She went to the fridge to pour herself a glass of orange juice.

"Waffle?" Nina asked from behind her. "I have plenty of batter."

"Sure, if it's no problem," Callie replied. "Can I help?"

"Okay—why not? Just pour half a cup into the center of the iron. The light will go off when it's ready." Nina watched over Callie's shoulder for a moment before sitting down with her own breakfast. She spoke again as Callie waited for her batter to cook. "We're going to head out soon to meet friends at a harvest festival. You know—corn maze, pumpkin picking . . . Do you want to come?"

Callie was tempted. Who could resist the lure of cider—and cider doughnuts? But being the only single woman in a crowd of families with young kids . . . not so appealing. Besides, even more attractive was having the house to herself for the first time in weeks. The light blinked off on the iron, and she opened it to reveal a perfectly round, perfectly browned waffle. "Thanks for asking, but I think I'll pass. You guys should have some nuclear-family time."

"You sure?"

Callie nodded. "Absolutely. Bring me home a pumpkin."

"We will get you the most biggest pumpkin we can find," Zoe announced.

Michael looked up. "Biggest. Not most biggest. And I think Aunt Callie might not need one quite that big."

Callie nodded. "Yeah, a medium pumpkin is fine for me."

After they left, Callie heaved a big, loud sigh, just because she could, without anyone asking her why. Then she brought her laptop down to the kitchen table and opened it up. Idly, she clicked on E! Online and read the story beneath a headline asking whether the heart of eminently eligible Nick Sykes had been captured by an adorable pop singer whose star was rapidly rising. As she continued to poke around, she discovered that the trailer for *Rerouting* had been released. Something clenched deep inside her belly. She clicked Play.

```
Ethan/Will/Nick whistles as he snaps a
suitcase closed on a bed.
     The phone in his pocket rings and
he pulls it out, smiling as he sees the
number. "Hey, Allison!" he says warmly.
```

Cut to Callie/Allison/Sarina biting her
lip and fiddling with an unusual pendant
in the hollow of her throat. Cut back to
Ethan/Will/Nick slumped on the bed, head
in his hands.

"What are you going to do, sit here
and sulk? Just because she's not coming
doesn't mean you don't get to move to the
left coast!" a friend exclaims to a sullen
Ethan/Will/Nick. "It'll be epic!" declares
another. The guys throw duffels into the
back of a big SUV. The SUV pulls away from
the curb; the brakes suddenly squeal as
it stops short. One of the guys jumps out
to pick up a bag forgotten on the curb.
Cut to them engrossed in a game of "I
Never" revolving around bodily functions
as they slide past their exit, a robotic
female voice announcing, "Rerouting."

The SUV pulls into a truck stop. As
the guys squabble over a bag of chips,
the car backs into a tractor trailer.
A massive man wearing a cutoff T-shirt
bearing the words "BITE ME" jumps out
of the cab. Cut to a friend frantically
explaining that they're trying to cheer
Ethan/Will/Nick up and that it wouldn't
help their cause if they all ended up in
the hospital. Cut to "BITE ME" and other
truckers at a bar with the guys, "BITE
ME" declaring, "You haven't heard about
heartbreak until you hear my story!"

More driving, turning right when the
robotic voice says, "Turn left . . .

Rerouting," the car stuttering to a stop
on a road surrounded by cornfields. Cut
to Ethan/Will/Nick sitting on porch steps
with a pretty girl. Cut to Callie/Allison/
Sarina, soft-focus. She opens a box containing the necklace she'd worn in the
opening scene. "Remember that pebble we
found when we hiked to the waterfalls?"
Ethan/Will/Nick asks. More driving.
Flashing lights. Drunken line dancing.
Another missed exit. "Rerouting," says the
robotic voice again.

The trailer ended, and Callie hit Play again to watch it a second time. It was surreal to see actors playing the parts of her and Ethan. And the more she thought about it, the more she thought how odd it was that Ethan hadn't contacted her. Not that he needed her permission—and maybe after what she'd done to him, she didn't deserve anything at all—but it would have been nice to have had some warning, some explanation before seeing such personal episodes of their lives being reenacted in a major motion picture. This wasn't just showing up at a film festival somewhere and dying—it was going to be released in theaters nationwide.

She closed the computer and slowly drank a glass of water, thinking about how long it had been since she'd seen Ethan's face—other than the photos she'd found online. She was happy that Nina, Michael, and Zoe were gone so she could pull the attic stairs down without anyone asking any questions. She climbed up and began sneezing, the dust immediately infiltrating her nostrils.

When she pulled herself together, she looked around, bending her head to avoid the beams. There were boxes and large Rubbermaid tubs everywhere, some neatly sealed and labeled, some bursting with stuffed animals and old quilts. She crept toward the back corner, and behind empty boxes that once housed a microwave, a juicer, and a television, she found an oversized shoebox. She pulled it out and carefully climbed down the attic stairs with it.

Behind her closed bedroom door, she sat down on the bed, staring at the lid. There was no label, just the name brand of the boots that had come in the box. She took a deep breath and lifted off the lid, sneezing again.

Callie wondered if anyone in the twenty-first century still had packets of actual letters, tied with ribbon. She certainly didn't. She and Ethan had spent so little time apart, they rarely even emailed each other. But she did have birthday and Valentine's Day cards, some ticket stubs, random sticky notes filled with Xs and Os, and lots of photographs. Callie had been late on the digital camera curve, so the photos she snapped in college were taken with film and printed on Kodak paper. A few of her favorites were in frames, and she'd stuffed those into the box as they were. In one, she and Ethan were sitting on a sofa in one of the dorm common rooms, surrounded by Shauna, Peter, Tim, and another girl she didn't recognize. Ethan's arm was draped around Callie, and she had her head on his shoulder. Jenna had taken the photo.

Another framed photo was taken by a tourist the summer they lived in San Francisco. They were at Fisherman's Wharf with Alcatraz in the background. It had been a chilly day, and Callie was wearing Ethan's sweatshirt. It had been a long time since she had looked at their younger faces—who they were before everything happened.

Callie riffled through the box; most of the other photos were of Ethan alone or with his friends, and some were of just her. She knew they had spent a lot more time with his friends than with hers—and that was okay at the time. She did it willingly—but she knew she wouldn't do it today. Among the photos were concert tickets for bands that Ethan liked and Callie had pretended to enjoy for his sake. He often scoffed at what he called the saccharine pop Callie preferred. The loud, angry punk he listened to was somehow more "legitimate." And though she had been known to turn up the volume on a handful of hard-driving songs, his choices tended to give her a headache. She smiled at the thought of how much of it she had listened to, just because she wanted to spend time with him. That she was so in love she didn't really mind. Even a few hours apart felt like eons. She couldn't imagine being so pliable now. *Have I gotten old and set in my ways? At thirty-one?* She shook her head at the thought. It wasn't that she wouldn't go to a concert she didn't like for the right person, but now she'd expect him to go to a concert for her, too.

Beneath all the scraps of paper was the silver heart bracelet Ethan gave her on her nineteenth birthday. She'd loved it, even though it wasn't her style at all. There was a carved wooden box he'd given her for their second Valentine's Day. All the way at the bottom, Callie found what she was looking for—the necklace Ethan had made for her. She lifted it out of the box and ran her finger over the smooth stone that had been turned into a pendant.

Callie heaved a deep sigh. No question, what she'd had with Ethan was special. Was it perfect? No—but what relationship was? What if all they needed was a break; could it have lasted? She wanted to have those feelings again—that breathlessness, that sense of floating on air. And maybe she could. Something was in the air, something that gave her hope.

She closed the box and tucked it into the back of her closet. Shutting the door firmly, she decided she needed fresh air. She packed water, paints, and a pad into her backpack and drove to a nearby nature preserve. She found herself giving big smiles to strangers on the trail as she crunched past them on the fallen leaves. Finally, she sat on a rock in the sun, trying to capture the brilliant colors of the day. As she walked back to the car, she was thinking about soup and planning to pick some up. And then she thought of her perfect waffle that morning. Even though Nina had prepared the batter and it was just a waffle—why couldn't she make soup herself? She dropped her bag on the passenger seat and scrolled through search results on her phone until she found a recipe for pumpkin soup with sage. She knew Nina wouldn't approve of the canned pumpkin, but you have to start somewhere.

She swung by the grocery store to pick up her ingredients—heavy cream, an onion, fresh herbs, garlic, some parsley for a garnish, and, of course, the can of pumpkin puree. And a loaf of crusty bread from the bakery section. While she waited in the long line at the register, she picked up a copy of *People*, wondering if it said anything about *Rerouting*. Leafing through it, all she found was a "stars are just like us" photo of Nick Sykes wearing a T-shirt and shorts and carrying a Starbucks cup: "Stars Drink Coffee." *Surprise, surprise.* As she replaced it on the rack, her eye was drawn to a cover blurb on *Glamour*: "How Do You Know When It's Really Over?" When she realized that the beautiful woman on the cover was Sarina Apple, she impulsively added the magazine to her basket.

At home, she dug out her old boom box, and with the music cranked loud, she followed her recipe and got the soup simmering on the stove. She closed the browser window on the recipe and clicked to check her email. There was a message from Emily letting her know about an upcoming art opening, a handful of coupons ("Today Only!" "Time to Save!" "Have We Got a Deal for You!"), and the monthly e-newsletter from Welford. Typically, Callie left those missives from her alma mater sitting in her in-box for about a week and then, out of a sense of obligation, pretended to read them before trashing them. This time, however, she clicked it open.

Applications for the incoming class were up and had come

from all over the globe. Several of the faculty were going to speak on a panel about the role of the US in the Middle East. The alumni weekend held the prior weekend had been a roaring success.

And then she saw it. "Ethan Rendel featured in *Magic Hour*," with a link to the article.

Apparently, *Magic Hour* was some sort of film-industry trade publication. There was a short introduction of Ethan as the screenwriter of *Rerouting*, and then a question-and-answer section.

> Q: *Rerouting* is your first film, and it has garnered significant prerelease attention. Did you expect it to be so well received?
>
> A: Expect, no. Hope, of course. It's a film I've worked on for a long time, and I thought it had a good mix of humor and sentiment. But, of course, it's almost impossible to judge your own work. I've been pleasantly surprised by all the buzz.
>
> Q: You said you've been working on the script for some time. Do you remember what inspired you to tell this story?

Callie held her breath.

> A: They always say, "Write what you know." Most of us went through breakups when we were young and had to find ways to get over them. I really wanted to tell a story about that, and about friendship. There are a lot of movies out there about the power of

women's friendships. I wanted to talk about
men's friendships in a way we don't often see.

Q: What about the title of the film? Having a
snappy, catchy title can be important for word
of mouth. Where did *Rerouting* come from as
a title?

A: It's a running joke throughout the movie.
The guys constantly fail to follow the directions the GPS gives them, so there's always
that robotic voice announcing, "Rerouting."
But there's also a larger meaning—what the
main character, Will, is talking about in the
conversation he has with his best friend in Las
Vegas.

Q: Tell us about that.

A: Well, it's basically about different routes all
arriving at the same destination. Sometimes
you find you're no longer on the path you intended to take, but that can be okay. If you're
meant to get to a particular place, you may
take a different route, but you'll get there. And
you can still enjoy the journey.

Callie continued to read. There were questions about future projects Ethan had in the works and what it was like being
part of film production. Nothing about his personal life, and
nothing further about what was behind the film.

"If you're meant to get to a particular place, you may take
a different route, but you'll get there." Callie kept rereading
that line, pinching the bridge of her nose between her thumb

and forefinger. Were she and Ethan meant to be together? What would have happened if she stayed with him? What if that summer had never happened? Would they have broken up anyway, or would they have matured together and made it work?

Callie shut the laptop, turned the flame off under the soup—which smelled delicious—and went into the living room. She flipped on the TV and scrolled through the movies, settled on *You've Got Mail*, and snuggled up on the sofa to watch.

She was in her own rom-com world when her temporary housemates returned, bearing four pumpkins, a bag of cider doughnuts, and a jug of cider.

"What's this?" Nina exclaimed, finding the soup in the kitchen.

"I made it," Callie called out, picturing the look of disbelief on her sister's face. Nina appeared in the living room doorway.

"Do you mean you bought a container of it and poured it into the stockpot?"

Callie stuck out her tongue at her sister. "No, I actually followed a recipe. Made enough for everyone."

"Huh," Nina said. "Will wonders never cease?" But then she smiled. "Good for you. Good for us!" Then she glanced at the TV. "Oh! I love this movie!"

"I know. You want to watch with me?"

"How about we eat and then start it again after Zoe goes to bed?"

"Fine by me." Callie heaved herself off the couch so the four of them could sit down to a meal of soup with big hunks of bread, followed by cider doughnuts for dessert.

CHAPTER FIFTEEN

After

Jump-started with *You've Got Mail,* Callie spent the rainy Sunday watching a marathon of romantic comedies. By the time Monday came around, her head was swirling with a jumble of memories, theories, questions, and fantasies. She was desperate for someone else's perspective—and didn't want it to be Nina's. She stuck her head into Tess's classroom before school started.

"Hey—coffee after school? Or wine?"

Tess looked up from the watercolor paints she was setting out on one of her tables.

"Wine, please. What's up?"

Callie shook her head. "Don't ask. I'll fill you in later."

She went through the rest of the school day mechanically dealing with what had become Liam's routine behavior. Today, he was hoarding all the toy cars and elbowing the other children who tried to come near him. Callie was relieved she had an appointment to meet with his mother the following morning.

Once the school day finally ended, Callie pulled on her coat and appeared at Tess's classroom door again.

"Ready?" she asked.

"Just about." Callie watched Tess stacking up some drawings and then put on her own jacket. Outside, it was gray and misty and romantic in a gothic sort of way. A perfect day to wear a wool cape and look out over the cliffs. If she were near any cliffs. Callie's day of rom-coms was obviously getting to her head. She mentally shook herself. *Just because a movie was inspired by me doesn't mean I'm actually* in *one.* She and Tess got into their separate cars and followed each other into downtown Brook Hill, then parked in a lot behind Main Street. She pulled up her hood, and they walked briskly to the wine bar, the Delicious Grape.

While *downtown* was still a bit of a misnomer, it had become trendier since Callie's parents had first moved there—hence the wine bar. There were also some ridiculously expensive women's clothing boutiques. More than once, Callie had been fooled into entering a shop displaying a sign reading "Sale: 90 Percent Off," only to discover that the sale rack had approximately ten items on it, and the remainder of the merchandise was priced at least three times what Callie was willing—or able—to pay. But the town was also home to an independent bookstore she liked to browse and a great toy store. The sidewalks were dotted with trees, neatly contained by low wrought-iron fences. In the spring and summer, the patches of dirt around the trees were explosions of flowers, but now, there was little color to be seen. Soon, the trees would sport red bows and wreaths for the holidays.

"So, are you going to tell me what's up?" Tess asked as they walked.

"Just wait. I brought my laptop. The movie trailer is out. I'll show you when we get inside."

Tess turned to look at her, her curly hair even curlier in the damp air. "Your ex's movie?"

Callie made a face. "No, *101 Dalmatians.*" She grinned, forcing herself to be lighthearted.

They reached the Delicious Grape and went inside. Callie ordered an Autumn Ale from their small but impressive beer menu. Once Tess had her Malbec, they settled at a table in the corner, and Callie pulled her laptop out of the bag and put it on the table.

"Okay, so let's see this trailer," Tess said, taking a sip of her wine. Callie kept the volume low, although the bar was fairly empty, and pressed Play. She watched Tess watch the film. Tess glanced at her during the breakup scene but otherwise didn't react. When it ended, Callie closed the computer.

Tess took another sip of her wine before turning to Callie again. "So—did you actually break up with him *over the phone*?"

Callie sighed. "Yes."

Tess looked appropriately astonished.

"He was three thousand miles away. What was I supposed to do?"

Tess shrugged. "I don't know. Water under the bridge, I guess . . . Except now hundreds of thousands of people will get to watch you do it."

"Thanks. That makes me feel so much better."

"At least you look great up on the big screen . . ." Tess rolled the stem of her wineglass between her thumb and forefinger. "But I don't think this is why you wanted to show me the trailer. What's really going on?"

Callie took a deep breath. "This movie has really thrown me, even more than I would have imagined it could. Then it hit me—I need to figure out what's getting under my skin so much. So I've been trying to see what else I can find out about it—you know, learn more, instead of trying to avoid it. I can't find much about Ethan, but it's amazing what's out there about these celebrities. No wonder people get obsessed with this stuff! I found some photos of Ethan on Sarina Apple's Twitter feed, and—" Callie stopped as Tess put up her hands.

"Whoa. Hold on! You're on some actress's Twitter feed? You're cyberstalking? You're as bad as what's-her-name, Meg Ryan's character in that movie."

"Annie. And maybe I am. I don't know. But that's not the point. The point is—there's *stuff* that maybe I never dealt with. Stuff that this movie has stirred up for me. And if I want to move on, I need to figure out how to put it to rest." She stopped to take a long swallow of her ale.

"And that stuff is?"

"I don't know. Nina thinks I'm still in love with Ethan. I think she's wrong, but having him back in my life—even in this indirect way—makes me think about how I felt about him back then, before I broke up with him. And how bad I feel about how I treated him."

Tess raised her eyebrows. "What exactly happened?"

"We were all set to move to San Francisco together. He was already out there, and I decided I couldn't go. So—like you just watched—I broke up with him over the phone."

"And . . . ? You're leaving out a lot of the story. *Why* couldn't you go?"

Callie bought herself time with another swallow of beer. She never knew how to answer that question without talking about things she'd long ago decided were just not shareable. "I was young. And though I loved him—I don't know—I guess I got scared about making that huge move. I wasn't ready." *It may not be the whole truth, but it will do.* She pressed on. "I know this is going to sound weird, but somehow this movie— even though I can't tell if I'm the villain of the story or what—it feels romantic. Like even if he wrote it years ago—which he probably did—it's about *us* and what we had. And it makes me remember how special it was, and I want to feel that way again. I don't know if that would be with Ethan—I mean, I don't even know if he's single, or if we'd even have anything to talk about—or with someone else. But I need to get it resolved. Finally. So, what I've been thinking . . ."

". . . is that you need to hire a detective and fly out to Seattle?"

"Very funny. So nice to know my best friend is taking me so seriously." Callie wrinkled her nose at Tess before continuing. "*Anyway*, what I was thinking is that I should get in touch with him. Maybe my friend Jenna can find him on Facebook, or get me his email address."

Tess's eyes widened. "Geez, Callie. It's sort of crazy."

"Maybe. But I feel like I have to do it. The thing is, at first I tried to ignore the movie being out there, but it wasn't working. It just keeps spinning inside my brain. It's made me remember what it's like to have that kind of relationship—and be past all that awkwardness when you're getting to know someone. And then I had that terrible date with that ad guy, Jason . . ."

Tess picked up her wineglass to take a sip and then plunked it back down abruptly. "Wait. What? You never told me about that. And don't make that face."

Callie hadn't realized she had "a face." She shrugged. "There was no chemistry," she said, thinking also of that ever-jiggling leg but keeping that detail to herself.

"After one date? You're so sure? Was there anything wrong with him?" Tess tapped her fingers on the table.

"Wrong with him?"

"Like, irredeemably wrong. He came to the date with a concealed weapon. He got drunk. He slugged the waiter . . ." Tess ticked each of these off on her fingers as if they were items on the standard checklist everyone consults on a first date.

Callie rolled her eyes. "By your standards, then, no, nothing was wrong with him. He was just . . . dull. He never got my jokes . . ."

"Well, maybe you weren't funny."

Callie stuck her tongue out at her friend.

"If you were in my class, that action would get you some time in the peace chair."

"Good thing I'm not in your class then." Callie smiled. "Anyway, there was just no spark."

"Look," Tess said, leaning forward in her chair. "I'm all for chemistry. But sometimes people just take longer to get out of the gate. Maybe he's uncomfortable on first dates. Have you heard from him again?"

Callie nodded gloomily. "Got an email from him the next day saying what a nice time he had."

"See? Sounds like a decent guy."

"*You* wouldn't want to sit through another dinner with him."

"So don't do dinner," Tess said, as if it were the most obvious solution in the world. Then she got a glimmer in her eye.

"What?" Callie asked warily.

"I've got it! A double date!"

"Are we in high school again?"

"Oh, stop being so difficult. No reason not to do a double date. How about you and—what's his name?"

"Jason."

"You and Jason and Brett and me all go bowling."

"Bowling?" Callie wasn't quite sure she'd heard right.

"Bowling," Tess said firmly. "No one can take themselves too seriously when they're bowling. I mean, the bowling shoes alone are too goofy! It gives you an activity besides just eating and talking, and us being there takes some of the pressure off. Why not?"

Callie took a deep breath. She knew that Tess would

logically counter any argument she raised. *Might as well wave the white flag.* "Okay, why not?"

"Good. That's settled." Tess finished her wine and put the glass firmly on the table. "Look, here's the deal. I didn't know you back when you were with Ethan. But obviously that was huge for you, and now that it's big as life, on film, I can see why you're curious. I promise I won't judge you for anything you decide to do when it comes to that. But I do think you need to try to move on. Callie, you're not just my best friend, you're literally one of the best people I know . . ."

Callie rolled her eyes.

"Nuh-uh. Don't do that," Tess said sternly, giving Callie the distinct feeling that she was a preschooler in her friend's class. "You're an amazing teacher; you're a brilliant artist. I know I said that Apple chick looks great, but you're ten times prettier." Tess held up her hand as Callie opened her mouth again. "I'm not done. I've never seen anyone pull off Converse hightops and a tiered skirt the way you do. It drives me crazy that you're single, living alone in that big house. I've never known anyone so deserving of the perfect guy. You should have your own movie, for God's sake—and it shouldn't show you crying, feeling bad about yourself, and breaking up with some guy over the phone, and then cyberstalking him ten years later. It should show you happy and in love."

"Geez, Tess, enough! You're gonna make me cry." Callie tried to joke, but her eyes stung.

"So I'll give you a tissue. But I'm going to finish what I want to say. That's what I want for you—to truly be happy. The only way that's going to happen is if you focus on someone else. I'm not saying you can't do this whole *Rerouting* investigation thing in the meantime. But like you said, you need to look ahead. And the first step is our double date. I'm clearing my calendar!"

Callie didn't know what to say. But it was good to know she had someone in her corner.

Back at home after sharing another round and an antipasto platter with Tess, Callie logged on to her laptop and replied to Jason's email, asking him out on the bowling double date before she could reconsider. The following morning, he'd replied saying that it sounded like fun, but that he'd have to put it off for a week due to a work trip. That was just fine as far as Callie was concerned. Perhaps between now and then he'd meet the woman of his dreams and elope.

In the meantime, she was determined to focus less on her fledgling personal life and more on getting to her early-morning meeting with Liam Switzer's mom, Ellen. She was briefly delayed by Nina's search for a heating pad; her sister was hoping it would help her backache. Callie finally found one underneath a stack of threadbare beach towels on the top shelf of the linen closet. Not for the first time, she wondered about the things her mother was unable to part with. *Maybe having trouble letting go is genetic?*

She raced to school, trying to catch every light. Conferences with parents could be tricky, particularly if there were issues of concern. It was rare that parents were willing to find fault with their own children.

It had been worse when she was at Pemberley. Back then, fresh out of school, she went into every parent meeting wondering why in the world they should listen to her. What did she know, after four years of education and psychology classes and years of babysitting, versus what they knew as the people actually responsible for their offspring's existence?

That first year, Callie was frequently steamrollered by intense New York City parents who were used to getting what they wanted if they could just throw enough money in the right direction: "Well, if the children are having problems sharing, you should just buy more toys for the classroom."

At one particularly unpleasant meeting, a parent whose child had excessive impulse-control issues told her that every single specialist who had examined the child had denied there was an issue. (All of these specialists were, of course, hand-picked, and had gained renown by opposing the diagnoses of children with social or emotional challenges.) After this, a fellow teacher opened Callie's eyes to a completely new approach.

"It's all in the presentation," her savior had said. "I don't care if the mom you're talking to has raised six kids of her own and has worked as a teacher for thirty years. You just act as if you have no doubt about what you're saying. You just *know*."

"But I don't know," Callie objected.

"Sure you do. How many hours do you spend with these kids every week? You're the one who's observing them with their peers. Their moms don't see that—no matter what they're like at home. And if you talk like you believe what you're saying, *they'll* believe it. Or at least respect you for it."

Callie anticipated an immediate smackdown the first time she tried it (*Who are you to talk to me like that, young lady?*). But the advice was sound. Over the years, she learned to couple it with focusing on making everything a team effort. She wasn't in this alone—she needed the parents' help.

It was with this attitude that she went into her meeting with Ellen Switzer. Confidence—even though the truth was that she wasn't entirely sure of the answer. But she did know that unless Ellen and she were a team, they would get nowhere.

When Ellen got to her classroom, having left Liam with the early-drop-off kids, she was less well put together than she had been on the first day Callie had met her. She was dressed for work, but there was eyeliner smudged next to her left eye. "I'm so sorry I'm late," she exclaimed as she blew into the room.

"It's fine, don't worry about it. I know how hard it is to get out in the morning," Callie said sympathetically. "Please, sit." She indicated one of the two adult-sized chairs set up for the occasion.

Ellen took off her long coat and sat down with it in her lap, folded in half over her arms. "So, I guess things haven't gotten better," she said, sighing.

Callie didn't want Ellen to give up before they'd even started. "Well, it was better at first—we had a few really good days."

"And then he started acting like a little shit again."

"I wouldn't say that, exactly . . ."

Ellen pinched the bridge of her nose between her fingers and closed her eyes. "I know, that was awful. I'm sorry. I'm just so tired." She opened her eyes and looked at Callie again. "It's not even like it's the kid's fault." She paused. "The thing is, things have been bad at home. There's no good way to say this, but my marriage is falling apart." Ellen looked away, and Callie could tell that she was trying to blink back tears.

"I'm so sorry."

Ellen spoke again, still staring at the spot on the wall where the poster counting the first hundred days of school hung, each day that had passed covered with a brightly colored Velcro dot. "Yeah, me, too," she said roughly, her throat clogged. "I probably should have told Robin this from the beginning—I'm sure it has a lot to do with what's been going on with Liam. But it's not easy to talk about."

"I'm sure it's not." Callie impulsively reached out to touch Ellen's arm. The other woman buried her face in her hands, and her shoulders started shaking. At first, Callie had the bizarre thought that she was laughing, but then it became clear she was crying.

"Oh my God, I'm so sorry," Ellen managed to get out between sniffles. "I am such a mess."

Callie retrieved a box of tissues from the other side of the room and placed it on the table. A moment passed before Ellen took one and blew her nose, crumpling the tissue up in her hands. "Oh geez, I didn't expect to come in here and have a nervous breakdown. I'm so sorry."

"Oh, please, don't worry about it. I can only imagine what you're going through," Callie replied, wishing she could come up with something more inventive to say. Her go-to "exude confidence" strategy was eluding her. While she'd had parents get emotional in the past, this was completely different. It was one thing when it involved a speech delay or the need for occupational therapy—dealing with a collapsing marriage was something else entirely.

Ellen exhaled a long, shuddery sigh. "To tell you the truth, you're practically the only person I've said anything to."

Callie raised her eyebrows. "Really?"

Ellen shrugged and a little laugh escaped her. "It's not something you want to talk about. Oh, hey, by the way, my husband says he doesn't think he loves me anymore. After being together for fourteen years. Right after we 'celebrated'"—Ellen made air quotes with her fingers—"our sixth wedding anniversary. And you keep thinking it will get better, and then even if you work it out, if you've told people, they'll always look at you as the couple who almost got divorced. You know, 'Did you hear about Ellen and Doug?'"

Callie didn't know what to say. Ellen's eyeliner was now equally smudged on both eyes. "You've been together a long time," she said weakly.

Ellen nodded. "We met the first week of college. Lived in the same dorm. If someone told me then that this was the guy I was going to marry, I would have said they were crazy. We were just kids. And now here we are. Obviously, it didn't work out the way we'd planned."

"I wish I knew what to say," Callie replied. And she meant it.

Ellen smiled faintly at her. "What is there to say?"

It suddenly hit Callie that they were the same age. She had gotten so used to assuming that her students' parents were older than she, the fact that she, too, was aging had somehow slipped past her. Clearly there was something worse than the conundrum she was facing in her own life—to be going through what Ellen was dealing with.

She almost never let her mind go there, but she couldn't avoid the thought that had things turned out differently, she could have had a child now, as well. The notion made her suck in her breath. If she and Ethan had stayed together, who knew? What if they had still broken up, but later? It never occurred to her before that, even if she had moved to California with Ethan, it might only have delayed the inevitable. And when would that have happened? What if they had had a child first and ended up in the same situation as Liam's parents?

Ellen cleared her throat and sat up straighter, plainly trying to pull herself together. "Anyway. We're not here to talk about me. We're here to talk about Liam."

"Of course. But you're right, I'm sure this is affecting him. Is . . . is your husband still living in the house?"

Ellen sighed and began shredding the tissue balled up in her hands. "Technically, yes. But he's been gone a lot. We've been telling Liam that Daddy has to travel for work. But Doug never used to travel, so this is totally different for him. And we try not to fight in front of him, but I'm sure he's picking up on things." Ellen's eyes welled up again. "That's what kills me. Liam didn't ask for this, and here he is, stuck in it."

"Kids are resilient." Callie hated the platitude as it came out of her mouth. "Which isn't to say this isn't hard on him. The best thing is to try to keep things as consistent as possible. And I'm really glad you told me. It's helpful for me to know."

"Thanks. I'm sorry to lay all this on you. And I don't know

how I can help you help Liam through it—I know it can't make managing your class any easier." Ellen continued to shred her tissue.

"It's okay. It's life, right?"

"I guess so, unfortunately." Ellen gave her a half smile. "Thanks for listening."

"Anytime." Callie hesitated, and then added, "Seriously, I mean that."

Ellen's smile grew a little. "Thanks."

Callie glanced at the window in her door and could see that the hallway had begun to fill. It was almost time for school to start.

Ellen stood, then put her coat back on and stuffed the shredded tissue in her pocket.

Callie paid extra attention to Liam that day—letting him choose his seat at snack first, giving him the privilege of being line leader, finding reasons to pat him on the head, and giving him a little congratulatory hug for sitting so well at story time. And he seemed to beam in the spotlight. Callie was happy she would have no misbehaviors to report to Ellen once the day ended.

Later that day, the Bouncy Castles teachers gathered for their weekly staff meeting. Callie shared the news she'd received that morning, and there were knowing nods.

"One of the toughest teaching challenges I had was a little girl with a single mom. She got involved with a man who moved in with them. Even though he was doing everything right, it really turned that kid's world upside down," commented Tess.

"I've had a couple of students whose parents split up. With one of them, you'd never have known anything was happening. But with the other . . ." Denise trailed off, shaking her head, the sadness on her face expressing what was left unsaid.

As the conversation wound down, Robin cleared her throat. "I really want to thank you, Callie, for taking this on. I didn't rise to the occasion. I'm sorry it fell to you." Robin twisted her fingers together and glanced at Judith. "The thing is, I haven't been feeling well. But it's actually for a good reason." She gave a small smile. "As Judith knows, I'm pregnant."

So that's what Judith was talking about, Callie thought, her eyes involuntarily straying to Robin's belly, which was still flat. She wasn't surprised—when Nina was first pregnant with Zoe, it was ages before she showed. This time, however, the bump rose almost immediately, as if her stomach now knew what to do and instantly expanded to accommodate its new tenant.

Robin accepted the flurry of congratulations. "Thanks, guys. I appreciate it. It's been a really hard first trimester, and I'm actually still having trouble, um, keeping anything down. So, thank you—especially you, Callie—for your support."

"Of course, Robin—I wish I'd known. But I understand why you didn't share the news sooner."

"I'm sure I speak for everyone when I say how happy we are for you, Robin," added Judith. "We'll be determining over the coming months how best to cover your time off in the spring. In the meantime, we have a more immediate question." Judith looked around the room. "Robin and I are both registered to attend the NOECE conference in LA in February. Robin won't be able to travel at that point, so we have a paid registration if anyone else is interested. We'll be able to cover half your travel expenses, as well." Judith's eyes again scanned the room, where she was met with resounding silence.

NOECE (which everyone referred to as "No-See") was the National Organization for Early Childhood Education. Callie had attended their annual conference once, when she was at Pemberley—which was financially able to send its teachers without expecting them to pick up half of the tab themselves.

It wasn't a bad event. There was lots of free stuff to be had from the many vendors who attended—toy manufacturers, children's book publishers, makers of ergonomic classroom furniture. Since then, the privilege of giving up a weekend—for which she would have to pay part of the cost—somehow never seemed particularly appealing.

"Well, don't all jump at the chance at once," Judith said dryly. "Anyway, you don't need to let me know now, but think about it."

Callie's mind raced. Los Angeles. Where Ethan lived. *What if...?*

"I might be interested, Judith," she said, before she could mull it over any longer. Callie avoided Tess's eyes, which she felt boring into her.

Judith smiled warmly. "That would be wonderful, Callie. Give it some thought."

Callie nodded. "I'll do that. And I'll look at my calendar." A snort came from Tess's side of the room.

"Great! Well then." Judith clapped her hands together as she might have when she was a classroom teacher. Callie could imagine her continuing with a cheery *Boys and girls!* Or, more appropriately, *Girls!* as there were only women in the room. But in fact, she said, "I think that's probably our business for the day. Unless anyone has anything else?"

As usual, everyone was eager to get home, and to swarm Robin with their congratulations. Denise gave her a long hug, announcing loudly, "Don't expect me to be politically correct when you start to show—I'm going to want to touch that belly and feel your baby kick!"

"Fine by me." Robin laughed as another teacher embraced her. The women buzzed around, declaring how wonderful babies were and how sorry they were that she wasn't feeling better. Callie could feel Tess hovering at her elbow, waiting to get

her alone. When she couldn't come up with any more plati-
tudes for Robin, she knew it was time to face the music.

She stepped away and toward the door, Tess close behind
her. In the hallway, Tess pounced immediately. "So, for the
first time since you've been here, you're interested in going to
the NOECE conference. Would it have anything to do with the
fact that it's in LA? Didn't you say this ex-boyfriend of yours is
in California?"

With an attempt at wide-eyed innocence, Callie replied,
"Can't I just want to go to Southern California for a few days in
the middle of winter?"

"Sure. All that way for a weekend. And I'm driving to
Boston tomorrow for breakfast and then turning around to
come back home."

"Okay, fine, yes," Callie said, giving up. "Ethan lives in
California."

"And does that have anything to do with your eagerness to
take this trip?"

"Eagerness? What eagerness? I said I *might* be interested,
that's all."

Tess waited.

"Okay, yes, it occurred to me that it might be a way to see
Ethan, if I decide that's a good idea. I haven't even gotten in
touch with Jenna yet. I have no idea how to reach him, much
less arrange to see him."

"Fine. I promised you no judgment, and I will follow
through with that. But more importantly. Our bowling date?"
Tess raised her eyebrows.

"Yes," Callie said resignedly. "I emailed him. He's up for
it, but not until next weekend. The weekend after Halloween,"
she clarified.

"Excellent! I'll get it on our calendar." She pulled her phone
out of her pocket and swiped the screen before tapping away.

"Done," she said, still looking at the phone. Then she looked up. "I'll cure you of this Ethan thing yet," she announced.

Callie laughed. "Let's get the diagnosis first, then we'll see if I need curing."

CHAPTER SIXTEEN

After

The following days were uneventful. Callie paid extra attention to Liam, which seemed to yield good results. Only one incident required the use of the peace chair.

After many stops and starts, she decided against emailing Jenna about Ethan's contact information. No matter how vague her message was, her friend would ask questions. Questions she wasn't prepared to answer. She needed to involve as few people as possible. She was already regretting bringing Tess into it. She adored her friend but felt wary of intrusion—even as she continued to cyberstalk her ex-boyfriend.

Callie logged on to the alumni directory at Welford and typed in Ethan's name. Sure enough, a Santa Monica address popped up, along with a phone number and email. It was odd to imagine Ethan in LA—he'd always hated it with its crazy traffic and what he called "lack of soul." It certainly made sense as the home of a screenwriter, but it was so strange that she had no idea what had led him down that road.

Callie set his contact information aside, knowing it would take a while to figure out what she was going to say in her message. Or maybe she would call him. She couldn't decide.

She considered checking her Connections account but didn't. She needed to clear her head. Over the weekend, she went for a long walk, raked the leaves in the backyard, and got to work with Zoe and Nina on adorning the house for Halloween. During the years she'd been back in Brook Hill, she'd bought a variety of decorations that she put out every year, including a witch who looked like she'd flown into one of the porch columns and webs with big, fuzzy spiders. With Zoe's help, she carved three jack-o'-lanterns—two goofy, one scary—and set them out on the porch. They decorated the fourth pumpkin with tempera paints. There was something to be said for having family around while she had so much on her mind.

On Monday morning, while most of her charges played, she set the table up for snack with Liam and Jacob as her helpers. The boys laid out a paper plate and a napkin in front of each chair, while Callie filled small Dixie cups with water. The cups at Bouncy Castles were always only half full (or half empty, depending on one's perspective) to avoid the worst spills.

Callie had just called the children to sit down and was beginning to pass out sliced apples when Judith appeared at the door. Callie looked up curiously.

"You had a phone call in the office," Judith said, her face giving away nothing.

"A phone call?" Callie was puzzled. Everyone knew to call on her cell phone while she was at work; she checked her messages periodically.

"It was your sister," Judith explained. "She asked you to call her right away."

Immediately, Callie's heart quickened. Was it their parents? Zoe? She glanced at the children, and Judith followed her gaze. "I'll stay with the kids," she said, and adopted the tone she used with the students. "Okay, boys and girls. Miss Callie has to step out a minute. You get to have snack with me!" She took the plate full of apples that Callie mechanically handed to her.

Callie left the classroom, pulling her phone from her pocket as she walked, and hit the speed dial for Nina's mobile number. A few rings later, Nina picked up.

"What's wrong?" Callie asked immediately, stepping into the office and partially shutting the door.

"I'm at the hospital. Can you come?"

Callie's stomach clenched. "What hospital? Why?"

Nina's voice was placid. "I went to the doctor this morning. She says I'm having signs of premature labor. She wanted me to come here right away."

"But . . . it's too early! You're not due until the end of January."

"I know," Nina replied calmly. And then her voice changed. "Callie, I'm scared." There was a pause as she seemed to be pulling herself together. "Michael's coming, but he was out on Long Island in a meeting, so it'll be a while. Please? I don't want to be by myself."

It was rare that Nina asked for help or displayed any weakness. *It must be serious.* "Of course. Give me a few minutes to get out of here. What hospital?"

"South Bergen. I'm in Labor and Delivery."

Callie ran back down the hallway to fill Judith in. Minutes later, she was in the car, her phone directing her to South Bergen Medical Center.

When she arrived, she quickly parked and found her way to Labor and Delivery, where she buzzed to be allowed in. The nurse at the desk seemed to be expecting her and directed her to Nina's room.

Nina was alone, lying on her side. Several IVs were hooked up, fluid running from bags into her veins.

"Nina! Are you okay?" Callie asked as she entered the room.

Nina shrugged listlessly.

"What happened?"

Nina took a long breath and spoke in a monotone, her eyes fixed on the window. "I called the doctor this morning because my back pain just wouldn't go away. She wanted me to come in right away, so I went as soon as I dropped Zoe at school. She said it was premature labor, and I needed to go to the hospital immediately. They're giving me fluids to keep me hydrated, and medicine to stop the labor." She waved her hand at the IV bags.

"Is it okay now?"

"So far, so good, I guess. They keep checking my cervix. It's not dilating anymore, apparently."

"That's good, right?"

For the first time, Nina showed some signs of life as she looked at her sister. "Yes, Callie, that's good," she said with exaggerated patience.

"Well, what do I know?" Callie asked indignantly. Then she immediately regretted her sharp tone. "And the baby is okay?"

Nina nodded. "See the heartbeat?" She pointed at the monitor, and Callie couldn't help but smile.

"When will Michael be here?"

"Hopefully in about an hour. He's on his way. He got a car service." Nina plucked at the cotton blanket pulled up around her.

"What about Mom? Did you call?"

Nina looked at her. "Why worry her?"

When did kids start protecting their parents, instead of the other way around? "I'm sure she'd want to know."

"Once we have something to tell her, I'll call."

Callie nodded. "Can I get you anything?"

Nina shook her head. "I don't think I'm allowed to eat anything. And I'm not hungry anyway."

Callie pulled the one chair in the room closer to the bed and sat down, wishing she could do something useful. Over the next hour, a nurse came in to check on Nina's cervix again—Callie left the room and stood in the hall—and Nina's doctor returned with an ultrasound machine. She was young and wore no makeup, her blonde hair pulled back from her face. It was only the stethoscope dangling around her neck and her ID badge reading "MD" that gave her identity away.

"How are we feeling?" she asked cheerfully. Callie wondered if doctors learned how to speak in the institutional "we" in medical school.

"Okay, I guess," replied Nina.

The doctor turned to Callie and put out her hand. "Hi, I'm Dr. Brody."

Callie took the extended hand. "I'm Nina's sister. Callie Dressler."

"Nice to meet you, Callie. Your sister and this little one gave us a bit of a scare, but we seem to have caught things in time."

"Glad to hear it."

Dr. Brody turned back to Nina. "I want to take a little peek at the baby. Do you want your sister to stay?"

Callie glanced at the machine, suddenly anxious. Nina's voice saying "Sure" seemed to be coming from very far away.

Callie took a deep breath as Dr. Brody adjusted Nina's hospital gown to bare her rounded belly. The doctor squirted some clear gel onto the bump and moved the wand over Nina's skin. With a lump in her throat, Callie watched the swirling on the monitor, but had no idea what she was looking at—even as Dr. Brody pointed things out: the head, the heartbeat, et cetera. There was something miraculous about the whole thing. She found herself needing to look away, blinking back tears.

Just as the ultrasound was wrapping up, Michael appeared at the door and immediately strode over to the bed to give Nina a kiss. "Are you okay? Is the baby . . . ?" His voice trailed off.

Nina smiled and pointed at the screen. "Perfect timing. You can see for yourself."

Callie wondered if Michael knew what he was looking at, or if he only knew all was well from Nina's smile, but he grinned from ear to ear. Then he turned to the doctor. "Can you tell me what happened?"

Before Dr. Brody began, Callie quietly excused herself. She went down the hall and found a vending machine, where she got a soda. While she waited, there was a sudden flurry of activity in another room, from which some very unpleasant moans were emanating. She tried not to listen.

When she saw Dr. Brody leave her sister's room, Callie went back down the hall. Nina and Michael were speaking quietly.

"If that's what she's recommending, then that's what we're going to do," Michael was saying.

"I just want to go home," Nina said, her voice cracking.

Michael put his hand on her cheek. "It's just one night, sweetie."

Callie cleared her throat loudly, and they turned to look at her. Nina quickly brought her hand up to swipe at her eyes.

"Everything okay?" Callie asked.

"The doctor wants to keep Nina overnight, just to make sure everything's okay. Then we're probably looking at bed rest for a while."

"Bed rest?" Callie couldn't imagine Nina being able to stay in bed for any length of time. She could barely stay seated long enough to eat a meal.

"I think it's overkill," her sister interjected.

Michael looked at her. "If it's what the doctor orders, it's what we're going to do."

Nina pursed her lips but didn't respond. Perhaps for the first time, Callie found herself agreeing with her brother-in-law.

Michael turned to Callie. "Would you mind picking Zoe up and bringing her back to the house? Nina's friend Holly took her home with her. I'll drive Nina's car back down later."

"Of course." She was happy to be useful—even as she wondered how things were going to work over the coming weeks if Nina was out of commission. "I still have her address in my phone." She walked over to give her sister a hug. "Hang in there, Nina. Maybe you'll at least get a good night's sleep."

Nina rolled her eyes. "I sincerely doubt that," she said. "But, Callie," she added. "Thank you for coming."

Callie waved her hand. *"Fuggedaboutit."*

Nina smiled, and Callie headed out to pick up her niece.

CHAPTER SEVENTEEN

Before

I wasn't sure why I was awake. I squinted at the digital clock—it was just after seven on an early March morning of my sophomore year. Across the room, I could see the shape of my roommate's body, curled up under the covers of her bed. Then I heard the knock on the door.

Confused and barely conscious, I swung my bare feet onto the floor and walked the few steps to the door. Ethan stood in the hallway, his hair tangled. He wore a T-shirt with a torn neckline and sweatpants. His feet were shoved into sneakers with no socks.

I grabbed his hand. "You're so cold! Where's your coat? It's freezing out." I pulled him into the room and wrapped my arms around him. Then I pulled back. "What are you doing here so early? What's the matter?"

"My dad had a heart attack," he said, his shoulders slumping.

Involuntarily, my hand went to my mouth. "Oh my God!" I exclaimed.

He walked past me to sit on the bed, then put his elbows on his knees and rested his head in his hands. I immediately sat beside him, twining my arm around his waist.

"Is he okay?" I whispered to not disturb my roommate, though she tended to sleep like a rock. I felt so dumb. I'd never known anyone who had a heart attack. *Were they always fatal?*

"I don't know." He shook his head in disbelief. "My mom just called. It was last night, after dinner. No one told me until this morning."

"Well, they probably didn't want to worry you. You're so far away."

He looked at me, his eyes angry. "They should have *told* me. I could have gotten a late flight out."

"Maybe they didn't know how serious it was," I said, and then paused. "Is it serious?"

"It's a heart attack!" he exclaimed, as if that should answer my question.

I instinctively glanced at the lump across the room that was my sleeping roommate, but she hadn't stirred.

Ethan spoke more quietly. "I have to go home."

I nodded slowly. That made sense.

"Will you come with me?" he asked.

I blinked, surprised. Of course, my heart immediately said yes. I met his parents once when they came for a visit—they told me to call them Harvey and Phyllis, and his dad had been lovely. But my mind raced. How many classes would I miss? How would I pay for the plane ticket?

"Do you think your family would want me there at a time like this?"

He put his hand on mine. "I need you to come."

• • •

It took us a while to figure out the particulars. I asked my parents if they'd pay for the plane ticket, which they agreed to, and I offered to reimburse them, which they refused. The only thing they were worried about was how much school I'd miss. I assured them it wouldn't be much, although I wasn't at all sure that was true. Ethan and I flew out from Albany to Chicago that afternoon.

I'd never been on a plane without my parents before, but Ethan was used to making the trip alone. We checked our bags and went through security. Ethan was quiet as we sat side by side in the waiting area. I hated the smell of jet fuel permeating the building. I commented on it to Ethan, and he nodded, but I could have said anything—*Look, that little boy over there is on fire*—and his reaction would have been the same. I couldn't blame him.

On the flight, I tried to read, but mostly I looked at Ethan's profile and at the fraying upholstery of the seat in front of me. Ethan's uncle—his mom's brother—picked us up at O'Hare and drove us directly to the hospital in Evanston. On the way, he told us that Ethan's dad was in stable condition in the cardiac care unit. They were waiting for test results that would determine if he had to have bypass surgery. I sat in the back seat, looking out the window. Funny how much it looked like a highway in suburban New Jersey. So weird that less than twelve hours before, I was asleep in my bed, never imagining that I would be in another time zone, en route to a hospital, within the day.

Ethan's uncle parked the car and the three of us walked to the hospital entrance, the glass doors sliding open with a whoosh as we stepped onto the rubber mat. Ethan grabbed my hand as we followed his uncle to the elevator.

On the fourth floor, a placard in bold blue type directed us to the CCU. And then we were in the waiting area. Turquoise vinyl chairs with wooden arms were clustered in groups on the dark blue industrial carpet. Boxes of tissues were placed around the room, along with well-worn magazines. Ethan's mom hugged him tightly.

"It's okay, Mom," he said, awkwardly patting her on the back. His brothers, Josh and Zach, hovered behind her. They were seventeen and fifteen. And then, suddenly, Ethan's mom hugged me, too.

"Thank you so much for coming," she said. "It's so sweet."

"I'm so sorry about . . . what's happened." I wanted to kick myself. I felt like my words were all wrong. But Ethan's mom nodded. It didn't seem like she thought twice about them.

Soon they were all headed into the CCU to see Ethan's dad. I extracted my hand from Ethan's. "You should have some time with just you guys," I whispered in his ear. Then I sat down and leafed through six-month-old magazines, barely reading the words about which celebrities were breaking up and checking into rehab.

The next few days passed slowly. We spent a lot of time at the hospital. I went in once to see Ethan's dad—I just couldn't call him Harvey. He looked gray, and so much older than I remembered, but he smiled and thanked me for coming. Mostly, I tried to stay out of everyone's way. I didn't want anyone to feel they had to entertain me.

I slept in the guest bedroom, which was small and located at the back of the house. There was a full-size bed with a patchwork quilt in shades of red. The dresser had one empty drawer where I put my things. The others were full of tablecloths and spare linens. The one window had white curtains and looked onto the woods behind the house.

Ethan was unusually quiet. I wasn't sure what to say to him, and I felt like everything that came out of my mouth was awkward and wrong. Josh and Zach were chatty—talking about movies, books, weather, sports, whatever they could come up with. It was as if neither of them could stand the silence and needed to fill the space.

The first night, I'd brushed my teeth in the bathroom down the hall and then went to my room, shutting the door behind me. I lay down in bed, and could see the moon through the curtains, which I hadn't completely drawn. I was wondering when I'd fall asleep when I heard the door open and shut behind me. I turned, and it was Ethan. Before I could say anything, he slid into bed next to me. I would have thought he'd be exhausted, but his hand snaked under my T-shirt and his lips were on my neck.

"Ethan!" I whispered, trying to move away from him. "We're in your parents' house!"

"I don't care," he whispered back. His hand moved farther up my shirt to find my breast. "I need you," he said roughly as he began to touch me, and I could feel his erection pressing against me.

I turned to kiss him, and his hands were all over, pulling off my pajama bottoms and my underwear. There was an intensity about him I wasn't used to. It was like he was trying to blot out anything other than my body, his body, and what we were doing.

Afterward, he coiled himself around me, and for the first time since that morning, I felt his body relax. Although I was worried about his mom catching us, I couldn't bear to wake him.

Over the following days, I came to expect it. I'd get into bed, and Ethan followed shortly afterward, immediately reaching under my clothes for my bare skin, making love to me like his life depended on it. But otherwise, he was quiet and still. He said nothing when they told us that his dad needed a triple bypass. He shook his head when I asked him if he wanted to talk. He was silent when his brothers tried to cut the tension with Adam Sandler videos. There were moments when I wondered what I was doing there—but then I felt guilty for even having that thought.

The surgery took place on Thursday, three days after we arrived, and it seemed to go smoothly. Ethan's dad would be in the hospital for a few days to recover, and then be moved to a cardiac rehab facility. I talked to Ethan and my parents, and we decided I'd fly back to school on Sunday, with Ethan following once his dad was settled in rehab.

Saturday was unseasonably warm for March, and Ethan suggested we go for a drive. I was happy to have some alone time with him, away from the hospital.

"Where are we going?" I asked, once we were in Ethan's dad's car.

"There's this place called Birch Lake," Ethan replied. "We used to go there for picnics and stuff when I was a kid."

Twenty minutes later, Ethan parked the car in a small lot. He took my hand as we walked toward a stand of trees, behind which lay the lake, smooth and glassy.

"Do you know how to skip stones?" Ethan asked, staring out at the water.

"Nope." I wondered what he was really thinking.

He turned to me, and for the first time in days it seemed like he was seeing me. My heart hurt for him.

"I'll teach you. It's all in the choice of stone, the wrist, and the follow-through." Ethan crouched down and picked up a few rocks, rejecting some and then choosing others. "See," he said, "the smoother and flatter the stone, the better it will work. Then, you hold it like this." He demonstrated. "And you flick your wrist, like you're cracking a whip sideways, and make sure you follow through." He did as he described, and the stone sailed over the lake, nicely skipping seven times.

"Wow!" I exclaimed, truly amazed.

Ethan threw a couple more and then turned to me. "Your

turn," he said. He helped me find some rocks, adjusted my stance, and showed me how to experiment with the flick of my wrist. It didn't go well. My rocks sank like, well, like stones.

"I just don't have the knack."

"Nah. It just takes practice." Ethan looked out over the water again. "My dad must have spent an hour with me out here one day until I finally got it."

So we continued. My arm got tired and my wrist got sore, but it seemed to mean so much to him that I learn. Finally, after it felt like I'd thrown at least a hundred rocks, I got one to skip twice.

"I did it!" I shrieked, literally jumping up and down.

"I knew you could do it," Ethan said, smiling. Then he wrapped his arms around me. I could have stayed there forever. He took a deep breath. "I want you to know how much it means to me that you're here. I'm sure it hasn't been fun for you, and I know I've been—"

"You've been fine," I interrupted.

He shrugged. "Anyway, I don't think I could have gotten through this without you."

My eyes welled up.

"I love you, Callie," he said, bending to kiss me, more gently than he had in days.

"I love you, too."

He smiled at me again and then started to look for more rocks.

"I don't need to do any more," I said quickly. "I'm good."

He took a quick look at me. "I just want to throw a few myself," he explained, before returning his gaze to the ground.

I sat down with my chin resting on my knees, my arms wrapped around them, watching him skip stones. Idly, I ran my fingers through the rocks on the ground near me, occasionally handing him ones that looked good.

I found a small flat stone with striations of color. "Look at this one," I said, holding it out toward him.

He glanced down. "It's too small."

"But isn't it pretty?"

He took it from me. "It is. Unusual," he said.

I went back to my search for skipping stones.

CHAPTER EIGHTEEN

After

Zoe and Callie were playing Candy Land on the living room floor when Michael came home from the hospital. As soon as she heard the door open, Zoe raced over.

"Where's Mommy?"

"She's not here right now, kiddo." Michael appeared in the doorway and looked questioningly at Callie over Zoe's head. Callie presumed that, in Michael's mind, it had been her responsibility to explain to Zoe that Nina wasn't coming home that night. Callie shrugged. Michael looked annoyed. "Mommy can't come home tonight," he said, his eyes back on Zoe. "She's not feeling well, so she has to stay at the hospital."

A moment passed. Then Zoe's lip quivered. "But I want Mommy!" she wailed.

"Mommy can't come right now," Michael replied. "She has to stay in the hospital to make sure the baby's safe."

"But I want Mommy!" Zoe wailed again. "I don't want the baby!"

"Zoe!" Michael snapped. "Don't say things like that!"

Zoe burst into tears.

"Michael! She's a child!" Callie went over to her niece and hugged her. "It's okay, Binks. Mommy will be here tomorrow."

"She can't say things like that," Michael said stubbornly.

Callie looked at him and tried to remind herself that it had been a stressful day. *But still, he shouldn't be taking it out on his daughter.*

"What do you want for dinner, Binks?"

Zoe's back heaved as she cried on Callie's shoulder. She didn't respond.

Callie picked her up. "Should we finish our game?"

Zoe shook her head. "Don't want to," she said in a shuddery voice.

"How about some TV?"

Zoe didn't respond. Callie carried her to the sofa, picked up the remote control, and found one of her niece's favorite cartoons. As a teacher, she cringed at the idea of television as a comforter, but as an aunt, she was okay with it.

Once Zoe was settled—her head resting on her knees and her thumb in her mouth—Callie went into the kitchen to figure out dinner. Michael was sitting at the table, a bottle of beer in front of him.

"Don't start," he said.

"I wasn't going to say anything."

"Of course you were." He adopted a falsetto tone. "'Michael! She's a child! She's scared!'"

Callie wanted to smack him but took a deep breath. "Well, then, you already know what I think. She's a little girl whose mom is home every night. Kids get scared when things change."

Michael took a long swallow of the beer and set the bottle back on the table. "Don't you think I know that?"

Then act like it. Give the kid a hug and tell her everything will be fine.

Callie opened the pantry door to take out a box of pasta and then went to the refrigerator to find some vegetables to throw in the sauce. She'd picked up a few things from watching Nina cook over the past few weeks.

Behind her, Michael spoke again. "This hasn't exactly been an easy day for me."

But you're an adult. She's a child.

"I know. Look, I'll take care of dinner. Why don't you go sit with Zoe?"

Michael didn't respond, but after another pull on the bottle, he got up and left the room. Once the pasta was on the stove and the vegetables were steaming, Callie walked quietly to the living room door and was happy to see two heads facing the TV, Michael's arm around his daughter.

The next morning, Michael took Zoe to school—with some difficulty.

"I don't wanna go!" Zoe shrieked.

Michael looked helplessly at Callie.

"Zoe," she said calmly. "You'll see Mommy after school, I promise."

"She'll pick me up?"

Callie bit her lip. "I don't know about that. But you'll definitely see her today." She hoped she was telling the truth. "And isn't it exciting that Daddy is driving you?" She forced enthusiasm into her voice.

Zoe seemed to sense the charade as she looked doubtfully at Michael. He looked up from his phone as if he could feel her eyes on him.

"Right!" he said with well-feigned gusto. "And we can stop for Munchkins on the way."

Zoe's eyebrows drew together. "Mommy never does that."

"But this is special Daddy-Zoe time," he enthused.

Callie had to give him credit as the two of them left the house.

Fortunately, Callie hadn't been lying when she said Nina would be home that day. By evening, she was settled upstairs in bed, where she would stay indefinitely. She was to get up only to use the bathroom and to shower.

Nina was not happy.

Zoe wouldn't leave her side and ate her dinner sitting on the floor next to the bed. Once she was in her pajamas with teeth brushed, she curled up against her mother's back and fell asleep. Michael carried her into her room, and then he and Callie sat with Nina to talk about the plan for the next three months.

"I really think I can go pick Zoe up at school," Nina said.

"You absolutely cannot," Michael replied.

"Well, I can't ask Holly to keep her every day until you get there." There was an edge to Nina's voice.

"Why don't I pick her up?" Callie suggested, not seeing any other way around it. "Some days she can stay later at school, and some days she can go home with Holly—or one of your other friends—and then I can get her after work."

"Every day?" Nina asked doubtfully.

"What other solution is there?" Callie asked. "Besides, it's not forever. I don't mind." Callie thought she should have crossed her fingers behind her back. But she was willing to do a lot for her niece.

Nina bit her lip. "I guess that will work."

"And maybe your mother can come up," Michael suggested.

She looked at him. "I can't ask her to do that."

"But, Neen. You know she'll offer as soon as she knows what's going on," Callie said. Whatever Lorraine's other flaws might be, Callie had no doubt she'd be there in a heartbeat if one of her girls needed her.

Michael nodded. "Exactly. We should call her. And there are my parents, too."

Nina gave Michael a look. Callie knew very well that Nina wasn't a fan of her in-laws. Now seemed like the perfect time to excuse herself.

The air got crisper and colder over the following days, and the wind picked up. As expected, as soon as Lorraine heard the news, she wanted to fly up immediately. Not quite ready to cope with her mother, Nina put her off until the following week. Callie located an old dorm fridge sitting in the basement—sometimes her mother's refusal to part with things was a blessing—and Michael set it up in their bedroom and stocked it with drinks, cheese, and fruit. Callie stacked books and magazines on the nightstand—next to the television remote and Nina's phone.

Each day was a new adventure as they juggled the schedule. Most nights, Callie brought in takeout for dinner, but one evening she broiled chicken and steamed vegetables—she could hardly call it "cooking," but at least it involved the oven. On Halloween, that Friday, Michael managed to come home early. Callie helped Zoe with her costume, delighted it was Dorothy from *The Wizard of Oz* and not yet another Disney princess. Zoe paraded in front of Nina, who got teary when Zoe asked if she could come trick-or-treating.

"It's just you and me, kiddo," Michael said. "Let's see how much candy we can get!"

Zoe grinned at her father and they headed downstairs.

"Damn hormones," Nina said as she wiped her eyes.

"Hormones?" Callie asked, her eyebrows raised.

"Well, they don't help! This sucks."

Callie nodded sympathetically. "Can I get you anything?"

"Permission to get out of this bed?" Nina replied hopefully.

"Nothing doing." Callie smiled. "I'm going down to deal with the trick-or-treaters. I'll be back up to check on you."

Callie loved Halloween. She liked to wait on the porch for the children, so she put on her coat—along with a tall, pointed witch's hat—and grabbed the large bowl of candy. It was dusk as she sat in one of the rocking chairs, watching the street. Several groups of kids, accompanied by parents hovering at the curb, climbed the steps in quick succession and rummaged around in her bowl for their favorites.

Callie watched the last bunch walk away, her smile fading. She had a sudden vision of herself standing on the porch of her parents' house, giving out candy on Halloween. All she needed were a couple of cats and an old housecoat and she'd be all set.

Maybe Nina was right. Here she was in suburbia, surrounded by families with young children and empty nesters. What other thirtysomething singles were in the area? None. Was she here just because it was convenient—and cheap—or was she hiding out?

Rearranging the candy so the chocolates and gummy candies were equally visible, she didn't notice the car pulling up in front of the house until the driver had exited the vehicle and slammed the door shut behind him. The sound startled her and she peered out, but the darkness had become too thick to see clearly.

As the person approached the house, he was illuminated by the porch light, but it wasn't until he was nearly at the top of the steps that she realized it was Ben, the architect.

"Hello!" she called.

Ben started and looked over. "Oh! I didn't see you there. Are you waiting to jump out at unsuspecting trick-or-treaters or only unsuspecting architects?"

Callie laughed. "The trick-or-treaters expect me to be here. It's where I am every year." *Oh God, I'm so pathetic.*

"Nice hat," Ben commented.

Callie had forgotten the witch's hat was perched on her head. "Oh!" She reached up to take it off.

"No, leave it," Ben said. "It suits you."

Callie raised her eyebrows as she readjusted the hat on her head. "I'm not sure how to take that."

He laughed. "That came out wrong. But it was supposed to be a compliment."

"Well, then, thanks. I think." She paused. "Anyway, I'm sure you didn't come here to compliment my hat. Or to beg for some candy . . ." She proffered the bowl.

He glanced inside. "Any Twix? That's my favorite."

"Sorry," she said, shaking her head. "I've got Kit Kats, Milky Ways . . ."

"Ah well. As you say, I didn't come for candy." He lifted his hand, which held a tote bag she hadn't noticed. "Our decorator had some samples she was going to take to Nina tomorrow, but I had a meeting with a prospective client not far from here, so I said I'd stop by this evening. I called Nina to let her know I was coming . . ."

Callie couldn't imagine her sister wanted to entertain her architect while she lay in bed in her pajamas. "I can bring it up to her—unless you need to see her?"

"No, that's fine. Not really my area, anyway. The decorating, I mean. So, how goes the trick-or-treating? Lots of kids?"

"They come in waves. Speaking of . . ."

Another group trooped up the steps, chorusing, "Trick or treat!"

Callie let them each choose two pieces of candy, and they tromped back down the steps.

"Extortion, really," Ben noted.

"True, but they're cute," Callie replied, wondering why he hadn't gone on his way yet, but realizing she was glad he hadn't.

"How's Nina doing?"

"Physically, fine. But she's going a bit stir-crazy."

"I can imagine."

"Yeah, and it's only the beginning. She could have three months of this."

"Yikes," Ben replied, leaning against the porch post, crossing one leg in front of the other. "Can't make things easy on you."

"I suppose not, but it is what it is. Probably a good thing they're here, actually. I can help out—and our mom is coming up from Florida next week."

"Oh, that's good." He paused. "Or is it?"

Callie smiled. "Good question. Overall, it'll be helpful. But you know mothers . . ."

He smiled, too. "Yes, I do," he said emphatically. "Mine is forever asking me if I'm eating properly. I think it's code for the fact that I don't have a wife cooking for me."

Callie laughed. "At least she's subtle. Mine is direct." She raised the pitch of her voice. "'You're not getting any younger, Callie. I don't know what you're waiting for.'" Callie's voice returned to its usual timbre. "It's a good thing she's not coming till next week. If she knew I had a date this weekend, I'd never hear the end of it." *Why did I bring that up? Why am I talking so much?*

Ben cocked his head. "Date? Someone special?"

Callie shook her head. "Hardly. A double date, actually."

"A double date." Ben's tone indicated that he clearly found this amusing.

"My friend suggested it. It's her and her husband, and me and this guy . . ."

"They're setting you up?"

"Um, no—we've already been on one date . . ." *Why am I talking about this?*

"How did you meet him?"

Of course he'd ask. "On Connections.com." She tried to keep the embarrassment out of her voice.

"Ohhhh," he said, once again amused.

"Hey!" Callie said, more sharply than she intended. "Lots of people do it—it works sometimes."

Ben hummed softly. "'If you like piña coladas, and getting caught in the rain' . . .'"

"What?" Her brow furrowed.

"If I ever sign up for one of those sites, that's what I'd start my profile with. Only people who get it need apply."

Callie laughed in spite of herself. "That's not a bad idea. Maybe I should change mine. 'I'm not into yoga; I have half a brain.'"

Ben chuckled. "See, isn't it perfect?" He lifted himself off the column and held out the tote bag. "Anyway, enjoy your date. Where are you all going?"

"Ummm . . . we're going bowling."

Ben laughed again. "Wow. This gets better and better. Hope you don't strike out."

Callie groaned. "That was awful."

"Yeah, you're right. That *was* awful."

Callie took the tote bag, and he turned to go down the steps as another group of children approached the house. Ben looked over his shoulder. "Say hi to Nina, and have fun bowling."

"Yeah, I kind of doubt I will."

Ben shook his head, smiling, and headed back toward his car.

Callie watched him go, over the heads of the kids poking around in the bowl. She was suddenly aware one of them was speaking to her.

"Excuse me," a small pirate asked. "Do any of these have nuts in them?"

She looked down at him, bringing herself back into the moment. "No, sweetie, no nuts."

"Great!" he enthused, and she watched him happily grab some candy.

CHAPTER NINETEEN

After

When Sunday afternoon rolled around, Callie was no more enthused about going on her double date than she'd been when Tess proposed it. She delayed leaving the house as long as possible, allowing herself to be sucked into combing websites for news about *Rerouting*. There seemed to be a romance brewing between Nick Sykes and an actress in the movie—but not Sarina Apple. When she couldn't procrastinate any longer, she pulled on a pair of ribbed black tights and cutoff jeans shorts with a chunky camel-colored sweater and added a pair of earrings—long, twisted silver ones studded with small multicolored glass balls.

She'd arranged to meet Jason at a bowling alley not far from Brook Hill and told Tess to be there shortly before the appointed time so she wouldn't have to be alone with him. Tess shook her head at that, but Callie didn't care. She was seeing this guy again only because Tess had insisted—although a voice in some part of her brain whispered, *Tess is right. There's nothing wrong with him. You don't give men a chance.*

She parked behind the bowling alley and resisted the urge to text Tess to make sure she was there. Stepping inside, she tried to remember the last time she'd been bowling. However long it had been, the distinct smell of feet and pizza hadn't changed. A couple of video game machines stood next to the door, where they had been since the 1980s. One of them was *Ms. Pac-Man.*

Accompanied by the *tock* sound of bowling balls hitting pins, Callie walked toward the desk where Tess and Brett loitered.

"*What* are you wearing?" Callie asked, her eyebrows raised.

Tess was decked out in a pink bowling shirt with a script letter *L* embroidered on the chest pocket in burgundy. Her jeans were tight and rolled up midcalf, exposing white socks peeking out of her short boots. A far cry from her typical flower-child look.

"Isn't it great?" Tess grinned from ear to ear. "Just call me Laverne," she added, pointing to the *L*. "I wear this every time I go bowling."

Callie tilted her head. How could she not have known about her friend's affinity for the game? "And exactly how often is that?"

Tess winked. "You'll just have to see how well I bowl."

"Don't listen to her," Brett interjected. "She's all talk." Brett was aggressively bald, having shaved his head years before. Callie thought it suited him, like David Beckham during his shorn-head phase. "So, Tess tells me we're here to pass judgment on your new friend."

Callie shot Tess a look. It was a good thing she'd known Brett nearly as long as she'd known Tess and felt almost as comfortable with him. When she'd told this to Tess, her friend had replied, "That's Brett, just one of the girls."

"No, you're here because it was the only way Tess could make me agree to see him again," Callie said, turning back to Brett.

"That bad?"

Callie sighed as Tess looked at her pointedly. "I suppose not. Our first date just wasn't very . . . exciting."

Brett nodded sagely. "Well, some bowling is *sure* to spice things up."

Callie was about to respond when she saw Jason approaching, wearing a ski parka and jeans. Callie waved to him and he came over, doing the same "do we hug?" dance that he had the first time, again not going through with it. Callie introduced him to Tess and Brett; Jason and Brett shook hands, and Callie caught Jason doing a double take as he took in Tess's outfit. He seemed to have a similar reaction to her own.

They paid for a lane and traded in their shoes for the oh-so-stylish bowling ones. Once they'd changed footwear, Tess insisted on snapping a photo of their feet to post on Instagram.

"Are you on Instagram?" Callie asked Jason.

"I have an account, but I don't really use it," he replied.

"See, something you have in common!" exclaimed Tess. "Callie isn't on Insta at all."

Callie was glad she was standing so close to Tess that she could surreptitiously poke her with her elbow. Brett took the moment to announce, "I think we need beer. Should I get a pitcher?"

"I'll go with you," Jason said immediately, and the two of them went to the bar while Tess started to enter their names into the scoring computer.

"So, he's not *bad* looking," she commented as she typed "Laverne" as Bowler One.

"Now there's a ringing endorsement."

"Well, looks aren't everything."

"I never said they were," Callie protested. "Did I say that I wasn't interested in him because he wasn't hot?"

"That's true," admitted Tess. "Anyway, you're giving him another chance. So," she said, changing the subject abruptly as usual, "how's your sister doing?"

"Okay. Cranky. But physically okay. My mom's coming up this week to help out."

Tess glanced at her. "Where's she going to sleep?" she asked, knowing that quarters were already tight.

"We haven't worked that out yet. Unless someone sleeps in the living room, we'll have to double up. Either my mom and me, my mom and Zoe, or Zoe and me."

"Sounds grand." Tess shook her head, negating her words.

The guys returned, bearing a pitcher of beer and four plastic cups.

"What are we talking about?" Brett asked as he began to pour. "By the way, this round's on Jason." He nodded his thanks toward Jason, who had removed his parka to reveal a crewneck sweater and then sat in one of the molded plastic seats. Almost immediately, the knee bouncing began.

"Callie's mom is coming up from Florida to help out with her sister," Tess explained. Then she turned to Jason. "She's pregnant and just got put on bed rest."

"Is she okay?"

Callie filled Jason in briefly, also explaining why her family was living with her.

"Ugh," Jason replied. "I had my apartment in Chicago redone. What a nightmare. They said six months. It took two *years*."

"Don't tell me that," Callie groaned.

"There's just so much that can go wrong. We'd thought all the pipes were up to code, but it turned out some of them were lead—so that was a nightmare. Then, we failed our electrical

inspection *twice*. Oh, and the wrong bathroom tile was de-
livered, which was supposedly *my* fault. Apparently, I was expected to have double-checked the lot number or something
before I signed off. And figuring out what a paint color looks
like from a square on the wall? Not that I really cared that
much, but . . ." Jason continued his catalog of renovation hor-
rors, failing to notice the look of gloom on Callie's face, until
Brett cut him off, slapping him on the shoulder.

"Okay, man. I think it's time to bowl!"

Tess insisted on going first. "I'm the only one who's dressed
for it!" she declared. She picked up a dark green bowling ball,
walked with it toward the lane, swung with commendable
form, and then released it so that it rolled directly into the
gutter.

Brett burst out laughing and Callie joined in. Tess turned
around and bowed comically. Jason laughed, too, a beat behind
the rest.

They fell into a rhythm, applauding some rounds, groaning
at others. Brett frequently pulled his phone out of his pocket to
consult it. Finally, Tess smacked his thigh. "Will you stop that
already?"

Callie looked over.

"Fantasy football. The bane of my existence. He's obsessed." Tess tilted her head toward Brett, who was smiling at
her affectionately.

"I've never understood how that worked," Callie responded.

"I'm in a league, too," Jason interjected eagerly, his knee
jiggling so fast it was almost a blur. "You put together a fantasy
team with real players. You get points based on how the players do in their actual games."

And this is exciting? "That's pretty cool." Callie forced enthusiasm into her voice.

"Totally! You trade players based on how they're doing—
makes you watch football a whole different way."

Callie laughed. "But . . . what if I don't watch football to begin with?"

"Then you suffer in silence like me," Tess declared.

Brett looked over at her. "In silence? You? Are you kidding me?"

Tess gave him a thin smile. "I love you, too, sweetie." But then she reached over and squeezed his knee, and Brett covered her hand with his.

"So, who do you have playing?" Jason asked Brett.

"And they're off to the races," remarked Tess as the men compared rosters, bemoaned their players' injuries, and bragged about successful trades.

Callie sat next to Tess and leaned toward her ear. "Well, at least he's enthusiastic about *something*," she said quietly.

Finally Tess grabbed a brief pause in their conversation to interject. "So, Jason, did Callie tell me you like to travel?"

Jason looked up, startled. Callie felt like she could see the gears switching in his brain. His knee momentarily stopped jiggling, then started up again. "Oh, yeah. Definitely."

"What are some of your favorite places?"

"Let's see. Hawaii's amazing, of course."

Callie nodded.

"And I love Vegas. I've been there at least a dozen times."

Callie cringed internally. She had been to Las Vegas once. It was enough.

"You like to gamble?" Brett asked.

Jason nodded. "It's one of the things I like about being in New York. You can go down to Atlantic City or up to the casinos in Connecticut and be there in a few hours."

"True," Tess said, glancing at Callie.

"Have you been to Europe?" Callie asked. She and Jenna had gone to Rome and Florence before Jenna's wedding three years earlier, and she longed to go back.

Jason shook his head. "I don't really feel comfortable when I don't speak the language."

"I don't mind it," said Callie. "I kind of like not being able to understand the conversations going on around you. You can just do your own thing in your own head. And at least the one time I went, enough people spoke English."

"I guess," Jason replied doubtfully as his leg bounced double time.

They bowled more and ordered a pizza. Callie tried not to yawn as the guys started talking about football again.

When the pizza pan was empty and they'd finished their third game, they were ready to call it a day.

"This was fun," Jason said to Callie. "I like your friends."

Callie was suddenly horrified, realizing he might think she'd introduced them because she was so into him. "They're fun people," she said weakly.

"Can I give you a ride somewhere?"

"No, I have my car. I'm good."

"Well, okay then." This time, he did give her a brief hug. "I'll call you."

"Great." She hoped she didn't sound as weary as she felt. "Drive safely."

"Will do," he replied, waving.

Tess and Brett appeared at her side.

"So," Brett said. "If I was looking for someone to watch ball with, or go with to Atlantic City, he'd be my guy."

"Now do you understand, Tess?" Callie asked.

Tess sighed. "He's not exactly a scintillating conversationalist," she admitted. "And what's with that leg of his? It never stops bouncing!"

Callie suppressed her chuckle. She wouldn't have pointed it out, but was gratified that the jiggling knee had made it on to Tess's radar, as well.

"Back to the drawing board," her friend continued. "Plenty

more guys out there. Who knows? They may have even emailed you already."

"Oh, Tess, leave her alone," Brett said, smiling kindly at Callie. "She'll find someone when the time is right."

"Is that like how you'll hang up those shelves in the bedroom 'when the time is right'?" Tess asked sardonically.

Brett smiled sweetly at her. "And I love you, too."

"I better go," Callie said. "I think you two need to get a room." She wiggled her eyebrows suggestively.

"God help me," said Tess. But she snaked her arm around Brett's waist and squeezed.

Callie felt a pang. *That's it. That's what I want.*

CHAPTER TWENTY

Before

It was a beautiful Sunday morning in October, and I was on my way to brunch in the dining hall. The foliage was at its peak, but there was a touch of warmth in the air. I collected my cereal, milk, and coffee and went to find a table. I was happy to see Jenna seated by the window. The room was fairly empty; sleeping late was a popular Welford sport.

"Hey, stranger!" Jenna said, closing the book she'd been reading as I placed my tray on the table and pulled out a chair. "What are you doing here this early?" Jenna's gaze moved past me, as if she was looking for someone. "And by yourself?"

"Ethan's still asleep."

Ethan and I had essentially lived together for the past four months. When we finished our sophomore year, we immediately left for San Francisco, where we spent the summer. Ethan did a language course and I did one in early childhood education at Berkeley. Through his cousin, we got a sublet from a grad student who was away doing research. It was pretty amazing—even if it was cold and didn't feel much like summer. We rented a car a few times. Once we drove down Highway 1 to Monterey and Carmel. Another time we went to Mission San Juan Bautista to see where *Vertigo* was filmed. And we went up to Point Reyes, where we walked to the lighthouse and saw the elephant seals, and then had to drive farther north to see the schoolhouse from *The Birds*—one of my least favorite Hitchcocks.

Ethan loved it all and was talking about moving there after graduation. I wasn't so sure. It was so far from my family, and we still had two years of school to get through.

But we didn't have to think about that yet. Back at Welford, we were in single rooms across the hall from each other. We slept in one and studied in the other. It was fun setting them up like our own little apartment. I got some big pillows to make the bed in the study more like a sofa, and we moved both desks in there. Since we weren't allowed to paint the walls, I covered the institutional gray with a bunch of my drawings and watercolors.

I tended to wake up early, but Ethan wasn't a morning person. And it wasn't fun to deal with his grumpiness if he was roused before he *had* to get up. But the night before, we'd slept separately. Ethan's brother Josh was visiting for the weekend, and the two of them camped out together in the study.

"I'm surprised you're up so early," I said to Jenna. "How was the concert?" She and Shauna and Jade had gone to see No Doubt the night before.

"It was amazing! You should have come."

I shrugged. "I'm not that into them." I spooned Cheerios into my mouth.

Jenna looked at me skeptically. "So then *why* do you have all their CDs?"

"I don't think I have them *all*," I protested. *Anyway, I haven't listened to them in a while—Ethan thinks they're annoying.*

Jenna raised her eyebrows.

"Anyway, I told you. Ethan's brother is here, so we all wanted to hang out."

After finishing a sip of orange juice, Jenna put her glass down. "What did you guys do?"

"We all had dinner, and then Josh wanted some time with Ethan. He needed 'brotherly advice' about some girl."

Jenna opened her mouth and then shut it without saying anything. After a moment she spoke again. "So, are you ever going to come running with me?"

"I should try to." I knew, as I said it, what a challenge that would be. Ethan and I liked to start our days together in bed. Though he wasn't a morning person, once he was awake, his whole body was up—literally—and very interested in doing all the things I liked.

We chatted awhile about classes and people. I'd finished eating and was settled back in my chair with a second cup of coffee, enjoying this unexpected time with Jenna—who I didn't seem to see much except in class—when a guy entering the dining room caught my eye. He was a transfer student who happened to be in one of my classes. I'd been struck by his smart comments—and by his fine cheekbones and chocolate-brown eyes.

It wasn't as if I hadn't noticed cute boys during the time Ethan and I were dating. As my girlfriends and I said, it's not like having a boyfriend means you go blind. But I had to admit—guiltily—that this one was a little different. I'd found myself wondering what it would be like to spend more time with him. I'd even dreamed about him—dreams I certainly couldn't tell Ethan about.

I forced my eyes back to Jenna, and my mind back to the conversation. *Is it a betrayal to feel attracted to someone else, even if you don't act on it?*

CHAPTER TWENTY-ONE

After

The week after the double date, Callie steered clear of Tess to avoid the inevitable questions about whether she'd gone back online. On top of her general dislike of internet matchmaking, watching Nina and Michael snap at each other hardly made Callie think fondly of coupledom, and no amount of rom-coms could remedy that. She knew Nina was testy because she was stuck in bed, but the sniping about everything—from how much time Zoe spent in their bedroom to whether they should redo Zoe's room back home to what TV show to watch—was driving Callie crazy. Perhaps there was something to be said for a life of celibacy.

Eluding Tess actually proved fairly easy since Callie was now racing out of school every afternoon to pick Zoe up. The earlier she got there, the less she had to fight the traffic. Zoe was also more at ease on the days Callie reached her immediately after school dismissal. The new routine was clearly stressing her out. Callie didn't think she could endure one more freeway tantrum. And that was saying a lot, considering she spent her days with children exactly Zoe's age.

So when Nina asked Callie to stop by her house in Wolcott, she was not enthusiastic.

"Please, Callie? It's so hard for me not seeing what's going on there every day."

"But I don't know the first thing about construction—and what they're supposed to have done. Besides, wasn't Michael just there over the weekend?"

"Yes, but I'd been going *every day*. Michael can't go during the week—he's getting into work late as it is, after bringing Zoe to school." Nina pulled on the cuffs of the oversized sweatshirt she was wearing. There was a stain across the lettering that spelled "Atlantis." It made Callie sad.

"But I won't even know what I'm looking at," she protested, already knowing she would lose the battle. "They could put the beams in perpendicular when they should be parallel, and I'll think it's all hunky-dory."

"Callie, I'm not expecting you to catch them making mistakes," Nina said exasperatedly. "Just to be a set of eyes that can tell me what's going on. You can take photos. I'll ask someone from HMK to meet you and walk you through."

"Well, then, what do they need me for? They'll know what they're looking at," Callie replied, even as she wondered if her guide might be Ben.

Nina sighed. "Having my *sister* check things out isn't the same as having someone I'm *paying* do it."

Ah, the sister card. Frequently played as trump.

"All right," Callie agreed reluctantly. "I'll go before I pick up Zoe. I don't want to be responsible for her at a construction site."

"Thanks." Nina looked away. "I really do appreciate it. I'd much rather be going myself."

"I know." Callie opened up the dresser drawer and found a

clean sweatshirt, which she tossed to her sister. "Here. The one you're wearing is stained."

Nina grabbed the shirt and gave Callie a half smile.

Callie stopped by the restroom after school. As she washed her hands, she looked at herself in the mirror. She fluffed her hair and on impulse rummaged in her handbag for a lipstick. The one she found was worn down to a nub, but she managed to apply some plum shine just as Tess entered the ladies' room.

"Hot date?" she asked. "I hope?"

"Hardly. I'm on my way to pick up my niece."

"Then what's with the lipstick?" Tess knew it wasn't exactly the norm for her.

Callie shrugged. "Why not?" She headed out of the bathroom. "See you tomorrow."

About half an hour later, Callie pulled into Wolcott. The homes she drove past were of similar vintage as the ones in her own neighborhood in Brook Hill, but a growing number of them were being added on to and upgraded as Wolcott became increasingly trendy. Nina and Michael's house was a center hall colonial, originally about the same size as the Victorian in which the girls had grown up. Now, it would be nearly double that. While Callie didn't think all that extra space was necessary—they had done fine without it—she could see the appeal of not being quite so on top of one another.

She hadn't been to Nina's house since the construction started, so it was a dramatic change. The original porch had been demolished, and a temporary wooden structure provided access to the front door. A large green dumpster sat in the driveway, and a matching Porta-Potty was tucked around the side of the house. At the back, she could glimpse the framed addition with large cutouts in the plywood where the windows would go. It resembled something her kids at school might build.

Callie parked behind a dark gray SUV as a broad-shouldered, sandy-haired man walked across the lawn. Swallowing her disappointment, she got out of the car to meet her tour guide.

"Hello!" she called.

He tilted his head and squinted at her.

"I'm Callie—Nina's sister."

"Okayyy . . . ," he said slowly, running his hand through his wispy hair.

This should be fun.

"I think you're supposed to be showing me around," Callie prompted.

"Really? I was just heading out."

Callie pushed down her twinge of annoyance. "But I thought this was all arranged. I couldn't get here before now."

The man's hand moved down to his jaw, rubbing slowly. "Well, I guess I can stay." *Doesn't he sound delighted?*

They both turned at the sound of a black sedan pulling up behind Callie's Toyota. A moment later, Ben emerged from the driver's side and strolled toward them.

"Hey, Mitch. Hey, Callie."

Callie couldn't help but smile. "Ah—I guess you're the one showing me around. I thought it was . . . Mitch." She tilted her head toward the other man.

"Nope. Sorry. You're stuck with me."

She pushed her hair behind her ear. "I'll try to deal with it."

Mitch was already moving toward the SUV at the curb. "'Night, Ben, miss," he called.

"Good night," she replied automatically, before looking back at Ben. "And Mitch is . . . ?"

"Oh—he's the general contractor. Good guy—but not much of a talker. Shall we?" He pointed toward the house.

"It looks like a lot has been done," she remarked as they crossed the yard.

"It does, doesn't it?" he said, looking up at the house. "That's the problem with construction. At the beginning, it seems to go very fast, and then you get into the long slog where it's electrical and plumbing and other unexciting things and it seems like the project is never going to end."

An angled plank provided access to the makeshift porch—not unlike the two-by-four raceway she'd created the day Liam joined her class. Ben swiftly moved up it and then turned, extending his hand to help Callie up. She looked warily at the plank and then took his hand, which was warm. He held hers firmly as she took the few steps, and for just a brief moment longer once she was safely on the porch.

He extracted a key from his pocket to unlock the door, and as his back was turned, he asked, "So, how was the big date?"

"Don't ask," Callie replied as he opened the door and stepped back to allow her to enter.

"Too late," he remarked, and she laughed. "What was so bad about it?"

"Well, I guess it wasn't *so* bad," she said, feeling a little guilty about her easy dismissal of Jason.

Ben glanced at her. "Then will you see him again?"

Callie looked at him. "Um, no."

This time he chuckled. "So it *was* that bad."

Callie glanced around; it appeared that the front part of the house hadn't changed. Center hallway with staircase, flanked by living room and dining room. But as she walked back, it was worlds different. The kitchen had been entirely demolished and the back wall of the house blown out to create what Nina was calling the great room. She turned to Ben. "There just wasn't any . . . *chemistry*. And we don't have much in common. He's just not what I'm looking for."

The corners of Ben's mouth turned up in amusement. "And what *are* you looking for?"

How, after only meeting this man—what, three times?—
were they having such a personal conversation? Somehow, it
didn't feel inappropriate. At the same time, how could she possibly answer that question?

"Maybe that's the problem," she said flippantly. "I'm not
sure I know."

"Oh, I'm sure you do. You just haven't found it yet."

"So it's like that Supreme Court justice who couldn't explain what pornography is, but said, 'I know it when I see it'?"

Ben raised his eyebrows, and Callie felt her face flush.

"Something like that," he said, with a quick wink. "Anyway,"
he continued, his tone shifting. "This is it. Chez Kagan." He
swept his arm wide.

"It's . . . big."

"Yes, that it is." While Callie took photos that she doubted
would tell Nina very much, Ben gave her a rundown on what
had been going on in the space over the past few days, and
then took her upstairs to see the upper floor of the addition,
where the master suite would be. She could envision the deep
sill that would grace the large window looking out over the
backyard, and nodded appreciatively as Ben pointed out where
they'd be able to tuck some bookshelves into an alcove. *Clever.*

"So, did you design all of this?"

"We're a team. One of the firm's partners heads all this up,
but I did a lot of the drawing. And since Nina and Michael
wanted us to oversee the construction, most of that falls
to me."

Callie nodded. "Have you been doing this long?"

Ben described how he made the jump from commercial
designing to residential. "I've been with HMK for about six
years," he concluded.

"And you like it? Aside from the clients, that is?" she added,
smiling.

He put his finger to his lips. "Shh. That part is just between us. But yes, I do like it. It's still exciting to see my drawings come to life. And to solve puzzles."

"Puzzles?"

"Figuring out how to give people what they want, even when it looks like their existing property and budget make it impossible."

Callie nodded. "That does sound neat." *Neat?*

"Should we check out the basement?"

"Sure." She followed Ben down to the unfinished basement, where he pointed out the large gap that had been created in one wall of the foundation to access the newly created portion.

"It's a lot of space," Callie remarked, looking around. "What's going down here?"

"Nothing right now. It will be unfinished for the moment."

Callie turned back to Ben, her lips pursed thoughtfully. "Hmm . . . maybe I can convince Nina to put in a skating rink."

"Hey! I thought you were on my side!" Ben protested. "Oh," he continued, looking like the proverbial cat that ate the canary. "I get it. You want to bring your dates here. Perhaps we should put in a bowling alley."

"Not nice," she said in mock rebuke. Then she couldn't help it—she smiled again. "Well, at least I'm not suggesting that she have the whole front of the house open up on a hinge."

"Oh, I can tell I'm going to have to be nice to you."

"Always a good rule to follow."

"I'll remember that." He grinned. "Anything else you want to see?"

"I don't think so. I'm not sure what I'm supposed to be looking at, anyway."

"Your sister just likes to check on things. Since she can't come, you're her designated scout. I'm sure you'll be back. And then you can compare where things were today to where things are then."

"It'll be like those puzzles where you compare two pictures that look the same but really have a dozen differences."

"Exactly," Ben said, laughing.

They went outside, and Ben locked the front door. Then he walked back down the plank and held his hand out for Callie's again. His grip was firm and sure. Was it her imagination, or did he hold it longer than necessary—again?

After he drew his hand back, he clapped both of his together. "Well. I guess that's it."

"I guess so. I have to go pick Zoe up."

"You're good to do all this."

She shrugged, embarrassed.

"I imagine I'll see you again?"

"I imagine so," she replied, and she turned to walk back to her car.

"Callie!" he called after her.

She turned expectantly.

"Give my best to your sister."

"Will do," she replied, with the sensation that someone had just punctured a balloon that had been rising lightly into the air.

CHAPTER TWENTY-TWO

After

Michael left work early the next day to fetch Zoe so Callie could pick up her mother. She navigated the maze of highways surrounding Newark Airport, and then followed the signs to Terminal A parking. As she walked toward the building, she wrapped her scarf more tightly around her throat and pulled on her gloves. Once inside, she checked the arrivals screen and settled in to wait. She was tempted to get a cup of coffee but, on principle, refused to pay twice the standard price simply because of airport real estate.

Eyes drawn to a bleached blonde in patterned tights and platform shoes digging for something in her large handbag, she heard her name called out in her mother's familiar nasal voice. Looking up, she did a double take.

For as long as Callie could recall, Lorraine had taken it as a personal triumph that she won every single battle in the war against her encroaching gray hair. At one point, she was getting it professionally colored every six weeks and touching up

on her own in between, empty bottles of dye filling the recycling bin and specks of Lorraine's chestnut brown turning up
on the faucet, on the tiled floor, and in the sink. But the woman
approaching her, who certainly had her mother's face, gait, and
wardrobe, had steel-gray hair. It was stylishly cut, with a side
part and a sweep of hair just skimming her right eyebrow, so
clearly she hadn't given up the beauty parlor.

"Mom!" she exclaimed. "Your hair!"

"Oh, this?" She patted it gently, as if it were a favorite pet.

"Yes, *this*." Callie imitated her mother's tone.

"Do you like it?"

"It's very nice. But when did you let . . ." All the years of
her mother's covering the gray suddenly made it feel like a bad
word. She would sooner have said *shit* in front of her. "When
did you let it go natural?" she asked finally.

"A few months ago, I guess. Just got tired of all the
maintenance."

"Wow." Callie couldn't get over it. "It looks great." She gave
her mother a hug.

Lorraine drew back. "You look thin. Have you been eating?"

*Most people would think that being able to fit into the same
clothes for ten years would be a plus.* Callie sighed. "Let's get
your bags."

A few minutes later, as they watched the luggage carousel
revolve, Callie turned to Lorraine. "How was your flight?" she
asked.

"Oh, it was fine. Had a nice long chat with the girl sitting next to me. She was on her way back up from visiting *her*
mother." It was a continuing sore spot with Lorraine that her
daughters rarely made the trip to Florida. Callie wondered how
her mother's seatmate would describe the conversation: *The
woman sitting next to me would not stop talking. Even though I
had my book open the entire time.*

Shortly after, they were in the car, Lorraine's two wheeled bags stowed in the trunk. As Callie shifted into reverse, her mom retrieved some hard candies from her purse. "Want one?" she asked, taking off one of the wrappers and popping the candy into her mouth.

"No thanks." Callie remembered her grandmother always having candy in her purse. Was it genetic? Would she start walking around with cellophane-wrapped butterscotch in the bottom of her handbag, too?

The traffic had gotten worse, and Callie navigated the tricky merge onto the highway.

"How's Nina?"

Callie wasn't sure how Lorraine thought things might have changed since she'd spoken to her older daughter just the night before. "Fine. You know. As good as can be expected." She glanced in the rearview mirror and scanned the road ahead of her. Out of the corner of her eye, she saw her mother shake her head. *Here we go.*

"I don't know how many times I told her that she needed to slow down. All this running around . . ."

"Ma, that had nothing to do with this."

"How do you know? Are you a doctor?"

Something twisted in her gut, but Callie pushed it back into its hiding place. "No. But Nina's doctor said that these cases are often inexplicable. It has nothing to do with what she did or didn't do."

Lorraine clicked her tongue. "Inexplicable. Well, maybe it would be *explicable* if she knew that her patient never rested."

"Of course she rested," Callie said exasperatedly. "I hope you're not going to say any of this stuff to her. She feels bad enough already."

"Why would I say anything? What's done is done. Nothing *I* can do about it now."

As if there was anything you could have done about it before. She hoped her mother would, in fact, be able to restrain herself.

Lorraine had the good grace not to start in on Nina immediately upon arrival. Callie was happy to see her sister was freshly showered and wearing a clean long-sleeved shirt. The area around the bed had been straightened up—which, of course, Nina shouldn't have been doing—the books and magazines neatly stacked.

"Nina!" Lorraine exclaimed, hugging her.

"Hi, Mom. What did you do to your hair?"

Lorraine touched it again as she had done when Callie had commented. "If Glenn Close can go gray, why not me?" she quipped.

Nina exchanged glances with her sister.

Lorraine sat down on the bed and rested her hand on her daughter's growing belly. "Hello, grandchild!" She looked at Nina. "You're not going to find out if it's a boy or a girl?"

Nina shook her head. Callie continued to be surprised by this. Considering how well prepared her sister liked to be, she couldn't understand why she wouldn't want to know what— well, *who*—was coming.

They chatted amiably about Lorraine's flight and the weather—"So much colder here than in Florida! I don't know how I lasted up here as long as I did!"—and then Michael and Zoe arrived, the little girl immediately rushing into her grandmother's arms.

Lorraine crushed her into a hug, then held her away so she could study her. "My goodness, you've grown in the past three months!"

Zoe beamed, and Lorraine looked over her head at Michael. "You've got a weed here, Michael."

"Hi, Lorraine." He stepped forward and gave his mother-in-law a stiff hug.

"I hope you're taking good care of my little girl." Lorraine's smile didn't reach her eyes.

Michael sighed. "Doing my best," he said with false cheer, his eyes on Nina.

Nina smiled back at him, *You're the one who wanted her to come* hanging unspoken in the air.

As they all sat in the bedroom to eat dinner—Michael having carried a couple of dining room chairs upstairs to go with the old TV tables Lorraine dug up in the basement—they confronted the subject of sleeping arrangements. Michael had bought an air mattress; the question was where it would go.

"So, Zoe is in Nina's old room?" Lorraine began. "Maybe she can move in with Callie on the air mattress and I'll take her bed."

Before anyone else could respond, Zoe wailed, "I want to stay in *my* room."

Lorraine raised her eyebrows, but Callie couldn't help feeling for the kid. She had already been relocated from home, and now her whole schedule was upside down. "Why doesn't Zoe stay where she is, and I'll take the air mattress in her room?" Callie suggested, hoping to forestall a long discussion that would likely end up with the same result.

They all looked at her, and she waited for someone to say *Are you sure?* or *Maybe there's another solution.* But no one did. Only Zoe piped up, "Yay! I get to sleep with Aunt Callie!" Then she turned to Callie and said quietly, as if sharing a special secret, "You can sleep in my bed with me if you want."

This is going to be fun.

Lorraine may have driven everyone a little crazy, but no one could say she wasn't an enthusiastic helper. She happily took over Zoe's school drop-off and pickup, which relaxed Michael and lightened the mood in the house. And Callie didn't mind not having to make the trip either. Lorraine also took on responsibility for meals. That meant boxed mac and cheese, canned soup, store-bought rotisserie chicken, or ordering in. ("I'm retired from cooking. It's not as if I didn't enjoy cooking for you girls all those years, but I'm done. Kaput. I told your dad, 'If you want home-cooked meals, you'll have to cook them yourself.'") Nina's lips frequently disappeared into a thin line when a prefab dinner appeared. Callie knew her sister longed to urge Lorraine to include some freshly steamed, organic produce—but after her initial attempts were rebuffed in no uncertain terms, Nina restrained herself.

The three women and Zoe ate dinner together in the master bedroom. "It's like a picnic!" Zoe said.

To Callie, it was an *Alice in Wonderland* version of the family dinners they had when she and Nina were growing up, Lorraine always trying to keep cheerful conversation going—even when Nina was a sullen teenager and Callie had no idea what was happening. Just as she had then, Lorraine filled the silences with stories about people neither of her daughters knew. ("Of course you know June! You met her when you were—oh, probably nine. She gave you that paint-by-number set.")

"You know who I ran into today?" Lorraine asked one evening. "Gerri Bender. You girls remember, Bobby and Gerri? They had those big German shepherds."

"You know, I do remember them," Nina said thoughtfully, spearing a piece of rotisserie chicken. "But I could never remember which was the husband and which was the wife." She popped the piece of chicken into her mouth.

Lorraine pointed her fork at Nina. "Gerri was . . . is . . . the woman. You know that."

Nina shrugged, as if it didn't really matter. Which it didn't.

After a moment of silence while they all chewed—except for Zoe, who had finished eating and was sitting on the floor coloring—Lorraine spoke again. "Callie—did I tell you that I saw the preview of Ethan's movie? What's it called? *Rerouting*?"

Callie nearly choked on her chicken and took a sip of her water before responding. She felt Nina's eyes on her.

"No, Ma. You hadn't told me."

"It looks quite good. Funny," Lorraine said in a tone of mixed surprise and admiration. "I might go see it when it comes out."

"I wouldn't have thought it would be . . . your kind of thing . . ."

Lorraine looked at Callie with her eyebrows raised. "Oh, us old ladies only watch period pieces or movies starring Diane Keaton or Meryl Streep?"

Callie rolled her eyes. "I didn't say that. And you're not old. I just thought . . ."

"Wait. I haven't seen the preview yet," Nina broke in.

"I'll show it to you," Callie mumbled.

"You watched it without telling me?" Callie wasn't sure if Nina's voice was hurt or annoyed.

Lorraine continued as if her daughters hadn't spoken. "My matinee club sees a movie twice a month. That's a lot of movies. We wouldn't normally see a road trip movie about a bunch of boys, but I think we need to add this one to our list." She took a bite of broccoli, and Callie very nearly breathed a sigh of relief—but then her mother spoke again.

"The actress who plays the young man's ex-girlfriend is very attractive . . . but she doesn't look anything like you. You'd think they'd find someone closer to your type if they're going to make a movie about your life." Her tone was casual, but her eyes were sharp.

Callie pointed at her mouth, making exaggerated chewing motions. She didn't know how to respond. Maybe there would be an earthquake. Or perhaps a tree would fall on the house. Not a big one—not one of the oaks that towered over the roof—just one they'd hear and have to run outside to look at.

In the silence, Nina spoke. "Ma, it's a movie, not a documentary. The actress is playing a character, not the *real* Callie."

Callie almost brought up some of the information she'd found online but knew it would be better to end the conversation altogether. Before she could do either, Zoe piped up. They had all forgotten she was there. "Aunt Callie is in a movie?" she asked, awestruck. Callie imagined that, in her niece's mind, she was swimming with Nemo or dancing at the ball with Prince Charming.

She shook her head. "No, Binks, I'm not in a movie."

"But Gamma said . . . ," Zoe began stubbornly before her mother cut her off with an impatient wave of her hand.

"Mom," Nina said, looking squarely at Lorraine. "Let's leave Callie alone about this." Callie was surprised by her sister's vehemence, let alone by her jumping to her defense.

"What am I doing?" Lorraine asked, her hands spread, palms up—the picture of innocence. "I just think it's interesting that Ethan made a movie about the two of you. I wonder what it means. I wonder if you get back together in the end . . ."

"Mom. Stop. All it means is that Ethan used their breakup story to get a nice, fat paycheck from a film company. Well, good for him. Meanwhile, Callie's never going to move on, get married, have a family—I know, I know, politically incorrect and all that, but that *is* what you want for her—if all she does is obsess over this." Then Nina turned to Callie. "By the way, I might be stuck in this room, but I know you've been trolling the internet for anything you can find out about him. Not to mention buying magazines you'd never in a million years pick up. Do you think *Glamour* can really tell you if you made the right decision?"

So much for defending me.

Nina turned back to their mother, her eyes narrowed. "She's been hung up on Ethan and what happened for way too long already. I don't think this fixation needs any encouragement."

Callie's skin got hot. She felt like she was a kid and her parents were arguing about whether or not they should sign her up for piano lessons. "Hello!" She pointed to herself. "Right here. In the room. You don't need to talk about me like I'm not here."

Nina looked at her and spoke more gently. "You know where I stand on this, Callie. Dwelling on it isn't doing you any good. I wish Ethan had never made this stupid movie."

Lorraine interjected. "Well, strictly speaking, it doesn't look stupid. It looks quite clever, and apparently the star is very well known. Of course, I've never heard of him—but I don't know who half the people in *People* magazine are anymore."

"That is *not* the point," Nina retorted.

"And what is the point?" Callie asked, standing up abruptly. This was exactly why she never told her family anything. *Damn that ridiculous alumni magazine.* "That I don't know what I'm doing and I'm alone because I'm stuck in the past? That I need you to tell me how to fix my life?" Thank God she hadn't told her sister about her plan to contact Ethan. She picked up her plate, which was still half full of food. "Well, my life isn't broken, thank you very much." She walked out of the room, ignoring Nina's voice calling after her.

Callie had nowhere to go. Her mother was literally by her side all the time. Lorraine didn't like solitude, so wherever Callie went—kitchen, dining room, living room—her mother appeared within moments as if by teleportation. Even her (new) bedroom was no safe haven until Zoe was snugly tucked in and off to dreamland.

Having no desire to continue the conversation that had

begun over dinner, Callie went for a walk. By the time she got back, Zoe was fast asleep, so she set up her laptop on the air mattress in the dark.

Whatever issues she had with her mother, Callie had to admit that Lorraine was an astute observer of people. While Nina was set on her assumption that Callie was stuck on Ethan and needed to get him out of her head, Lorraine was much more in tune with Callie's own mindset. She had the same question. What did all of this *mean*? To which Callie added, *And what's the harm in finding out?*

Sitting cross-legged in the glow of the laptop screen, she pulled up a travel website and plugged in flights from Newark to Los Angeles for the dates of the NOECE conference. She could book a flight for under $500. One advantage of living in her parents' house—although it was hard to see any at the moment, as she sat in the dark on an inflatable bed—was that she'd been able to save money. The cost of the travel wasn't going to keep her from making the trip.

And if she did go, what then? Would she show up at his door? And if he opened it and saw her, how would he react? How would she want him to react? *Only one way to find out.*

Callie opened up her email. Since the moment she'd looked up Ethan's email address, she had been composing—and discarding—various versions of the same message. Tone was everything. She didn't want to sound too friendly or flattered, but she didn't want to come across as offended that he hadn't contacted her about the movie. As her inbox loaded, she began a new draft in her head.

But before she could hit the Compose button, she saw an unopened message in her inbox, dated the day before. The email address began ethan_rendel. The subject line: "Rerouting." Her stomach felt like it had plunged down an elevator shaft, and her heart raced. She clicked to open it.

Dear Callie:

So strange to be writing to you after all these years. I got your email address from the alumni directory. To be honest, I never imagined I'd be contacting you again, but, as they say, truth can be stranger than fiction.

As you may know, my big news is that a screenplay I wrote—*Rerouting*—is being released in January. If you've seen anything about it, you've probably figured out that the story kicks off with a big breakup. I can't pretend that I didn't get the idea from us.

I wanted to let you know that the film goes in an entirely different direction after that. It's a guy road movie—not the autobiographical piece it was when I first wrote it nine years ago.

Anyway, I will be in New York for the premiere the second weekend of January. Perhaps we can get together and I can explain it all in person? Let me know what you think.

    —Ethan

CHAPTER TWENTY-THREE

After

The words of Ethan's email swirled in Callie's brain over the following days. Part of her was surprised that he felt he owed her an explanation—that he didn't think she deserved whatever she got. After all she'd put him through, did he still care about her? Why did he *really* want to see her?

She'd been struggling for weeks to figure out what to say to him—and now, he'd reached out to her. She couldn't help thinking it was some sort of message from the universe—but she didn't know what that message was. And as she drafted and redrafted a response, she realized she had no clue how to reply. Once, she had to shut her laptop quickly to conceal her latest version from Lorraine, who, as usual, appeared in the kitchen while Callie sat there with the computer and a cup of tea.

A few mornings later, Judith called to her as she arrived at Bouncy Castles. Callie stopped, unbuttoning her coat as she stood in the office doorway. Judith sat at her desk, which was cluttered with gifts from students over the years—"Best Teacher" pencil cups, ceramic apples, and countless decorative ladybugs from a period when rumor had it that Judith collected them.

"What's the latest with Liam?" Judith asked, putting down her pen.

"Things are pretty good. We have our rough patches, but paying more attention to him seems to help. And I've been in touch with his mom every week." Since their first meeting, Callie and Ellen had spoken regularly. Callie had the distinct impression Ellen was trying to make up for her lack of involvement during the first weeks of school when Robin had been Liam's teacher. She also had the feeling that Ellen felt a connection with her, ever since she'd shared her marital troubles. In each call, Callie asked hesitantly how things were going—not wanting to pry but thinking it would be worse if she ignored what Ellen had revealed.

Judith smiled. "I'm glad to hear it. You've got a way with people, Callie."

Praise from Judith was uncommon. "Thanks," she replied, pleased.

Judith picked up her pen again, seeming to indicate that Callie was dismissed, but just as Callie began to turn away, she spoke again. "Oh—what about the NOECE conference? Have you figured out if you'll be able to attend? I'm still holding two hotel rooms."

"Oh," Callie said, stalling. Since getting Ethan's email, she had set aside her internal debate about the conference. Now that she might see him in New York, there was no need to go. But what if, depending on their meeting here, she might want to see him in LA after all? If not, there was certainly nothing wrong with going to a professional conference. She might learn something.

If there was one thing she'd learned in the last few weeks,

it was that overthinking got her nowhere. "Yes, I think I'll be able to go."

Judith offered her an even broader smile. "Wonderful! It will be a great experience for you. There's so much to see there—it will be good to have someone to look at it all with."

Callie reflected Judith's smile, but on a smaller scale. It occurred to her that she hadn't simply agreed to a conference. She had signed on for weekend with her boss. *Perhaps overthinking wasn't so bad after all.*

One day the week before Thanksgiving, Callie was again on Zoe pickup duty. While Lorraine was in New Jersey, she was taking the opportunity to see her old doctors. "I don't trust those Florida doctors," she'd said. "They're so used to treating old people, they just expect all their patients to die anyway. They don't think they need to do anything to stop it. Sometimes I think they even want to push us along. The funeral homes probably give them kickbacks." On that particular day, she'd been able to take advantage of a cancellation at a much-in-demand dermatologist's, so Callie stepped in to fetch Zoe. At the last minute—just as she pulled into Nina's friend Holly's driveway—Nina called to ask her to stop by HMK to pick up some new drawings.

Callie sighed. She didn't necessarily mind possibly running into Ben—but now it was too late to go there first. A few minutes later, Zoe was strapped into the car seat and Callie restarted the car, looking over her shoulder to speak to her niece. "We just have to stop by the architect's office on the way home."

"I don't want to." Zoe fixed her gaze on Callie in the way only a preschooler could.

"It'll be quick. We just have to pick something up for Mommy."

"I want to go home." Zoe's voice got shriller.

"I know, Binks, but we have to stop first."

Callie might as well have told her they needed to pull out her fingernails, considering the shriek Zoe emitted. If there were a wineglass in the car, it would have shattered.

Facing forward again, Callie stared at the garage door on Holly's house. Zoe was still screaming in the back seat, the reverberations of the sound throbbing in her ears.

She had no choice. She was going to have to go down the road she—and so many parents and caregivers—had sworn they'd never go down. She reached into her purse to retrieve her smartphone and turned to face Zoe again. Like a magnet, the phone drew Zoe's attention, and the screaming stopped.

"So, what games does Mommy have on her phone for you?"

Zoe bit her lip, clearly thinking about this extremely important question. "I like the Mickey Mouse one."

"Okay, the Mickey Mouse one." Callie pulled up the app store and did a search. After several consultations with Zoe, she downloaded the correct game. "Now," she said, holding the phone aloft, "you can play your game, but I don't want to hear any more complaining. Promise?"

Zoe looked at her solemnly. "Promise," she said, reaching for the phone.

Callie finally put the car into reverse to back out of the driveway.

They parked near HMK Design, and Callie let Zoe keep the phone while they went upstairs. They went through the frosted glass door, and Callie was greeted by the same girl at the reception desk, the one with the bright red asymmetrical hair. The girl pointed at Zoe, whose eyes were fixed on the phone as it worked its magnetic power. "I know you," she said. "Zoe! And you're Nina's sister," she added, looking at Callie. "I remember—you were here before. I'm Kat, by the way."

"I'm Callie. Zoe, say hello."

"Hello," said Zoe, her gaze never wavering from the screen.

Callie shook her head disapprovingly, but Kat grinned. "Oh, I get it. Those games can be addictive. I've got a thing for *Candy Crush*, myself."

Callie smiled politely, thinking of the worsening traffic as rush hour drew near and worrying about how much battery power the phone had left.

"Well, you must want to get her home." Kat nodded toward Zoe. "Let me get Ben for you."

Callie's chest did a funny little skip. Perhaps the climb up the staircase had winded her.

Kat buzzed Ben via intercom, and moments later, he came out of his office. As usual, he was wearing khakis and a button-down shirt. The sleeves were folded up, as if he'd been doing something other than tapping on his computer keyboard, and he carried some rolled-up papers. His hair was a little shorter than Callie remembered it. She stopped herself just before she commented on his haircut. She didn't want him to think she was looking at him that closely.

He smiled. "Hello, Callie. And we have Zoe today, too." He glanced at the phone. "Ah, the electronic babysitter," he added, turning his gaze back to Callie.

"You do what you've got to do," she replied.

He nodded knowingly and took her into the conference room where they'd been before. Without even looking up, Zoe backed herself into a chair in the corner and sat down. Callie suspected she'd been here before, doing the same thing, only on Nina's phone.

"So, how are you?" Ben asked as he rolled the papers out on the table and secured the corners with the paperweights.

"Oh, I'm fine," Callie replied, hoping he didn't notice she answered a beat behind his question. She'd been noticing his forearms, which looked strong and sinewy and had just the right amount of hair on them. She hadn't anticipated that. "So what's this?" she asked, looking down at the diagrams on the table.

"Nina and Michael have decided they want to finish the basement now after all." Ben looked up from the drawings, his eyebrows raised. "Did you have something to do with this?"

"Why? Are they asking for a skating rink?"

"An indoor swimming pool," said Ben gravely.

Zoe's head popped up, momentarily released from the pull of the phone. "Really?" she asked, her eyes like saucers.

Ben glanced at Callie before responding. "Sorry, Zoe—I was just kidding."

The little girl's face fell.

"But you're going to have so much space to play down there you won't even know what to do with it all," he added enthusiastically, and both Ben and Callie sighed with relief when Zoe turned back to her game.

"They're always listening," Callie said softly.

"Yeah, I stepped right into that one."

"Nice recovery, though." She grinned.

Ben smiled back at her. Not for the first time, Callie noticed his nice smile. And there was that little skip in her chest again. She cleared her throat and looked down at the papers. "So, what *are* they doing?"

"That remains to be seen. We have a few versions here— that's what I wanted to show you so that you can show Nina."

Callie found herself wondering if it was really necessary for her to translate these diagrams for her sister, who had been living and breathing this project for months. Wouldn't Ben know that Nina could do this herself? But she obediently looked down as he pointed out the distinctions in the different plans.

Just as he was explaining how the location of the office on version two was different from version one, Callie heard a ping—a text coming into her phone. Reflexively, she glanced over at Zoe, who had looked up. Her niece held out the phone. "Someone wants to see you, Aunt Callie," she said.

Callie's brow furrowed and she took the phone. Despite her age, Zoe was starting to read. The message was from Jason. He'd contacted her a few times since the bowling excursion, and she kept telling him that she had a conflict. This latest text read, I know you've been busy, but I hope that I can see you sometime soon.

She took a deep breath and expelled it slowly.

"Problem?" Ben asked.

She shrugged and held up her phone. "It's Jason. The bowling date guy."

"I thought that wasn't going anywhere."

She sighed. "It's not. He just hasn't caught on yet."

He cocked his head and raised his eyebrows.

She bit the inside of her lip. "You're a man," she began.

Ben glanced down at himself. "Last time I checked."

Callie allowed a half smile. "If you went out with someone a couple of times and she didn't want to see you again, would you want her to tell you straight out? Or if she turned you down a couple of times, would you figure out that she wasn't interested?"

Ben pursed his lips. "Hmm. That's tough. No one is ever not interested in me."

"Of course. That goes without saying," Callie replied dryly. "But if you could put yourself in someone else's shoes . . ."

"The average Joe." He pointed at the phone. "Or Jason."

"Yes. The poor schmo who doesn't have women falling at his feet wherever he goes."

Ben tapped his mouth with his index finger. "Well," he began, with mock seriousness. "There's something to be said for honesty."

"Ugh. That's what I was afraid of." Callie dropped into the rolling chair next to her as she handed the phone back to Zoe.

"Sorry. I calls them as I sees them," he said, shrugging. "My brother used to have a rule. If he asked a woman out twice and she declined both times, that was it for her."

Callie looked up at him. "And how did that work out?"

"Okay, I guess. He's married."

Suddenly Zoe spoke. "Mommy says Aunt Callie won't get married until she gets over Ethan."

Callie's face grew hot as Ben gazed at her. "Zoe!" she exclaimed. She wondered if Zoe even knew what she was talking about.

"But that's what Mommy said," Zoe said stubbornly, looking at Ben and adding, "They're in a movie together."

Great. Now he'll think we made a sex tape.

"Go back to your game," Callie said, her head in her hands. She sensed Ben sitting down next to her and uncovered her eyes. He had spun the chair in her direction.

"This sounds interesting," he said.

"You can't believe everything kids say." She aimed for a light tone but knew her cheeks were probably glowing, and not in a good way.

"Oh, I don't know about that. When my niece told me that her mom only takes out the vase I gave them when I come to visit, it turned out to be true."

"Yes, well, that's only if they've picked up on accurate information. When Nina was five, she told her best friend that Mr. Trapani next door was the tooth fairy, because Joey Trapani had told *her* that his dad was the tooth fairy. That certainly wasn't true."

"So what you're saying is that Nina *did* say it, but that she's wrong."

"I suppose that's the logical conclusion."

"And this movie?"

How to answer that one?

"My ex-boyfriend from college is a screenwriter. My sister thinks his screenplay—he wrote *Rerouting*—is about me."

"Well." Ben paused. "I suppose I wouldn't want you to believe everything my brother might say about me."

Callie exhaled. "Exactly."

"And I can't imagine living in such close quarters helps matters," Ben added.

Callie smiled at him gratefully. "No, it really doesn't."

Ben tapped on the table. "Oh, I met your mother the other day. Nina asked that I give her a tour of the house."

Callie tried to read his expression. She could imagine how that would have gone. It was likely that whatever layout choices Nina had made, Lorraine would have made the opposite. "And how did that go?"

"Let's just say at least she didn't suggest that we put the front of the house on a hinge so it could be opened with a garage door opener."

Callie laughed. "Consider yourself lucky. But to be fair, having her up here has been a big help." Although traffic was bound to be worsening every minute that passed, Callie didn't really want to leave. "Are you from around here?"

"Depends what you call 'around here.' Long Island. So just a traffic jam away."

"Are your parents still there?"

Ben nodded. "They're not together anymore, but they're both still there. They complain more about the winters now, but with their grandkids in the city, I'd be surprised if they go anywhere. They put a lot of pressure on my brother to move out near them, but my sister-in-law would sooner stab herself in the eye."

"Yes, I'm quite sure Michael is delighted that our parents moved to Florida full-time." Grudgingly, she glanced at her watch. "Oh, wow, look at the time." She turned to Zoe. "We should get going, Binks."

Robotically, Zoe stood, still intent on the screen.

Ben rolled up the drawings and handed them to Callie.

"Anytime your sister needs something, she's welcome to send you as her errand girl."

Callie inclined her head. "Well, thank you very much." She hesitated and then added, "I'm happy to come."

They looked at each other for a moment, and then Zoe broke the silence. "Are we going?"

"Yes, Binks, we're going." Callie placed her hand on her niece's shoulder and steered her out of the room.

When Callie arrived home from work the following day, she found Zoe curled up on the living room couch, watching Noggin. She kissed her niece on the head and then went up-stairs to get her book. As she neared the top of the stairs, she heard voices.

"Don't you think I keep asking myself what I might have done to end up stuck in this bed?" Nina's voice fairly trembled with rage.

Lorraine's tones were clipped. "I'm not suggesting you *did* anything. I'm just saying that it's too bad you had to do so much running around with the move here, and taking care of Zoe, and dealing with the construction . . ."

"And how else would it get done? You do know that women in other parts of the world work in the fields until their babies literally drop out of them, right? And because they have no birth control, they have babies well into their forties . . . in case you were going to bring up my age again."

"And what are the infant mortality rates in those places?" Lorraine asked sharply.

Callie could picture Nina's face—the tightness of her features as she tried not to scream. She wondered if she should try to smooth things over. Or at least bring this useless debate to a halt. She was about to continue up the stairs when Lorraine spoke again.

"Anyway, it's a shame Michael can't help out more." Lorraine's tone was light, as if it were a throwaway comment, but Callie knew the feelings that lay beneath it. *Oh no, this won't be good.*

Nina's voice was little more than a hiss. "Michael helps in his own way. He works as hard as he does to make a good life for us. Do you think he likes being gone twelve hours a day? He doesn't. But it's what he has to do." Nina paused. "After all," she began again, her tone having shifted. "It's not like we get any help."

"What are you talking about? What am I doing here, spending winter in New Jersey? I could be in eighty-degree weather right now, looking out at the ocean," Lorraine said sharply.

"That's not what I'm talking about, and you know it," Nina replied, her inflection harsh.

"Oh, I see. This is about your sister again."

What?

"Why shouldn't she live here in the house? It's empty and paid for. She's on her own, living on a teacher's salary. It's different for you," Lorraine continued.

When Nina spoke again, her anger had dissipated, replaced by resignation. Clearly, this was not the first time they'd had this conversation. "Mom, plenty of single people actually manage to support themselves, without free housing. You're not doing Callie any favors."

Silence. Callie could picture Lorraine looking blankly at Nina. Callie herself was now glued to the top step, afraid to move on the creaky old boards and reveal that she'd been listening. More important, she wanted to know what Nina was going to say. At least, she thought she did. Part of her wanted to cover her ears and sing, the way she'd have done as a child when her parents told her it was time to go to bed.

"You're enabling her. You're letting her not grow up. No, don't look at me like that. She hasn't built up any confidence that she can really take care of herself. Make smart decisions. Recover from mistakes. She can hide out here, safe and sound, and continue as she always has."

Who the hell made her a psychologist? Or an expert? Or anyone who even really knows me? Does she have any idea how good I am at my job? How good I am with kids? Yes, maybe the rest of my life isn't exactly where I'd like it to be, but, well, that's just the way things are at the moment.

The blood rushed to Callie's ears and she didn't catch Lorraine's response. No longer caring about the creaky stairs, she stomped up the last step and into her room and shut the door. She stopped herself just before she slammed it. No need to give Nina any other reason to call her a child. But that didn't keep her from picking up one of Zoe's stuffed animals and hurling it against the wall. The poor monkey didn't know what hit it.

CHAPTER TWENTY-FOUR

After

The Friday before Thanksgiving, Nina had an appointment with her obstetrician. Michael left work early to drive her, and when they came home, Nina—unsurprisingly—declined to go upstairs. No one could argue with her decision to spend the rest of the evening on the living room sofa. "I feel like I've been let out of prison," she declared.

Since overhearing Nina and Lorraine's conversation a few days earlier, Callie still felt a prickle—or more—of resentment whenever she looked at her sister, and had been steering clear of her. It was one thing for Nina to expound her version of tough love directly to Callie. It was another to talk about her behind her back. And to their mother, of all people.

But there was no avoiding the conference that took place in the living room that night to discuss Thanksgiving dinner. Nina stretched out on the couch, propped up on pillows. Lorraine was in one armchair, and Michael was in the other. Callie took a seat on the floor slightly behind Nina's head so she wouldn't have to look at her. Everyone said, "Callie, you can't sit on the floor," but it wasn't at all clear what the solution was, so she stayed where she was. Nina offered, in a tone Callie interpreted as halfhearted, "I can shift my feet so you can sit on the sofa." Callie's "No, thanks" was clipped.

"So," Nina began. "What are we doing about Thanksgiving dinner?"

Since their parents had relocated year-round to Florida, Thanksgiving had become Nina's responsibility. Every year, she lamented the days of preparation and the hours in the kitchen, but Callie knew she secretly loved it. Not necessarily all the work, but the beauty of the table once it was laid. There was always a gorgeous seasonal centerpiece, and Nina would pull out their wedding china—simple, classic Vera Wang. She tried new recipes from her glossy cookbooks. Her stuffings featured wild mushrooms and leeks or oysters and bacon, and her sides included things like herbed asparagus with shiitakes and sweet-pea-and-mint puree. It was a sea change from the canned carrots and peas they'd grown up on.

The first year Nina hosted, Callie said she'd bring dessert. She was proud of herself for not picking up a pie at the bakery or buying a box mix, and instead followed a recipe for pumpkin cake with cream cheese frosting. Callie thought it tasted delicious, even if she had to admit it wasn't the most appealing-looking confection she'd ever seen. The following year, Nina told her to please not worry about it, that she would take care of dessert.

"Maybe I can do some of the meal," Nina continued.

"Absolutely not," Lorraine said firmly.

Michael nodded. "For once, I agree with your mother."

Lorraine looked at her son-in-law. "Will wonders never cease?"

"Come on. This is getting us nowhere," Nina cut in. "I can sit for the prep. You can all help."

"Forget it, Nina. We're not risking your health and the baby's health." Michael's voice was firm.

Nina glared. Or at least, from the set of her shoulders and the appearance of the back of her head, Callie assumed she was glaring.

"You know what, why don't *I* cook?" Callie proposed from her perch on the floor.

Everyone turned toward her.

"You?" Nina asked.

"You don't cook!" exclaimed Lorraine.

"Well, no time like the present to start."

Before Lorraine could speak again, Nina interrupted. "Maybe you could do that delicious soup as an appetizer."

Callie was pleasantly surprised by her encouragement.

Nina began again. "And I can give you my file. I've been collecting recipes. There was a really nice-looking stuffing I found online. And we haven't done brussels sprouts before. I thought we could roast them in balsamic vinegar . . ."

Oh no, this isn't going to be the Nina show.

"No, thanks, I'll figure it out."

"But . . ."

"Nina, I've got it." The words came out more sharply than she'd intended, and Nina swiveled to look at her.

"You don't need to bite my head off. I'm just making suggestions."

"Right. Your *suggestions*." Callie felt everyone's eyes on her.

"What's with you?"

This was not the time or place. Callie didn't know when the time or place would be, but this wasn't it. "Nothing. Long day, that's all."

Nina's eyes remained on her, and Callie knew she wasn't sure whether to believe her. But then Nina sighed and turned away.

"Well, that's settled, then," Lorraine said, with an air of finality.

"Excellent." Michael clapped his hands together. "You ready to go upstairs, Neen?"

"I'm comfy here. Why don't we stay and find a movie to watch?"

As they channel surfed, Lorraine and Callie went into the kitchen.

"What's with you and your sister?"

"Nothing." Callie chewed her cuticle and avoided her mother's eyes.

Lorraine looked at her with narrowed eyes. "Good. I'm glad to hear it. It's the holidays. Your dad is coming. Nina has enough on her mind. Whatever it is—and I *know* it's something—this isn't the time." She put her hands on her hips. "So—what's this soup Nina was talking about?"

"I made pumpkin soup a few weeks ago. Not hard—and it was yummy."

"Sounds great. And then we can do the old standards. I haven't had green bean casserole in years!"

"We? I thought you were retired from cooking."

"Well—Thanksgiving . . ."

Callie shook her head. "You can be my assistant. I'll plan the menu."

Lorraine looked appraisingly at her daughter. "Okay, then," she said, her tone a mixture of surprise and amusement.

Callie opened her laptop and searched recipes, jotting ideas on a pad of paper while Lorraine dug through the pantry.

"How old is this flour?" she asked.

"I have no idea. It might be here from before you moved."

"Callie!"

Was it because she didn't label the contents of her pantry by date? Or because she didn't bake? Callie wasn't sure what was so objectionable—but maybe there *was* something to be noted about the fact that she'd done so little to make this *her* kitchen and not Lorraine's.

Lorraine walked across the room to toss the (possibly perfectly good) flour in the trash. "You know who I had coffee with today?"

Callie shook her head and resisted saying, *But I'm sure you'll tell me.*

"Sharon Kershaw."

Someone she actually knew. "How is she?"

"She's good. Thinking about retiring soon. She asked about you."

Sharon Kershaw was a friend of Lorraine's from one of the many evening enrichment classes she had taken when Nina and Callie were young. Callie couldn't remember if it was knitting or macramé or conversational French. Or something else entirely. Lorraine had gone through a period when she was signing up for all sorts of things. In retrospect, Callie suspected it was her mother's way of finding adult conversation after long days alone with her two girls. Several nights a week, as soon as Martin came home, Lorraine jumped into her Volvo and zipped out of the driveway.

Whichever class they'd met in, Lorraine and Sharon continued to stay in touch, despite the fact that Lorraine was a stay-at-home mom and Sharon worked full-time as an administrator at a prestigious private school in northern New Jersey.

When Callie was a junior in college, Sharon offered her a job in their summer program—but Callie turned it down to spend the summer with Ethan in the Hudson Valley. Even then, it felt a little silly to have forgone such a promising opportunity just to be with her boyfriend. She remained so embarrassed about her choice that she didn't apply to work there after she'd graduated and was no longer going to the West Coast.

"Is she still at the same school?" Callie asked.

Lorraine nodded. "She's dean of the lower school. It could have been a good place for you to teach. Could still be. I'm sure she'd be happy to talk to you—a lot of time has passed now."

Callie sighed. "Yeah, it has been a long time. But I'm happy where I am."

Lorraine shrugged in a "suit yourself" way and opened the door to the cabinet where the spices and seasonings lived.

"I'm actually beat. I think I'm going to go up to bed," Callie said. "I'll finish this menu tomorrow."

"Good night, sweetie," Lorraine replied absently, studying a container of paprika, likely attempting to carbon-date it.

CHAPTER TWENTY-FIVE

Before

It was spring of junior year, and I sat on the bed in our dorm room waiting for Ethan to come out of the shower. I'd just hung up the phone and was excited to share my news, but there was a bubble of unease in my stomach that wasn't there before I spoke with my mother.

The door opened and Ethan walked in, a towel around his waist. I didn't understand how he could walk down the hall practically naked. Even after nearly three years of dorm living, I still wore a heavy terry-cloth robe as I padded to and from the shower. Ethan picked up a second towel and rubbed furiously at his hair.

"So, I just got off the phone with my mom," I began.

"Hmm?" Ethan removed the towel from his head and dried his chest.

"I was just talking to my mom," I repeated. When Ethan didn't respond, I continued. "Remember I told you how I saw her friend, the one who's at that private school in New Jersey, when I was home for the holidays?"

"Mm-hmm," Ethan said, retrieving his boxers from the dresser and dropping his towel to put them on. I knew he was trying to distract me, but it wasn't going to work—no matter how cute his glutes were.

"They're going to be hiring a couple of people for their summer camp, including in the kindergarten program. They don't usually hire from outside for camp—most of their teachers stay on through the summer, especially with the little kids. But Sharon—my mom's friend—told my mom that if I'm interested, the position is mine."

Ethan's eyebrows drew together. "I thought we were staying up here this summer."

"I know we talked about it, but this is a great opportunity. It will be good for my résumé, and good experience, too."

Ethan sat on the bed. "But I already have my internship lined up at the radio station. If I want to get into journalism, I need that broadcast experience."

I bit my lip. "Well, maybe it makes sense for us to do our own things this summer."

He frowned. "Where's this coming from?"

"Nowhere. It's just . . . we both have good opportunities, but they're not in the same place."

"This is our last summer in college. Our last free summer. You don't want to spend it together?" There was no mistaking the hurt in his voice.

Nearly all my friends complained about boyfriends who "needed their space," or who disappeared as things got intense. I couldn't relate. Ethan wanted me by his side nearly all the time. The way he loved me so much made me feel safe, and I adored being with him. But I also felt a little bit, well . . . *caged* was the word that kept coming to mind.

Sometimes, I wished I could sleep in the study without hurting his feelings.

"I'm not saying I don't *want* to spend it together. I'm just saying it might make sense. It's just a few months—and I'll only be two hours away. You have your car—you can come and see me. Or maybe I can borrow my mom's car and come up here."

Ethan returned to the dresser for a pair of jeans. When he spoke again, his back was still turned. "It's just not what I had in mind. We've always said it would be nice to spend time in the Hudson Valley over the summer. Go to a Tanglewood concert. A weekend at Lake George. This is our last chance."

I bit my lower lip again, harder this time. It was true.

He swiveled to face me again. "It's not like anyone in San Francisco is going to have heard of that school. It's not like it's—I don't know—Andover or something. So it's probably not any better for your résumé than anything else."

I opened my mouth and closed it again. Maybe it wasn't the best time to bring up the fact that I wasn't as set on California as Ethan. No matter how great our summer there was, it didn't feel like home to me. Ethan kept saying he'd found his place in the world. But I wasn't sure my place was three thousand miles away from my family. And I wasn't sure I was such a fan of the Bay Area—not long term, anyway. It was overwhelming to think about life after graduation.

Ethan sat on the bed again, cross-legged this time, and faced me. "Come on, let's stick with the plan. It'll be great." He touched the necklace I was wearing—the one he'd had made for me as my twenty-first-birthday gift. With his index finger, he traced the stone that lay in the hollow of my throat—the pretty one I found the day he taught me to skip stones. I hadn't realized he'd slipped it into his pocket.

He leaned his forehead against mine.

"I guess," I sighed. "How can I ever refuse you?"

He smiled. "That's my girl." He kissed me and then drew back. "I've got to run to class. See you at lunch?"

I nodded. Of course I'd see him at lunch. And at every other meal.

CHAPTER TWENTY-SIX

After

Callie and Nina's dad, Martin, arrived the Monday before Thanksgiving. He immediately went upstairs to see Nina and, after hugging her, he stood awkwardly at her bedside. Uncomfortable with anything smacking of "women's problems," he was clearly afraid any question he might ask about how she was feeling or how the baby was doing might lead down the rabbit hole.

Callie had devised a Thanksgiving menu of simple and traditional items—glazed carrots, brown-butter mashed potatoes, herb-roasted turkey, sautéed green beans, and wild rice-and-mushroom stuffing. She brought in a pumpkin pie from a local bakery. It was a little overwhelming, and the kitchen looked like a tornado had touched down—twice—but she and Lorraine had more fun than she would have anticipated working together.

The six of them sat down to eat in late afternoon. There had been some resistance to Nina's plan to come downstairs to eat, but it was halfhearted. It was Thanksgiving, after all. And Callie's anger had faded—she could never hang on to it long, which was probably a good thing.

The turkey sat on the well-worn carving board, and the accompaniments were loaded into Corningware dishes Callie remembered from childhood—white, with cornflower-blue flowers. Unlike in some families, where silence settled on the table once people's plates were loaded, talking at the meal was continuous. Lorraine never had any trouble keeping up a stream of steady chatter. For years, when all else failed, she could always discuss what had happened the night before on *ER* or *NYPD Blue*. One might have thought that John Carter and Nurse Hathaway were actual members of the family, considering the familiarity with which Lorraine spoke of them.

Now, as they began to eat, Martin spoke first. "Nina, your house is really coming along." He popped a heaping forkful of stuffing into his mouth. Michael had driven him over that morning for a tour.

Nina smiled ruefully. "Thanks, Dad. It's so frustrating that I can't see it—except for the photos Michael takes on his phone."

"Just think what a wonderful surprise it will be when you get over there," observed Lorraine. "It'll be like one of those home renovation shows on HGTV. 'The big reveal.'"

"Do you really think that's the kind of thing I'd go for?" Nina asked, her eyebrows arched.

Michael laughed. "Hardly. I think if I ever got us on one of those shows and they redid something without your input, you'd kill me."

"No kidding." Nina moved the green beans from side to side on her plate. "Maybe you could take me over this weekend?"

Michael shook his head. "No."

"Come on, just once," she wheedled, putting her fork down. "I won't ask again."

"Let's not start. You're not walking up and down the stairs. You know the doctor just told you she wants you to stay on the same restrictions. She wouldn't say it if she didn't think it was necessary."

Nina snorted. "It's CYA."

Zoe looked up from her plate, where she'd made a mash-up of the side dishes. "What's CYA, Mommy?"

"Change your attitude," Nina said promptly as she picked up her fork again. Callie was impressed. "Are you eating your food or just playing with it?"

"It's kind of weird," Zoe objected.

"Well, eat the turkey then. You like turkey."

Zoe speared the smallest piece of turkey she could find and slowly put it in her mouth.

A rare, but tense, silence settled over the table for a moment.

Hoping to change the mood, Callie spoke. "By the way, I'm going to LA for work in February."

"What's in LA?" Lorraine asked.

"A conference on early childhood education. One of the other teachers was supposed to go, but she can't, so I'm taking her spot."

"Well, isn't that nice," Lorraine enthused. "Getting out of the cold for a few days."

Callie served herself some more potatoes, feeling Nina's eyes on her as Lorraine prattled about a friend whose son lived in San Diego. She knew she was taking a chance by announcing the trip, but figured better now than trying to keep it a secret. Nina would inevitably find out anyway and entertain suspicions about her motives. At least for now, Callie was keeping her date with Ethan in New York a secret. Days after receiving his email, she'd finally responded. She kept it short and friendly, saving all questions until their meeting.

"Oh, Callie," Martin interjected. "I think you're right about the house needing painting. We should look into that in the spring. And we should have the roof looked at, too."

Before Callie could respond, Nina spoke. "Dad, are you sure it makes sense for you guys to keep putting money into this house?"

"You have to do routine maintenance. It'll come back to bite you if you don't."

Nina fiddled with the fork in her hand. "That's not what I'm saying."

Callie had the distinct feeling that Nina was assiduously avoiding looking at her.

Nina continued. "I'm saying that you haven't lived here for seven years. What's the point?"

Callie cleared her throat. "Um, *I* live here."

"You can find your own place," Nina replied shortly. "It's not their responsibility to house you."

"I didn't say it was," Callie countered, putting down her fork. "What business is it of yours anyway?"

"It's my business because they're my parents, too."

"What does that have to do with anything? You just think it's unfair. And that ticks you off." Callie heard her voice rise several decibels, and she glanced at Zoe, who was burying her green beans under a pile of mashed potatoes.

"It has nothing to do with fairness. Though you're right. It isn't fair," snapped Nina.

"Girls!" Lorraine cut in. "This isn't the time."

"Well, when is the time?" Nina asked angrily. "It's a serious issue. You need to be thinking about your long-term future. Making sure you have the funds to take care of yourselves. The real estate market is back up. If it's as hot this spring as it was last year, it could be a great time to sell. That would be a nice nest egg."

"You don't need to worry about our finances," Martin said calmly. "We're fine."

"I have a friend who's a real estate agent. She'd be happy to come in and give you an idea—"

"Enough," Lorraine said warningly. "We're not ruining our holiday meal talking about this."

Nina opened her mouth and closed it abruptly before putting her fork down with a clatter.

Zoe looked up from her plate, where not a single green bean could be seen under the mashed potato blanket. She cocked her head and gazed at each of them in turn. "Is it time for dessert?"

CHAPTER TWENTY-SEVEN

After

Callie and Nina avoided each other the rest of the holiday weekend. Nina once tried to bring up the subject of the house again, but Callie refused to engage. The arrangement she had with their parents was none of Nina's business.

"Nina, let's drop it. We have to live in this house together for the next two months, at least," she snapped. *This house that wouldn't be here for you to live in rent-free during your construction if Mom and Dad had sold it.*

Callie wasn't sorry to go to work on Monday. Aside from the smoldering hostility between her and her sister, a viral outbreak had begun on Saturday. First, Zoe's nose started to run. By Sunday, the runny nose was accompanied by a fever, Michael was sneezing, and Lorraine had a hacking cough. They all tried to keep their germy selves away from Nina, but Callie wasn't particularly concerned for herself. After years of working with children, who were often literally covered with snot, she had built up an immunity that any pharmaceutical company would have been happy to bottle and market at a very high price.

Aside from the phlegmy hacking, the house was enormously crowded. Martin originally tried to share the twin bed with Lorraine, which Callie thought was ridiculous. Clearly, they ended up thinking so, too, because now he was bunking on the couch in the living room. Callie felt a little guilty for not offering to move down there herself, but she'd already relocated twice. And she knew Zoe didn't want to share with Grampa. ("He snores!") On the upside, Martin was headed back to Florida that Monday afternoon—happy to escape before the epidemic caught up with him. Callie didn't point out that he'd already been exposed. Undoubtedly, many people would disembark from that flight with an unwanted gift from the unobtrusive man with the silvery hair.

Over the weekend, she'd also gotten a message from Liam's mom, Ellen, asking to set up a meeting. Callie was surprised. Things with Liam had been going fairly smoothly. But she'd emailed back saying that of course she could meet. Ellen's reply further puzzled her. She wrote that she hoped she wasn't overstepping, but she needed some advice. They arranged a four o'clock meeting for that Monday. Callie was glad for the excuse not to go straight home. Ironclad immunity or not, the more time away from the germ factory, the better.

While she got settled in her classroom that morning, smiling at the kids' construction-paper turkeys, Callie wondered what Ellen wanted to discuss. And as she thought about how to occupy her time from the end of her workday at two thirty until four o'clock, it occurred to her that they didn't need to meet at the school. She quickly shot an email to Ellen suggesting that they get coffee instead. Although it felt a little strange, it sounded like Ellen's desire to meet wasn't for a typical parent-teacher conference—so why not change up the setting?

Ellen emailed back almost immediately, saying she'd be happy to meet wherever was convenient.

That afternoon—after a long day of trying to corral children who, after not being in school for four days, had forgotten everything they knew about sitting still, following directions, and listening—Callie went into downtown Brook Hill.

On her way to the toy store, intending to search for Hanukkah gift ideas for Zoe, she passed Alouette, one of the boutiques whose high prices typically kept her far away. But she was struck by a beautiful waterfall cardigan in the window, which was accented with a herringbone scarf. *Why not check it out?*

She stepped inside, the bells on the door tinkling gently. Because she could fit into nearly all of the clothes she'd worn for the past ten years, she rarely bought anything new. Perhaps she could justify a more expensive purchase after all.

Wandering through the store, she touched the soft fabrics and admired the unique pieces. These were things she'd never find at the mall. Maybe that's what customers were paying for here—the uniqueness. As she looked at a pretty sweater dress in a beautiful and unusual shade of deep orange with a plunging cowl neck, it occurred to her that she should give some thought to what she should wear for her "date" with Ethan.

They'd arranged to meet on the night of the premiere, at the bar of the boutique hotel in TriBeCa where he was staying. Other than a few short email messages back and forth to confirm the time and place, they'd had no further communication. For her part, Callie didn't know what to say—and figured it made more sense to delay real conversation until they saw one other.

There was no hint in the impersonal messages that they'd had any sort of history together. But, of course, they had. Callie kept wondering how much of that history had made it into *Rerouting* and continued to poke around for information about the movie. She'd read the interview with Sarina Apple in *Glamour*, but it hadn't told her much other than what items the actress carried in her purse and who her acting influences were—an odd combination of Audrey Hepburn and Reese Witherspoon. She did find some stills from the movie, though. The one that she kept looking at was of Nick/Ethan and Sarina/Callie. Sarina was wearing a necklace remarkably similar to the one Callie had at the bottom of her shoebox of mementos. Nick was standing behind her. The two of them were both looking into a mirror, presumably at the necklace, but really at each other. Callie knew it was just acting, but she remembered what it felt like to look at someone like that—and have them look at you the same way. *What would it be like to look into Ethan's eyes again after all this time?*

Browsing the rack of clothes, she found the orange dress in her size, and then continued to pick up other items—a forest-green sweater, a cream silk blouse, a pair of wool slacks. Nina would say they were grown-up clothes. Callie went into one of the small dressing rooms—there were only two, with heavy brown velvet curtains looped up on single hooks. After slipping off her own clothes—a short pleated gray skirt over black leggings, a red sweater, an infinity scarf looped around her neck, and her old Doc Martens—she tried on her selections. Nothing grabbed her until she stepped out of the dressing room in the orange dress and looked at herself in a standing oval mirror with a heavy pewter frame.

"Oh, don't you look gorgeous!" A salesgirl appeared behind her.

In the mirror, the dress hugged her curves, the scoop of the neck showing off her collarbones. The color, although unusual, set off her skin and eyes, making her think of a luminous fall day. She smoothed the skirt and met the salesgirl's eyes in the mirror. "Thanks."

"You *have* to get that."

Callie knew she was trying to make a sale, but she also knew the salesgirl was right.

A few minutes later, with the dress neatly wrapped in tissue paper inside a chic black shopping bag with ribbon handles, Callie stepped back outside. Checking her watch, she saw she still had time to kill. For the heck of it, she stepped into a nail salon.

Shortly before the appointed hour, her nails freshly painted an unusual shade of mauve, she went into Sip, the café where she frequently met Tess—and ordered a hot chocolate. With the frosty air that had swept in after Thanksgiving, it felt like that kind of day. Ellen hurried in a bit later, her cheeks flushed from the cold and her hair falling out of its clip.

"I'm so sorry I'm late," she apologized as she pulled off her gloves.

"Don't worry about it—it's fine. Relax. Get yourself something to drink."

Ellen smiled gratefully and went up to the counter to order a coffee. When she returned to the table, she sat, warming her hands on the cardboard cup. "Thanks so much for meeting me. I know this is a little unorthodox."

Callie waited while Ellen looked down at her coffee and looked back up again.

"I guess the only way to say this is to just say it. Doug— Liam's dad—and I talked over the holiday weekend. For a long time." She sighed, absently pushing loose strands of hair behind her ear. "It's definitely over." Ellen pinched the bridge of her nose and momentarily closed her eyes as if the words themselves were painful.

"I'm so sorry."

Ellen's shoulders lifted and dropped again. "I don't think it could have turned out any differently. In some ways, it's a relief that we've made a decision."

"I guess that's a good way to look at it."

"Anyway, I wanted to talk to you because Doug is looking for a place to live, and as soon as he finds one, he's moving out. We don't know how to tell Liam." Ellen looked pained. "I know that we're going to end up screwing him up, but if we could screw him up as little as possible, that would be good."

"You're not going to screw him up!"

"Thanks for your confidence. But we don't know where to start—and I thought maybe you'd have some advice." If anyone could look simultaneously hopeful and despairing, it was Ellen at that moment.

"Wow." Callie felt overwhelmed. This was not in her wheelhouse. "Well, I'm not a child psychologist, and I think it would definitely be good for you and Liam's dad to talk to a professional who could give you better guidance—but I can give you some thoughts."

"Anything. I'd be so grateful."

So Callie talked about saying only what was necessary—not getting into details that Liam wouldn't understand or care about. And emphasizing that the new living arrangement had nothing to do with him, and that both of his parents loved him as much as they ever did. Callie said she'd check the school "library"—the bookshelves behind Judith's desk—for some books, both for Ellen and Doug and for Liam. She also offered to ask Judith for names of family counselors. Ellen took notes, explaining, "If I treat this the way I would any other project, maybe I won't cry all the time."

After Callie offered a few more ideas, Ellen put her pen down. "You have no idea how much this means to me. I've been dealing with this basically on my own," she said.

"What about your family? Or friends?"

"I haven't said anything to my parents yet—they're in Wisconsin, so I've been able to keep them in the dark. They're going to freak out. And I'm just not ready to face my friends around here—we're the first couple I know to get divorced." Ellen sighed. "I talk a little to some old friends from school, but they don't know what to say."

"That has to be hard." Callie imagined how she'd react if Jenna called with this kind of news—and suspected she wouldn't do any better than Ellen's friends.

"I just never expected this. It's totally a cliché, but I thought we'd be together forever. Now I wonder if we were just too young. How could the person you love at eighteen still be the right fit for you when you're thirty?"

"Oh, I can see how it's possible," Callie offered, her voice unconvincing to her own ears.

"Possible, but probable?" asked Ellen. "I mean, I'll always be grateful that we have Liam. So I can't say it was a mistake. But I keep wondering if we were just staying together because it was easier. Inertia. If we should have dated other people. If we could have figured out sooner that this wasn't going to work for the long haul."

Callie's head swam. She and Ethan weren't Ellen and Doug. She didn't even really know this woman sitting across from her. But she couldn't dismiss the feeling that she was staring at an alternate version of herself. Would she and Ethan have made it if they'd stayed together? Was this an after-the-fact cautionary tale, suggesting that she had made the right decision? Or, in some perverse way, did it mean that the decisions you make at that age can be so foolish—and that Callie had made the worst mistake of her life by ending things?

With a mental shake of her head, she reminded herself that dissecting the past was pointless. In just about six weeks, she'd see Ethan, the man she'd loved when she was eighteen. Was she about to reach the end of the wiser path? Now that they'd grown up separately, was this the time for them?

She was starting to think that instead of coffee, she and Ellen should have met over a bottle of wine.

Ellen spoke again, and Callie pulled her head back into the moment to focus. "It is what it is. There's no point in going over and over the past—although knowing that, and actually being able to stop doing it, are two different things."

Callie knew all too well how right the other woman was. She walked back out into the cold a few paces behind Ellen, feeling both unsettled and excited. Stepping back in order to move forward wasn't easy.

Callie was on her break the following day when Nina texted, asking that she call when she had a chance. With Lorraine and Zoe still sick, Callie worried that one of them had gotten worse—or that Nina had caught whatever they had.

Nina sounded tentative. "I know you're not very happy with me right now. And I know you're going to hate this. But it turns out we can't get the trim tile we wanted, and now we need to rethink the master bathroom. Margo—you know, the decorator—got some samples for us, and we need to decide what we're ordering, like, *yesterday*. I would've had Mom pick them up when she took Zoe to school, but, obviously, they didn't go, and Margo can't make it down here today—"

Callie interrupted her. "Fine, Nina, I'll go."

"Really?" Nina's tone suggested that Callie had agreed to walk on hot coals.

"It's fine. I'll go," she repeated. She could do without the drive, but she didn't mind the thought of possibly seeing Ben. No, she didn't mind that at all.

"Great!" Nina gushed. "Thank you *so* much, Callie. I *really* appreciate it. I'll let Margo know you're coming."

A few hours later, Callie was once again walking up the stairs to the glass door at HMK Design. She opened it to find Kat at her desk, talking to another woman who was much more conservatively dressed—and with much more conservative hair.

"Speak of the devil!" Kat exclaimed. "This is Nina's sister. Callie, right? This is Margo. We were just saying you'd be here soon."

Callie took Margo's proffered hand and shook it, not able to prevent her eyes from flickering toward Ben's office door, which was closed. She suppressed a sigh of disappointment.

Margo had Callie follow her to her own office, where a number of tile samples were laid out on a table. She talked to her about shower tile, floor tile, bullnose, edging, and counter-top stone, and Callie realized she was looking at four different options for the bathroom. As far as she was concerned, any one of them would be lovely, and she was glad that it wasn't her decision to make. Margo grouped each set of samples into separate large envelopes and then put two envelopes into each of two tote bags.

"So, are you the sister who made that adorable sign for Nina's daughter?" Margo asked as she packed everything up.

"That's me," Callie replied, surprised.

Margo looked up. "It's so sweet! Nina showed it to me to give me ideas for colors for her daughter's room."

Huh. Who knew?

"You know," Margo continued. "People pay a lot of money for that kind of custom artwork. Have you done others?"

Callie shook her head. "I draw and paint a lot, but not usu-ally stuff like that. Although I did paint the bookshelves and a mural in my classroom. I'm a teacher."

"Well, if you're interested, you could put together a little portfolio, and I can keep you in mind for my clients doing kids' rooms."

It was an idea out of nowhere—but it immediately struck a chord. "Wow. Sure. I never thought about it. But I will."

Margo walked her out, as far as the glass door. Ben's door was now open, but the angle didn't allow Callie to see inside. She went downstairs and stopped before stepping outside to put on her gloves and readjust the bags—which not only felt like they were full of rocks, they literally were. She'd just pushed the door open when she heard a sound behind her. Glancing back up, she saw Ben stepping out of the office, wearing a puffy winter jacket.

"Oh, hello!" she called up to him, wondering if her slouchy knit hat was on straight but not having a free hand to adjust it.

He smiled as he walked down. "Hey. What are you doing here?"

Did he really not know? "Picking up some tile samples for Nina." She swung the bags as proof.

"Those must be heavy. Let me take one."

She passed one over gratefully and stepped outside, then headed toward her car with Ben following. Then he spoke again. "Actually, I'm on my way to get coffee. I have a new-client meeting tonight and I need some caffeine. Want to come?"

Does the sun rise in the east?

"Sure. It'll save me from turning right back around to drive home." It would also get her snarled in rush hour traffic, but she was willing to make the sacrifice.

Ben suggested they drop the tile in Callie's car and then walk to Cuppa Joe, the café in which they'd met the day of Zoe's friend's birthday party. After a brisk walk in the cold, he held the door open for her, the warm air and aroma of coffee enveloping them as they stepped inside.

As it had been when Callie was there with Zoe, the glass case was full of brightly colored, buttery-looking baked goods. Callie found herself thinking about how long it had been since lunch, and her eyes scanned the heaped plates on the shelves.

"Are you going to get something to eat?" Ben asked.

"I'm tempted by those cupcakes, but I'm afraid they'll be disappointing. I can't say I've ever found bakery cupcakes to be as good as they look."

"I know what you mean. They're dry, or the frosting is too sweet. That said, you want to take a chance and split one?"

"Sure, why not?"

They agreed on a decadent-looking chocolate confection, and Ben paid for it, along with their drinks.

"You can get it next time," he said, when Callie protested. She liked the sound of there being a next time.

Soon they were seated at a round table next to the window, and Ben carefully began slicing the cupcake in half.

"Are you sure you don't need a measuring tape?"

"Sorry. It comes with the engineering training." Ben grinned as he finished cutting the sweet treat into two equal parts.

Callie slid her plastic fork into the cupcake. "Well, here goes nothing." She popped the rich-looking chocolate into her mouth, and her eyes widened. "This is actually good!"

"Yeah?" Ben tried a bite. "You're right. A cupcake that actually lives up to expectations."

"Who'd a thunk it?" Callie took another bite.

"So how was your Thanksgiving?" Ben asked as Callie chewed.

Callie told him how overcrowded the house was, and about the illness that had felled them one by one.

Ben nodded. "Ours is always complicated since my parents split up. They'll have the meal together now, but it's awkward. My dad and his wife don't like to go to my mom's and vice versa, and my sister-in-law doesn't want us all in their small apartment."

"What about your sister-in-law's family?"

"They're in Connecticut. Nobody wants to drive up there, but that's often what we end up doing because it's neutral territory and they have the room for everyone. That's where we were this year, actually."

"And how was it?"

Ben sipped his coffee and put his cup down. "Fine. No major drama—the best we can hope for."

"How long have your parents been divorced—if you don't mind me asking?"

Ben sighed. "A long time now. Over twenty years. You'd think things would have gotten better by now."

"So you were a kid."

"Thirteen. My brother was fifteen."

"Geez." Callie took her last bite of cupcake and shook her head as Ben offered some of his. "One of my students—he's four—his parents are splitting up. It's hard."

Ben nodded sympathetically. "I wonder if being so young will make it easier for him. He won't remember much about them being together, and it'll just be the way things are."

"You think it was worse for you and your brother, being teenagers?"

Ben pressed the back of his fork into the cupcake crumbs to collect the last bits of chocolate. "Who knows? I only know what we went through. But it was pretty crappy. We knew what was going on—had to deal with more information than we probably should have. My brother, Nate, had a really rough time with relationships for ages. He was just starting to date and didn't trust *anyone*. It was like he assumed being with someone meant getting hurt. I can't tell you how many nice girls he dumped—all to avoid getting close enough to anyone." Ben looked thoughtful. "At least, that's my armchair psychologist assessment of the situation."

"But it seems like he worked things out. He's settled now, right?"

"True. And it probably helped me. Watching what he was doing made me think long and hard about relationships. I managed to avoid making the same mistakes." He grinned. "Although I'm sure I made some other ones."

"Don't we all," Callie replied ruefully.

Ben held out his coffee cup. "I'll toast to that."

Callie tapped her cardboard cup against his.

"So, how's the kid in your class doing?"

Callie signed in relief that he hadn't asked about her own mistakes. "He's okay. A bit off-kilter, but that's to be expected."

Ben nodded. "Do you like teaching?"

Callie talked about how much she enjoyed the kids, despite the challenges. And she surprised herself by sharing that what she liked best about working with kids was seeing the world through their eyes—experiencing the wonder she was sure she herself once felt but had long forgotten. Ben's eyes widened in understanding. Once again she noticed how very lovely they were.

"I know what you mean. A while ago I took my niece and nephew to the Museum of Natural History. Going with them to see the whale—it was like it was the first time I was seeing it. I'd forgotten how awesome it was. And the dinosaur skeletons. I could see how they were imagining them—like *Jurassic Park* come alive. If that makes sense."

It certainly did make sense to Callie. What didn't make sense to her was how such a bright, understanding, good-looking man was single. Perhaps he had a girlfriend? But if he did, she wondered, would he be sitting here having coffee with her? Maybe he had a boyfriend? She took the last swallow of her coffee and put the cup down, clearing her throat and trying to get her head on straight. "Do you see much of them? Your niece and nephew?"

"About once a month. They always have a lot going on—dance and tae kwon do and who knows what—but we try to find a weekend day when we can, or I go have dinner with them. They're good kids. Seems like you have a nice relationship with Zoe."

"Definitely. She's great. I mean, she has her moments, of course . . ."

Ben laughed. "Who doesn't?" He drained his coffee cup and glanced at his watch. "I hate to say it, but I need to head off for my meeting."

"Well, at least you're caffeinated now." Callie inclined her head toward the empty cups.

"Good thing, too. Otherwise I might nod off while they tell me how they want to turn their three-bedroom house on a quarter-acre lot into a five-bedroom McMansion on an acre."

Callie's eyes widened. "Is that what they want?"

Ben smiled wryly. "That's what they *all* want."

Callie laughed.

"Anyway, thanks for keeping me company." Ben smiled again, more warmly.

Callie felt a flutter inside her chest. "Anytime."

"I'll hold you to that."

Callie busied herself putting on her coat. Ben picked up her hat, which had fallen to the floor, and when she looked up from buttoning her coat, he arranged it on her head. "Cute hat," he said, adjusting the brim.

"Thanks." She felt her face flush and hoped it wasn't obvious. "Good luck at your meeting." She willed her voice to be light.

"Thanks. Safe drive home."

"You, too." They left the café, headed in opposite directions. *Was she imagining the way he looked at her?* Callie didn't think so—but it had been a long time since she'd met anyone who she hoped would look at her that way.

CHAPTER TWENTY-EIGHT

After

Callie pulled into her driveway, wondering how she'd gotten there. She'd driven home on autopilot, her mind on Ben and on all that can go awry in relationships. Pushing those thoughts out of her head, she turned off the engine, retrieved the bags of tile from the back seat, and went into the house.

When she appeared in the master bedroom doorway, her sister looked up. Zoe was curled next to her, and the television was tuned to a cartoon about a mouse in a ballerina costume.

"Thank you *so* much, Callie," Nina exclaimed as Callie brought the bags over to her.

Lifting out the envelopes, Callie tried to remember what Margo had told her so that she could point out which piece was meant for which part of the bathroom. Soon Nina had three options arrayed around her on the bed; she had rejected the fourth immediately.

Callie had just stepped away when Nina called her back.

Callie turned, and Nina bit her lip. *What now?*

"I was thinking about this trip you're taking to LA."

Callie raised her eyebrows and was silent.

"Are you planning on seeing Ethan?"

Callie blinked. "What are you talking about?"

"Callie. Don't play dumb with me. I read the article in the *Quarterly*, remember? It clearly said he lives in Santa Monica."

Callie was silent. She'd known this moment would come.

Nina sighed. "I thought so." She looked down and back up again. "Callie, you need to let this go."

"No offense, Nina, but you don't know anything about it."

"Maybe you're right. But what I *think* is that you're wondering if you made a mistake. Especially now that he's made this stupid movie. It's stirred up all this stuff for you."

As much as she wanted to, Callie couldn't deny it. "Fine. I agree it's stirred stuff up. But beyond that I can't say. To be honest, I don't even know what *I* think about it."

Nina slid some of the tile samples over and patted the bed. Callie sat down obediently, even as she wondered why she did.

"Do you remember when we were home for the holidays your senior year?" Nina asked.

Callie tried to think back. Her sister would have been thirty.

Nina looked straight at her. "You asked me how people know if their relationships are going to last."

"I did?" Callie had no memory of this.

"You did. You were wondering how people know if they're meant for each other. If they've found the person they want to marry, grow old with, have kids with."

As Nina spoke, Callie conjured vague images of the conversation she was describing. She was sure Nina wasn't making it up; back then, it wasn't unusual for Callie to go to her for advice.

Nina plucked at the bedding. "It was pretty clear to me that things had started to go south for you guys. Or at least for you. This whole plan about moving to San Francisco seemed to scare you, and I was pretty sure you were going to break up with him. And I wouldn't have thought you were crazy if you did. You'd been together a long time for a college relationship, and if you were having doubts, it would have been smart to see what else was out there. You were so young."

"Nina, why are you saying all this? As if you know better than I do why I broke up with Ethan? Believe me, I know why." Callie fought to keep her voice measured. "And you keep insisting I'm stuck on him when I've hardly mentioned his name for *ten years*. It's not like I've been starving myself and pining away."

"No—but you also haven't opened your heart to anyone else. And ever since this movie came up, he's obviously been back in your life—even if only in your mind." Nina sighed. "It's like you've never been sure that your reasons for breaking up with him were good enough. But—whatever those reasons were—I think you have to trust yourself that they *were*." Her sister paused, then continued with more conviction. "And what happens if it turns out that he *does* want you back? What makes you think you'd be happier now than you were then? When he's ten years different, and you're ten years different, and you live three thousand miles apart?"

Callie pressed the heels of her hands into her eyes and then dropped them again. "Look, I don't know. I just need to find out. I want to know what the last ten years have done to us. How we've changed. Or not."

Nina sighed again. "It's your life. It's your choice. I just worry about you."

Callie felt a spark of anger flare up, and she rose from the bed. "I'm a big girl. I really *can* take care of myself, even if you don't think so."

"Oh, Callie! Stop getting so caught up in this thing about how you think I treat you."

Callie raised her eyebrows. "Fine. Then stop telling Mom she's babying me."

"What? When did I say that?"

"Come on, Nina. It's your whole thing about me living here. You can't have it both ways. You can't be the big sister giving me all this advice because I don't know what I'm doing, and then tell Mom that she needs to kick me out so I can grow up."

Nina closed her eyes and then opened them again. She was clearly struggling to keep her voice calm. "That's not what I said."

Callie glanced at Zoe, whose eyes remained glued to the pirouetting rodent on the screen. "I don't want to have a fight. Let's just stop."

"Fine. Subject closed."

Callie nodded firmly. "Good." She turned and left the room.

In bed that night, she stared at the ceiling, Nina's words swimming in her head. She'd started to drift off to sleep when there was a soft whimper and the rustle of Zoe's bedcovers. Callie's eyes popped back open. The whimpering grew louder.

Callie sat up. "Zoe? What's the matter?"

Zoe was crying.

Callie found Zoe's back in the lump under the covers and rubbed it. "Are you feeling okay?"

Zoe emerged, reaching her little arms out. Callie picked her up and felt those arms wrap around her neck. She wished she could live up to the confidence the tightness of Zoe's grip conveyed—the belief that she could fix whatever was wrong. But if she couldn't solve her own problems, how could she solve someone else's?

Callie sat back down on her bed with Zoe curled in her lap. "Does something hurt?"

Zoe shook her head.

"Did you have a bad dream?"

Again Zoe shook her head.

Callie continued to stroke her niece's back. Finally, Zoe turned her face up. It was wet with snot and tears. "Is Mommy ever going to get out of bed?"

At least this was something she could deal with. "Of course! Even now she gets out of bed to go to the bathroom, right? And to go to the doctor? And when the baby comes, everything will go back to normal."

"I don't *want* the baby!" Zoe threatened to break into tears again.

Callie took a deep breath. "I know that's how you feel. I know this is hard for you. But it'll be okay."

Zoe sniffed loudly.

Callie took her little wet face in her hands. "You know what, Binks?"

"What?"

"You know how Mommy is my big sister?"

Zoe nodded, suspicious.

"Well, if Gamma only had one baby—your mommy—there'd be no me. There'd be no Aunt Callie. I'm not so bad, right?"

Zoe shook her head.

"Well, maybe the baby won't be so bad either."

"It's not fair," Zoe said stubbornly.

Ah, so it begins.

Callie stopped herself before saying the words every parent has repeated since the beginning of time—*Life isn't fair.* Instead, she said, "I know, Binks." She felt Zoe's wet face soaking through her T-shirt. "Why don't we try to go back to sleep?"

Zoe sniffed again. "Can I sleep with you?"

Nina had a strict rule about Zoe sleeping alone. "We're not

going to get into that bad habit," she had said, more times than Callie could count. But Callie wasn't Nina. And suddenly worn out, she just wanted to sleep. "Okay, Binks."

She lay down with her arm curved around her niece.

"Aunt Callie?"

"Mmm?"

"Why don't you have a baby?" *Oh God.*

"It's just the way things are right now," Callie replied lightly.

"Ohhh," Zoe said a moment later with an air of discovery. "You need to get married first."

"Exactly." She was just getting it from all sides today, wasn't she?

"You should do what Mommy said and get married."

"Yes, Binks," Callie said patiently. "It's sleep time now."

Callie moved her hand to Zoe's back. She could feel her niece's breathing begin to settle and then become slow and rhythmic. It was amazing how children could be talking one minute and sleeping the next.

She wished she could do the same.

CHAPTER TWENTY-NINE

Before

I was a college graduate. The postgraduation barbecue was over, and our parents and grandparents and third cousins had returned to their hotel rooms. A bunch of us gathered in the common room of Jenna's dorm, and the sounds of Nickelback, Linkin Park, and Alicia Keys were coming from the iPod dock someone had brought out. Six-packs of beer were strewn around, and we were all feeling a bit maudlin.

I was curled up in the corner of one of the couches. Ethan stood in a far corner of the room talking with Tim and Peter. He absentmindedly picked at the label on his beer bottle. How often had I watched him cause little bits of paper and glue to flutter to the floor?

Jenna had made photo albums as keepsakes for Amy, Shauna, Jade, and me. Mine was back in my dorm room, where I'd gone through it earlier. There was a cute photo of Jenna and me in Halloween costumes (we were both cats, wearing shorts with black tights, black turtlenecks, and cats' ears—very original), and a group photo I loved from Jenna's twenty-first-birthday dinner at a restaurant in Glover. Five of us had piled into Ethan's small car, and the rest of the group crowded into two other cars. In the picture, I was laughing so hysterically at something that tears were rolling down my face, but I couldn't for the life of me recall what was so funny.

Amy wandered over, holding her own album in her hand. "Aren't these great?" she asked. "Jenna is so amazing to have made them."

"Can I see yours?"

"Sure." She held it out to me.

I took another sip of my Sam Adams and then held it upright between my legs while I flipped through the album, which was a bit thicker than mine. As I turned the pages, there were lots of occasions I had no memory of. Photos of the girls being silly. Photos taken at the No Doubt concert I didn't go to—the weekend Ethan's brother had been visiting. Photos taken on day trips—to Woodstock, to a nearby Hudson Valley mansion—that I vaguely remembered being invited to go on but had begged off. I suddenly closed the album as a lump rose in my throat.

I couldn't believe four years of college were over. I glanced again at Ethan, who was laughing. Thinking back to all the poker nights he'd had me join in on as an honorary "guy" and all those Wednesday night movies, I doubted he had any regrets. There probably wasn't anything he'd wanted to do that he missed out on. But what about the things *I'd* missed? It had been my choice to skip stuff he wasn't interested in—and I'd been happy to be with him doing whatever he wanted to do—but I couldn't help asking myself: What did I lose out on that I could never get back?

Jenna sat down beside me.

"Hey," she said. "What's up?"

I cleared my clogged throat as surreptitiously as possible and held up the album. "Feeling a little sentimental."

Jenna pushed her hair behind her ears. It was as blonde as ever, but now she sported a bob instead of her long ponytail. "I know. Can you believe it? Four years. *Pfft!* Like that." She snapped her fingers for emphasis.

"No kidding." She wasn't making me feel any better.

"So, when did you say you leave for California?" She pulled her feet under her.

"Not until the end of the summer." I took another sip of my beer. Ethan was going to spend a few weeks with his family in Chicago and then drive out to San Francisco. He'd wanted me to join him at his parents' house and drive with him, but I wanted to spend the summer in New Jersey. He'd been upset, but—for once—I held my ground. "I'm going to be moving three thousand miles away from my family. I haven't spent a summer with them since high school," I'd explained, over and over again.

Ethan had been talking about it for so long. We were watching the sea otters in the bay in Monterey when he came up with the idea. It started with six simple words. A wish, really: "Let's move out here after graduation." And he'd repeated it so often it turned into reality, without my ever making a conscious choice. Now the plans were made, the plane tickets purchased. But instead of excitement, I felt a vague sense of dread. As if I'd lost control of my life.

Jenna and I continued to talk. She'd be going home to Connecticut for a job at a community newspaper. "It's not the *Times*, but it's something," she'd quipped when she first told me. While we chatted, Ethan perched on the arm of the sofa beside me, his hand resting lightly on my shoulder. Slowly, people began to depart. It was clear everyone was exhausted from the long day, but reluctant to bring an end to it.

"I think that's it for me," Jenna said finally, yawning widely as she stood up.

I stood, too, and gave my friend a hug. "I'm going to miss you," I whispered.

"Me, too. You better come see me when you're back visiting your family."

"Definitely." I suddenly felt teary again as I watched Jenna head toward the stairs.

Ethan looked around at the thinning crowd. "Ready to go?"

I nodded, and he put his arm around me.

The air was cool as we walked toward our dorm, the stars bright in the inky black sky. I was still wearing the dress I'd had on under my graduation robes, but I'd pulled an oversized sweater around me.

"I can't believe this is all over," Ethan said, slipping his arm off my shoulder and grabbing my hand. He gazed at the stars as he walked. "Can you imagine how different it would have been if we hadn't found each other?" He chuckled. "I mean . . . if I hadn't spilled my Coke all over you?"

"Mmm" was all I could manage in response.

We continued in silence until we arrived "home." While Ethan headed down the hall to the bathroom, I pulled off my dress and put on a T-shirt and pajama bottoms and went to brush my teeth. When I got back to the room, Ethan was already in bed. I slipped under the covers and curled up on my side with my back to him, wanting nothing more than sleep.

He put his arm around my waist, pulling me closer. "How am I going to manage without you for the next three months?" It would be, by far, the longest we'd been apart. When I didn't respond, he spoke again. "Are you sure you won't come out sooner?"

I sighed. "Let's see how it goes." I wished I'd been clearer about my doubts, and now it felt too late, like I was on a train whose brakes had failed.

He kissed the back of my neck and I relaxed, despite myself. "It's going to be good, you know," he whispered.

I let my body melt, and I felt his hardness as his hands began to caress my body. This was where we always fit. This was what I'd miss.

CHAPTER THIRTY

After

On December 10, Callie turned thirty-two. By definition, she was in her last year of her early thirties. Whether that was good or bad, she wasn't sure.

When she was a kid, it was so hard to sleep the night before her birthday, and it felt like it would be *forever* until she could blow out her candles and open her presents. In high school, birthdays meant a decorated locker, movies, and ice cream. When she turned seventeen, there was the driving test and the excitement of slipping the brand-new laminated license into her wallet. She kept coming up with excuses to look at it, although it was, without a doubt, the worst photo ever taken of her.

In college, there was always Ethan. A romantic dinner and a gift. After college, during the years she was in New York, she and her roommates—sometimes joined by Jenna, who took the train in from Connecticut—went out for drinks and dancing.

On her twenty-fourth birthday, she even met someone. She'd pointed out a cute guy to Amy, who was drunk enough to think it was a good idea to tell him that it was Callie's birthday and that she'd like a kiss. Callie was mortified, but the guy obliged. They went on a few dates after that, but it soon fizzled.

Since moving back to New Jersey, her birthdays had varied. One year she met Emily at a hot new restaurant in Manhattan. Other years, Tess and Brett took her out—once, a friend of Brett's joined them, "unexpectedly." "My surprise gift to you!" Tess had whispered to her. Callie couldn't help but laugh, even as she was exasperated.

The morning of her thirty-second, she got out of bed while Zoe was getting ready for school. One thing about having a preschool roommate—she no longer needed an alarm clock. By the time she showered and dressed and went downstairs, Lorraine was just about ready to take Zoe to school. Callie braced herself for a cheery "happy birthday" greeting—but none came. All she got was the usual hug from Zoe and "Have a good day" from her mother. Could her own mother have forgotten her birthday?

She had a cup of coffee and toast, humming "Happy birthday to me" in a dirge-like cadence. Coffee finished, she rinsed her mug and put it in the dishwasher before grabbing a banana. As she gathered her things, she called goodbye to Nina from the bottom of the stairs. Nina yelled goodbye back. Still no acknowledgment of her birthday. Callie pulled her phone out of her pocket to check the date. Nope, it was definitely her birthday. If someone had asked her if she wanted people to make a fuss, she would have said no—but it was infinitely worse to be forgotten.

Callie was in her classroom getting things set for the day when Tess poked her head in the door. "Good morning, birthday girl!" she sang. Then she saw Callie's face. "What?"

"You're the first person to remember."

"See!" exclaimed Tess. "If you were on Facebook, you would have had eighty-seven birthday greetings already."

"Sure. From people I went to elementary school with and don't even remember."

"Well, if you want to be picky about it!" Tess grinned. "I even have a card for you." She dug into the voluminous tote bag on her shoulder and pulled out a bright pink envelope.

Callie took it and gave Tess a quick hug.

"Don't read it in front of the kids." Tess winked.

"I think we're okay. Last I checked, they couldn't read."

"You never know. They're sneaky little buggers." Tess smirked. "What are you doing tonight to celebrate?"

"I don't know. I think I might go to the mall and get a little present for myself. Although I did buy a dress at Alouette the other day." That dress had reminded Callie about the buzz she got from new clothes, and she decided she should indulge herself more often.

"I'm glad you're treating yourself. But call me if you want to go out, okay? Or just come over. Brett and I have no plans." Tess began to step out the door, but then stepped back in. "Hey—Judith mentioned you're going with her to the NOECE conference?" It was a statement but ended with a question mark.

Callie nodded.

"So—what's that about? A *belated* birthday treat? Have you contacted your ex?"

"Look, it's my birthday. No interrogations. But yes, I'm going. And no, I haven't told him I'm coming." She chose not to mention the reason for that: her upcoming date with Ethan in New York. That would certainly trigger Tess to break the new rule Callie had just instituted.

"Okay—it's your birthday—no *interrogations*. But don't think this conversation is over." Tess wagged her finger at her before heading to her own classroom.

When school ended, Callie checked her phone and discovered a voicemail from her mother. "Happy birthday,
Callie!" she exclaimed. "I didn't want you to think I forgot."
There was a pause. "Well, I suppose I did have a momentary
lapse of memory. But." Clearing of throat. "Of *course* we have
to celebrate! Unless you have other plans?" There was another pause, as if her mother expected to get a response despite the fact that she was speaking into voicemail. "Anyway,"
she began again, "we'll have a special dinner tonight. See you
later!"

Callie sighed. Neither of the invitations she'd received was
very tempting. As much as she loved Brett and Tess, the idea of
being the third wheel on her birthday was less than appealing,
even though she knew they'd do their best to make her feel
like a queen. But she refused to feel sorry for herself. Though
her actual birthday might end up being nothing to write
home about, she could still feel that sneaking thrill that had
planted itself deep inside her when she decided to embrace her
thoughts about Ethan and his movie. Something was happening. Perhaps it was her own form of *rerouting.*

She drove to the mall, forgetting until she saw the crowded
parking lot that it would be a zoo two weeks before Christmas.
Sure enough, there were shoppers everywhere, particularly
as she approached the Santa display. A velvet rope closed off
the entrance where a sign indicated that Santa was feeding his
reindeer. Beyond was a line of at least two dozen families waiting for Dasher and Dancer to finish eating. Callie didn't envy
the moms and dads trying to keep their little ones calm as they
waited in their red velvet dresses, white tights, and fancy holiday sweaters. Nor did she envy Santa, who was sure to come
back to some very cranky children who would not be interested in sitting happily on his lap.

Callie skirted the crowd and headed into one of the few
stores she patronized on her infrequent visits to the mall.

While it was a chain, it carried an eclectic mix of items. As she looked at some pretty sweaters, she heard her name.

"I thought that was you," said a woman about Lorraine's age. Her hair was dyed golden brown and she wore a smart shearling jacket. Callie couldn't place who she was. *One of Lorraine's friends?*

"Oh, hi!" She hoped her enthusiasm would mask the fact that she didn't have a clue who she was talking to.

"So good to see you," Mrs. X said. "Are you home for the holidays?"

Callie hated these conversations. "No, I live here."

"Really? Your parents must be delighted. You've settled down here?" Her eyes skimmed over Callie's ringless left hand.

"I don't know about settled. But I'm here now," Callie said lightly, fighting the urge to stuff her left hand into her coat pocket.

"Are you staying with your parents?"

Why did some people think they were entitled to administer the third degree? *Oh—no children yet? Are you and your husband having . . . difficulties?*

"My parents are in Florida. I'm living in their house." Callie wished that didn't sound as pathetic as it did. Maybe Nina had a point after all.

Mrs. X nodded knowingly. Callie could imagine her conversation with Mr. X later. *I ran into Callie Dressler today. So sad. She was a bright girl. Too many kids these days can't get their act together.*

Callie could feel the thrill at her core dissipating. In the silence, she supposed she should ask about Mrs. X's family, but she still couldn't remember who she was. Gamely, she tried to engage. "So . . . how are you and yours?"

"Oh, we're wonderful. Roger is married with two kids— they live in DC. And Lauren just got engaged."

Lauren! How could Callie have forgotten? Or maybe she'd

tried to forget. Lauren was one of the "mean girls" in high school.

"That's great. Congratulations!"

"Thank you, dear. So much work to do, planning a wedding." She prattled on, talking about all the choices that needed to be made and how expensive it all was, but Callie recognized the humblebrag when she heard it.

Callie was finally able to extricate herself when the other woman announced she was on a desperate search for a holiday gift for her future son-in-law. Taking a deep, cleansing breath, Callie went back to her browsing.

After she found a cream-colored angora boatneck sweater with interesting cabling on the sleeves and a suede skirt with a patchwork design, she walked back past the long line for Santa. The big guy was back in his chair, resolutely smiling despite the howling boy in his lap. The mother was desperately trying to pick her other son up off the floor. Callie recognized the little boy's posture—it looked like he'd turned his bones to liquid. *How do all children innately know how to do that?*

By the time she got home, it was dark. The unhappy reality of the shortening days. Callie picked up her shopping bag and headed inside, surprised to find how quiet it was. The kitchen light was on, but no one was there. The rest of the downstairs was dark and silent. As she dropped her things on the kitchen table, her bag tipped over, the contents—including the birthday card from Tess—spilling onto the floor. *Just perfect.* She knelt down to gather everything up, and as an afterthought pulled the card out of its envelope and used a magnet advertising a local plumber to stick it on the refrigerator door. Then she hurried upstairs, calling Nina as she went.

"I'm in here," Nina responded from the bedroom. "Where else would I be?"

"Where is everyone?" Callie asked, glancing at her watch. It was just past five.

Nina yawned. "After dance class, Mom took Zoe to some puppet show at the Wolcott library. They hit traffic on their way home and Zoe was hungry. Mom just called—she's taking Zoe out for pizza and is going to bring one home for the rest of us. She said to tell you she's sorry it won't be much of a birth-day dinner, but she couldn't take Zoe's whining. I could have told her it wouldn't work to make her wait that long to eat. Oh—but wait! Look what I have."

Nina reached over to the nightstand and presented a sin-gle Hershey's Kiss. It must have been a leftover from the gift basket her friends in Wolcott sent.

"Pathetic, I know, but it's the thought that counts, right? Happy birthday!"

Callie couldn't help but smile at her type-A sister. Bed rest had definitely had an effect. No way would Nina have settled for such a gift before. She would have come up with a way to make *homemade* Kisses if she'd been able to.

"Thanks, Neen," Callie said, unwrapping the chocolate. "Do you need anything?"

Nina shrugged. "I'm okay. Oh, Ben is on his way."

Callie hoped any reaction she had to that news was well concealed.

"Apparently, the contractor forgot to have us choose base-board moldings and now they need to order them, *immedi-ately*. So, he's bringing us some samples. He should be here pretty soon, actually."

Callie wondered why Lorraine couldn't have picked them up, but she kept her mouth shut. "Do you want him to come up?" she asked instead.

Nina glanced around the rumpled bed and shook her head. "Not unless he needs to see me. You look good, by the way. Thirty-two must suit you."

Callie looked down at herself. Circle skirt with a geomet-ric print, openwork sweater with a tank underneath, boots.

"Thanks!" she said, and then headed into the bathroom, where she brushed her hair and, for the heck of it, her teeth, too. She was just going back downstairs when the doorbell rang. She willed her feet to descend the last few steps at an ordinary pace. When she opened the door, Ben stood on the other side wearing his parka and holding up three pieces of wood like an admission ticket.

"Come in. Nina told me you were coming."

He stepped into the foyer. "It's cold out!" he said by way of a hello. His gloveless hands were a little red. "These are for your sister." Ben handed over the molding samples.

"Thanks. Do you need to see her?"

He shook his head. "Not unless she needs to see me."

"Nope. She's good. Can I get you anything?"

"Some water?"

"Sure."

Ben followed her into the kitchen. She retrieved two glasses from the cabinet next to the sink, noticing how outdated everything looked. Funny how you could see something every day and not think twice about it, but when you look through someone else's eyes, you suddenly perceive what's really there. Callie suddenly hated those sad Formica countertops.

She put the glasses down on the table and turned to the fridge for the water pitcher. No in-door water and ice dispenser for them. "You can take your jacket off, if you like," she said as she picked up the pitcher. Ben hung his parka on the back of one of the chairs, and as she poured the water, he wandered over to the fridge, looking at the plethora of magnets and random photos that had been there for so long that Callie didn't see them anymore. There was a newborn photo of Zoe, and a picture of her and Nina at a cousin's bar mitzvah, clipped there by her mother years earlier. Then Ben's gaze rested on the brightly colored card featuring a drawing of two women holding fancy-looking cocktails.

"Someone's birthday?" he asked as he took the glass of water.

Callie took a sip from her own glass. "Mine."

"Today?"

She nodded.

"Happy birthday! What are you doing to celebrate?"

"Not much," she replied. In response to his knitted brows, she added, "There's been a lot going on. It's not really on anyone's radar this year."

"Well, it's on someone's." He pointed to the card.

"True. That's from my friend Tess." She forced a smile. "But it kind of feels like that movie where Molly Ringwald's family forgets her birthday because her sister's getting married."

Ben raised his eyebrows. "I seem to recall that in the end the cute boy saves the day."

"Does he? I don't remember that part," Callie lied, taking another sip of her water to avoid looking at his little smile.

Ben set his glass down on the counter. "Well, you can't do nothing on your birthday. How about I take you out to dinner?"

Callie fought to keep her own smile from growing too broad. "You don't have to do that."

"Of course I don't have to. But I'd like to. And it's too late for you to say you have other plans."

"Okay, then. That would be lovely." A bloom of warmth flooded her body.

"You'll just have to tell me where we should go. I don't know this area too well."

"Okay. I'll let Nina know. I'll be right back."

She headed up the stairs, grabbing the molding samples on her way. She wasn't sure what to tell her sister but concluded that less was more. She dropped the moldings off and told Nina she was headed out for dinner with a friend and texted her mom to tell her not to worry about dinner—she had other plans anyway. Then she stopped in the bathroom to scrutinize herself in the mirror. She didn't want to do anything obvious, but she smudged some earth-tone eye shadow on her lids and applied a little blush before going back downstairs.

Ben had come out into the hallway, where he stood in front of the table displaying family photos. He'd picked up the frame containing Callie's high school senior portrait. Not for the first time that day, Callie regretted living in her parents' house.

"Please don't look at that awful picture," she said as she approached.

"Oh, it's not bad. You should see mine." He carefully replaced the frame.

They put on their coats and went outside to Ben's car. Callie slid into the passenger seat when he opened the door, and oddly had a flash of getting into Ethan's decrepit Volkswagen and leaning over to unlock the door for him. Of course, Ben had an electronic key fob that unlocked all the doors with a cheerful chirp, so no stretching across the driver's seat was necessary. A moment later, Ben was behind the wheel and they were pulling away from the curb. Callie directed him to a nearby bistro, and it wasn't long before he was navigating into a parking space.

"After you," Ben said, holding the restaurant door open for her. As Callie stepped in, she thought she felt his hand on her back, but wasn't sure through the bulk of her jacket. The hostess brought them to a booth and left them with menus.

"So, what's good here?" Ben asked.

Callie told him what she'd previously ordered, and as they were discovering they both liked scallops and disliked spinach, a waiter approached their table to offer them drinks.

Callie hesitated but then ordered a Sam Adams.

"Sounds good," Ben said. "I'll have one, too."

The waiter stepped away toward the bar and Callie put her menu down. "I always feel like I should get a glass of wine."

"Why?"

"I don't know. It seems like the thing to do."

"Do you like wine?"

"That's the problem. I really don't."

"Well, then. There you go. Apparently, my dad forced himself to learn to drink coffee when he was in his twenties because he felt weird not ordering it when he was out to dinner with friends. I never understood that. Just don't order coffee if you don't like it," Ben said matter-of-factly.

The waiter returned with a tray containing two bottles, two tall pilsners, and a basket of bread. After they gave their orders, Ben flipped back the napkin covering the bread to reveal warm rolls. They each took one, along with a gold-foil-wrapped pat of butter.

Ben ripped his roll in half and began to butter one side. "It's always a good sign when the bread comes out warm."

Callie agreed, and they chewed in silence for a moment. "So, do you live in Wolcott?"

"Not far. Chestertown. I'd been renting for a while, and then I bought a townhouse a few years ago."

"What brought you to New Jersey?"

Ben swallowed the bread in his mouth. "A girlfriend, actually."

"Oh?" Callie took a sip of her beer. She hoped her reply sounded casual.

"I met her when I was working in the city. She lived in Hoboken, and I was in Brooklyn. When I wanted to switch to residential design, she convinced me to look in New Jersey, and I got an offer out this way. For a while, I was doing the reverse commute, but when my lease was up, I moved to Hoboken."

Callie nodded. "And then?"

Ben finished sipping his beer and put his glass back down. "We broke up. And I got tired of driving from Hoboken and paying Hoboken prices."

The waiter came to refill their water glasses, and Ben buttered the other half of his roll. "So, what about this ex of yours? The movie guy?" he asked, his eyes on the knife passing across the bread.

Callie cleared her throat. *Why is Ethan always cropping up?* "He was my college boyfriend. We broke up the summer after college."

Ben looked up from his bread. "Are you in touch?"

Callie shook her head. "We haven't seen each other since then. What about you and your ex?"

"Nah. There's no reason. Someone from school, though—you probably have friends in common, still bump into each other . . ."

"Ethan's in California, so no chance of that."

Ben nodded and took another bite of his roll.

"How did you get into architecture?" Callie asked.

Ben looked at her for a long moment, licking a bit of butter off his lip, before he spoke. "When I was a kid, I was always creating these crazy structures out of blocks and boxes and all kinds of things. And I just loved buildings—imagining what they'd be like inside, why they were designed the way they were. Like most architects, I went into it thinking I was going to design great buildings—theaters, skyline-changing office buildings, cathedrals . . ." He popped the last bite of roll in his mouth as the waiter brought their salads.

"What happened?" Callie picked up her salad fork.

"Reality. There just aren't all that many great buildings being built." Ben speared a piece of tomato with his fork.

"Was it hard? Having to switch gears?"

"A little, at first—it certainly didn't seem like I'd be creating anything special. But like I said the other day—I enjoy coming up with ways to make people's living spaces the way they want them to be. I like to think I'm making at least a small difference in their lives."

"How was your meeting the other night? New business pitch, right?" Callie asked, carefully moving the onions to the side of her plate.

Ben pointed with his fork. "Don't like onions?"

"How could you tell?"

"Just a good guess." Ben grinned. "Let's see—the meeting. It was fine." Ben tilted his head. "I had the bad luck of being the first architect they were meeting with."

"Why is that bad?"

"They're not really sure what to ask, or even what they want. You spend a lot of time educating them on the process—which means they're bound to have more-productive meetings with the people that come after me. Sometimes, though, it can work in your favor—if you build a good rapport with them. Remains to be seen."

"Sounds like parents checking out preschools. Sometimes they get really attached to the first one they see, but other times they don't even know what to look at when they come to observe a classroom for the first time."

As the waiter came to take their salad plates—Ben's completely clean, Callie's containing a small pile of purply-white onions—and then returned with their entrees, they talked about childhood memories, which gave way to family vacations and sibling gossip: the time Nina thought it would be a good idea to cut Callie's hair, Ben's brother's attempt to convince him that he'd been left on the doorstep by aliens.

When Ben excused himself to use the restroom, Callie pulled out her phone and saw that Tess had texted. Are you around? I hope you're doing something to celebrate your birthday. Do you want to go out for dessert?

Callie texted back. You're so sweet. I'm actually out for dinner. Rain check?

She was slipping her phone back into her purse when

Ben came back to the table. Soon afterward, their plates were cleared, and the waiter brought them the dessert menu.

"I don't think I could eat anything else," Callie said, looking at the decadent choices on the laminated card in her hand.

"You have to order something. It's not a birthday without cake. Besides, we can share."

"Well, if I have no choice . . ." Callie glanced up at him and back to the menu. "How about the double chocolate layer cake?"

Ben put his menu down. "Sounds perfect to me."

A few minutes later, the waiter brought out the cake, shielding it with his hand. The rest of the waitstaff followed.

Callie looked across the table at Ben with her eyebrows raised.

He smiled. "No birthday dinner is complete without a moment of complete mortification. You're welcome."

The delegation in black pants and black shirts arrived at the table, and the waiter placed the cake, with its single glowing candle, in front of Callie. She resisted covering her face with her hands as they sang "Happy Birthday" to her, accompanied by several other diners who grinned in her direction as they chimed in. Amid the sprinkling of applause, Callie blew out the candle illuminating her pink face. Then she picked up her knife and handed it to Ben. "Do you want to do the surgery?"

He reached for his fork instead and stuck it into the edge of the cake. "I think we can share it this way."

She shrugged and took a forkful herself.

After finishing dessert and two leisurely cups of coffee, they headed back to Callie's house. Ben pulled up to the curb and switched off the engine.

"This was really nice," Callie said. "Thank you."

"You're welcome." Ben pointed toward the house behind her. "So, this is where you grew up?"

Callie nodded. "My parents moved here when Nina was a baby."

"I guess you've been dropped off at this curb by lots of guys."

Callie's eyes widened. "Lots?"

"Well, I don't mean *lots*. I mean, the appropriate amount."

Callie laughed. "I don't know what the *appropriate* amount would be, but I'm not sure I ever was."

"No?" Ben sounded surprised.

Callie thought about it. On the rare occasions Ethan visited her here, he'd pulled into the driveway. And the few men she'd dated since moving back usually walked in with her. No reason to drop her at the curb. "No, no curb drop-offs. I didn't really date in high school."

"Huh. I'm surprised."

"Really? You saw that photo inside." Callie made a face.

"I did see that photo. You were cute," he protested. "You must have gone to school with idiots."

Callie laughed again and felt a rush of heat spread throughout her body.

"Well, in that I don't like to think of myself as an idiot," Ben began again. "I hope we can do this again."

Added to the heat came a swarm of butterflies. "I'd like that."

Ben pulled out his phone and tapped her number into it. Callie sat for a moment as he slipped his phone back into his pocket. His eyes held hers, and for a moment she wondered if he'd kiss her. But then his eyes slid away and the spell was broken.

"Well," she said as she put her hand on the door handle.

"Well," he repeated. "I'll give you a call. Have a good night. And happy birthday."

"Thanks," she said, and headed inside, glad he couldn't see the broad smile on her face.

CHAPTER THIRTY-ONE

Before

The day after graduation, Nina, my parents, and I loaded up the two family cars to haul my stuff home. I still referred to the house in Brook Hill that way, though it had been four years since I'd spent more than three weeks there at a stretch. As I sat beside my mother for the drive—half listening to her prattle about the people she'd met at last night's barbecue, about the buffet breakfast that morning, about the other cars on the road—I thought about Ethan. I should've been desolate at the idea of not seeing him for three months. But I wasn't.

Over the following days, I settled into my childhood bedroom. After four years of having absolutely no privacy—no place I could go to shut the door and know that no one would bother me—it felt positively spacious. Luxuriously "all mine." The change was marvelous.

I cleared out old clothes that had been living in my dresser drawers, forgotten and unworn, and reorganized. Nina was thriving in Manhattan, about to move into an apartment she bought in TriBeCa. So, it was Mom, Dad, and me in the house—as it had been after Nina graduated from high school. Ethan and I spoke on the phone every day, but our conversations felt empty. Somehow, there wasn't enough to fill them.

I registered with temp agencies. After a couple of one- or two-day assignments, I landed a six-to-eight-week stint at an insurance agency, subbing for a receptionist who'd had emergency surgery.

My first morning there, I chose my clothing carefully. I didn't have too many office-appropriate options, but I was reasonably pleased with my lime-green sleeveless boatneck top and cream slacks. Automatically, I reached for the necklace Ethan had made for me, but after a moment, I put it back down. Instead, I found the crystal pendant my parents gave me for my high school graduation and fastened it behind my neck.

It turned out to be a nice place to work. I became friendly with three of the women there, all in their early to midtwenties. The reception desk where I sat was like Grand Central Station. They hung around to chat, and we talked over lunch in the staff room. It was all light—*The Sopranos*, *Big Brother*, J. Lo's marriage to Marc Anthony, Mary-Kate Olsen's eating disorder, what stores were having good sales—and somehow, I never mentioned the boyfriend I was supposed to be moving in with in California. It was liberating to be just *me*—and not half of "Ethan and Callie." The other women were single. Debi had recently moved to Hoboken with some friends, and the others often went there to bar hop and meet guys.

At the end of my second week, they invited me to join them on Friday night. I couldn't remember the last time I had made plans with friends without feeling I had to check in with Ethan.

That was how, at about nine o'clock that Friday evening, I found myself crowded around a small round table, itself crowded with beer bottles and a nearly empty bowl of mixed nuts, with my three coworkers and another friend of Debi's. The bar was loud and teeming with bodies, all in varying stages of drunkenness. Two guys had insinuated themselves into our group. I gave them credit for approaching a cluster of five women.

Debi nudged me and leaned close so I could hear her above the din. "There's a guy looking at you." She tipped the neck of her beer bottle across the room, and my eyes slid in that direction.

The guy Debi was indicating had dirty-blond hair, light blue eyes, and great bone structure—angular, with strong cheekbones. Like most of the men in the bar, he was wearing khakis and a collared short-sleeve shirt.

Debi looked at me and raised her eyebrows, and I shrugged slightly.

"He's pretty hot," she said.

It would have been a good time to tell her that I had a boyfriend. But I didn't. Instead, I spent the rest of the evening peeking through my eyelashes across the room. It was a strange sensation—being in a bar as a "single" woman. Not that I really was, of course, but no one knew that—unlike during the past four years when, even if he wasn't with me, everyone knew me as "Ethan's girlfriend." Over time, I'd stopped thinking about how I looked when I went out. It wasn't like I should have been attracting attention anyway.

That morning, however, I'd chosen my outfit knowing I'd be going out. Happy that my office had a casual-Friday policy, I'd pulled out a short skirt and a sleeveless top that hugged my curves. And in the ladies' room at the end of the day, I put on makeup the way Nina had taught me on a rainy Sunday afternoon. She called it "the smoky eye." So, I suppose it wasn't surprising that someone had noticed. And Debi was definitely right—I caught him looking my way more than once.

The mystery man never approached, however, and I felt

simultaneously relieved and disappointed. When I got home, I called Ethan—something I hadn't been doing. He'd been the one dialing me most of the time.

Another week passed, and I found myself again en route to Hoboken, riding in the back seat of my coworker Grace's car. After circling for a parking space, we ended up at the same bar. When it was my turn to get the next round of drinks, I pushed myself closer to the bar to get the bartender's attention. There was a jostling on my left and I looked over. It was the cheek-bones guy from the previous Friday.

He smiled at me and leaned in. "I've been kicking myself all week for not saying hello when I saw you here last Friday. If I didn't talk to you tonight, I'd have to throw myself out of my apartment window."

I laughed in spite of myself. "Geez, that sounds pretty awful."

"Well, I live on the first floor, so . . ."

I laughed again, harder this time. "I'm glad I don't have to picture you plunging thirty-seven stories."

He smiled. "I'm Tom."

"Callie," I replied as the bartender appeared in front of me. I ordered the drinks for my table, and Tom helped me carry them back. Debi glanced from me to Tom as we approached.

I learned that Tom built websites at a graphic design company. I didn't understand it, but it sounded interesting. He was a couple of years out of college and lived in Hoboken with a roommate. He also played guitar in a band that had a gig coming up the following Thursday. As he leaned toward me to be heard, I felt his breath on my ear. It was nice. And he smelled nice, too—something citrusy. When I told him I was temping because I'd be moving across the country at the end of the summer, I knew I should mention Ethan. But I didn't. *I'm only having a conversation with someone I'll never see again.*

A few hours later, when Grace was ready to go, Tom asked for my number, and I hesitated.

"Okay, how about this?" he asked. "Promise me you'll come hear my band on Thursday."

What harm could there be in that?

That Thursday, only Debi was keen on going, so I drove my mom's car into Hoboken alone and met her outside the Salty Dog, where Tom's band was playing. We headed toward the back where a small crowd was gathering. Tom, wearing a black T-shirt and jeans, was helping set up the amps. The T-shirt was snug, and I couldn't help noticing that his back was broader and more defined than Ethan's. Then he turned and saw me. He walked over, smiling. "I'm glad you came," he said, squeezing my shoulder.

The band was actually good—a cross between Creed and 3 Doors Down. Tom sang backup and played guitar, and watching him, I understood why musicians attract groupies. When their two sets were over, a sweaty—in a good way—Tom approached Debi and me again.

"You guys were great," I exclaimed, and his face broke into a wide grin.

"Thanks. Can you hang around until we get the equipment put away so we can have a drink?"

A little while later, Tom and one of his bandmates joined us. There was a lot of laughing, and I couldn't help but notice how often Tom touched my arm. It was getting harder and harder to tell myself that I was just making a friend. Finally, we all reluctantly agreed that we needed to call it a night. Tom's friend took off in one direction, and Tom, Debi, and I walked to the corner together.

"Where's your car?" Debi asked.

I pointed farther up the street.

"I'm this way." She indicated a side street.

"I can walk Callie to her car," Tom said quickly. "If you're okay going on your own," he added.

Debi looked at me, and we said our good nights before Tom and I continued up the street.

"So glad you came," he said, his hands stuffed into his pockets.

"It was fun."

"Maybe we can get together again?"

I bit my lip. "Look," I began. "I'm only here for a couple of months before I move. I don't think—"

Tom interrupted me. "We enjoy each other's company, right? What's wrong with spending more time together?"

I swallowed. Based on the facts Tom knew, he made perfect sense.

"It's supposed to be a gorgeous weekend," Tom continued. "Some of us were talking about going down the shore. Maybe you and your friends want to come?"

I knew I should say no. "Why not?" I said instead.

CHAPTER THIRTY-TWO

After

The morning after Callie's birthday dinner with Ben, Tess pulled up next to her in the parking lot and they walked into school together. "So, your family remembered your birthday after all?"

"My mom brought home a cake. And she bought me this." Callie indicated the loosely woven infinity scarf around her neck.

"Nice. But I thought you said you were out to dinner."

"Oh, right . . ."

Tess's eyes sparkled. "Have you been on Connections again?"

Callie shook her head as they entered the school.

"Well?" Tess stepped in front of her and swiveled, blocking her path.

"I was out to dinner with my sister's architect." Callie moved to step around Tess.

Tess matched her movement by sliding to her left. "Oh? Do tell."

Callie stepped to her left, and Tess mirrored her. "Fine," Callie said exasperatedly. "I met him when I had to do some errands for Nina. He's nice. He found out it was my birthday and took me to dinner."

"And?"

Callie glanced at her boots and then looked up again. "I don't know yet."

"But you like him," Tess said knowingly. "I can tell."

Callie shrugged and managed to slip past Tess.

"You can't fool me, Dressler!" Tess called after her, laughing.

Callie went through the day as if she were floating slightly above the ground. Was this all because of Ben? She hadn't met anyone in ages she was even remotely interested in. And she didn't think she was wrong in thinking he liked her, too. If she were fourteen, she'd be repeating every word he'd said, every glance he'd thrown her way, to her sister and her best friend, asking for their assessment: *But do you* really *think he likes me? Or do you think he's just being nice?* She had the sound on her phone turned off as usual while she was in the classroom, but periodically she slipped it out of her pocket to see if he'd called or texted—just in case she'd somehow missed its insistent vibrating against her thigh.

There had been no communication by the time she left school, but she told herself it didn't mean anything, and that if he'd reached out already, she'd think it was stalkerish. She mostly believed herself.

When she arrived home, Lorraine and Zoe were playing Chutes and Ladders at the dining room table. Callie waved hello and declined their invitation to join them before going upstairs to power up her laptop.

As she'd gotten in the habit of doing, she checked some of the entertainment websites for anything new about the movie. Nothing—but she followed a link that took her to a fan site for Nick Sykes, where she got absorbed reading about *The Summit*, the TV show he'd starred in, and all the convoluted story lines that led to Nick's character sleeping with nearly every girl in the cast.

Shaking her head at herself, she clicked the browser closed and opened her email. The ethan_rendel email address jumped out at her immediately. A new message from Ethan. It was short, and she scanned it quickly. His hotel reservation had changed; he'd now be in the Meatpacking District. He suggested shifting their meeting place to the bar there. The closing line threw her: "I'm looking forward to seeing you again after all this time."

Callie put her head in her hands and massaged her temples. Why was this getting to her, anyway? She'd finally . . . finally . . . met someone she wanted to get to know better, and yet here was Ethan, continuing to haunt her. Except he wasn't just haunting her. He was back in her life, sending her emails.

Callie was distracted for the rest of the evening. When she went to the refrigerator to get milk for Zoe, she stood there for a full minute staring at the shelf, not remembering what she was supposed to be doing. Later on, she loaded up a basket full of laundry and took it down to the basement, along with her cell phone. She poured the detergent and closed the lid, set the spin cycle, and started the machine. As it filled with water, she sat down on the bottom step and dialed.

Jenna picked up on the second ring.

"Hey, Callie! How are you?"

"Good—you?"

"Good. Busy. Getting ready for the holidays." They chatted a bit, Jenna telling Callie about juggling the holidays between her family and Rob's, and Callie filling Jenna in on Nina's bed rest and Lorraine's arrival. After a pause, Callie took a deep breath.

"So—you know this movie of Ethan's . . . ," she began.

"Yes . . . ?"

"Well—he got in touch with me."

"He did?" Callie couldn't tell if what she heard in Jenna's voice was only surprise or something else. "What did he say?"

"He wanted to tell me that the movie isn't really about us—well, obviously, it is in part—but not about our whole relationship. And he asked to see me when he's in New York for the premiere in January."

There was a silence. "Wow. What are you going to do?"

"We're going to meet for a drink."

Another silence.

"Are you still there?" Callie asked.

"I'm here. Just trying to wrap my head around this. Look, I have to ask—are you thinking you could get back together?"

Callie let out a long exhale. "Oh, Jenna—I don't know. It's been ten years. I'm not the same person I was. I don't know who he is now. I don't even know if he's single. It's just—this movie has gotten me thinking about things, about the choices I made, about where I am in my life. It finally hit me that this whole situation has hung me up somehow. Maybe seeing him again can help me put it behind me—whether it turns out there's still something between us or not."

"Do you have any idea what he's thinking?" Jenna asked carefully.

"Honestly, I don't know. He says he wants to explain how this whole movie thing happened . . ." Callie trailed off.

"Don't you think he's looking for answers himself?"

"What do you mean?"

"Look, even after all these years, I still don't know why you ended it with Ethan. I've made my own assumptions—I always thought he was a little possessive, and maybe that finally pushed you away. I mean, I've never said anything—and please don't take this the wrong way—but back in school I sometimes wished you'd break up. I hated how you were so tied to him—and not in a good way. You gave up so much for him."

Callie couldn't deny it.

"But when Ethan called me ten years ago looking for an explanation, I had nothing to say to him. He might still want answers. Are you ready to give them?"

Callie didn't know. But it was an excellent question.

"You don't have to answer me. But you do need to think about it. Whatever you're hoping for in this meeting—you might not get it. And it might be rough. Even if he's moved on, he might still be pissed. You should be sure you really want to do this. That you've thought it through."

Callie nodded, even though her friend couldn't see her. "I hear you. But I feel like I need to see him."

"And then, whatever happens, you'll be able to let it go?"

"That's the plan." As the washing machine started to agitate loudly, Callie stood and moved toward the other side of the basement. "The funny thing is—I might have actually met someone."

"Wait, what? And you didn't lead off with that?" *Jenna—ever the journalist.*

Callie laughed. "Well, I don't know. His name is Ben, and he's Nina's architect. We've spent some time together—not real dates, but he talked about us getting dinner sometime." Callie didn't feel like explaining what had happened on her birthday.

"And you like him?"

"I think so. Honestly, I'm so mixed up right now. But he's nice and funny . . . and cute. It's crazy that this is all happening at the same time."

"Maybe. But maybe not," Jenna said thoughtfully. "If this movie has gotten you thinking about your past, and where you are now, and what you want—maybe it's also making you more open to what's out there."

Perhaps there was something to what her friend said. "I *have* felt like there's something in the air."

"Well, no one deserves to be happy more than you. I hope it all works out—whatever that means."

They wrapped up the call so Jenna could meet Rob for dinner, and almost immediately afterward, Callie's phone rang. The number was unfamiliar, and her mind was still on her conversation with Jenna. She knew her friend well enough to read between the lines that Jenna didn't think meeting Ethan was a good idea. Callie answered the call distractedly.

It was Ben. There was that flutter in her chest again. He asked how she was.

"Fine." *I was just obsessing over my ex-boyfriend and telling my friend that I may have a thing for you.* "You?"

"Good. Crazy day. I'm glad tomorrow's Friday."

Callie murmured agreement.

"So, I'm headed to Long Island this weekend for my mom's birthday—it's her sixty-fifth—but I wanted to see if we could make a date for dinner for next Friday night."

Callie couldn't help smiling, even though he couldn't see her. "That would be great."

They chatted about the dinner for his mom, which led to them sharing stories about mishaps at family functions over the years, and before Callie knew it, they'd been on the phone for nearly an hour. She couldn't remember the last time she'd felt this comfortable with someone so quickly. After they said their good nights, Callie clicked the Off button and started upstairs. Thoughts of her conversation with Jenna came floating back as she trailed her hand along the railing. What *was* Ethan expecting from this meeting? What was *she* looking for? Would either of them get it?

CHAPTER THIRTY-THREE

Before

When I suggested the beach to my new friends at work, Debi and Grace were in right away. So that Sunday morning, the two of them, along with one of Debi's roommates, met in front of my house. Then the four of us—along with assorted beach chairs—piled into my mom's car.

I couldn't remember the last time I went to the shore. I'd spent so many summers away, I missed the weekend trips my high school friends took when they were home from college. But I remembered the route, and soon we were cruising down the Garden State Parkway. Progress slowed as we reached the shore exits, but finally we were parking a few blocks from the Point Pleasant boardwalk.

Tom had been right; it was a perfect beach day. Bright blue sky with only a few clouds, no humidity, and a bit of a breeze off the ocean. We found the guys on the boardwalk; they'd beaten us there by a few minutes. Everyone introduced themselves, and then we paid our beach admissions and went in search of a spot to lay claim to. There was a disagreement about how close to be to the snack bar and restrooms and how far to be from other people, but we finally agreed on a location and got settled.

I wasn't surprised when Tom set his chair up next to mine. I felt self-conscious when I pulled my beach cover-up over my head, and wished I'd chosen a one-piece bathing suit rather than the bikini I was wearing—patterned with sunbursts. But seeing the other girls in two-pieces, too, I felt better.

I dug in my bag for my sunscreen, which I applied to my legs. It was a good distraction from Tom taking off his shirt. As had been suggested by the tight T-shirt he'd worn when performing, he was ripped. Six-pack and all. He sat down as I moved on to sunscreening my arms and shoulders.

"Your hair looks cute that way." It was up in a high, messy ponytail. My bangs were still growing out, so they were wispy around my face. "Do you want me to get your back?" It was like something out of those beach-blanket movies.

I passed him the tube, and he squirted the lotion onto his hand. I turned away and felt his hands on my back, assiduously making sure they gave sun protection to every inch of my skin, including under the straps of my swimsuit top. Debi caught my eye and raised her eyebrows.

We spent the day enjoying the sun. The guys brought a Frisbee, and some of them went to the water's edge to toss it back and forth. A few went swimming. I walked in up to my calves, but Tom swam. He walked back to our encampment dripping wet, his swim trunks clinging to his thighs. We all went to the boardwalk for pizza. Tom laughed at my jokes, even the bad ones. When the sun shifted behind us, we talked about heading back.

We gathered our things and trudged to the boardwalk. The other girls went to use the restroom while I washed the sand off my legs at the outdoor shower. As I stood on one foot trying to dry the other, Tom put his hand out to help me balance. When I had both feet on the ground again, he continued to hold my hand, his index finger gently stroking the inside of my wrist.

"So, what do you say? Are you willing to have dinner with me yet?"

His touch on my wrist was making my pulse throb faster. I found myself thinking about the last time I'd had sex. Almost exactly five weeks before.

"Well? What about it?" he asked again, leaning toward me. "It's just a meal. You have to eat. Why not have company?"

I knew I should say no. After all, I should have said no to drinks, to this outing, to everything he offered from the very beginning.

"Okay," I said. "We can have dinner."

CHAPTER THIRTY-FOUR

After

The next week, Callie alternated between happily anticipating her dinner date with Ben and pondering her conversation with Jenna, trying to figure out what she hoped to accomplish by reconnecting with Ethan. She considered emailing him to say she couldn't make it after all, but the thought of canceling turned her stomach. She was afraid that feeling would never go away until she did something about it. She needed to either close the door with Ethan once and for all, or walk through it.

When Friday arrived, she pushed Ethan firmly onto the back burner. She put on the new outfit she'd bought on her birthday—the sweater and suede skirt—with tights and tall boots and carefully did her makeup.

Ben was due to pick her up at seven, and the last thing she wanted was for Nina or Lorraine to know who she was going out with. She wanted to keep this spark to herself for now—to nurture it in peace without endless questions or advice. So she hovered by the front window in the dark living room, watching for his car.

"What are you doing here in the dark?"

Callie jumped as Lorraine suddenly spoke behind her.

"Nothing." How did her mother still have the ability to make her feel like she was sneaking around like a child? And in her own house, no less? Perhaps because she *was* sneaking around . . . in the house that still belonged to her mother.

Callie was spared any further questions as she saw headlights pull up in front of the house.

"I've gotta run. Have a good night, Mom."

As Callie pulled the door shut behind her, she thought she heard Lorraine speaking, but pretended she didn't. At least now she wasn't behaving like a seven-year-old. She'd moved on to her teenage years.

Ben had just gotten out of the car when Callie started walking down the path.

"Hey, you're not letting me be a gentleman and come to your door."

"I'm saving you from my mother," Callie replied as she approached the car.

"Well, then, at least I can open the car door for you." Ben bent to do just that.

When they were both inside and Ben was pulling away from the curb, Callie asked, "So where are we going?"

"I made reservations at this really nice Indian restaurant near me, in Chestertown. If we save room, there's a terrific dessert place down the street."

"Sounds great."

Chestertown was larger than most of the suburbs, with a village green lined on one side with a string of hotels and office complexes. Restaurants, bars, and boutiques bordered the other sides. Ben pulled into one of the municipal parking lots, and they walked to the restaurant.

"I so rarely think to come here, but there's so much going on," Callie commented.

"Have you been to any of the shows at the Playhouse?" Ben referred to the theater a block from the village green.

"Not in a long time. Something else that I should do more often."

"I've seen some really good stuff there. Maybe there's something coming up that we could see." He glanced at her as they walked.

Callie liked his way of thinking. "That sounds great," she replied.

They paused their conversation as they entered the restaurant and were seated at their table, but then picked up where they left off.

"I was actually briefly involved in theater back in high school," Ben said as he dipped a piece of papadum in tamarind sauce.

Callie shook her head. "Not me. I have no problem standing in front of a classroom of kids, but the thought of being onstage gives me hives. What shows were you in?"

"Just one. *Grease.*"

"Cool! Who did you play?"

Ben shook his head ruefully. "It's pretty embarrassing."

"Why? Were you one of the Pink Ladies?"

"Very funny." Ben made a face at her. "Remember when I said my high school portrait was worse than yours? I was Eugene Florczyk."

Callie laughed. "I'm sure it was all makeup and costumes," she replied reassuringly.

"Oh, absolutely." Ben winked. "After that, I stuck with stage crew."

The waiter brought their entrees, rice, and naan in

hammered-copper bowls, and they stopped talking long enough to dish their meals out onto their square white plates.

"I had a friend in college, Jade, who liked her Indian food so spicy that her nose ran as she ate it," Callie commented as she took a bite. "Mmm. This is really good."

"The first time I ever had Indian food, it was crazy spicy. It was a long time before I was willing to try it again. But I'm glad I did."

They ate and talked about food and about trying new things, and the time flew by. Before Callie knew it, the waiter was clearing their plates, and Ben was asking if she was interested in dessert there or down the street. "They have all sorts of Italian pastries and gelato," he explained.

"You had me at pastries."

Ben paid the check, and they made their way to their next stop. Ben opened the door, and this time Callie was sure that his hand was on her back as she walked through.

"Oh my God, it smells so good in here," she exclaimed.

"I know, right? The only problem is deciding what to order."

"If that's my biggest problem, I'll take it."

In the end, they both got decaf cappuccinos, and Callie ordered a cannoli while Ben got a napoleon, both of them planning to share. They carried their desserts to a table near the back.

Callie could feel Ben's eyes skimming over her as she took off her coat and hung it on the back of her chair.

"I didn't say it before, but you look really nice," he said.

"Thanks." She sat and adjusted her skirt.

Ben sat, too, and they were momentarily quiet as they savored their pastries.

"For the longest time, I wouldn't try cannoli," remarked Callie. "When someone told me that they were filled with cheese, it sounded so gross. When I think about all the cannoli I could have eaten, it's very sad." She shook her head dolefully.

Ben pointed at the one in front of her with his fork. "Well, it's good you're making up for lost time, then."

They slowly ate their desserts and sipped their cappuccinos while they talked. When their cups and plates were long empty, Callie looked around. "We seem to be the only ones left."

Ben glanced at his watch. "Not surprising. It's nearly eleven. They probably want to close up."

Callie turned toward the counter. Sure enough, the woman behind it was wiping down the surface, while across the room, a young man with long hair was sweeping.

"I guess we should go before they kick us out."

Ben helped her on with her coat, and they stepped outside, then crossed to the opposite side of the street where the brightly lit movie theater marquee glowed against the darkened storefronts. As they passed, Ben pointed at one of the glass-encased posters. "Isn't that your ex-boyfriend's movie?"

Callie looked, and sure enough, it was a poster for *Rerouting*, underneath a placard that read "COMING SOON." Central to the image was a car with four guys draped across it. Dotted around the car were round photos with blurred edges; among them were pictures of the Las Vegas Strip, the car being towed, and Nick Sykes walking through the woods with Sarina Apple.

"Yeah, it is."

Ben seemed to be waiting for her to say more, and then his shoulders lifted in the slightest shrug. "Maybe I'll see it when it comes out," he said as he started walking again.

Callie's mouth was dry, and she was silent.

"Hey, have you seen that new movie with the guy who used to be on that hospital TV show—the one based in Boston? I forget what it's called," Ben suddenly asked.

"No, but I heard it's good." She was relieved he'd moved on.

"Yeah, me, too. Seems like most of the stuff he's done since the show ended has pretty much bombed."

"It must be tough when you're so identified with one character."

"I suppose that's why I gave up acting after my run as Eugene Florczyk."

"That was very wise," Callie said solemnly, but with a smile.

They arrived at the car and quickly got inside. Callie rubbed her hands together. They were cold, even in her gloves.

"Chilly?" Ben asked, glancing over.

Callie nodded. "It almost seems colder in the car than outside."

"Maybe because we're sitting still." He reached over and put his gloved hands around hers. "Better?"

Callie noted silently that it was not only her hands that felt warmer. "Much."

He smiled and left his hands there for another moment before putting them back on the wheel. Too soon, he was pulling up in front of her house.

"Door-to-door service," he said, turning off the engine.

"I would expect nothing less. Thanks for tonight. It was really nice."

"I thought so, too. So . . ." He paused, looking past her at the house for a moment. "I guess if you've never been dropped off at the curb by a guy, you also haven't had a good-night kiss here."

Callie shook her head and was suddenly aware of all the nerve endings in her body.

"Well, there's a first time for everything." Ben's hand, now gloveless, found her cheek, and he leaned toward her. Callie closed her eyes and felt his lips on hers. They were soft, but the kiss was firm. And lovely. Not like so many first kisses that somehow go horribly wrong—even if in the long run they work themselves out.

Ben drew back momentarily and looked into her eyes. And then he kissed her again, and her hand moved up to his neck. As she wished the kissing would never end, she thought it was a good thing so many people were sharing her house at the moment, or she would be sorely tempted to invite him inside. Even though it was a first date. Although, perhaps, one could consider their excursion for coffee their first date. And her birthday dinner their second. Which would make this their third. Nonetheless, she was glad her houseguests thwarted her desire to give in to temptation.

And then the kissing ended. Ben sat back in his seat, and Callie sighed softly.

Then Ben sighed, too, but it didn't sound as happy as hers had been. She glanced at him, but his eyes were trained straight ahead through the windshield.

"I really like you, Callie," he said. "I can't remember the last time I felt this way about someone."

The words were divine. But Callie's blood ran a little cold at his tone. There was a "but" coming. She knew it. Was he married? He'd told her he wasn't, very early on. Gay? Starting the process of gender reassignment? Moving to New Zealand? She searched his profile for some clue, and he bit his lip.

He turned toward her. "Maybe I'm overreacting. But my last girlfriend—when we met, she was on the rebound, and I didn't know it. It took a while for me to figure out that the problems we had were because there were three of us in the relationship. Her, me, and her ex. It's made me a little—I don't know if it's gun-shy, or paranoid." He paused and faced forward.

Callie waited, but the warm glow from the kiss had been replaced by an anxious roiling in her middle.

Ben looked at her again. "I need to know if there's any reason I should be worried about this ex-boyfriend of yours that your sister says you're not over."

Callie knew what the right answer was. Unfortunately, she didn't know if the right answer was true. After all, she was planning to meet Ethan in New York. And she liked Ben. She liked him a lot. But she didn't want to start off on—well, not a lie, but a half-truth. Her brain was muddled, and she struggled to find words that would both be honest and set his mind at ease.

But she hesitated too long before speaking. She could tell by the change in the set of his jaw as he watched her. His handsome, strong jaw that was just beginning to show how long it had been since he shaved that morning. She had felt the traces of stubble when they kissed. Which now felt like a lifetime ago.

"I'm working on it." She heard how unconvincing the words sounded as they echoed in her ears.

Ben looked away, and all Callie wanted to do was take it back, and say, *No, of course you have nothing to worry about.*

"It's just that this movie coming out has thrown me a little. That's all," she said hurriedly.

Ben swallowed and turned to face her again. "I want to believe you," he said, holding up his hand as Callie opened her mouth to speak. "I'm not saying you're lying. It's just—I saw your face when I asked you about the film. There's something unfinished there. And no matter how much I like you, I don't want to get hurt. Especially because I think we could really have something good here."

Callie pressed her lips together. What could she say? She couldn't promise that she wouldn't hurt him. How could she? "Can you give me a little time?" she asked, hesitantly putting her hand on his. He squeezed her fingers and she felt momentarily relieved.

But then he spoke, and her relief dissipated. "I don't know."

Tears stung Callie's eyes and she blinked rapidly.

Ben's face softened a little as he looked at her. "I'm sorry."

"No, I'm sorry," Callie said thickly. She cleared her throat. "I'm going to go inside now."

Ben nodded. She let herself out of the car and walked to the front door. She fumbled a little with her key and wondered if he would come after her. He didn't. But he waited until she had let herself in and shut the door before he pulled away.

CHAPTER THIRTY-FIVE

Before

Tom called a few times during the week following our trip to the shore. I felt guilty that seeing his number on the caller ID activated a buzziness in my brain—and elsewhere. He wanted to come out to Brook Hill to pick me up, but I told him I'd meet him in Hoboken. How would I explain him to my parents if he showed up at our door? Even though my stomach, which had been in turmoil for a while, wasn't on board, the rest of me was.

We met at a restaurant in uptown Hoboken, the Grill on Fourteenth—inventive name. It had a rooftop bar and a view of New York City. I was wearing a polka-dotted summer dress. As I walked toward the restaurant, it occurred to me that this was my first real "first date." Ethan and I had met up at a campus movie. Crazy as it seemed in hindsight, I hadn't been sure that it *was* a date. All of a sudden, I felt more like a grown-up. And more like a cheater.

"Hey," Tom said as he spotted me. "You look great."

I flushed. "Thanks."

We had a drink at the bar while we waited for a table. When we were finally seated, I was happy to be off my feet in their high-heeled sandals. I could barely taste my grilled chicken with roasted peppers. It was as if I were watching myself from above, observing a girl in a sundress on a date with a good-looking guy in a polo shirt.

Tom turned to me as we stepped outside after dinner. "How about we walk over to the water?" He tilted his head toward the Hudson River.

"Sure," I said, even as I knew I shouldn't.

We walked past the factories that had been converted into high-priced lofts and arrived at the waterfront. As always, the skyline was beautiful—glittering and imposing. I put my elbows on the railing and looked across, wondering if it was possible to glimpse Nina's building downtown. Tom had his own elbows on the railing, but his back was to the skyline. I glanced at him and found his eyes on me.

"What?" I asked.

"Just looking at you. I like to look at you."

My face got warm and I lifted my arms from the railing to stand up straight. I knew I should say I had to go home, but before I could get the words out, he reached out his hand and traced my left arm from my elbow up to my shoulder. Then his hand moved toward my neck.

"Tom. I don't think—"

"Good. Don't think," he interrupted, and bent to kiss me.

I didn't mean to, but I kissed him back. My muscles had lost all connection with my brain. His tongue was entwined with mine, and I found myself thinking he'd probably kissed a lot of people. He was very good at it. Finally, I pulled away.

"Do you know how long I've been wanting to do that?" Tom asked, his fingertips running along my arm again. "Since that first night I saw you and didn't introduce myself."

I swallowed. "I think I should head home." I knew it wasn't the kindest thing to say, but I shouldn't have been encouraging him anyway. Of course, I shouldn't have kissed him either. Or met him for dinner. Or given him my number. The list was endless.

He looked at me, puzzled. "Are you okay?"

I nodded. "Just . . . it's just late. It's the downside of living with your parents." I felt bad throwing them under the bus. They were probably asleep. But on the long list of things I should have felt bad about, that was nowhere near the top.

He took my hand and we walked toward my mom's Honda, which was parked on Washington Street, Hoboken's main drag. We stood beside it, and he brushed a piece of my hair out of my face. "I think it goes without saying that I want to see you again."

I looked up at him. He was a few inches taller than Ethan. *Ethan.* And then he was cupping my face in his hand and kissing me again. I could feel his kisses deep inside, in places no one but Ethan had ever touched. His other hand moved down to the small of my back and pressed me against him.

I knew he was trying to get me into bed. It was probably all he was interested in. I was clear from the beginning that I was leaving town. Moving three thousand miles away. As if he could read my thoughts, he stopped kissing me long enough to murmur against my lips, "Are you sure you have to go?"

His words were a sharp breeze blowing away the fog. I shakily drew a long breath and took a step backward. "I do."

"Okay, then. I'll call you."

He waited while I walked around to the driver's side and let myself into the car, and I saw him waving in the rearview mirror as I pulled away from the curb. A few blocks away, at a traffic light, I put my forehead against the steering wheel and shut my eyes. The blare of the horn behind me jolted me back to reality, and I headed home.

I didn't intend to see him again. I really didn't. But then he called—as I knew he would. Debi kept asking me about him, her eyes sparkling. I wished I could confide in her. But, of course, I couldn't.

There was no one I could share this with. I certainly couldn't talk to anyone who knew about Ethan. And people who didn't know about Ethan wouldn't understand. Unless I told them the whole story—and was willing to face the judgments they were sure to pass. So, I talked to Ethan and pretended everything was fine. And I agreed to meet Tom again for dinner, still feeling nauseated, but also wanting to know what life had to offer besides what was on this road I'd been traveling for four years.

Tom suggested we get dinner at a restaurant a few blocks west of Washington Street and then go hear some music at the Salty Dog, the bar where he and his band had performed. I drove toward Hoboken beneath a darkening sky, wishing I'd brought an umbrella. I kept telling myself I was going to end it tonight. Maybe even at dinner. And then I would head home, safe and sound.

But dinner came and went. He made me laugh with stories about his clients, and it felt natural when he reached across the table to cover my hand with his. We shared something called "chocolate decadence" for dessert, and Tom picked up the check. When we stepped outside, it was drizzling. He didn't have an umbrella either.

"Well, unless we go back in and have a second dinner, I guess we have no choice," Tom remarked.

He draped his arm around my shoulder, and we started walking. But almost right away, the rain fell more heavily. We'd barely made it a block when he pulled me under the awning of a corner deli that was closed for the night. We watched the rain coming down in sheets.

"Doesn't look like it's going to let up," I commented, noting the water rushing beside the curb.

Tom shook his head. "Nope. I'd say we have three choices."

I looked at him.

"We can stay here under this awning. We can run the four blocks to the Salty Dog and get completely soaked. Or we can stop at my place. I'm about half a block further on. We can dry off and pick up an umbrella."

I bit my lip, continuing to look at him. His face appeared open and guileless. And his eyes, lighter blue than Ethan's, were steady on my face.

As if he could read my mind, he smiled. "No matter how powerful you think I am, I can't control the weather. This wasn't a ploy to get you back to my apartment."

I wasn't sure what other choice we had. I nodded in agreement.

We sprinted the half block but nonetheless were drenched when we got to his brownstone. He unlocked the heavy exterior door; led me down the hall, which was overlaid with small, diamond-shaped tile; and let me into his first-floor apartment. The living room was all large leather sofa and big TV. Clearly a guy's place—but remarkably neat. Had he straightened up with me in mind?

"Where's your roommate?"

"Golf trip. Let me get some towels." He disappeared down the hallway but continued to talk, his voice carrying back toward me. "Our clients are always giving us all kinds of crap with their logos on it, so I have a big-ass collection of T-shirts. I bet there's something you could wear so we can dry your dress."

I looked down. My dress was soaked through. Good thing it was black.

"Ah, perfect!" he shouted, returning to the room with

towels and a forest-green T-shirt that he unfolded and shook
out for me to see. "It's an extra-extra-large." It was at least
as long as my dress and definitely contained more material.
Across the chest was the logo of a natural food company
whose granola bars I had tried once. I didn't like them. "You
can change in the bathroom." He handed me the shirt and a
towel and pointed back down the hall. "The dryer is in there,
too. You can throw your dress in."

I kicked my sandals off by the door and took the items from
him before walking down the hall barefoot. Shutting myself
into the bathroom, I looked in the mirror. My hair hung in wet
strands around my face. *How exactly did I get here?* I pulled
off my wet dress and dropped it on the floor. Even my bra was
damp, and it felt snug—did the rain shrink it?—but there was
no way I was taking it off. I drew the T-shirt over my head and
looked down at myself. Even though it covered more skin than
the dress had, I felt exposed, my bare legs appearing beneath
the hem. I tossed my dress into the dryer and turned it on,
thinking I couldn't delay leaving the bathroom much longer.

When I got back to the living room, it was deserted. I sat
on the leather sofa, curling my legs under me and assuming
Tom was changing in his bedroom. Sure enough, he appeared
a few minutes later, in a fresh shirt and shorts, rubbing his hair
with a towel. "Can I get you something? A drink?"

I couldn't go anywhere until my dress dried. *Why not?*
"What do you have?"

He went into the kitchen, and I heard the refrigerator door
open. "Not much." He reappeared in the doorway holding two
long-necked bottles of summer ale.

"Sure."

He brought them over along with two glasses and a bottle opener. I watched him pop the tops off and pour the beer
into the glasses. I thought back to the flyers various women's
groups used to pass out on campus, and was glad to see my

drink go directly from the bottle into the glass. No chance for him to slip me something. Not that I thought he would—but really, how well did I know this guy? Nowhere near the way I knew Ethan. I pushed that thought out of my head.

He passed me my drink, and I took a big swallow before putting it down on the glass-and-chrome coffee table.

"So the shirt worked." He gestured toward it.

I nodded and thought of my straggly wet hair. "Yeah, but I look like a drowned rat."

He shook his head. "Nah. It's sexy."

The blood rushed in my ears. He put his drink down on the table and deliberately moved closer to me. I couldn't pretend I didn't know where this was headed. And there was definitely a part of me that wanted it.

His hand was on my wet hair and his lips were on mine. His kisses grew more urgent, and his tongue explored my mouth. Somehow, even though I'd been sitting on the hem of my T-shirt, he got his hand under it. First it moved up my back, and then around to my front. He stopped kissing me. "Your bra is wet," he said. "I think we should take it off."

Before I could respond, he reached behind me and un-snapped it. Under the voluminous T-shirt, it was easy for him to slip the straps off my shoulders, and the bra slid down. And then his hand was moving around toward my chest again. Finding my bare breasts. I heard myself moan. My entire body was humming.

Then, somehow, the shirt and bra were off, and Tom's shirt, too, was on the floor. My hands explored the muscles of his chest as his lips moved down my body. When he started to slip his fingers inside the waistband of my panties, I came to my senses. My hand found his and grabbed it.

He lifted his head to look at me.

"No. It's too fast."

A shadow crossed his face, but he pulled his hand back.

"Do you have any idea how much I want you?" He dropped another kiss on my lips, and his hand found my breast again.

"You don't play fair," I whispered.

He laughed softly. Sexily. "I never said I did."

And then, he was kissing me again, and I was kissing him back, and we were shifting onto the sofa so he was on top of me, his hardness pressing between my legs. My skin was on fire, and when he tried again to pull off my last article of clothing, I didn't stop him. He reached for his shorts and fumbled one-handed in his pocket for a condom—as if he was afraid that, if he got up, I'd change my mind again. But at that point, my body had taken over any sense I had left—and I wanted to know what it would feel like to truly be with someone else.

He was poised over me, but the angle was wrong, and it took a minute for us to connect. He moaned as he entered me, and his eyes were shut in pleasure. I closed my own eyes and tried to go with it. Maybe it was the couch. Maybe it was us. Maybe it was me. But somehow, all I was aware of was friction and body parts—and then, it was over. He collapsed on top of me.

"Wow," he whispered. "That was amazing."

I swallowed. "Mmm" was all I could reply. I hoped he wouldn't ask if I'd finished—I just wanted this to be over. He didn't—he just got up to clean himself off. I pulled my clothes, such as they were, back on, and sat up.

When he returned, he put his arm around me. "You're incredible," he said. "Gorgeous." I let him kiss me, because it seemed silly at this point not to, but all I wanted was to slide to the other end of the couch.

"So now what? Movie?" He picked up the remote control.

How ironic. "Sure," I said, wondering how soon I could leave. I sat through *Legally Blonde 2* with his arm around me. The film finally ended, and I got up to go to the bathroom. I retrieved my dress, which was thankfully dry, and put it back on. Feeling more nauseated than I had before, I turned the water on in the sink, loudly, suddenly needing to throw up. Afterward, I rinsed out my mouth, using toothpaste I found in the vanity drawer.

Tom looked at me, surprised, when I came back out to the living room fully dressed. "Are you going?"

I nodded. "Parents. Gotta get home."

"Can I walk you to your car?"

I shook my head. "No, I'm fine."

He got up to kiss me goodbye, but I turned it into a peck and went downstairs, suddenly remembering the rain. Thankfully, the storm had cleared, and I headed outside, wondering how I had become this person. A person who would betray her boyfriend in the worst way. No wonder I felt sick.

CHAPTER THIRTY-SIX

After

Time was quickly skidding into the holidays. Hanukkah had already begun, a bigger event for Callie than usual now that she was living with Zoe. Her niece bounced up and down every evening, eager to light the menorah so she could get her present.

Callie tried to throw herself into sharing—or at least being entertained by—her niece's joy, but it wasn't easy. She'd splurged on Magna-Tiles for her—magnetic plastic squares that could be configured and reconfigured into a dazzling array of structures. She and Zoe sat on the floor building, but Callie couldn't keep her mind from wandering. It was the same when she decided to make latkes. They cooked them at Bouncy Castles every year, but she'd never tried at home. They all sat in Nina's room—which, like the rest of the house, had been decorated for Hanukkah with blue-and-white paper chains and sparkly Stars of David that Callie had made as projects with Zoe—to eat them with applesauce and sour cream. But as

Callie looked around the room, all she could think was *What a lovely family home. But it's not exactly mine.*

Not only was her romantic life screwed up, she was thirty-two years old and didn't have a home of her own. Moving into her parents' house was supposed to be temporary. Now it had been more than seven years. It had been easy and cheap to stick with the status quo, but were those good enough reasons? She thought—painfully—of the day Ben stopped by, and how she'd wished that the home he'd seen her in had been decorated with photos and objects she'd chosen herself. Somewhere along the way she'd gotten stuck. And worse, she hadn't even realized it. No matter what happened with Ethan, it was time to move on. She needed to create a life that was truly hers, in the here and now.

Tess and Callie went for coffee at Sip the last day before the holiday break.

"So?" Tess asked, swirling the plastic stirrer in her cup. "What's up with the architect?"

Callie felt a pang. More than a pang. She shook her head.

"What happened?"

Callie pushed her fingers through her hair and pressed the heels of her hands against her eyes.

"That bad?"

Callie peeked between her hands. "I'm a disaster."

"What did you do? Ask him how many kids he wants?"

Callie sighed. "I wish. I as much as told him I wasn't over my ex."

Tess looked at her as if she'd sprouted three heads. "What the fuck is wrong with you?" she asked incredulously. Callie couldn't blame her.

"I don't know," Callie said gloomily. She laid out the conversation to Tess as it had happened, and Tess shook her head.

"Discretion? Ever heard of that? No need to be so honest. It was a first date!"

Callie put down her cup without having taken a sip. "I know. But he's a good guy. At least I think he is. I couldn't lie."

"Why the hell not? It wouldn't be a lie. It would have been . . . withholding the whole truth. It's not like you're even in touch with this other guy."

Callie picked at her cuticle.

"You're not, are you? What have you been keeping from me? Is this about your trip to LA?" Tess's eyes narrowed.

Callie sighed. Time to come clean. "I actually heard from him—Ethan. He emailed me. He's going to be in New York for the premiere after New Year's."

"And you're going to see him," Tess said flatly.

Callie nodded. "We've emailed a few times. We're meeting for a drink."

"And what do you expect to come of this?"

Callie looked at her friend. "The thing is, ever since this movie thing came up, I can't get him out of my head. I need to find out if I screwed up all those years ago."

"And seeing him is going to help you with that? Are you planning to throw yourself into his arms?"

"No! And I'm sure he's going to want answers, too. That phone call I told you about . . . when I broke up with him. I wasn't very . . . forthcoming."

"Why doesn't that surprise me?"

"All right, Ms. Know-It-All. But the bottom line is, maybe seeing him, no matter the outcome, will let me finally put this behind me."

"No matter the outcome," Tess repeated. "But you're still going to LA . . ." She let her voice trail off.

"Hey, I'm going for an educational conference. So, Ethan or no Ethan, it'll be worthwhile."

"Right," said Tess disbelievingly. She took another sip of her coffee and looked at Callie over the rim of her cup. "All I can say is, whatever happens, I hope he sees the amazing person I do. And I hope you do, too."

Callie felt a surge of warmth toward her friend. "What would I do without you?"

The days of the holiday break felt extralong as they ticked by before Callie's meeting with Ethan. When she wasn't thinking about that, she was thinking about Ben, fearing that she'd made the biggest mistake of her life. It suddenly occurred to her that for so many years she'd wondered if breaking up with Ethan was her most significant blunder. What did it mean that her thinking had shifted?

She tried to distract herself by creating the "portfolio" Margo the designer had suggested. The more she thought about it, the more excited Callie was about the chance to moonlight by putting her artistic streak to use. She'd taken photos of the bookshelves and mural at school, and was working on drawings of animals, trains, fairies, trucks—anything that children might like—as well as sample alphabets in different styles. But even as she created, her mind swam.

She wasn't sure if it was good or bad that her dad had come up for the holidays. He was back sleeping in the living room, and the house felt chockablock with people—especially with Zoe's school closed and Michael, remarkably enough, taking a few days off. On the one hand, it made Callie crazy to be constantly surrounded by people. On the other, it was a distraction from her ever-circling thoughts. On yet the third hand, she'd been questioning more and more whether she wanted to continue living in her parents' house and wondered when the right time would be to bring that up.

On the evening of Christmas Day, while Nina, Michael, and Zoe were watching a *Frosty the Snowman* and *A Charlie Brown Christmas* marathon upstairs, Callie was loading the

dishwasher after their annual Chinese food takeout dinner, and her parents sat at the kitchen table. Lorraine flipped
through a stack of catalogs, commenting on nearly every page.
"Who in the world would spend eighty dollars on a heated
steering wheel cover?" "Martin, look at these sheets. Don't you
think they'd be nice in our guest room?" "These are such cute
dresses. Maybe we should get one for Zoe . . . Wait! Are they
kidding? Who buys a dress for a four-year-old that costs over a
hundred dollars? I wouldn't spend that on a dress for me, and
I'm not growing anymore. Well, maybe sideways!"

Meanwhile, Martin had procured a pad of paper and a pen
and was making a list. He was big on making lists. Callie wondered if it was a way for him to look busy so he wouldn't be
drawn into every inane conversation Lorraine tried to start.

"Callie, I'm putting together a list of house things we
should deal with come spring," he said.

Callie glanced over and saw a string of blue ink on the
lined paper.

Maybe this is the time. Callie picked up the dish towel
from the counter and dried her hands as she turned. "Actually,
Dad, I've been thinking of getting my own place."

Martin looked surprised, but it was Lorraine who spoke.
"What are you talking about? This *is* your own place."

"No, Ma, it's not. It's your place."

"Don't be ridiculous." Lorraine paused to fold down the
corner of the page she was on and closed the catalog. "Is this
because of your sister?" Her eyes narrowed.

Callie hung the towel on its hook. "No, it's not because of
Nina."

Lorraine's facial expression suggested she didn't believe a
word of it.

"Well, maybe she got me thinking about it," Callie allowed.
"But it's really that I'm not a kid anymore. I haven't been for a
long time. I should be living on my own." She held up her hand

as Lorraine opened her mouth. "I mean, in a place I'm paying for. And that has my stuff in it. Not yours."

Lorraine snorted, but Martin gave her an appraising look.

"You have a point, Callie," he said as Lorraine glared at him. "What if you paid us rent? And made some changes here?"

"I don't know, Dad. This is still your house. I don't need all this space."

"This is ridiculous," interjected Lorraine. "The house is here. We're not selling it. Why shouldn't you be living in it?"

"Lorraine," Martin began, shifting toward his wife. "It's up to Callie." He glanced at his daughter. "We don't need to decide now. But it's something to think about. You let us know what you want to do."

"Thanks, Dad." Callie smiled at him.

He gave her a mischievous smile back and squeezed her hand. "Our baby's growing up," he said.

"Dad!" she exclaimed, and though she rolled her eyes, she didn't really mind.

CHAPTER THIRTY-SEVEN

Before

The morning after I slept with Tom, the first thing I did was throw up. When there was nothing left inside me, I splashed water on my face and gazed at myself in the mirror. I looked the same—just a little green around the gills, as my mother would say. How could I have the same face, when inside I wasn't the same at all? I didn't know who I was.

Tom called, but I let it go to voicemail. I went through the weekend in a fog, spending most of it in bed. I told my mom I'd picked up a stomach bug. The second time Tom called, I answered the phone and told him I couldn't see him again. He was confused, but I couldn't tell if he was hurt or just puzzled. He'd only known me for three weeks, I told myself. He'd get over it. The way I treated him was nothing compared with what I'd done to Ethan.

I talked to Ethan every day and wanted to cry every time I heard his voice. Not only because of what I did—but because I didn't know what to do next. How could we ever get past this? Did I even want to?

I pulled myself together for work on Monday morning because I didn't want to lose the job. I ran the shower while I threw up so my mom wouldn't know I was still sick. Or whatever I was.

When I got to the office, Debi asked how my date was—and then looked at my drawn, gray face and said, "That bad?"

I shrugged. "I was sick over the weekend, that's all. It was okay, but I'm not going to see him again."

Debi opened her mouth, presumably to ask why, but luckily the phone rang and I had to answer it. I kept my head down the rest of the day and didn't eat lunch in the staff room. I wasn't hungry anyway and told everyone I needed to run errands.

Every day that week I went to work feeling sick to my stomach and spent my lunch hours wandering in and out of shops near the office. On Thursday, I was looking at nail polish in the drugstore on the corner when the cramping started, somewhere deep in my middle. The pain was so bad I had to crouch down on the floor, bottles of polish remover staring back at me when I opened my eyes. Every time I thought I felt better, another wave crashed over me. One had just subsided when I saw two pairs of feet. I looked up—it was a woman holding a little boy's hand.

"Are you okay?" she asked, her forehead creased with worry.

I wanted to tell her I was, but I didn't think it was true. The boy was wearing shoes with Velcro straps. I focused on them as something clenched inside me.

She bent down. "Do you need help?"

"I don't know." I could barely choke out the words.

"Let me help you up."

I took her outstretched hand and stood, still hunched over. I felt wetness between my legs. My period. I hadn't been paying any attention to the calendar and didn't have anything with me. The thought of finding the right aisle was overwhelming. I looked at the woman, who had smooth, straight golden-brown hair.

"Do you have a tampon? Or anything?" I asked.

She let go of her son's hand and told him not to move. He ran his fingers along the shelf, pausing at each price sticker and then starting again. She rummaged through her bag and produced a pad in a pink wrapper.

I took it as the cramping began again. "Thanks. I think I just need the bathroom." I tried not to let the pain show on my face.

The woman at the pharmacy counter directed me to the toilet in the stockroom, clearly not meant for public use. I pulled down my pants—blood was everywhere. Soaked through my underwear and my thankfully black pants, and streaking the insides of my thighs. I sat for a while, hunched over and panicked, feeling like someone was reaching inside my gut and squeezing. I had no idea what to do—so I called my mother.

Remarkably, she didn't ask any questions. She picked me up and drove me straight to her gynecologist's office. I had no idea how she got them to see me right away, but she did. The first thing they asked was the date of my last period. I didn't know. I'd always kept track when I was at school, but I hadn't thought about it since I got home. It had been a while. Too long. They took blood, put me in the stirrups for an exam, and brought in an ultrasound machine. I didn't ask any questions. I didn't want to know.

But then the doctor pulled over a chair to talk to me. I was wearing a gown, open to the back, with nothing under it but my bra. She was about my mother's age, maybe a little younger. The fine lines around her eyes made her look kind.

"Callie," she began. "Did you know you were pregnant?"

Were. I shook my head.

"Well, you were. I'm afraid you've had a miscarriage. I'm sorry."

A miscarriage. Was it Ethan's? Tom's? It had only been a week since I'd had sex with Tom. It had to have been Ethan's. But he always wore condoms. Except . . . A memory of graduation night came back to me in a rush. In the dark, he'd whispered in my ear that he wanted to feel what it was like to be inside me with nothing on. Just once, before we were going to be apart for so long. He promised he'd pull out and put a condom on—and he had. But I guess it hadn't been enough. The doctor was still talking. Something about a procedure to clean out my uterus. About there being no reason to worry about my being able to carry future pregnancies to term. And then she was asking me if I wanted my mom to come in. *Yes, I do.*

The next few days were a blur. My mom was amazing. The last thing I wanted her to know was that I was having sex. Clearly, that cat was out of the bag. But she didn't ask any questions—which, for her, was nearly incomprehensible. She just held me while I cried, and I found myself telling her about Tom, how confused I was, and how terrible I felt. She rubbed my back, told me everything would be okay, and made the arrangements for the D&C.

Afterward, I spent a day in bed. Mom brought me soup and sat next to me while she updated me on the neighbors—who was getting divorced, who called the town to report someone putting up a deck without a permit, who refused to pick up after their dog. For once, I didn't mind listening. She told Dad that I had to have an ovarian cyst removed. Being Dad, he asked nothing and avoided the topic entirely.

When I was alone, I thought about the terrible things I'd done. I was pregnant with Ethan's baby, and I didn't know it. I slept with someone else. I lost the baby. I couldn't pretend anymore. I knew I wasn't going to California. It wouldn't be fair to

Ethan. It wasn't right for me. No matter how hard it would be, I had to call and tell him. He didn't need to know the whole story—it would only hurt him more. But I had to make that call. It was time.

CHAPTER THIRTY-EIGHT

After

The day before New Year's Eve, Michael went to work, and Lorraine and Martin took Zoe to see a movie about a talking beaver. Callie was invited along, but she declined. For some reason, a talking beaver wasn't much of a draw.

Instead, she was in "her" room, "reading" the new Jojo Moyes novel Tess had given her for the holidays. Her eyes scanned the same page again and again as her mind wandered. She finally put the book down and reread Ethan's last email, which confirmed the day and time of their meeting and said he looked forward to seeing her. It was at least the sixth time she'd read the message, but she hadn't discovered any deeper meaning behind his words. She was about to pick up the book again when there was a knock on the doorframe. It was Nina.

"What are you doing up?" Callie exclaimed.

"If I can walk to the bathroom, I can walk down the hall," her sister said dryly.

"Get back into bed!"

But Nina stepped inside. "One bed's as good as another." She navigated her bulky belly and the rest of her onto Zoe's pink bedspread, pulling up her legs and making herself comfortable while Callie watched. "Besides, I'm thirty-six weeks now. This whole bed rest thing is ridiculous." Nina pulled a piece of hair in front of her eyes as if examining it for split ends and then pushed it back again. "Anyway, I wanted to talk to you."

Callie sat down on the air mattress, leaned back on her hands, and looked at Nina quizzically.

"So, Mom's pissed at me."

Callie raised her eyebrows.

"She thinks it's my fault you want to get your own place. She says I shouldn't have given you a hard time. That I have a good life, and I shouldn't care if things seem 'fair.'"

Callie cocked her head. "*Do* you care?"

Nina sighed. "Sure I do. I don't think there are many sisters who wouldn't be at least a little annoyed that their sister gets to live rent-free in their parents' house when those same parents don't do anything to help her financially. And yes, I know we're in completely different circumstances, but I'm human. Sue me."

"If you haven't noticed, you're living here now. It's not like you get nothing from them." Callie started to push herself off the air mattress. The air mattress she was sleeping on because her sister and her family were now sharing the house with her, "rent-free."

"Yeah, and I had to beg you for it. No one offered. I had to ask."

That's true. Callie leaned back again.

"Look, I didn't come in here to fight." Nina rolled her head as if her neck was sore. "I came in to say that you shouldn't feel you have to move out on my account. But I appreciate your being willing to."

Callie looked at her sister, surprised. "Thanks." She glanced away and then back again. "But the truth is, I think maybe you're right. I shouldn't be here. I should be on my own. Truly on my own." She bit the inside of her lip.

Nina smiled. "Good for you."

Callie chose not to be annoyed by her sister's patronizing tone. "We'll see how it goes. I still have to figure it out."

As Callie watched her, Nina's smile faded a little.

"What?" Callie asked warily.

"So . . . Ethan's movie is coming out in a couple of weeks. Are you going to go see it?"

Callie took a deep breath. She'd told Jenna; she'd told Tess. Why keep her plans a secret from Nina? She was tired of secrets anyway. Her life was full of them.

"I'm going to do more than that," she said quietly.

"What do you mean?"

She steeled herself, ready for further disapproval. "I'm going to see him."

Nina passed her hand across her face and sighed. "Look, I know what happened."

Callie's eyebrows drew together. She was truly baffled. "What do you mean?"

"I know about you and that guy."

"What guy?"

Nina peered at her as if trying to determine if she was telling the truth or playing dumb. "The guy you kissed on the street in Hoboken."

How could Nina possibly know?

"I was there." Nina sighed. "I'd met some friends for dinner and we were walking on Washington Street. Suddenly, there you were, holding hands with a tall blond guy. I couldn't believe it was you, but then I looked at the car you were next to. It was Mom's car, with the Welford and Loyola stickers."

Callie couldn't grasp what Nina was saying. "Why didn't you say anything?"

"Um . . . because you started kissing him. And as far as I knew, you were about to move in with another guy."

Callie shook her head to clear cobwebs from her brain. "But why didn't you say something afterward?"

"I guess I thought you'd tell me about it. When you didn't—how was I going to bring it up? Especially after you and Ethan broke up—it was just weird. Once I didn't say something right away, the moment had passed. Why didn't *you* tell *me*?"

"What was I going to say?" Callie asked, digging her fingernails into her palms as she clenched her fists. "'By the way, I cheated on Ethan.' Who wants to admit that?"

"I'm your sister. You could have told me."

"Why? So you could tell me what a terrible person I am?"

"I wouldn't have done that!"

"Really?" Callie looked at her wide-eyed, her eyebrows nearly at her hairline.

Nina looked at her hands. "Okay. Fine. I understand why you think I'd be . . . judgy. But still . . . I always felt bad that you didn't think you could tell me the truth. When you and Ethan broke up, I kept pressing you. I was trying to let you know I was there for you. That you could tell me anything." Nina paused and looked away, her voice husky when she spoke again. "Honestly, it hurt that you didn't tell me. There was a time you told me everything. Or at least I thought you did."

Callie remembered those conversations. She'd thought Nina was being nosy. Implying that Callie had made a mistake. She pulled her knees up and rested her chin on them. A silence floated between them.

"What happened with the guy?" Nina asked after a moment. "I mean, I never saw him again. It wasn't like you were suddenly with someone new."

Callie took a deep breath. Hadn't she decided she was tired of secrets? "Nothing happened. We went on a few dates." She paused. "And I slept with him—the week after you saw us." She waited for Nina to respond, but her sister was quiet.

Callie continued. "There wasn't anything there. I stopped seeing him, but I was a mess. I kept talking to Ethan, feeling horrible about what I'd done, but not knowing what to do." She paused, her eyes on Nina's rounded belly, and sucked in her breath before she began again, her voice barely a whisper. "And then, a week later, I started bleeding."

Nina's eyes widened.

Callie had never described aloud what she'd been through, and she had to swallow the hard lump that had lodged in her throat as her eyes filled. "I'd been feeling sick, but I didn't put it together. It turned out I was pregnant. I had a miscarriage."

Nina sat up straight, her hand on her mouth. "Oh, Callie! I can't believe you went through that alone."

Callie managed a rueful smile. "Actually, I didn't. I had Mom." Nina's eyes widened farther. "She was great. Took me to the doctor, took care of me."

"I can't believe you never told me any of this. I can't believe *Mom* never told me any of this," Nina exclaimed in astonishment. "Was it Ethan's baby? Or the other guy's?"

Callie bit her lip. "I think it had to be Ethan's. But just the fact that I had to ask myself that question . . . I knew we couldn't go on like that. I couldn't go to California. I had to end it." She could still hear the hurt and bewilderment in Ethan's voice. He was devastated. Devastated enough by the fact that she was breaking up with him—and he didn't even know the whole truth. Something still twisted deep inside when she thought of the pain she'd caused. She looked down at her hands. "You were right the other day when you said I was a mess. I was a complete mess, Neen. I look back on that time and it seems like a dream, like it happened to someone else. I *couldn't* tell you—I mean, you were off living your perfect *Sex in the City* life . . ."

Callie felt the air mattress shift. Nina had sat down next to her. "What are you doing?" Callie asked, alarmed. "You're supposed to stay still."

"Shh," Nina said, putting her arm around her. *This must be how Zoe feels when Nina comforts her.* Nina leaned her head on Callie's and gave her a hug. "And shut up about my *Sex in the City* life, when you were obviously the one having sex in the city."

Callie pulled away and glared at her.

"Just teasing." Nina smiled sadly at her sister and squeezed her hand. "I'm so sorry for all of it."

Callie bit her lip. There was one other piece in this puzzle. A piece she'd carried deep in the recesses of her heart. The question she was afraid to ask. She looked down at her hands again, now intertwined with her sister's. "Neen—do you think *I* caused the miscarriage? Because I didn't know I was pregnant? Because I had sex with someone else?" That had been all she could think about when the doctor had told her. When Lorraine had gone on and on about the neighbors. And in the weeks—and months—that followed. Callie held her breath as she waited for her sister to speak.

"Oh, Callie! Look at me." When Callie didn't, Nina put her finger under her chin and turned her head to face her. "Listen. The miscarriage wasn't your fault. Do you know how many pregnancies end during the first trimester? It just didn't work out. It had absolutely nothing to do with you."

Callie looked at her doubtfully.

"Seriously, Callie. You need to believe me. Look. Do you want me to tell you how many times Michael and I had sex while I was pregnant with Zoe?"

Callie shook her head vigorously.

"Well then." Nina smiled. "Just believe me when I tell you it was a lot. There are actually studies that say sex is *good* for the developing baby. Please stop being so hard on yourself."

Callie turned away and looked down at her lap.

"Have you felt guilty all this time?" Nina asked quietly.

Have I?

Nina raised her sister's head again. "You want to know what I think?"

"Even if I don't, I bet you'll tell me," Callie said, with a half smile.

"I think you sabotaged things with Ethan. I think you wanted to end it and couldn't get yourself to do it. So you forced your own hand."

Callie's immediate reaction was to disagree. *And yet . . .*

Nina put her hand on Callie's. "And you ended up paying some major consequences. More than Ethan ever knew. Maybe even more than you realized yourself."

Callie had been so focused on what she'd done to Ethan that she'd never considered how much her own heart had ached. And not just because she'd hurt Ethan. She had been so ashamed about what she'd done, and about the miscarriage, she'd never stopped to think about what she lost that summer. She thought she deserved the pain—physical and emotional. Suddenly, she was blinking back tears again.

"You have to let it go," Nina said softly. "You were barely an adult. He was the only person you'd ever been with. People make mistakes when they're young."

"And stupid."

"Stop punishing yourself. I'm sure you did plenty of that at the time," Nina said, as if reading Callie's mind. "And it seems like Ethan is fine. Clearly you didn't destroy him."

Callie looked at her sister. "How do you know?"

"That he's fine? The guy has a major movie. Even if he fell apart then, he pulled himself together."

But all these years later, had Callie pulled *herself* together? Had she forgiven herself for what she'd done to Ethan? And what about what she'd done to herself? Had she even acknowledged that?

CHAPTER THIRTY-NINE

After

The days passed, and Callie grew increasingly anxious as her drinks date with Ethan approached. School had started again, and she felt Tess's eyes on her all the time. Martin had flown back to Florida—tired of the couch and eager to return to the golf course. Meanwhile, Nina became more and more resistant to staying in bed and kept turning up around the house. Callie felt like her sister—along with Tess—was always watching her.

The day before "E-Day," Nina's doctor officially ended her bed rest, although, as Michael kept reminding his wife, she was still supposed to "take it easy." The doctor clearly didn't know Nina very well. Taking it easy wasn't in her vocabulary. She got Lorraine to drive her to her own house immediately after the appointment and came back exclaiming giddily about the progress. Callie had expected her sister to have a list of complaints about what had taken place while she was out of commission, but she was genuinely delighted. Callie couldn't help but smile, watching her act like a kid who'd visited the most incredible candy store imaginable.

The following day, Callie pulled out the dress she'd bought at Alouette and put it on, then went into Nina and Michael's room to pirouette in front of the full-length mirror. It was as perfect on her as she'd remembered. She did her makeup—the smoky eye and all—and used a curling iron she unearthed under the bathroom sink to touch up the ends of her hair.

Downstairs, she poked her head into the kitchen, where Nina was looking at paint swatches. "I'm heading out," she said.

"Oh no. I need to see what you're wearing."

Callie stepped into the kitchen.

"Oh, Callie! You look amazing! That dress is gorgeous on you. See—I always knew you could clean up nice."

Callie wrinkled her nose at her sister but flushed at the compliment. Suddenly, Lorraine was behind her.

"Oh my! Where are you going looking so beautiful?"

"Just into the city for drinks." Callie had given Nina permission to tell Lorraine where she was going after she was out the door. Callie didn't think she could handle her mother's reaction, especially having just revisited that awful time with Nina. Looking back on it, it was suddenly clear how wonderful her mother had been—never questioning her choices, never criticizing her, and never breathing a word of any of it to anyone. She gave Lorraine a quick but tight hug. "I love you, Mom."

Lorraine narrowed her eyes at her, as if surprised by the unexpected show of affection. But then she broke into a wide grin. "I love you, too, sweetie."

Callie took the train to Penn Station and walked up the stairs like a salmon swimming upstream. Rush hour had begun, and the crowds were flooding in the other direction, heading toward the trains destined for the suburbs. She waded through to the subway, took the A train to Fourteenth Street, and then headed west to Ethan's hotel, where she entered through the revolving glass door.

Callie spotted Ethan before he saw her. He was seated in an overstuffed chair, looking at his phone. He looked basically the same, though, true to the photo in the *Quarterly*, he had filled out, having lost some of the boyish lankiness she'd been so familiar with, and he wore no glasses. But his hair still flopped in his face. When he looked up and spotted her, she had the distinct impression that he'd had to catch his breath. But then he smiled, and she decided she'd imagined it. And in that instant, she realized she felt nothing. No desire for him. No regret about her choice.

As she walked toward him, he rose out of his seat. He was wearing a beautifully cut midnight-blue suit, no tie, and a crisp white shirt. All clearly expensive. "Wow," he said. "You look exactly the same."

She smiled. "Thanks. I don't. But thanks anyway."

He stepped toward her awkwardly, and they hugged as if neither of them knew where to put their arms. They quickly drew apart.

She glanced at his outfit. "You look great. A big step up from flannel."

He smiled, embarrassed. "It's Hollywood. A stylist put this together for me. It's so silly—no one will be looking at the screenwriter anyway. Not when they can goggle at Nick Sykes and Sarina Apple."

"Well, maybe they should. Without you, there'd be no movie."

"True. So, should we go to the bar?"

Callie wasn't sure when she'd needed a drink more. "Sure," she replied, and they crossed the lobby.

It was darker inside the hotel bar, where the decor was dark wood and black lacquer. There was jazz playing in the background. They found a table near the back, and Callie took off her coat. Ethan's eyes skimmed over her. "You look amazing," he said quietly.

"Thanks," she replied, pulling out a chair to sit down. A moment later, a waitress appeared to take their order.

Callie glanced at the drinks menu. "A Sam Adams, please." It was what she'd always drunk at Welford and it felt like the right choice.

Ethan looked at her. "Same drink," he said. "Sounds good." He looked at the waitress. "Make that two." He turned back to Callie. "Nice to get a beer. My girlfriend is a wine drinker, so I usually join her."

Callie nodded, and Ethan's eyes lingered on hers as if awaiting a reaction. Callie couldn't decide if his mentioning his girlfriend within the first three minutes was normal.

"Oh, umm . . . is she here? In New York, I mean? For the premiere?"

"Oh, no. I mean, she went with me to the one in LA but couldn't go to this one. She had to be back at school. She's a teacher. Like you . . . slash aspiring actress."

"Well—"

"I—"

They laughed awkwardly. "You go ahead," said Ethan, in a gentlemanly manner. Callie wished he hadn't been so polite. She wasn't sure what she was going to say.

"Boy, this is weird" was what she came up with.

"I'll drink to that."

The waitress returned, and they were spared further conversation for a moment while she poured the beers into glasses. "Let me know if you need anything else," she said and stepped away.

"So," Ethan began. "How are you? You said you'd be coming into the city after you got out of school for the day—so I know you're teaching. But that's about it. What have you been up to for the past ten years?"

Was that a dig? If so, Callie was sure it was deserved. "Well, I teach at a preschool in the town where I grew up."

Ethan raised his eyebrows. "Are you living with your parents?"

What kind of question is that? "No, they're in Florida now." Callie conveniently left out that her place of residence was the house they still owned. "Are your folks still in Chicago?" She wondered how long they'd be able to sustain this courteous small talk.

"Yep. Same house. I get back to see them every few months."

"That's great. How's your dad doing?"

"He's good. Nice of you to ask." Ethan glanced at her again, and Callie could hear the unspoken *after all these years* loud and clear. "Anyway, he's had no further issues." Ethan rapped his knuckles on the table. "Knock on wood. He's gotten into running—he's actually healthier than he's been in years."

"So glad to hear it." Callie smiled warmly, meaning it. "And when did you move down to LA?"

"About seven years ago. I'd started to take screenwriting classes up in San Francisco and then decided to go for my MFA. One of my teachers had gone to USC, and it sounded like such a great program, I was willing to put aside my feelings about Southern California. And, I guess, it's worked out well." He shrugged.

Callie nodded. "Congratulations, by the way. Looks like the movie's going to be a hit."

"Thanks." He paused. "Do you plan on seeing it?"

"Of course."

He put his glass down and traced the moisture the beer bottle had left on the table with his index finger. "I wondered if

I'd hear from you when it came out." There was something in his tone she couldn't quite identify. Part wistful, part bitter—but she wasn't sure which sentiment was dominant. "All along I felt like I should reach out to you about it. After all, you were sort of the 'inspiration' for the screenplay. But I kept putting it off. I kept telling myself it made more sense to wait until things were more concrete—and then, as production started, I guess I just didn't know what to say. It's not like we'd left things on the best of terms." He looked at her. "I mean, I didn't even know if you'd talk to me."

Ethan took another swallow of beer before continuing. "You know, I started writing pretty soon after you dumped me. I was a mess for a long time." He paused, and Callie thought she could see some of that remembered hurt reflected in his eyes. "I was trying to stay super busy, and I heard about this screenwriting class. I figured, what the hell—I'd give it a try."

"And that's when you wrote the film?"

Ethan nodded. "I guess I thought it would be—cathartic." He exhaled roughly before continuing. "At first, it was all about us—how we got together—but it had no arc. It wasn't a good film. My teacher hated it. So I changed it. And kept on taking classes and writing more—and, like I said, I ended up going for my MFA. One of my teachers at USC hooked me up with an agent he knew. I gave him a couple of other scripts I'd written. He didn't think they were commercial, but he liked my writing. So I pulled out the only other screenplay I had and gave it to him. It was this one. I wanted to go back and edit it. Make it less about you and me. But then I figured, why spend more time on it when it might not go anywhere? But then it did. He got it optioned, and they actually put together the funding and started casting. And now, here we are."

Callie nodded. "Here we are," she echoed.

He sighed and rubbed his palm over his face. When he dropped his hand, his eyes were dark. "Callie, do you have any idea what you did to me?"

She looked down at her fingertips pressed against the table. The skin around her nails grew white with the pressure. She forced her gaze up to meet his. "I think so."

Ethan's eyes focused on the ceiling, and his jaw tensed. Then he looked back at her and shrugged. "You broke my heart. It sounds clichéd, but it's true."

She bit her lip. "I'm so sorry."

"After four years, I think I deserved more than a phone call."

Her eyes welled with tears and her throat clogged. "You did," she whispered.

Ethan looked at her for a moment and then looked away again as he took a sip of his drink. Callie waited. She didn't know what to say.

Ethan put his drink back down. When his eyes found Callie's again, he shook his head. "I never did anything to you. I didn't cheat on you. I didn't . . . I don't know . . . treat you badly. When you called, it was like getting hit by a freight train I never saw coming." He paused. "For years I wondered what I'd say to you if I ever saw you again."

Callie bit the inside of her cheek.

"My brother Josh—I can't even tell you how many hours he spent listening to me—would say it's not even worth getting into. It's over. Long over." He shrugged and, after a pause, spoke again. "So, you know, in the movie, the ex-girlfriend wants the guy back in the end."

Callie nearly choked on her beer. "I didn't know that."

"Yeah, I guess you can't spoil the Hollywood ending in the preview. But in the movie, she calls him and asks him to get back together. It's not the way I originally wrote it. But the studio said it's what audiences want."

She nodded slowly, and he raised his eyebrows. "Did you think that was why I emailed you? Did you think I might want you back?" he asked, his voice harsh.

Callie felt a spark of anger at his tone. She took another sip of beer to compose herself. "I guess I did wonder that. But I didn't know why you'd written the film in the first place. I didn't know what to think about any of it." She paused. "When I said I'd meet you, did you think *I* might want *you* back?"

"I think you've hurt me enough for this lifetime," Ethan said lightly, taking a long swallow of his beer.

Callie quickly looked away, blinking fast.

Ethan ran the back of his hand across his mouth as he put the glass down. "That was a joke."

She looked back at him, her eyebrows raised.

"Well, sort of." He laughed joylessly.

Callie swallowed. "I deserved that. I know I hurt you. I wish . . . well, I wish it could have been some other way."

Ethan took a deep breath and exhaled slowly. Then he leaned forward in his chair, tapping his fingers on the table. "I just didn't get it. I still don't. After all these years—it's never made any sense to me. I thought we were good. I had no idea we weren't."

Callie nodded, and part of her wanted to extend her hand and rest it on his. But she didn't. She didn't want there to be any misunderstanding. And she didn't want to feel him jerk his hand away either.

"I know," she began. "And that's my fault. I should have talked to you. I should have had the courage to break it off sooner. Because the truth is . . ." She took a deep breath and started again. "The truth is . . . I hadn't been happy for a while."

Ethan shook his head. "But you seemed like you were."

"Oh, Ethan, I'm not sure you really saw me. You saw us. And what you wanted us to be. And I didn't realize it myself for a long time. But then it hit me that somewhere along the way I'd gotten lost. Being with you felt safe . . . but I was giving up who I was, and what I wanted."

"I never asked you to give up who you were," he protested.

"But it's what happened. I loved you so much, and for a long time I was willing to go along with anything you wanted. But after a while I started to realize what I was missing out on, and it bothered me. I tried to push back, but somehow you always managed to talk me into doing things your way. I didn't want to let things slip by me. We were so young. You were ready to begin an adult life. You seemed so sure. And I just wasn't. I wasn't sure about anything."

Ethan drew a long breath. "You could have talked to me about it. You should have. What you did sucked."

Callie couldn't disagree. "I know it doesn't mean much, but I really am sorry. Breaking up with you wasn't an easy thing, Ethan. I hurt myself at least as much as I hurt you. And I handled it horribly. You're right. It sucked."

Ethan nodded slowly, as if absorbing what she'd said.

Callie hesitated. It would be so easy to stop talking now. But if she was coming clean, she should go all the way. She knew that Tom wasn't the point. She'd wanted to end things with Ethan before. Tom was just a convenient excuse. Something that finally pushed her to do what she'd needed to do for a long time. But after all these years, after all she'd put Ethan through, he deserved the full truth. And if it meant that he got to paint her as a cheater, well, it wasn't as if it wasn't true. "There's something else I should tell you . . ."

He looked at her quizzically.

She took a deep breath. "You asked me then if there was someone else . . ." Ethan's eyes narrowed, and Callie rushed ahead before she chickened out. "I said there wasn't, but that wasn't the truth."

He stared at her, waiting for her to continue.

"It wasn't anything serious. I met this guy. We went out.

He . . . well . . . he wasn't the point. It didn't come to anything. But I knew it was wrong. I shouldn't have done it. You deserved better. That's when I knew I had to end it with you. It's like—I couldn't do it just for me, just because I wanted something else. But I had to do it for you. Because you shouldn't be with someone who'd treat you like that."

As she spoke, Ethan was shaking his head. Callie couldn't tell if it was from disbelief, disgust, or some combination of the two. Then he let out a sound that was almost a snort. "So you were protecting me," he said incredulously.

"Well, would you have wanted to be with someone who'd cheat on you?" The word stung, but it was true.

Ethan was quiet for a moment. "I wanted to be with someone who loved me the way I loved her," he said finally.

Callie's nose clogged and her eyes stung, but she forced herself to speak. "And you should have been. And that wasn't me anymore. *I* wasn't me anymore. I needed to find myself again."

Ethan stared past her for so long, Callie began to wonder if he'd ever speak to her again. But finally his eyes refocused on her face. "Jesus. I never would have expected that from you. Not that I expected you to dump me either. But why didn't you tell me the truth?"

"I don't know. I could say I was trying to protect you. Maybe that was part of it. But it was probably more because I was ashamed. That wasn't the person I wanted to be."

Ethan sucked in a long breath and let it out before he spoke again. "Maybe it's better you didn't tell me. I don't know if you could've hurt me any more than you did, but if you could have, that would have been the way to do it. Imagining you with someone else was a visual I definitely didn't need." He paused. "So, this guy. Did you sleep with him?"

Callie flinched. She'd hoped Ethan would assume she had, and she hated the thought of delivering that final blow.

She was about to open her mouth and say that she did, just that one time. That one time that was so meaningless yet had changed everything.

Ethan quickly spoke again. "Never mind. I don't need to know."

In that moment, Callie knew she couldn't tell him the rest. It wouldn't change anything, and why give him the added pain of "what might have been" if he knew she'd been pregnant? That would be the piece of the story she'd continue to bear on her own, but at least now she didn't blame herself. At least not the way she once had. "I never meant to hurt you," she said quietly.

Ethan nodded slowly. "I know," he replied, not looking at her.

He picked up his glass again and tipped it back, taking a long swallow until there was nothing left. As if she'd been watching, the waitress was at the table in an instant, asking if they'd like another round.

Ethan's eyes flickered to Callie's. "I have a little more time before the red carpet. I could use another before I have to face the madness. You?"

She looked at the inch of beer that remained in her glass. She was exhausted. She wanted to leave. She'd said her piece. What more was there to say?

As if he were reading her mind, Ethan spoke again. "Just one more drink. For old time's sake?"

Suddenly Callie wanted to laugh. Wasn't this exactly what had always happened between them? He wanted one thing, and she wanted another—and then he'd twist her arm. But fine, she figured. One more drink, as a final apology for the pain she'd caused.

"Sure," she said, looking up at the waitress. "Same again, please."

In moments, there were two more bottles at the table,

along with a bowl of nuts. As the waitress poured the beer into their glasses, Callie looked across the table at Ethan, marveling that he seemed like a stranger. The idea that he had seen her naked—many, many times—was almost impossible to believe. She felt an ache in her chest. Had she really thrown Ben away for . . . this?

There was silence between them for a while, and then—after taking a big swig from his newly refilled drink—Ethan asked how her family was doing. She told him more about her parents moving to the year-round sunshine, and about Nina and her family. He talked about his brothers—Zach was getting into sportscasting, Josh was doing something with information technology. And they swapped stories about college classmates—unsurprisingly, she knew little to nothing about where his friends had ended up, and vice versa.

And he talked about his girlfriend, Paige, with whom he was living. Callie wasn't sure anyone could be such a combination of smart, funny, athletic, and beautiful, but she didn't comment.

"So, what did she think about you meeting me?"

"I didn't tell her." He picked at the label on the beer bottle that still sat on the table.

Callie raised her eyebrows.

"She doesn't know about you," Ethan said then, looking back at her.

Callie nodded slowly.

"I mean, she knows I had a college girlfriend, but she doesn't know about the whole movie connection thing. We weren't together when I first wrote the screenplay."

"Huh," Callie said, surprised.

"I mean, why give her something to worry about?"

Callie wasn't sure that a college relationship that had been over for ten years was anything that Paige should be uneasy about. But the fact that her live-in boyfriend was keeping a secret from her was another story.

"So, how about you? Are you with anyone?"

Callie couldn't help but wonder if the question was as casual as he intended it to be. But it didn't matter. She knew what she wanted—which wasn't to be with him again. She shook her head. "Not really."

"Not really?"

"There's this guy, but I don't know. Nothing to talk about." The last thing she wanted to do was talk about Ben, who she wished was sitting across from her right now instead of Ethan. Ethan gave her a long look and seemed about to say something, then almost visibly shook himself and was silent.

Once the check was paid, they left the bar, and Callie walked with him to the lobby.

"So," Ethan said.

"So," Callie echoed.

"I guess this is it, then. Unless we become Facebook friends," he quipped.

"I'm not on Facebook."

"I know," he replied, with a small smile. Embarrassed, perhaps, to admit that he'd looked for her there.

"Well . . ." Ethan reached to give her a hug. This time, it wasn't so awkward, and he held her for a moment, which surprised her. "Your hair smells the same."

Callie quickly pulled back from his embrace. "Same shampoo," she replied matter-of-factly. She cleared her throat. "Anyway, I'm glad you're doing well," she said, meaning it. "You deserve it. Good luck tonight."

"Thanks."

"I'd tell you to say hello to Paige for me, but . . ." Her voice trailed off.

Ethan smiled and shrugged, and for a moment, she felt a

little sorry for Paige. And perhaps for Ethan, too. But what she really felt was another pang of regret about Ben, and how foolish she'd been.

"Anyway." Ethan spoke again. "Have a safe trip home. Maybe we'll talk in another ten years."

"Maybe." But even as she said it, she doubted it. She could finally close this chapter. He wasn't the one who got away, he wasn't the one she needed to hold on to now. He was just someone she used to love. And perhaps more important, she'd apologized—and even if Ethan hadn't completely forgiven her or heard her full confession, she had forgiven herself.

Some things in life were simply out of our control, Callie reflected. Falling in and out of love, tripping and stumbling, making bad decisions and suffering the consequences—that was the stuff of life, not cause for shame. In fact, it was the very reason you had to keep going, even at the risk of falling again. All this time, and she'd never learned that lesson until now. She hated to admit it, but Nina was right.

Perhaps it would be better not to tell her.

CHAPTER FORTY

Now

I wheel my roller bag through Newark Airport, happy to be off the plane from Los Angeles. I'd caught a seven o'clock flight this morning, but with the time difference it's already after three in the afternoon here in New Jersey. The weekend at the NOECE conference was unexpectedly interesting, but also exhausting, and I'm thrilled to be back on the East Coast. I follow the signs to ground transportation and wait in the mercifully short taxi line, giving the driver an address in Wolcott as soon as I shut the door.

As it turned out, the conference coincided with Nina and Michael's move-out date. I spent days helping them pack before I left—assistance they desperately needed now that Nina has the new baby to take care of.

Daniel Matthew is four weeks old and gorgeous, if you want to take a besotted aunt's word for it. Nina went into labor a few days after her bed rest ended, and all went smoothly. Zoe is alternately enamored of her tiny baby brother and frustrated by him. "Look how cute he is! Can I kiss him?" "Daniel is yawning! How does he know how to do that?" "He doesn't *do* anything! When will he be able to play with me?" And she is constantly at Nina's side, clamoring for attention. Watching her, I can't help but wonder if this was how Nina behaved when I was born. Perhaps that was the beginning of our turbulent relationship—although I truly think we're on the upswing these days.

My dad flew up to meet Daniel ten days after he was born. Then, he and my mom returned to Florida a week later. I thought they'd stay to help with the move, but my mom was done. Having to be a hands-on parent and grandparent for months had taken its toll, and being constantly awakened in the middle of the night was the last straw. But more than ever, I appreciate how admirably she rises to the occasion when it really counts.

The cab pulls up in front of Nina and Michael's house. Michael lets me in and gives me a kiss on the cheek. "Welcome back. Nina's in the family room." He jerks his thumb toward the back of the house.

There are boxes everywhere. I can't believe my sister isn't hyperventilating in this mess, but I find her on the sofa nursing.

"Hey," she says wearily. "How was your trip?"

"Good. Fine. Glad to be back. What can I do to help?"

She sighs. "Honestly, I don't know. And you've been traveling all weekend. You shouldn't have to do anything. Why don't you just go up and find Zoe? She's supposed to be getting her room organized. I don't even want to know what that means."

I grin, trying to imagine that myself, and head upstairs. When I arrive in Zoe's doorway, I'm momentarily stunned. Hanging on the wall above her bed is the "Zoe's Room" sign I made. The paint color, the rug, the new throw pillows on the bed—they're all perfectly coordinated with it.

"Hi, Aunt Callie!" Zoe looks up from the floor where she's surrounded by stuffed animals. "Do you like my new room?"

"I love it, Binks," I say, overwhelmed. I spend an hour or so helping her unpack books and toys and games and animals. Zoe has very specific opinions about where everything should go. Unfortunately, those opinions change every few minutes. She's still rearranging when I tell her I need to go.

She flings her arms around me. I'm kneeling on the floor, and she nearly knocks me over.

"I'm going to miss you, Aunt Callie!"

I stroke her curls. "Don't be silly. You'll see me all the time."

Zoe draws back and looks at me solemnly. "Mommy says I'm not old enough for sleepovers. But you are. You could come sleep over. I'll make room in my bed."

I laugh. "Sounds great, Binks," I say and give her a squeeze before stepping out of the room. Once in the hallway, I pull out my phone. I find the number I need and press the call icon. He picks up on the first ring.

"Are you back?" Ben asks. I feel a little thrill at the sound of his voice.

"Yep. I'm at Nina's. I could use a ride."

"Hmm, I think I can do something about that. I'll be there in about twenty minutes. I missed you."

The words wash over me like sunshine. "I missed you, too," I reply before turning off my phone, and then I stand for a minute in the hall, just smiling. I can't help it.

When I left Ethan's hotel after meeting him for drinks, my mind was churning, trying to come up with words that would convince Ben that, despite what I'd said only weeks before, my ex-boyfriend was entirely irrelevant. I called him the next day, not knowing if he'd even pick up the phone, but he did. And although his voice was guarded, he agreed to see me.

I drove to his office to meet him—it was Saturday, and he

was there doing some drafting. I climbed the stairs to HMK, a hard knot in the pit of my stomach. He opened the frosted glass door to let me in, and we sat on the sofa adjacent to the receptionist's desk.

I perched on the edge, my hands in my lap. Then I shifted and crossed one leg over the other. I wasn't quite sure what to do with my limbs. Meanwhile, Ben looked at me expectantly.

"So. I wanted to talk to you," I began.

He raised his eyebrows.

"I saw Ethan last night. My ex. He was in New York for the movie premiere."

A muscle worked in Ben's jaw, and I plunged ahead.

"I need you to know that I have done a *lot* of thinking. About my relationship with him, about breaking up with him, and about what I want now. I know now that I was one hundred percent right to end it, but I felt bad for a long time about how I handled things. It was that guilt that was keeping me from truly leaving it behind."

Ben waited, and I took a deep breath.

"But I'm ready to move on. And the person I want to move on with is you. You said you couldn't remember the last time you felt this way about someone. Well, neither can I." I bit my lip as I looked into his rich brown eyes, trying to read what was going on in his mind.

And then he smiled, and it was like the sun came out. "Do you know how many times I thought about calling you over the past few weeks?"

I shook my head and reminded myself to breathe.

"I kept thinking that I had been unfair to you. That everyone has baggage, and it's not right to expect you not to have any—just because of the particular baggage *I* carry."

"No, I get it," I protested. "I probably wouldn't have wanted to get involved with me either."

He leaned toward me, closing his hand around mine. "So

if I asked you the same question today, your answer would be different?"

I liked the feel of his hand, his thumb lightly stroking the back of mine. "Yes," I replied, nodding quickly.

He looked at me, smiling wider now.

"So, things are okay now?" I asked.

He ran his finger along my cheek. "Yes, things are okay now." He leaned farther forward and kissed me gently. "Better than okay, I think," he added, before he kissed me again.

Since then, it's been amazing. We talk every day and see each other almost as often. The night he cooked dinner for me at his townhouse—delicious chicken with mozzarella and prosciutto and Caesar salad—he took me to bed for the first time. And no matter how good I thought sex could be before, this was something else entirely.

Tess is insisting on meeting him, but so far I've kept him to myself—though I know that will soon change. "No bowling this time," she promised. "Just dinner with Brett and me. I have to see the guy who's put that goofy smile on your face."

When I walk downstairs, I find Nina putting dishes away in the cabinet while Michael is hooking up the large-screen TV. Daniel is sleeping in what Nina calls "the bucket"—his car seat with the big handle.

"Neen, why don't you rest?" I ask, leaning against the shiny granite countertop.

Nina looks over her shoulder at me. "I can't rest with the house like this."

Of course. I help her with the dishes but keep looking at my watch. The fourth time, Nina calls me on it.

"So, is Ben on his way?" she asks, a smile playing around the corners of her mouth.

I nod, realizing I am grinning from ear to ear.

"I'm so glad you're happy." She reaches out to squeeze my arm.

"Thanks, Neen."

"And by the way, Callie, thanks for everything."

I wave my hand as if swatting a fly.

"No, seriously. You were a trooper through all of this. It can't have been easy for you."

"Well, it wasn't easy for you either," I say lightly. And then I remember. "Oh, and I love Zoe's room!"

"Well, I had great inspiration for it. Margo told me she asked you for a portfolio?"

I nod again. "I gave her one that I put together over the past few weeks. She actually has two clients she wants to introduce me to."

"That's amazing, Callie."

I grin again as a text pops up on my phone telling me that Ben is outside.

"Okay, I guess I'm out of here."

Nina winks at me suggestively. "Have fun."

I smirk at her and then turn toward Michael, who is kneeling, headfirst, into a cabinet. "Bye, Michael."

He eases himself out. "Bye, Cal. Thanks."

I pause. "You know, I really prefer Callie."

Michael looks surprised, then shrugs. "Okay, Callie. See you later."

Ben's small black car is at the curb, and as soon as I see it, butterflies fill my stomach.

I quickly cross the lawn to meet him and slip inside after popping my bag into the trunk. "Hey. Thanks for getting me," I say, leaning over to kiss him. His hand immediately slides behind my head, pulling me closer as his lips capture mine. When I finally pull away, I have to catch my breath.

He smiles at me and squeezes my hand. "Sorry I couldn't pick you up at the airport—I'm not sure I was on my game pitching new clients anyway when all I could think about was you." He kisses me again. "So, your place or mine?"

"Mine," I say.

We drive about twenty minutes and pull up in front of an adorable Craftsman bungalow, which I still can't believe I can call home. Well, it's my name on the lease anyway. It's on a street among similar homes, about halfway between Bouncy Castles and Ben's place.

It all happened so quickly. I'd mentioned to Ben that I was looking for a new place to live, and days later he told me that a bicoastal HMK client had redone this bungalow as a pied-à-terre for when he needed to be in this area, but that he'd been relocated to Hong Kong and was looking to rent it out as soon as possible.

So, over the last couple of weeks, in addition to helping Nina pack, I was also boxing up my own things and ferrying them to the bungalow. I'd given Nina the key so her moving truck could deliver my bed while I was in LA.

Ben pulls into the driveway and turns off the ignition. As I pull my roller bag out of the trunk, he takes a shopping bag out of the back seat. I look at it curiously.

"Dinner," he says. "Chinese."

"Yum, I'm starving."

We walk up the path to the wide front porch, and I open the front door. There are boxes everywhere on the wide plank hardwood floors, but I can envision how I'm going to set it up. The kind of sofa I want, and rug, and coffee table. The bistro-style table and chairs I plan to put in the small dining area. In my mind's eye, I can see my books filling the built-ins on either side of the fireplace, and some of my favorite paintings hanging on the wall. I wander through, and poke my head into the bedroom to check on the delivery of my bed.

I laugh as I flip on the light. Despite everything Nina had on her plate, she made the bed with my linens and comforter—the same ones I'd put on for her and Michael when they moved into the Brook Hill house last fall.

I go back out to the kitchen—white Shaker cabinets and soapstone countertops—where I find Ben pulling Chinese food cartons out of the bag, along with chopsticks.

"Where should we eat?" he asks.

"I guess we'll have a picnic." I head out to the living room, and inside one of the boxes I find the fleece blanket I bring when I go outside to sketch, and spread it out on the floor.

A few minutes later, we're seated cross-legged, passing white cartons back and forth as we eat directly out of them. I fill him in on my trip—the acres and acres of booths hawking early-childhood-education-oriented wares; the session I attended about empowering children, which I thought I could have led myself since I was already doing everything that was being recommended in my own classroom; the dinner with Judith where she got unexpectedly tipsy on two glasses of wine.

"Oh—you know, you never told me about how it went with Liam's mom last week," Ben remarks as he pops a shrimp into his mouth.

"Oh, gosh—I didn't? It was good. She and her husband are actually going for couples' counseling," I reply, around a bite of baby corn.

Ellen and I have been in regular contact about Liam, who has more better days than worse as time goes on. At our meeting last week, I was surprised to discover that there was a chance for his parents' marriage after all.

Ellen had laughed. "Oddly, we're getting along better now that we're living apart. It actually seems worth it to try again. And he's agreed to counseling, so we're giving it a shot."

"That's great," I'd replied.

"We're not telling Liam anything; we don't want him to get his hopes up. But to be honest, *my* hopes are up." Ellen had shrugged. "I never imagined I'd be in this position, but if it's meant to be, I guess it will work out."

It made me think of what Ethan had said in his interview about *Rerouting*. Sometimes life takes you on a different path, but if you're meant to get somewhere, you will. On the other hand, there are also times that you stay on the wrong path too long, and what you really need to do is be brave enough to leave the road and go in an entirely different direction. Maybe your destination won't be what you thought it would be, but it could be something better.

I smile across the takeout containers at Ben.

"What?" he asks.

I shrug. "Nothing. It's just good to be home."

Ben gestures around the room. "Your very own home. I can't wait to see what you do with it."

"Me, too." I grin.

We carry the boxes into the kitchen, and while I put the leftovers in the fridge, Ben shows me a small bakery box. "Look what I have," he says, lifting the lid. It's two of the double chocolate cupcakes we shared the day we first had coffee together.

"Oh, I love you!" I spontaneously exclaim, feeling my face grow hot. "I mean . . ." But then I stop. I had meant it the way you'd say it to a plumber who rescues your heirloom ring from the U-bend under your sink, or to the roadside assistance guy who gets your car to start in a freezing parking lot in the middle of the night. But now that I've said it, well—maybe there's more to it than that.

Ben looks at me. "It's okay. I know what you meant." He puts his hands on my shoulders. "But just so you know, if I said it, it wouldn't be just because you get so excited by chocolate cupcakes."

I press my lips together before I speak. "I'm not sure I only meant it because you *bring* me chocolate cupcakes."

Ben pushes my hair out of my face. "The truth is, I think I started falling a little bit in love with you when I saw you in that witch's hat back on Halloween," he says, his eyes meeting mine.

"I didn't know that was such a good look for me." My heart beats a little faster.

"Oh, it is. You should wear one more often. But only around me." He bends to kiss me, and my hands go up around his neck while his slip under my sweater, finding the bare skin of my back. With his tongue tangled in mine and his fingers pressing into me, I can feel heat rising in my cheeks and between my legs. While I don't ever want to stop kissing him, I'm also grateful when he pulls back just far enough to whisper against my lips. "So, you've got a bed in that other room, right?"

"Yep. With sheets on it and everything."

The corners of Ben's mouth turn up. "Well then," he says, and suddenly he picks me up, carries me into the bedroom, and deposits me on the bed. I reach for him, and his lips land on mine as he hovers over me before rolling onto his back and pulling me on top of him. We separate long enough for him to lift my sweater over my head. And then he stops.

"What is it?" I ask, my breathing shallow.

He gazes up at me, his eyes dropping from mine to my lacy bra and then back up. "I just want to look at you. I missed you this weekend. You have no idea how much time I spent thinking about this."

"Oh?" I ask teasingly. "How much?"

"Let's just say that I haven't fantasized this much about breasts since I was a teenager."

"And was that a lot?"

"You don't want to know." He grins.

I raise my eyebrows. "Wow. That's a lot of pressure. I hope I can live up to expectations."

"I don't think you have anything to worry about," he says huskily. And with my eyes on his, I reach behind my back and unhook my bra, then drop it to the side of the bed. He groans and reaches for me. I can feel the hardness in his jeans as his hands and lips cover every exposed inch of my skin. And then he's pulling off my jeans and with them the silky panties I've started wearing again. His hand moves between my legs, and I hear myself moan.

"I love making you make that sound," he whispers as I start to tug at his fly.

It's a flurry of hands and mouths and sighs as we try to prolong the exquisiteness of the foreplay, enjoying the delicious anticipation of our coming together—but we can only restrain ourselves for so long. He touches my cheek and looks into my eyes as he positions himself above me—and then he's entering me, and it's like coming home. I've never felt so full—in more ways than one—and we quickly find our rhythm, moving together as his lips once again crush mine. My hands slide down his back, loving how familiar the texture of his skin has already become, and I wrap my legs around his hips, making him groan, as I knew it would. Even as I can barely catch my breath, I feel like I could live inside this moment forever—and then, as his breathing quickens along with the movement of his hips, he tips both of us over the edge.

He presses his forehead to mine and whispers, "Welcome home," making me shiver, even as the heat rises off my skin.

"Good to be home," I whisper back.

A few moments later, I'm curled up against him, my cheek on his chest, his arm around me.

"That was incredible," he says.

"Mmm," I reply articulately.

"Now this is a time I'd like to be twenty-one again," he muses.

I raise my head to look at him. "Why?" I ask.

He strokes my waist. "Because then we could go again right now."

I put my head back down. "As nice as that would be," I say,

"I like being where we are now. I'm a lot smarter these days than I was then."

He kisses my head. "Actually," he says, "so am I."

ACKNOWLEDGMENTS

I feel enormously blessed to be in a position to be writing these acknowledgments. It has been a long and winding road to get to this point, and it wouldn't have happened without the support of so many people.

First and foremost, I want to thank my initial editor, Sarah Branham Velez, who "got" *Typecast* right from the start, and who was a wizard at guiding me to make it better. It has always amazed me that Sarah came up with the same big idea for the book that I was considering myself—if that's not kismet, I don't know what is.

I also want to thank Michelle Cameron and my Writer's Circle friends and classmates—particularly Elizabeth Schlossberg, Mally Becker, and Suzanne Moyers. I'm so glad that one week I dropped the ball on the other manuscript I was working on, and brought in *Typecast*—which was then known as *Rerouting*—instead. That was the beginning of a new revision that made the book even better.

To Amy Gash—thank you for believing in my fledgling novel based on your early read of it. I've been so grateful for your guidance and advice.

To Angela Terry—thank you for the wise counsel you gave to a virtual stranger, and for introducing me to Christina Henry de Tessan at Girl Friday Books.

To the team at Girl Friday—including not only Christina but also Kristin Duran, Katherine Richards, Georgie Hockett, Laura Dailey, and the rest of their terrific crew—thank you for your careful attention to detail and for making the process not only smooth but fun.

To my friends who read various versions at various stages— Heather Gittleman, Hazel Siegel, and Ulrika Lerner—I am so appreciative of your time, encouragement, and insight.

To my bookstagram community—who know me as @books.turning.brains—thank you for helping keep me immersed in women's and contemporary fiction!

To my parents—my mom, who recently left us, and my dad, who has been long gone—thank you for always encouraging me and believing in me. I'm grateful that I was able to tell my mom that *Typecast* was going to be published.

And last, but far from least, to my husband and my boys—I love you more than you could ever know, and am so grateful that you put up with me in all my moods. The path that took me to you is definitely the one I was meant to be on.

ABOUT THE AUTHOR

Andrea J. Stein is a lifetime lover of books. Born in Brooklyn, she was raised in New Jersey before attending a small, quirky liberal arts college and a large, preppy university, both in New York State. A book publicist by profession, she lives with her husband and sons in suburban New Jersey—where the boys attended preschool at a place much like Bouncy Castles. She spends an inordinate amount of time taking pretty photos of books. Things that make her happy include strong tea, turtles, sunshine, sheep, and the ocean. For more information, go to andreajstein.com.

CPSIA information can be obtained
at www.ICGtesting.com
Printed in the USA
JSHW061002150722
28138JS00004B/4